CREATIVE TEXTS PUBLISHERS
PO Box 50, Barto, PA 19504

Creative Texts Publishers products are available at special discounts for bulk purchase for sale promotions, premiums, fund-raising, and educational needs. For details, write Creative Texts Publishers, PO Box 50, Barto, PA 19504, or visit www.creativetexts.com

ROLAND
by N.C. Reed

Published by Creative Texts Publishers
PO Box 50
Barto, PA 19504
www.creativetexts.com

The following is a work of fiction. Any resemblance to actual names, persons, businesses, and incidents is strictly coincidental. Locations are used only in the general sense and do not represent the real place in actuality.

ISBN: 978-0-692-60587-5

For those who rise to the occasion.
For those who protect the helpless.
*For those who **do**.*

ROLAND

by

N.C. Reed

CHAPTER ONE

From the field diary of Roland Stang;

How did it come to this? How did we get here, from being the most powerful nation on Earth?

I mean, no one else is any better off, mind you. Some nations don't even exist anymore except as vaguely defined territories between the lines on some map. But we're still in bad shape. For us it's worse, in a way. Many other nations were accustomed to the violence. The bloodshed. Random, pattern less, mind numbing, blood and chaos. Even now, as I try to write this, to leave some kind of record of what we've been through, I shudder at some of the things I've seen in the last two months. Seen? I shudder at some of the things I've done in the last two months.

Things I had to do to survive. To help others survive. For the first time in my life, I'm glad I don't have any family. I'm glad I'm alone. Glad I don't have to watch as my children suffer from hunger. When they cringe at the sound of gunfire, or the approach of a vehicle.

When they stoically nod their understanding when daddy or mommy don't come back. When they don't come back because they died trying to find something for their children to eat. Or worse, when they just keep walking, leaving their children among an ever growing group of orphans, abandoned by parents who 'can't take it anymore'.

Cowards. Only the most callous and uncaring coward could abandon these kids. Some of them barely out of diapers, most in their tween years, along with a handful of teens who simply don't have anywhere else to go.

And how the hell did I wind up looking after them? That's a question I keep asking myself over and over. There are still a few adults around, but I'm having to watch them pretty close. There are three teenage girls in the group that the men are starting to look at in ways I don't care for. And even the women are looking at the kids as if sizing them up, considering what they could get for the kids if they sold them.

N.C. REED

None of them bother looking my way, and so far, I haven't encouraged them. The less they think about me, the more surprise I'll have when they make their move.

And they'll move soon, I think. The food is almost gone. Maybe another three, four days. One couple has already voiced that the 'rug rats' shouldn't be getting as much, since they aren't doing anything. Again, I said nothing. But I've made sure that the kids are eating as well as I can. And I've put one of the teen girls in charge of making sure that all the kids get vitamins I nabbed from a drugstore I cleaned out a while back.

I've got caches, if I can get to them. Enough to help get these kids away from this hell hole of a city, and into some kind of safety. If I knew where that was. God help me, there's twenty-nine of them, and one of me. The teenagers, the three girls, and three boys, will probably be of some help, but I don't know how much. One of the boys is a loner, quiet and tough. He's already backed me a couple times, silent but ready. I think I can consider arming him when we go, but the others I'll just have to hope will watch the kids for me while I try to get us somewhere safe.

Safe. It's like a bad joke. Where is safe, anymore? With hordes of gangs, or 'tribes' as many have taken to calling themselves, everywhere, killing indiscriminately. It didn't take long for the worst in society to come out and play.

I guess I'm one to talk. Twenty-four years old, and a stone killer. Two tours in Afghanistan, another in Iraq, and one more in Africa in seven years. I guess technically I'm AWOL, but no one seems to be keeping up with that anymore. The Army stood strong for a couple of weeks, but without effective leadership, it began to melt away as soldiers left their units to take care of their families. In the end, I was the only one left in my platoon, so I started caching things I might need later, and looking for a hole to hide in. Big bad soldier boy gonna hide till the monsters are gone.

Pathetic. It's all I can do to look in the mirror.

And then I stumble across this outfit. And these abandoned kids. Who look at me so desperate, so hopeful. Like I'm going to save them from all the bad things that are happening. Like since I'm here, everything will be okay.

That's how it came to this, I guess. For me anyway. I saw plenty of kids abandoned in other countries. Left to die, sometimes sent to die, being used as a soldier, or a weapon. Dammit, this is America. We're supposed to be better than this.

Here comes the 'quiet' one. James I think his name is. He rarely comes to me at all, and speaks even less, so something must be up...

"Sir?"

Roland Stang looked at the tall, rangy teenager.

ROLAND

"Yeah, kid?" he smiled briefly. "James, right? What's up?"

"Yes, sir," James nodded. "I could be wrong, but I think that bunch are up to something. Something bad," he added, using his head to indicate the group of adults now gathered by the door. Stang looked over at them casually, letting his eyes take in the whole warehouse, rather than settle on them.

"What makes you think that?" Stang asked, keeping his motions casual. He stretched, allowing his hand to come to rest where his gun was lying out of sight.

"They were talking a little loud, earlier, sir," James replied. "And Wright, the big one with the hygiene issues? He's been a little. . .insistent about the girls, if you know what I mean. I've heard him and his little buddy with the hat mention what 'something like them is worth'. I think those were their exact words."

"I'm concerned," he admitted. Stang had 'known' James for two weeks. Concerned was a word he'd never heard the youth use before.

"Well, I admit I was expectin' this," Stang confided in the teen. "Was hoping' it was a little further down the road, though."

"You expected it?" James' voice was calm, but questioning. Not suspicious, but interested. Like he was trying to learn something.

"Yeah. Look kid, that bunch ain't exactly the cream of society, ya know? The best of 'em is worse than most people I've known in my life. The fact that it took 'em this long to work up to something shows us a little about their lack of intestinal fortitude. I think we've stayed here about as long as we're gonna be able to."

"I was thinking that too, sir," the teenager nodded seriously. "But we won't get far with them following."

"They won't be following," Stand said grimly. "I want you to find Maria, and tell her to announce its candy time to the little ones. The rest of you help her round up the little ones, and move them toward the back. I think it's time we rid ourselves of that bunch."

"Do you need any help?" James asked.

"Nah, I think I got it. Appreciate it, though. Go on, now, and do like I said." James moved away, going on his errand.

Soon the teens were corralling the smaller children toward the eating area, with the promise of 'candy time', the white lie they had invented to get the kids to take the vitamins. The fact they were candy flavored had helped with that.

But it seemed that at least one of the group's malcontents was paying attention.

"Hey! Greaser girl! Where d'ya think you're goin'?" Wright bellowed at Maria, a pretty Latino girl with her hair in a long pony tail. She looked at Stang, fear in her eyes. He nodded to her, and she kept going.

"She's taking the kids to get their vitamins," Stang replied in her stead. "Nothin' to worry 'bout."

"Who the hell put you in charge?" Wright demanded.

"Nobody," Stang shrugged. "Just tryin' to take care o' the ones that can't take care o' themselves. That's all."

"Well, it's time they earned their keep," one of the women, Juney, Stang thought, piped up. "We been takin' care o' that pack o' brats, and it's time we got ours back."

"In what way?" Stang asked, nothing but curiosity in his voice, though his hand tightened around his gun.

"We're gonna start tradin 'em off, that's what way," Wright informed him. "Startin' with that little wetback!"

"I don't think that's gonna work out for ya," Stang said slowly, smiling ever so slightly. "Fact is; I don't think that's healthy for ya at all. Best just let that idea go, and you folks pack it on up and head for greener pastures." He was giving them a chance. They probably wouldn't take it, but Stang was giving them a chance to save their lives.

Just the one, though.

"Say what?" Hat man asked, a look of incredulity in his face. "Who the hell do you think you are, anyway?"

"I'm the fella protecting' these kids," Stang smiled. "Ya'll move on, now."

"There's six of us, and one o' you," Wright sneered. "And that rifle o' yours ain't loaded," he added. Stang chuckled.

"Oh I know that," he surprised them. "I knew the minute you tampered with it. That's why I'm using' this." He brought an ugly looking shotgun out from under the tarp next to him. "And I assure you, it's loaded. To the gills, in fact." He flicked the safety off as the short, wicked looking KSG suddenly got the drop on them.

"You've got one chance. Take it, and go," he ordered.

"You won't shoot," Wright bluffed. "And we ain't leavin' here without them girls, at least."

"You had your chance," Stang sighed, and pulled the trigger.

ROLAND

CHAPTER TWO

It took almost an hour to calm the little kids down. The older children, especially the teenagers, seemed more relieved than anything. I guess I had underestimated how much attention they were paying Wright and the others. Sometimes I don't pay enough attention to things like that, I guess. But what do I know about children, anyway? I was raised in an orphanage for the most part, when I wasn't in and out of foster care anyway.

I joined the army as soon as I could get someone to sign for me. I was still seventeen, but had a diploma, and the orphanage people were glad to be rid of me, it seemed like. I hadn't been a trouble maker, but I really wasn't one to 'toe the line' either. I never have liked bullies, and don't let anyone tell you that bullies don't work for Social Services, cause it's a damn lie. They do.

We can't stay here in this warehouse. If it was just me, or me and the teens, maybe we could make it, but the younger kids, they need to be where they can get fresh air, and sunshine once in a while. My recent encounter with Wright and his happy little band pretty much proved this wasn't a place for that.

What a mess. There's no way to walk out of here, not with the little ones. They just can't make it. I've got a HUMVEE stashed nearby, but there's no way to cram them all inside. What I need is a bus. And a shop. If I could find a working bus, and then spend a few hours in a good vo-tech school working on it, I could get them out of here.

But to where? I'm looking at my map, and we're a long way from anywhere that would be even remotely safe. Nashville was a good town before things went crazy, but now it's just over run with people like Wright, and some a whole lot worse. And I'm just one guy. I guess even worse, in a way, is that all I've ever had to be responsible for was me. Now, because of some genetic pre-disposition to be a do-gooder, I've saddled myself with nearly thirty kids. Kids that need to be fed, clothed, and educated. Sweet mother, I have no idea what I'm gonna do about all that.

First things first, though, I guess. I need to get us out of the city.

~*~

"Any of you guys know where we could get a bus?" Stang asked, looking at the assembled children.

"A school bus, or a public transit bus, either one. School bus is better, though."

"There might still be buses at the service center," one of the girls spoke up. Dinah? Diana? Deanna? Hell with it.

"What's your name again?" Stang asked.

"Deena," the little brunette said shyly.

"Okay, Deena, do you know where this service center is?"

"Yeah, but it's pretty far," she admitted.

Of course it is, Stang thought to himself. Why wouldn't it be?

"Anyone else?"

"They were using buses to evacuate people from schools, when things first went south," James mentioned. "Might find one at any of the evac points. But there's no guarantee of that."

"Anyone know where the nearest school is?" Stang asked.

"Prater Elementary is only a mile or so," one of the other boys chimed in. Ralph, maybe?

"Ralph, right?" Stang asked, and the boy nodded.

"Okay, Ralph, think you and me can make it to that school, Prater you said, and see what's there?"

"Yes, sir," the boy nodded. He didn't look too enthused about it, but then Stang wasn't either.

"All right, here's the deal," Stang announced. "Ralph and I are gonna see about finding us a way outta here. Maria, you're in charge of the kids while I'm gone. I hate to do that to you, but you're good at it. I expect the rest of you to help her. James, I want you on look out. If someone tries to get in, hide, and stay quiet. I'll deal with it when we get back. Everyone good?"

"We need to try and let the little ones eat," Maria suggested. Fine girl, that Maria.

"That's fine, just do it quietly. Hopefully we'll be out of here soon enough. Ralph, let's make tracks."

~*~

ROLAND

"I don't believe it," Stang almost breathed it. Ralph nodded his agreement.

Sitting right there, in front of the school, was a fairly new Bluebird school bus.

"I wonder if somethin's wrong with it," Ralph asked, ruining Stang's good mood.

"Way to jinx us, Ralph," he muttered. "You may be right, though. I can't see another reason to leave the bus here. Let's check it out. Be careful, and keep your head on a swivel, kid. We want to see trouble before it sees us."

"Amen," the boy nodded, his head already turning to scan their surroundings. Roland made his way to the bus without difficulty, and opened the door. The bus smelled of stale air, but nothing worse, which had been a real possibility. Easing onto the vehicle, he cleared it quickly, then motioned for Ralph to join him.

"Well, the keys are here, anyway," Ralph pointed. "It might start."

"One way to find out," Roland nodded, and sat down in the driver's seat. He turned the key, and the diesel engine spun. It was slower than he liked, but it was turning.

"Well, that's something, anyway," he shrugged, and tried it again. This time the engine caught, sputtered for a moment, then died.

"Maybe it's out of fuel?" Ralph suggested. Roland looked.

"Half a tank, if this gauge is right. Let's try it again." The key went forward, and Roland was rewarded with a sputtering cough, a backfire, and then a running engine.

"Man, this thing idles rough," Ralph noted.

"Hasn't been run in a while," Roland reminded him. "Let's get outta here. We'll take it slow, and maybe the engine will smooth out some."

~*~

Roland had intended to modify the bus at least some, but realized that might not be so easy without power. If he could find a place with a generator, that would help. Of course, then he'd need fuel for the generator, and he needed more fuel for the bus.

Sighing, he took out a notebook and started making a list. The ride back had been uneventful, and the bus was now inside the warehouse. But they were far from safe.

"You wanted to see me, sir?" James asked. Roland looked at the boy and nodded.

"Can you drive, James?" he asked.

"I don't have a license, sir," James replied evenly.

"I don't think anyone cares about that anymore, buddy," Roland laughed. "Can you drive?"

"Yes, sir," James nodded. "Almost anything. Including that bus, if you need me to."

"Really?" Roland was surprised.

"Really."

"Well, that's good to know. You got any idea if the others can drive?"

"I don't really know them very well, sir," James shook his head. "I only met them when all this started."

"How'd you come to be here, James?" Roland asked, curious. "You have any family?"

"Not that I know of, sir," the boy answered reluctantly. "I was in foster care. My foster parents didn't come home from. . .from whatever started all of this."

"Greed, mostly," Roland told him. "Money and greed. I spent a lot of time in foster care, growing up. Your foster folks okay to you?"

"They always treated me decently, sir. More than I can say for others."

"I know that tune," the soldier nodded back. "Anyway, if you can drive nearly anything, then we can make some better plans. I've got a Hummer stored not too far from here, with a trailer. Know what a Hummer is?"

"Yes, sir," James replied.

"You know, you can call me Roland, James."

"Yes, sir. Roland." Roland sighed.

"Anyway, I was thinking that you and me could go and collect that Hummer, and see what else we can see or find. I want to take that bus, and whatever supplies we can find, and get out of this town. Take these kids somewhere at least marginally safe. You game to help me with that?"

"Of course, Roland," James replied at once. "Whatever you need."

"Can you handle a gun, James?"

"I can, sir. Roland," the teen corrected himself.

"Ever fire an AR?"

"AR, AK, shotgun, and handgun, sir," James nodded. "My foster father was a hunter, and a shooting enthusiast. I learned from him."

"Do you think you could kill someone, if you had to?" Roland asked. "It's okay if you can't."

"I was going to kill Wright and his friends, before you took that on," James said softly. "He was too evil to live, at least around these children. I can kill anyone who threatens any of these children, and be fine with it, Roland."

ROLAND

"That's a good answer, James," Roland smiled. "You know, I think together, the two of us, and the others, just might be able to save these kids. At least get them out of the city."

"That's a worthy goal, sir," James smiled for the first time Roland could remember seeing it.

"It sure is. So, here's my idea. . ."

CHAPTER THREE

I've had to re-think my sketchy plan. I realized I can't just load this bunch up and head out to the country side, moving by the seat of my pants. For one thing, I need a place to go. That, I think, I got figured out.

But then, what happens when we get somewhere reasonably safe? Kids need stuff. They need clothes, shoes, food, toys, and things to keep them occupied. Things to learn with. Geez, I need school books. And who's gonna teach them? I sure can't.

This is enough to give a man a migraine. And I don't suffer from migraines. Not for the first time, I'm thinking how nice it would be to track down the bastards responsible for all this misery, and shoot them. With a LAW rocket.

In the face.

Anyway. So now, in addition to all the other things I need, I have to start trying to scavenge for the stuff we'll need when we get where we're going. Which will probably mean we'll need another vehicle.

Which means one of those other teenagers better be able to drive. James, Ralph, and the other teen boy, Willie, I think, are currently removing unneeded seats from the bus. We need seating for only thirty, at most. The rear seats are being removed so we can use that part of the bus for storage. You know, for all that stuff we need that we don't have, and I have no idea where to get.

~*~

"We're done with the seating, sir," James reported for all three of them.

"Good deal, Lucille," Roland smiled. "Now, you boys know this area some?" All three nodded.

ROLAND

"Good, 'cause I don't. Here's what we need. First, we need food. That's obvious. We need water, too. Again, obvious. But we also need clothes, blankets, tents, cookware, shoes and socks, hand tools, and the list goes on and on. Get me?" All three nodded.

"So, where can we get those things? And forget Wal-Mart, Target, and places like that. They will have been picked clean already. Think storage places. Warehouses like this one. Come to think of it, has anyone looked to see what's in this warehouse?" Roland mentally scolded himself for not having thought of that sooner.

"Mechanical items, mostly, so far as I've seen," James replied. "Parts for vehicles of all kinds."

"Anything useful?" Roland asked.

"Not unless we need a car part."

"Well, I guess that was too much to hope for. This area is basically one large storehouse district. Other than fuel, we might find everything we need in these warehouses. I doubt it, but it's worth checking out. Ralph, Willie, that's us. James, you're in charge until I get back. Let Maria and the others deal with the children, I want you making sure this place is safe, okay?"

"I'll take care of them Roland," James said quietly, but firmly.

"Okay, you two go get ready," Roland ordered Ralph and Willie. "James, do me a favor and go get Maria."

~*~

Maria approached him a little hesitant, worry on her face. She didn't know Roland from Adam. The fact that he had protected her and the others from Wright didn't mean he wasn't a threat.

"Take a seat, Maria," Roland told her. When she did, Roland smiled.

"I know you're scared. So am I," he admitted, and saw surprise on her face. "I figured it was time I let you know what I had in mind. And to get your input. What I want is to get us out of this city, to somewhere that's at least marginally safe. To do that, we need transport, hence the bus. But we need a lot of other things, too."

"Clothes, food, shoes for the little ones," Maria started. "Medicine and first aid supplies, and a way to filter water. Cooking equipment, maybe some tents. . ."

"Well, you already got this figured out, I see," Roland chuckled.

"I've been thinking about what I'd need, if I escaped from here," she admitted.

"Still want to escape?" Roland asked. If she left, he was screwed. No one was better with the little ones than Maria.

"I don't know yet," the girl admitted. "I'm weighing my options."

"Fair enough. I would ask that if you decide to go it alone, please let me know ahead of time. I'll have to see if someone can fill your shoes, or if I have to learn to take care of the young'uns myself. That sound fair?"

Maria studied Roland for a long time, and Roland waited patiently, even though he really didn't have the time. Finally, she spoke.

"I'm not going to lie. I'm not sure you aren't as big a threat as the others were. It's difficult for me to trust you."

"I can understand that," Roland shrugged. "Even sympathize. Is it something in particular I've done, or maybe just a good, cautious nature?"

"It's because you're a gringo," Maria admitted, her voice slightly bitter.

"Ah. . .oh, you mean white?" Roland had to guess at that. Maria nodded.

"Well, again, I guess that's fair. I'm not a bad guy. . .well, that's not true," he stopped himself, and she looked surprised.

"How old are you, Maria?" he asked suddenly.

"Nineteen," she didn't even think about lying.

"Adult, then," Roland nodded, sitting down. "Look, I'm not really a good man, to be honest. I mean, I'm not like Wright, or the others, but. . .I'm a soldier, Maria, or I was before the world imploded. I've been all over the world, meetin' new cultures and killin 'em." Her eyes widened at that, and he held up a hand.

"It's an old joke, Maria. Sorry. But it is sorta true. Thing is, I've never seen myself as evil, just. . .well, not good, per se. I only meant to stay here overnight. It was raining, and this was a good shelter. I didn't count on seeing all of these kids, alone. I… I can't just leave 'em. I'm not that bad. I've got to get them somewhere safe."

"To do that, I need your help, if you're willing. If not, I understand, and if you want to go, I'll try and make sure you have everything you need to make it. And no hard feelings, either. You should have your whole life ahead of you, and taking on a responsibility like this isn't something you should have to do."

"I don't mind," Maria said softly. "I worked in day care before. . .before," she said firmer. "I love children. I was studying to be a teacher."

"What happened to you, Maria?" Roland asked softly. He knew the signs, and Maria had them all. She's suffered some kind of trauma. Recently.

"Nothing that hasn't happened all over the world," the girl didn't quite snap. "So long as you're on the level, then I'll help you. At least until the rest are safe. I make you no promises beyond that."

"I couldn't ask for more," Roland nodded. "And thank you."

"I'm not doing it for you," she said flatly. "I'm doing it for them."

ROLAND

"Works for me."

~*~

"James, you said you've used an AR. Can you show me how to disassemble this, check it, and reassemble it?"

James nodded, and quickly and efficiently stripped the civilian model rifle, checked if for dirt and debris, then correctly reassembled it, slamming the magazine home with authority, but not chambering a round.

"I'm convinced," Roland nodded, handing the teen a bandoleer. "Be safe, and please don't shoot anyone by accident. Especially me," he added, grinning.

"Never by accident." James actually told a joke.

"All right, we're outta here. James, keep a good watch. We'll be back."

"We'll be here."

~*~

The warehouse next to theirs was a bust. Empty except for a few odd and end boxes of junk. Roland and the boys searched the office, and found some snacks, peanut butter crackers and the like, which they bundled up for the smaller kids. There were also two cases of bottled water. Roland sent the two boys off to deliver the food and water to the warehouse. When they returned, the trio set off for the next building.

A chemical warehouse. Mostly petroleum based products, like grease and motor oil, machine oils, and so forth. Nothing here really that they could use. Roland did set two cases of two stroke motor oil near the door, intending to take it with him when they left. Never know when you'll want to run a chainsaw.

There was another small find of water and food in the office areas of this warehouse, so the bounty was once again sent away to their own warehouse. This cycle went on for the remainder of the day. Despite the smaller successes, Roland found nothing of real use in any of the warehouses they searched. With the light fading, he decided it was time to call it quits.

It was a dejected trio that wandered back into the warehouse they were using for shelter. Although they had found some things that would extend their supplies, the day was pretty much a bust except for that.

"There's always tomorrow," Roland reminded them. "Tomorrow we'll head out and around the neighborhood some, and see what we can see. I'm sure there are a few things lying around we can use. Cheer up!"

The two boys grinned slightly, then went to their bed rolls. They were tired.

They're not getting enough to eat, Roland realized. *None of us are. I've got to do something about that, but what?*

He still didn't have an answer when sleep claimed him at last.

ROLAND

CHAPTER FOUR

I'm trying to be upbeat, but it's getting harder every day. We've spent three days going through every building within walking distance. Twice we've been shot at by unseen attackers. No one's been hit, but that's due more to dumb luck and poor shooting than anything else.

I used to think I could tackle any obstacle and overcome it. In combat, I was always able to get the job done, no matter what, and then RTB. I'm learning that when there's no Base to return to, and no logistics to support you, things are a lot tougher.

I've got a few MREs stashed with my Hummer, but I'm not sure how well the kids will handle them. And let's face it, twenty-four MREs, which could last me for two, even three weeks in a pinch, would last less than two days with as many as there are here to feed. I want to save them for a real emergency.

Providing I can get to them, of course.

Today we're trying something different. Din. . .Da... Deena, yeah, Deena, looked through the phone book last night, and may have found the answer to our food situation. A warehouse foods company about five miles from here. It's possible there's food left there that would be more palatable for the younger children. Ralph, Willie, Deena, and myself are going to take the bus and check it out. If there's food there, we'll cram everything we can find onto the bus, and then come back here.

We're still working on our list, and starting to pick things up as we go, hoping to assemble all we need so we can get the hell outta here. We need to be able to plant a garden when we get where we're going. And we need to get going there soon, so we can plant the garden, and get some food from it for winter.

I honestly have no idea how people cope with being responsible for the lives of children. I've never been as stressed over anything as I am the care of all these children.

Please, God, help me find a way to take care of them. Don't desert them now.

~*~

"There it is," Deena said softly from her seat behind Roland.

"Well, it looks intact, anyway," Roland nodded, pulling into the empty parking lot. "I think we'll head around back, out of sight. I'd rather no one knew we were here."

He maneuvered the bus into the rear of the building, pleased to find four cargo doors. Opening the rear emergency door on the bus, Roland backed into one of the cargo bay doors.

"All right, let's see if there's anything to find, here, boys and girls."

Roland had to pry the walk through door open with a crowbar, which he considered a good sign. If the door was still locked, maybe no one had been here. Most people thought of grocery stores when they thought of food. This place supplied grocery stores, so maybe no one had been here yet.

He was relieved they hadn't encountered anyone on the way here. The populations were probably thinned some since the Crash, with all the wanton destruction, but there were still plenty of people running around. He wanted to avoid them if at all possible.

Once inside, it was dark. The only light came from the open door. Roland muttered curses under his breath at his carelessness. Of course it's dark. No windows in a place like this.

"Here," Ralph said, handing Roland a headlamp. He took it, noticing the others had one also.

"Where did you get these?" Roland asked. "Good thinking, by the way. Better than mine."

"James had them," Ralph replied. "Said we might need them." James slid upward another notch in Roland's estimation. Good kid.

"Okay, let's see what we can find. Stay together. If we encounter trouble, head to the bus immediately. Got it?"

"Got it," all three whispered in tandem. They followed him, lamps searching everywhere for labels and signs.

"This is a pallet of cereal," Deena called softly five minutes later. "We don't have milk, but the kids can eat it dry as a snack."

"Good call, Deena," Roland grinned. "Remember where it is. We can look for powdered milk, too."

"Hey, this is canned tuna," Willie announced. "Lots of it," he added.

"Another good one. Deena this looks like a good trip. We all owe you." The girl was grateful that no one could see her blush in the dark.

ROLAND

In thirty minutes they had located more than enough food stuffs to keep the children and themselves going for some time. Now, it was time to start loading.

It would have to be done by hand, since there was no way to get the pallets into the bus. With nothing else for it, Roland placed Deena on watch, and he and the boys started muscling the pallets for loading with a pallet jack.

"Fill the seats, too," Roland ordered. "We'll eat some of this stuff long before we can leave. We'll find another way to carry it if we have to."

It took two hours of continuous, back breaking work to get everything loaded. Two hours in which Roland sweated furiously over being spotted. Deena turned out to be an excellent choice for over-watch, her eyes keen and her mind sharp. Twice she had called a halt to their work from her perch atop the bus. Each time she and Roland watched as battered convoys of "technicals" prowled the streets and highways around them.

Roland decided then and there that the bus had to be painted. Sitting on a giant yellow target made his skin crawl.

Finally, they were finished. The last thing crammed aboard was a pallet's worth of bottled water.

"I think we can go now," he said to the exhausted boys, and grateful girl. "Let's load up and get the hell out of here." They had left a narrow pathway between the seats, and while the teens took that route, Roland closed the overhead, then came through the walk through. He secured the door with a block of concrete, hoping no one would notice. He'd already decided that if they could find a box truck, they'd return to fill it before leaving.

With the bus heavily loaded, handling was a little tricky. If they had to move at any real speed, turns would be a problem. Roland eased the bus along, everyone's eyes scanning around them.

"Hold it!" Deena called as they approached an intersection. "There are vehicles approaching the intersection on the cross street! I can see them through the alleys!"

Roland slowed at once, and turned the bus into a through-way alley, hopefully hiding. Without being told, Willie exited the rear door and ran to the alley entrance to watch. He was back in five long, stress filled minutes.

"They're gone, and the coast is clear," he announced a little breathless from both exertion and fear.

"Good job, Willie. You too, Deena, way to be looking," Roland praised, and started them on the way home again.

When did I start to think of that place as home?

~*~

The teens were all glad to see them back, and thrilled with the food. But there was a small problem.

"Can opener?" Roland looked at Maria as if she's spoken some long dead language.

"Yes, a can opener," the small woman sighed. "You know, to open all these cans you brought back?"

"Ah. . .ya know, I don't. . .I mean no one probably thought about that..."

"I'll look in the break room," Maria sighed again. "Perhaps there's one in there."

"Hey, good thinking!" Roland encouraged her. "And ask James. He seems to know where a lot of things are."

"James is. . .creepy," Maria objected.

"In what way?" Roland demanded.

"He never says anything."

"Maybe he ain't got nothin' to say," Roland shrugged. "That don't make him creepy. Just makes him a man that keeps his own council."

"He's not a man!" Maria huffed.

"Are you are girl, then, or a woman?" Roland shot back, teasing. "James is doing a man's work, same as you're doing a woman's. And by that I mean an adult's work. I treat anyone who *acts* like a grown-up *like* a grown-up." Maria was about to say something else, probably a witty comeback, when the import of what he'd said seem to hit her. She looked at him closely for a moment, then nodded.

"I'll go find a can opener."

ROLAND

CHAPTER FIVE

Had the dream again last night. Funny, this is the first time since everything went to hell. No idea why. I thought all that therapy crap had really worked. Like this stupid journal. I write in it nearly every day, no matter if anything happens or not.

Today is a 'not' day. I decided that we need to rest, and eat. The kids that are helping me need to get their strength back, and now we've got plenty of food, they need a day to eat and rest.

Maria, bless her heart, has been working almost non-stop with the little ones, Deena and the other girl, Terry. . .no, that's a guy's name. Teri? You know what, who cares. The other girl is helping to, and so are a couple of the younger kids, two girls and a boy each thirteen or fourteen I guess.

I looked through the stuff we took from Wright and the others. Wasn't much. Two knives, one crap and one good one, a revolver with eleven rounds, and a little .25 auto with seven. I cleaned them up last night before I turned in. I've got my rifle and my shotgun, but I've pretty much given the rifle to James. It's not a military rifle, but a civilian AR model, my own. Kinda hate to part with it, but I've got other rifles waiting for me in storage.

Speaking of which, I think it's high time I went and collected my gear. It's not that far away, and I can hump it in about three hours. I've been going over what all I stored in the trailer in my head. When I loaded it, it seemed like everything I could possibly need to lie low for a while, and see what happens.

Now, with all these children to see after, I'm seeing holes in my gear that I could never have anticipated. How could I?

But you know, I should have thought further ahead. I mean, I knew things had gone to shit. Everywhere you looked it was crazy. Blood literally running in the streets sometimes. All over money.

N.C. REED

Someone, somewhere, decided that the dollar wasn't any good anymore. I never stopped to think about how that might affect the rest of the world. Had no idea how much the rest of the world depended on the dollar to make the wheels go 'round.

When the dollar 'fell', if that's the right word, the wheels came right off, too. Things didn't turn ugly until 'check day' rolled around, and there weren't any checks. That was the start. Riots in the streets all over the country, with people who depended on the taxpayer for sustenance showing their disapproval of the situation.

At first the newsies were almost cheering them on, some of them. Others were actually telling things like they were, only too many people didn't listen. For once, being a loner, and a product of multiple foster homes and orphanages had stood me in good stead. I always kept a duffel full of things I'd need if anything ever happened. Anything.

Too many times I had been trapped in a bad situation because I didn't have a way out. So I started squirreling away money, clothes, camping gear, stuff like that, when I was probably twelve or so. Once I was in the Army, I started collecting silver coins, since I read that no matter what happened, silver would always be good. Real money. I probably had two hundred dollars in face value of just quarters. But I also had dimes, halves, and a few silver dollars.

Of course, I never planned on there not being anywhere to spend it. Jokes on me this time, I guess.

But I do have a lot of stuff. What I didn't have was enough food for everyone, but now I do. If I only had more hand tools, especially garden tools, and seeds, I'd take a chance and head out of here tomorrow.

Thing is, if I don't get that stuff here, I may not have a chance to get it when we're in the country. I have no idea what's still available, and no way to find out, either. So...

Tomorrow, when I go out, I'm going to look for them. If I get lucky, and find what we need, then we're leaving the day after. If not, then I'll keep looking for a little while longer. But every day we have to stay here is another day where someone comes looking around, and finds us.

What I wouldn't give for just three or four guys from my team to help out. But they're gone, now. Just like I should have been.

Only that's not an option, now.

~*~

"Maria, you got a minute?" Roland asked. The petite woman looked at him and nodded, eyes wary.

ROLAND

"Come on over to where I keep my gear, so we can talk. I need to tell you what I'm planning." Other than James, Maria was the person he most depended on. She followed him, uneasy as always.

"First things first," Roland told her. He picked up the good knife and the small automatic, handing them to her.

"Know how to use a gun?"

"Yes," she nodded, looking at him as if he were about to bite.

"Then take this one, and this knife. Pretty good knife, so it should serve you well. When I get back, I'll sharpen it better, but it should do in a pinch like it is."

"Back?" her eyes narrowed. "Where are you going?"

"I'm going after my truck and trailer tomorrow," Roland replied, sitting down. "And while I'm out, I want to look for garden tools, and seeds. If we're gonna survive once we leave town, we've got to have a way of growing food. I know how to scavenge in the wild, but it'll never be enough for so many. And the kids; they need better food than that, anyway."

"You're thinking long term, then," Maria said. A statement, rather than a question.

"Ain't really got a choice, seems like," Roland shrugged. "They can't look after themselves. Not yet. Not for a long time, for some of them. Where ever we wind up, I need to be able to grow food. We can hunt meat, but kids need vegetables. And that means we have to grow them."

"You keep saying 'we', but I told you I may not stay," Maria pointed out.

"There'll still be 'we' if you go," Roland shrugged again. "I hope you decide to stay, but if not, I still have to feed all these children. 'We', as in all of us," he waved a hand to encompass the others, "will have to eat. Have to survive."

"I still haven't had a chance to think about clothes and shoes for all of them," he sighed, remembering that little detail. "That's something else I need to do. Damn, I had forgotten that."

"There are second hand stores that may not have been trashed. You can try them." Maria was looking at him 'funny'. Roland didn't like that.

"Yeah, that might work. Thanks," he nodded. "Anyway, take these," he thrust the pistol and knife at her again, and she reluctantly took them. "I'll be leaving early. I'll make it a point to come straight back, and unhook the trailer, before I start looking for clothes and the like."

"You need to take someone with you," the younger woman spoke.

"No, not this time," Roland shook his head. "It's a fair ways, almost five miles from here, as the crow flies. And I can't fly," he added with a grin.

"It isn't safe for a man alone out there," Maria insisted.

"I've been worse places than this on my own, Maria," Roland spoke softly. "And when it's just me, I don't have to worry about someone else getting hurt."

"My father's business will have many of the things you need," she said flatly. "He was a landscaper. And a gardener. He and our neighbors always had a community garden. His storage building will have many of the tools you want, as well as some seeds. Heirloom seeds. Which you will need."

"I don't know what that means," Roland admitted.

"Heirloom seeds will reproduce. You keep part of the yield from your garden for the next year's crops. It is the old fashioned method of growing food. Many no longer use it because they can, or could, simply buy new seeds each year. I believe that will no longer be an option, no?"

"Well, that's true. I didn't know that. Thanks, Maria. I guess I should try to find a bookstore, and get some reading material on gardens. I seem to have a lot to learn."

"Books are another thing we have need of," Maria nodded eagerly. "For entertainment, and for information. To teach the *ninios*."

"I had thought about that, at least. School books, anyway. Hadn't thought about just having books to read for entertainment. I guess we'll have to find something before we leave, if we can. Anyway, like I was saying, I'll be heading out early, probably well before dawn. I'd like to be close to where I'm headed by the time its daylight. Truth is, I'm thinking about leaving at midnight. If I hurry, I might can get back before daylight, and avoid being seen altogether."

"You should not go alone," Maria said again. "Too much depends on you. Someone needs to be with you."

"I need everyone here," Roland insisted. "And I work better alone. Once I get there, I'll be fine. Now, I'm going to rest up, and then eat a bite before I go. You look like you could use some rest, too. Try to get some sleep, if you can."

"I will be fine," she almost snapped.

"Okay." With that he turned to his bedroll, and stretched out. Maria stood there for nearly a minute before turning and walking away. Stomping might be more accurate.

Wondering what kind of 'gringo' problem he'd caused this time, Roland nodded off to sleep.

ROLAND

CHAPTER SIX

Stupid women.

Maria says she can't trust me, she doesn't like me cause I'm 'gringo'. She won't say she'll stay and help, yet, so who do I find, ready and waiting for me when I wake up just after midnight, intending to slip outside and be on my way?

You guessed it. Maria. With a look on her face that screams 'don't argue'. Like I'm gonna not argue.

Truth is, I don't want her around. I'm trying to like Maria, and I respect the hell out of her for taking on so much responsibility with the children, but her attitude toward me makes my skin crawl. She sometimes looks like she's just waiting for an excuse to knife me. Maybe I shouldn't have given her that Kershaw. Or the gun for that matter.

I admit, just to myself, she makes a good argument. She knows where her father's place is, and what we need. She knows how to raise food, for that matter, which I don't. Handy skill to have in days like this.

I pretty much have to let her come along, but I can't just up and say that, since she'll get the idea that she's in charge. Well, actually she's already got that idea, looks like. And maybe this will convince her

I'm not going to do anything to her.

Which makes my tingle meter peg out, right there. If she can't trust me, and isn't sure I'm any better than Wright and his bunch, then why the hell does she want to go out there, alone, with me?

Stupid women.

~*~

"I told you before, I'm fine on my own."

"You need someone to watch your back," Maria insisted for probably the tenth time. Her tone indicated she was tired of saying it. Which was good, since Roland was tired of hearing it.

"I can watch my own back," Roland replied. "And if someone's with me, then that's someone else to worry about."

"I can take care of myself," Maria huffed slightly.

"Why do you want to go?" Roland asked.

"I told you, my papa will have many of the things you need."

"Where is your papa, Maria?" he asked carefully.

"Gringo's killed him and my mother, and my brother, just after the world went crazy," she stated flatly. "They. . .they are dead," she hesitated, slightly, indicating that there was more to it than that, but Roland didn't press her.

"I'm sorry, Maria," was all he could think to say.

"You aren't the one who did it, so there is no need for sorrow on your part," was her dull reply. "You will need me to guide you to where the tools and seeds are. Simple as that. I am going." She hesitated again, then spoke more softly.

"It will also give me a chance to see if my home is still there, and perhaps gather some of my own things. Clothes and... personal things."

Roland considered that. This was probably as close as she could come to asking him for a favor. Finally, with a great sigh, he nodded.

"All right," he gave in. "But when I tell you to do something, you do it, understand?" She nodded her agreement.

"Okay, we'll leave in half-an-hour." She nodded again, and turned away, walking back to where she slept. Shaking his head, and muttering more than one curse, Roland prepared for his journey.

~*~

"James is in charge until we get back," Roland ordered the other teens. "Deena, you and Teri will have to pick up the slack while we're gone. Willie, you and Ralph help out as much as you can, where you can. And all of you try to get some rest while the young ones are asleep. If everything pans out, we might be leaving in a day or two. Any questions?" Surprisingly there were none.

"Okay, get gone, then. James, wait for a minute if you will." When the others had gone, Roland eyed James.

"We should be back in a day. By tomorrow, at the latest. If something happens, I honestly don't know what to tell you. Do the best you can. Try to keep everyone safe. Including yourself, okay?"

"We'll be fine," James told him simply. "You will too."

ROLAND

"Hope so, kid," Roland grinned.

With that, Roland collected Maria, and headed out.

~*~

"Where are we going?" Maria asked, as they hit the parking lot.

"To where my truck and most of my stuff is stashed," Roland replied, his eyes looking left and right into the darkness. He had a pair of night vision goggles, and was wearing them. He didn't have another set with him, so Maria had to follow blindly.

"Where is that at?" she asked.

"About five miles from here, at a storage place called Big Al's U-Store," Roland told her.

"Sounds very legit," she observed.

"Are you seriously complaining about the name of the place?" Roland asked, his voice a little snappish. "And are you going to talk all the way there? Someone we don't want to hear might be out too, you know."

"I will be silent from now on," Maria promised, and he detected a slight amount of genuine contriteness in her voice.

"Good, now let's get moving. Stay close, and I can tell you if the footing gets rough."

There was faint light from the half-moon, but among buildings, the shadows simply made it harder to see. They made good time despite Maria being essentially blind. They couldn't risk a light unless it was absolutely necessary. About half-way to their destination Roland's warning about uneven pavement was late, and Maria tripped, falling into him.

"I thought you were to warn me of rough footing," Maria said accusingly as Roland set her back on her feet.

"And I thought you were gonna be silent," Roland shot back. "I was trying to warn you, just too late. I'll try and do better. Let's keep moving."

Several times during the trip, Roland could hear people talking, and more than once they heard gun shots. Fortunately, Roland had been right about people not being out late at night. Most were asleep already, since night time activities were limited due to a lack of electricity.

Without Maria along, Roland could have made it in a couple hours walk. With her along it was breaking day by the time they reached the storage facility.

Big Al's wasn't very reputable due to the kind of people who rented from him. He asked no questions, and answered none. He respected his customer's privacy and enforced that privacy among the many renters. No one was allowed to 'snoop', and he never revealed what he might know about anyone's storage.

Because of that, a lot of people who were otherwise disinclined to be trusting of others trusted Big Al's. Roland was no different. The things he had in his trailer were of. . .questionable, origins at best, and would have made the most even and fair minded cops crazy if they were discovered. Not that the police were looking.

But others would be. He held up a hand in the dim light of a new day, motioning Maria to stop. He studied the door for a minute, locating his tell-tales. All were in order.

"What are you looking for?" Maria asked.

"I left little bits of stuff here and there to let me know if anyone had messed with the door. They haven't. Should be okay."

"Interesting," was all she said. Roland sighed and unlocked the ridiculously strong padlock. The door slid upwards with almost no noise, thanks to the oil and grease he had used on it. Inside sat his truck.

"Wow," Maria exclaimed quietly. "You weren't kidding about being a soldier, were you?"

"No. Why?" Roland asked.

"Not everyone tells the truth," Maria shrugged. "Especially..." she stopped.

"Especially 'gringos'?" Roland finished for her. She had the grace to blush, not that Roland could see it in the near darkness. And he wasn't looking anyway, busy inspecting his trailer. It hadn't been tampered with, and was securely hooked to the hitch.

"Sorry," she offered.

"I don't care," Roland shrugged. "You got a problem with me being white, I get it. Not my fault, you know," he added. She said nothing.

"Anyway, get in," he ordered. "I want to get going before people get a chance to wake up and see or hear too much." She complied, still somewhat ashamed. Roland hit the switch and was rewarded with the powerful rumble of the engine.

"That a girl," he said fondly, patting the dashboard. "Buckle up," he ordered, doing the same himself. He put the rig in gear and eased out of the storage unit carefully. Once clear he headed out, not bothering to secure the door. If Big Al was still working he would know the place was available again when he saw the open door.

Out on the road, it was getting light enough that Roland didn't need the head lights, and he left them off. Bad enough to be moving in daylight with the noise the Hummer was making. He didn't need light attracting even more attention.

"There's a lot of stuff in here," Maria finally spoke again. She had been silent for a while.

"Yeah. Which way?" he asked her. She looked at him quizzically for a moment, then started.

"Oh, right. Turn left at the next light. We're only about ten minutes from my home."

"Sounds good," Roland nodded, making the turn.

"Four more lights, and then left again. That will be my street." Roland counted off the lights, staying quiet.

"You're very quiet," Maria said almost accusingly just after the second light.

"Got nothing to say," Roland shrugged. "Didn't figure you'd want to hear it if I did." Maria flushed at that, and this time Roland noticed, but decided against saying anything. He reached the fourth light, turning off onto a side street.

"That's my house," Maria pointed to a nice two-story brick with a large shop in the lot next to it. "My father's shop," she added. Her voice was small, almost subdued. Roland pulled the Hummer to a stop parallel to the house, still in the street.

"What do you want to do first?" Roland asked.

"I would like to go inside just for a minute," Maria replied after a moment's thought. "Alone."

"Not happening," Roland said at once. "I'm going where you go. I won't look over your shoulder, but for all you know someone has taken up residence in your house. You're not going alone."

"I can take care of..."

"So can I, yet you're still here," Roland cut her off. "Let's go. We're wasting time." Maria huffed, but accepted his argument, and the two went to the door. It was unlocked.

"Wait," Roland ordered, and pushed the door open, entering with his KSG held at waist level. The inside was trashed he hated to see.

"C'mon in, but step light. Someone redecorated for you." Maria stepped inside, and gave a small gasp at the condition of what had been her home.

"Why do this?" she asked no one, bending down to handle some broken figurines. "These were my mother's."

"Some people don't need a reason, Maria," Roland said softly. "They do things like this because they're mean, or because they can. It makes them feel powerful. They're cowards, deep down, and doing things like this makes them feel tough." She looked up at him, a tear trailing along one cheek.

"You sound like you speak from experience."

"You could say that," Roland nodded. "I've known a lot of bullies. On a basic level, they're all the same."

"I will only need a few minutes," Maria promised, picking up a backpack that had probably been stored in the closet it was next to.

"Take whatever time you need," Roland told her gently. "I'll stay here, and keep watch." Maria gave him a grateful look and went to collect her things. Roland watched her go, and then eased back to where he could see the street from the door. They were exposed here, and it made his skin crawl.

But Maria needed the time. She needed this to help her heal. Roland knew all about the need to heal.

~*~

Maria had been gone about ten minutes when Roland heard them. Voices, low and urgent. He sighed, knowing that wasn't good. He moved slightly to see further down the road, and spied five gang types working their way toward the house. Two were especially interested in the Hummer.

"I say we just take the truck and run for it," one said. He was wearing a leather jacket, even though it was a little too warm for it.

"Yeah, well, you ain't runnin' this show, now are ya?" the largest shot back. "I'm bettin' that little gal has come back to get some of her stuff. She got away the first time, but I aim to have me some o' that. Then we take the truck and go."

"She might have someone with her," the skinny one argued. "Let's just take the truck. No tellin' what's in that trailer!"

Big One punched Skinny in the back of the head, sending him flying.

"Shut up! I give the orders around here, not you. Got it?"

"We all get it, Foot," the Fat One said, hands up in a placating manner. "Rip was just offering suggestions. His way is safer, you have to admit."

"I don't have to admit nothin'!" Big One snarled, but he didn't offer to punch Fat One. Roland took note of that. More to Fat One than met the eyes, apparently.

"Fine," Fat One sighed. The other two, Roland decided to call them Dummy One and Dummy Two, since they didn't offer to speak, nodded in unison. Skinny One got up, rubbing his head.

"I want that girl," Big One said again. "Rest o' you can have'er when I'm finished. Then we'll take the truck and go. If anybody's with her, we kill him, and take his stuff. Anybody got a problem with that?" No one spoke.

ROLAND

But Roland had a problem with it. Not only that, but from listening, these idiots were responsible for death of Maria's family. That would make killing them that much sweeter.

Roland felt a rush fall over him, all too familiar. This time he didn't even try to fight it. His Calm was on now. He walked out on the porch, looked at the five morons in front of him, and shot Big One in the chest. The double-ought buck spread him all over Dummy One and Dummy Two, and left three of them paralyzed in shock for a few seconds.

But not Fat One. His hand moved like lightening, streaking to his waist and pulling a handgun.

Looks like I was right about him, part of Roland's mind smirked, even as he worked the slide on his shotgun and shot Fat One right in the middle of his large belly.

That's what you get for still being fat when everyone else is starving, he thought with malicious glee, working the slide again without the need for thought. By now Skinny One was running. Dummy Two was trying to get his rifle off his shoulder, while Dummy One was yanking on his pistol, trying to free it from his waist band.

Amateurs, Roland snorted mentally, shooting Dummy Two. Dummy One watched his friend fall, then raised his hands in surrender.

"Wait! I surrender! I give up! I didn't want to, Foot, he. . .he made me! Yeah, he made me! Threatened to..." He stopped when a round of buckshot disconnected his head from his shoulders.

Skinny was long gone, now, running down the street. There was no way buckshot would get him from this distance. Pulling the shoulder stock out on the KSG, Roland flipped a switch underneath, and took careful aim.

The Hornady Ballistic Sabot round left the short barreled shotgun at over eighteen hundred feet per second. Skinny lost that race before it ever started. Hearing a gurgling sound, Roland turned to see Fat One struggling to move. Roland drew his knife, and knelt down over him.

"You were *almost* fast enough," Roland told him, smiling. It wasn't a pleasant smile. "But you weren't. Never start a fight you can't finish, know what I mean? Did you enjoy wrecking that girl's life, jackass? Tearin' her home all ta pieces? Tell me something, ass-wipe. Was it worth it?" With that he drew the razor sharp knife over Fat One's throat, and the gurgling noises stopped. Roland wiped the blood from his knife on Fat One's clothes, and returned it to its sheath.

Standing among the dead bodies Roland calmly but quickly reloaded his shotgun. He could feel the adrenaline running through his body, straining for release, but there was no more release. He breathed deep, trying to rid himself of the urge to do more violence. Finally, he felt the tide begin to ebb and his mind start relaxing. He turned back toward the house, to find Maria standing in the door, the little pistol he had given her in hand.

The look on her face was enough to tell him she'd seen it all.

ROLAND

CHAPTER SEVEN

"Maria, are you. . ." Roland started toward her.

"Stay back!" she almost screamed, and lifted the little pistol with a trembling hand. She used her off hand to steady it, but there was still a tremble or two.

"Maria, it's okay," Roland stopped, raising his hands, and letting the shotgun fall in its harness. "They can't hurt you anymore."

"What about you!" Maria demanded, tears in her eyes. "You. . .you just killed them!"

"Yes, I did," Roland nodded. "They had it coming. From what they said, they were the people who killed your parents. And the big one had very ugly plans for you. He came here looking for you specifically."

"How can I know that?" Maria demanded. Suddenly Roland felt the Calm hit him, and nothing he could do would stop it.

"You know what?" he said, his voice very low. "I don't care. I'm sick and tired of this shit. You say you can't trust me because I'm a gringo, then demand to come with me. Now, when I just kept you from being their plaything forever how long they decided to keep you alive, *I'm* the one you can't be sure of?"

"I'm sorry me being white offends you. . .no, you know what? I ain't sorry. I can't help the color of my skin. I think this is where you and I part ways, Maria." Roland started for the Hummer. He didn't want to leave her alone, but he was sick of this. Whatever her issue was, she needed to deal. Lord knows he had plenty to deal with every day. And night.

He was almost to the truck when she called out to him.

"Wait!"

"No," he threw back over his shoulder. "I'm not waiting. I'm done. You want a lift back to the warehouse, I will give you that, but you and me are done. I can't trust you, Maria. Sooner or later you're gonna stab me, cut me, or shoot me. Probably with a weapon I gave you in the first place. I don't intend to let that happen. You're a walking time bomb, full of hate for the wrong people."

"And I'm definitely the wrong people." He stopped suddenly, almost out of breath. That was probably more than he had spoken to her since they'd met. He was worn out with worrying over Maria.

"You need me!" Maria shouted. "You need my help."

"I don't need anyone's help that bad," Roland shook his head. "And you weren't planning on staying, anyway. We'll have to learn to get by without you sooner or later. Might as well be sooner, to my way of thinking." He opened the door, and started to get inside.

"Roland, wait!"

And he waited. Maria had never called him by his name. Gringo was usually the best she had, if she bothered to address him by any name at all. Despite himself, he looked back at her.

The gun was hanging by her side, and she was shaking like a leaf. Concerned, he stepped back out, looking at her.

"Are you all right?" he asked. He didn't approach her, and kept his hand on the pistol grip of his shotgun. She was unstable and he didn't want to get shot.

"No, I'm not," Maria admitted, sliding down the porch post she was leaning against to sit on the porch.

"I haven't been for a good while. I'm. . .I'm sorry."

"For what?" Roland asked gently. Her sudden change was worrisome.

"For being so mean," she sobbed softly. "I have been so afraid for so long, and I hid it by trying to be tough all the time, and keep everyone at arm's length. It's. . .it's been hard since my family died, with no one to depend on."

"Well, I can understand that," Roland offered a small olive branch. Just a small one, since he didn't want to get hit with it. "I mean, I ain't never had a family, not that I can remember anyway, so I've never had that. Not 'til I joined the Army."

"I'm sorry for you, if you've never known the love of a family," she told him, looking up at him with a tear stained face.

"Can't miss what you never had," Roland shrugged. "James is pretty much the same way. Though he talks like he had a good foster home finally, before things went nutty." He paused, looking up and down the street. So far the shots hadn't drawn anyone, but he couldn't count on that to last.

"Look, Maria, I know this is a bad time for you, but we really need to get moving. Someone probably heard those shots." Maria nodded, wiping her face.

ROLAND

"Let me get my things and we will take what we need from Papa's shop." She disappeared back into the house, emerging five minutes later with her backpack, a small suitcase, and what looked like a comforter. Placing them in the back of the Hummer, she led him over to the shop building.

The door had been jimmied, and the place ransacked, but she ignored that, going to one of several storage boxes. Maria opened the box, revealing a number of air tight containers, each with a freezer tape label.

"Seeds," she said simply. He nodded, and started moving the containers to the trailer. Maria began locating the various hand tools they would need. They worked in silence, neither feeling the need to say more than they already had. Roland looked around the shop, wondering if there was anything else they might need.

"There is a small generator," Maria told him, pointing to another cabinet. He was amazed that it was still there. They hauled it to the trailer as well. There hadn't been a lot of free room in there to start with, and it was disappearing fast.

"There may be fuel," she added. "If it is still there, we should take it. And the chainsaw. We will need fire wood." Roland nodded, and the two went back once more. He grabbed the chainsaw, and two five gallon cans of gas. Maria took another two, and managed to make it to the trailer with them as well.

The very last trip was for one remaining fuel can, and her father's tools. Files, wrenches, any and every kind of tool a man in his trade might need.

"We should go," Maria announced as they loaded these last items. "They had friends who might come looking for them. I wish not to be here when they arrive."

"Sounds like a plan."

Maria didn't look back as they drove away. She had said goodbye. Her new life now lay ahead of her. Somewhere.

~*~

A very relieved looking James was waiting with the cargo door open when they returned. Twice they had detoured to avoid what looked like makeshift roadblocks. That worried Roland more than he let on. Something like that could stop them from leaving.

"Good to see you, Roland," James smiled.

"Good to be here, James," Roland grinned back. "Let us rest a while, and get some chow, and I've got some stuff for you to look at."

"Okay," the teen nodded, and took his station at the walk-through door again.

N.C. REED

Maria was very subdued, but smiled as the smaller children all clamored to see her back. She had kind words and a smile for each of them, calling them by name. Terry and Deena both looked equally happy to see her, Roland decided. He couldn't help but smirk a bit.

Roland took an MRE, leaving the better food for the children, and sat down on the hood of the Hummer, looking at a map. He carefully noted the roadblocks on it, and scribbled some notes in his field book.

Slowly he was getting an idea of what lay beyond the industrial park their warehouse was in. He had stayed here idle too long, forced to watch over the children.

I should have killed that bunch sooner, he thought to himself, sourly. He immediately chastised himself for thinking that. He had to wait until they gave him a reason. Killing someone because they might be a problem later was socially unacceptable. *Got to remember that.*

He needed a truck. One he could haul stuff in. He needed to find the things he needed to strengthen the bus so it could take on a roadblock. The Hummer was up-armored. That was more luck than anything, since he had grabbed the first one he'd come to. That made it a gas guzzler, but the tanks were full and there were four Jerry cans of gas in and on the truck itself. It would make it.

What he really needed was a technical. Technical was a wide term for any modified vehicle, and he needed a strong one, reinforced to take a pounding. Something that could blow its way through even a determined roadblock and open the way for the other vehicles. Something to draw fire away from the bus.

I need, I need, I need, Roland thought wearily. *What don't I need? At this rate we'll never get out of here.*

He paused in his morose thinking to steal a glance at Maria. She was helping the children get fed their evening meal. They reminded him of a bunch of baby birds, chirping for more.

I need to try and find some candy for them, he thought suddenly. *Just a little something for a treat, every now and then. Help keep their spirits up. Wouldn't hurt to try and find some toys, too.*

These thoughts brought him full circle back to his morose feelings. There was so much he needed to give the little kids any kind of decent life. Every time he stopped to look around, he saw something else he needed.

And the teens needed some relief, as well. They were working their ass off just like adults, when by rights someone should still be taking care of them. What a messed up situation. Shaking his head, he returned what was left of his meal to the package, and set it in the seat of the Hummer. He suddenly wasn't hungry anymore.

ROLAND

"You wanted to see me, Roland?" James' gentle question jolted Roland from his cloudy thinking.

"Sure did," he managed a grin. "You said you were familiar with a pistol, right?"

"Yes, sir, I am."

"Ever fire a Beretta? Ninety-Two model?" Roland held one out to him.

"Yes, my foster father had one. He let me shoot it on several occasions," James nodded, taking the weapon, and checking that it was clear before examining it.

"I've got a rig you can wear, drop down holster, all that stuff. I'm counting on you not exaggerating how well you can shoot."

"I never said I could shoot well," James replied solemnly. After a few seconds he grinned. "But I can."

"Don't scare me like that kid," Roland let go a breath he hadn't realized he was holding. "I need help.

And you've got to be that help. There's no way I can take care of all of you alone."

"I know," James nodded somberly. "We'll make it."

"You're pretty upbeat, aren't you?" Roland smiled.

"I decided long ago not to be otherwise," James shrugged. "I've learned to make the best of whatever situation I find myself in, just like the Apostle Paul."

"I did that too," Roland nodded in approval. "We foster kids gotta stick together, right?"

"Right!" James laughed. Everyone else turned to see what was funny, but all they saw was Roland and James exchanging a fist bump.

"Do me a favor, and go find Ralph and Willie. We need to have us a talk."

~*~

"Okay, before we can plan too much, I need to know what you fellas know how to do. Anyone of you know anything about cars?" Ralph raised his hand.

"I worked on older cars with my grandfather all the time," he said. "And I know a little about newer cars, too. Depends on what's wrong whether or not I can fix 'em, but I can service 'em and keep 'em running."

"Sounds like a plan," Roland nodded. "How about welding. Any of you know how to weld?"

"I do," Willie nodded, and Ralph nodded as well.

"Outstanding!" Roland felt better suddenly. "Can anyone hot-wire a truck?"

None of them answered. James looked at the ground, however.

"Well, I can," Roland grinned. "Just checking'. Anyway, here's the deal. We need two things. Well, three. First, can either one o' you drive?"

"Oh, me!" Ralph raised his hand. "Got a license and everything!"

"What kind of vehicles have you driven, Ralph?" Roland wanted to know.

"Well, my mom's car, my dad's truck, my grandfather's tractor, and..."

"Wait, you know how to drive a tractor?" Roland was interested in that.

"My grandfather is. . .well," the boy hesitated a minute. "He was a farmer, anyway," he finished in a mumble, his excited mood gone in an instant. "I used to help him in the summer time. Learn to drive early on a farm."

"So you could handle a big truck, then?" Roland asked. "Like a U-Haul, maybe?"

"Sure," Ralph agreed.

"Even if it was loaded?" Roland pressed.

"Can't weigh more'n soy beans," Ralph shrugged. "Drove many a load o' soy beans to the elevators for my gran."

"Well, boys, we may just have us the beginnings of a plan, then."

ROLAND

CHAPTER EIGHT

I slept harder than usual last night, and now I'm sore and stiff. And cranky. I managed to brew me a cup of MRE coffee, and good thing, since I needed the caffeine jolt.

Today, I'm planning on taking Ralph and Willie, and seeing if we can find a box truck. If we can, then the next thing is to find the materials we need to armor the bus up a little. We need to scout for fuel along the way, but I don't expect to find any. If we're lucky, we'll find a truck at a U-Haul place that's either full, or has a tank on site.

If we're not lucky, then I'm not sure what we'll do. I'll probably have to give up the road block buster option. Or use the Hummer, which I really don't want to do. We need something bigger, and heavier, if we can find it, and get fuel for it.

Maria hasn't said much to me since we got back. I haven't said anything to her, unless she spoke to me first. She still looks at me with wariness, but maybe it's a little less, now. I'm not sure. I've just got a feeling she's trouble for me, somewhere down the line. And I don't need any more trouble.

Terri and Deena are really taking on a lot more with the kids, and it's a big relief. Neither is out of high school yet, but they're both pretty mature. Terri's so shy it's painful to watch her try to talk. And a little funny, though I'd never laugh at her.

I just realized I don't know any of the little kid's names. I need to spend more time learning that stuff. Right now though, I'm so busy, I just don't have the time. Or the energy.

Maybe that will change, once we're out of the city.

The more I think about it, the more pissed I become. Where the hell are the social services and emergency services? The people who were...

Oh. Never mind. I'm a soldier, and where am I?

N.C. REED

When things really started going to crap, emergency services types stopped coming to work, choosing to stay with their own families. Can't blame them I guess. Does kinda leave people like me hanging' though.

But then I should still be on base, shouldn't I? I mean, wouldn't do much good. I don't think anyone was left in my company other than the officers and non-coms on HQ staff. A few enlisted without family, maybe. Only my company sergeant was left in our company chain of command, and no one from my platoon.

He had looked at the empty barracks one morning, and then at me. I'll never forget the look on his face when he said 'good luck'. Every time I play that scene over, I realize that I disappointed him that day. But I stayed 'til the last. We weren't doing anything. Just sitting there.

At least now, I'm doing something.

~*~

Roland looked around him and blew his breath out in a long whoosh. There were so many things he needed to do. So many things he needed. Wanted. Not for himself, but for the little children in the group. For all of them.

He needed a place of safety. He had several ideas, but there were problems. Were the places still safe? Were they already occupied? There had been a lot of refugees leaving the larger cities. They had to go somewhere. If Roland could think of it, so could they.

His original plan was in doubt, now. He lacked the fuel, he lacked the Intel to know what lay ahead of them. He had to devise an alternative. More than one. And he had to gather as much as he could supply before he left.

What if he could find a viable community? He hadn't thought of that before. It wasn't like everyone had died off. It was true that many people had died. Roland didn't know the exact number, and doubted if anyone did.

He rubbed his hands across his face, and sat down heavily. This was too much. There were too many unknowns. He had no help, no Intel, no communications. No support of any kind. He didn't need any of those things if it was just himself.

But it wasn't just him, was it.

What am I going to do?

~*~

ROLAND

"Okay, we're looking for a truck, like a U-Haul. Deena checked the phone book again, and got the closest ones to us. I want you two to take a look at the map, and see if anything looks familiar to you." Both Ralph and Willie did as ordered, eyeing the map through the plastic, looking at the marks Roland had made. Reluctantly both shook their heads, no.

"That's all right, we can find them, no problem," Roland assured them. "I asked because if either of you had been there, you might know more what we could expect to find. Are you two ready to go?"

"Yes, sir," both answered in unison.

"All right, let's load up."

~*~

The first place was a total bust. Roland didn't even bother to pull off the road.

"Not much here to pick over," he smiled at the two boys. "Let's head for the second."

But the second, and then the third were both equally worthless for their needs.

"Well, just one more and we can go back," Roland tried to keep upbeat. It took twenty minutes to reach, and was the farthest from the warehouse. At first look, things looked promising. Roland cautiously pulled into the lot.

There were two large trucks still on the lot, but one had two flats. He ruled it out right away. It would take hours to fix, and they had no way to air the tires without electricity.

The other looked older, but in decent shape. There was also a small truck. It would be handy for hauling, but lacked the weight to drive through a road block if needed. It would have to be the older one.

"Okay, we need to grab the keys if we can find 'em," Roland ordered. "I want to check them all for fuel. There might be some gas we can siphon from the other two for the one we're taking." They moved inside cautiously.

"Ralph, take Willie and find the keys," Roland ordered when no one challenged them. "I'll keep watch. Let's hustle, but stay quiet. Okay?"

"Yes, sir," Ralph nodded. "C'mon Willie." The two went to the desk, and Roland was pleased that they made very little noise.

"Got'em!" Ralph whispered loudly, holding up three key rings.

"Good deal," Roland nodded. "Let's check."

They quickly and quietly moved to the truck Roland intended to take. He inserted the key and gave it a turn. He didn't try to start it, not yet. He simply watched the fuel gauge.

The gauge rose slowly, stopping just below a half tank. Much better than he had hoped. He shut the key off, and quickly checked the other two. The truck with the flats was empty. The smaller truck, however, still had more than a quarter tank of fuel.

Roland took a siphon from his Hummer, and quickly attached the hoses, pumping the fuel from the small truck by hand. He had two small fuel cans, and after he filled the first, Ralph and Willie hauled it to their truck, while Roland kept pumping fuel.

They managed to get a total of eight gallons, more or less, before the siphon began sucking air. Roland was grateful for the fuel, but wished it had been more. He would have to be happy with what he had, however.

The larger truck now had three quarters of a tank of fuel. It would have to do. As he had feared, their chosen truck refused to start, or even turn over. He produced a set of jumper cables, hooking them to the Hummer. After a few minutes of letting the Hummer run, the U-Haul sputtered to life. Roland quickly closed and secured the hoods on both trucks.

"Well Ralph, here's where the rubber meets the road," Roland grinned at the teen. "You said you could drive."

"I can handle it," Ralph promised solemnly.

"Then let's head out. I'll lead the way and you follow. Can you find your way back from here?" He nodded.

"Okay. Willie, go with him. If anything happens, if we're attacked, let me deal with it. You two run for it. If you have to, dump the truck and make your way back on foot. Don't lose your bags," he pointed to the two backpacks he had put together for them.

"If you have to bail, grab them and go. Leave anything else."

Roland hated having to use the two boys for this, but he really didn't have any choice. He couldn't do all these things alone. He didn't have enough hands. If he had just one more adult...

"We're ready," Ralph called from the truck. Willie was strapping in beside him.

"I'll lead," Roland told him. "Use the radio only, *only*, in an emergency. Someone tailing you is an emergency. Needing to use the bathroom, not an emergency." The radios were GRMS/FRS hand-held, so anyone who happened to be on the same frequency would hear them. But it was better than flashing lights and blowing horns, which attracted unwanted attention.

Ralph nodded his understanding, and handed the radio to a now strapped in Willie. Roland took one last look around, then headed for the warehouse. The U-Haul pulled smoothly onto the street behind him and closed up cleanly.

ROLAND

Ralph really could drive. Good boy.

CHAPTER NINE

Even though he was paying attention, things spiraled out of control before Roland even realized it. A pair of technicals burst out of an alley behind the truck just as they crossed the halfway point to the warehouse.

Someone must have seen the truck, along with the Hummer, and decided it was something worth taking.

"Mister Roland, Mister Roland," Willie's scared voice came over the radio. *"There's somebody 'hind us, Mister Roland!"*

"I know, buddy, no problem. Tell Ralph I'm going to pull over a bit, and you guys speed up and go around me, okay? Don't stop, no matter what."

"Yes, sir!"

As he made room, the big truck eased to the left and started coming around him. Ralph really did know how to drive pretty well; Roland was pleased to see. The U-Haul wasn't built for speed, but it was steady. Roland readied his rifle, now a select fire M-4 courtesy of Uncle Sam, and braced it on the window sill of the driver's side door. The U-Haul came even with him, and he could see Willie's scared face peering down at him from the higher cab. Roland winked at the boy, and then grinned, and Willie grinned back at him just a little as Ralph picked up speed in the larger truck.

The two technicals had been reinforced with parts from other vehicles, odd and end pieces of steel, and even some chain link fencing. Roland couldn't see any crew served weapons in his mirror, but they had small arms and were shooting like ammunition wasn't a problem.

The two cars split, just then, with one pulling behind the Humvee while the other stayed on the U-Haul. Roland ignored the one behind him. They could shoot their under-powered rifles at the armored Humvee all day, and not do more than scratch the paint. Instead, he concentrated on the one following the boys. As soon as they pulled even with him, Roland opened fire, spraying the entire vehicle with rifle fire.

Just two seconds or so too late to prevent one of the thugs inside from hitting the rear tires on the U-Haul's passenger side. Roland was sure Ralph tried to keep the big truck straight, but he doubted anyone could have. The truck was doing fifty miles an hour and gaining when the tires were hit, leaving shredded rubber all over the road. Roland ducked on instinct when a large piece of tire from one of the dual wheels hit the windshield in front of him, but managed to stay on the road.

He watched helplessly as the events played out in slow motion. The truck's now tireless rear wheels slammed into the pavement with the truck still moving. As they dug into the street, it was like the boys had tossed an anchor out, and hung it on an immovable object.

The truck pulled to the right and began to slide. Roland could only imagine what Ralph was going through, trying to control the big truck. As he watched, the truck began to tilt up on its left side. For a second Roland thought it had stopped, and would settle back on its wheels, but instead the truck fell onto its driver's side, and started sliding down the road, still traveling at a good rate of speed.

Bullet's careening off the rear of the Humvee reminded Roland that he had problems too. The first technical, the one that had disabled the truck, had fallen back, apparently taken out of service by Roland's rifle fire. The second was still on his tail, and still firing.

Roland quickly reloaded his rifle, managing to keep the Humvee between the gang and the truck. He could see the truck coming to a halt, its forward energy finally used up in the slide down the street. Roland maneuvered the Humvee around the front of the truck and slid to a halt, rifle slamming rounds at the remaining technical.

The thugs in this one were smarter than the first, and stopped maybe three car lengths away, dismounting. Roland saw at least five people leaving the vehicle, managing to catch two of them in a hail of rifle fire, dropping them to the ground.

Sparing a glance through the windshield of the truck, he could see the two boys working to free themselves. Roland could smell fuel, and realized that their hard work gathering fuel for the truck was lost, now. He turned back to the thugs in front of him, snapping a few shots off to keep them honest. The hail of return gunfire forced him to duck behind the upturned front of the truck for cover.

He glanced again at the U-Haul, to see Willie working his way out of the passenger window, now pointing skyward. Ralph was kicking out the windshield in front of him, already splintered by their wreck.

"Willie! Don't go out that window!" Roland yelled. "Follow Ralph and come to me!"

"I'm coming, Mister Roland!" Willie shouted, still pulling himself out of the window.

"Willie, get back!" Roland shouted again, motioning for the teen to drop back into the truck. He never knew if Willie heard him, or understood.

Willie's head popped out of the window. As he struggled to pull himself out, he was torn to pieces by gunfire.

Roland froze as the small body slumped against the frame of the door. Ralph yelled Willie's name, trying to get to him. Roland would vaguely remember waving Ralph away, motioning for him to get out of the truck.

Then, he snapped. A cold feeling came over Roland as the Calm settled over him in a way he'd never encountered. Coldly furious at the needless death of brave, scared little Willie, Roland shut down emotionally.

He walked calmly to the Humvee and pulled his pack out. Setting it on the ground, he helped Ralph from the truck, stopping twice to fire back at their attackers, forcing them to keep their distance.

"We gotta help Willie, Mister Roland!" Ralph exclaimed as he extricated himself from the wrecked truck.

"Willie. . .Willie's gone, Ralph," Roland told him calmly. Too calmly. Ralph looked at Roland and froze.

"I want you to get in the Hummer, and get outta here," Roland ordered. He stuck his rifle around the front of the truck and emptied the magazine in random fire. He let it fall into his hand, and tossed it through the window of the Humvee.

"What about you?" Ralph asked. "And we can't just leave Willie!"

"I'll take care of Willie," Roland promised sincerely. "You need to do like I told you. Tell James that it's up to him until I get back. And you. . .you help him, Ralph, all you can. Okay?" Ralph nodded, not knowing what else to do.

"Off you go, then," Roland tried to smile, but it died on his lips. "Don't look back, and don't stop until you're back inside the warehouse. Go!"

Ralph hesitated for a second, looking up at Willie's body. Gulping, he ran. When he started pulling away, Roland stepped out from behind the truck and opened fire.

~*~

There were nine of them that he could see. The crew from the other vehicle must have caught up with the action his mind told him, somewhere far off. Roland didn't care. Not anymore.

ROLAND

Cold and calculating, Roland started shooting. He had always had an aptitude for it, which had surprised his instructors since he had never even held a weapon before joining the Army. After testing him on several different rifles and handguns, the head shooting instructor had simply shrugged and called Roland a 'natural'.

Some people are just born shooters, the Warrant Officer had told him.

And now, Roland shot. Again and again and again. Taking his attackers by surprise, he had killed three of them before they could react, and then rolled a grenade under their vehicle, destroying it. That would prevent them from following Ralph.

He slipped behind the truck again, running to the back of the overturned U-Haul. From there, he attacked again, hitting his assailants from a new angle. Apparently it had never occurred to the idiots that he could or would do that. Nor had they tried to flank him.

Amateurs.

Roland shot two more, then felt a tug at his left sleeve, which he ignored. Thumbing the selector switch to full auto, he emptied the remainder of his current magazine into the figures trying to move away from the car. At least one fell, but Roland couldn't tell if he had hit the fallen attacker or if they had been injured by the car blast.

And he didn't care, either.

Dropping the expended magazine, Roland ran back to the front of the truck, and this time kept running toward the buildings along the road. He snapshot another of the attackers, seeing him fall, before taking cover in a doorway. Leaning out quickly, he took a look at the scene before him. There were seven of nine now down, though not necessarily out. He saw movement through the smoke behind the burning vehicle, and snapped a three round burst in that direction, grinning ruthlessly when he heard a cry of pain.

"I know you're out there!" he called mockingly. "Your buddies are all down, and now I'm coming for you!" There wasn't an answer, but he hadn't expected one. He just felt like taunting the survivors.

"I'm going to kill all of you!" he sing-songed to the wounded. "You killed a little boy who didn't even know how to use a gun. And now I'm gonna kill you all. And I'm gonna hunt down your family, and kill them, too!"

"You leave my family outta this!" someone yelled back, and Roland smiled. One of his rocks had hit a dog.

"Not gonna happen, tough guy!" Roland called back. "Only way you can protect your family from me is to kill me! Only I don't think you got the stones for it, know what I mean?"

"I'll kill you!" someone screamed, and Roland heard feet pounding the pavement. Smiling, he leaned around the door frame, to see a lone man running toward him.

"AHHH!!!!" the man screamed, firing his rifle from the hip, just like in the movies. Roland smirked, and shot the man in the head.

"Dumb-ass," Roland shook his head. "I don't even know where your family lives." Leaving the cover of the door frame, Roland worked his way to the body, finding his aim had been true. Satisfied, he started checking the rest.

He could feel exhaustion creeping over him, now that his Calm had gone. His rage was still there, boiling beneath the surface, but there was no one to take it out on anymore.

He heard a cough, and smiled again. Turning, he saw one of the thugs trying to crawl away.

"Wait a minute, now," Roland called, unsheathing his knife. "You can't leave now, we're just gettin' started! What will the guests think?" The man crawled faster.

"Now, now, I know the party isn't everything you hoped for, but still, is this any way to be?" Roland taunted, following along. He caught up to the crawling figure, and a hard kick to the ribs turned him over on his back.

Only it wasn't a him. It was a her.

"Le… leave me… a… alone!" she gurgled weakly.

"Now why would I do that?" Roland asked, head tilting slightly. "Maybe you didn't hear me earlier? About killing all of you? I can't hardly do that by leaving you alone, now can I?"

"Y… You're crazy!" the woman almost screamed, her face showing fear. Roland leaned down, the smile still on his face.

"That's what the doctors tell me," he whispered, right before he cut her throat.

The rest were already dead, having died from their wounds, or bled out afterward. Roland walked slowly to where his pack was sitting, weary and light headed. It was time to get out of here before…

He never felt the pavement come up and hit him in the face.

ROLAND

CHAPTER TEN

"...st a lot of blood, but the wound wasn't all that bad. He should be fine." From deep in the depths of wherever he was, Roland heard a female voice, quietly talking.

"That's a relief," he heard a male voice answer. Did he know that voice? It sounded familiar for some reason.

Roland stayed still, regulating his breathing, allowing himself to come fully awake. He didn't know where he was, so the first thing he had to do was...

Suddenly the memory of Willie's lifeless body sprawled across the door of an overturned U-Haul came to him, and Roland forgot his discipline. He sat straight up.

"Whoa, Sarge! Take it easy, bro, you took a round, and lost some blood. But you gonna be alright, my grand done fixed you up shiny and new." Roland felt an arm on his shoulder, and suppressed the urge to break it. Instead, he looked up at the source of both the arm, and the voice.

"Jesse?"

"Aw, you remember me," Jesse Fuller grinned, his white teeth contrasting with his dark skin. "How you hangin' Sarge? Found you in the street, almost bled out. Looked like you'd had some trouble."

"Willie," Roland replied. "There was a little boy on the truck, named Willie. Did you...?" Jesse shook his head sadly.

"Sorry, Ro'. Boy was gone. I brung him along, and buried him. I'm sorry."

"He was just a kid," Roland whispered. "Fifteen years old."

"You know well as I do, Sarge, age don't mean nothin' to the Reaper. Bill come's due, you pay it," Jesse shrugged. "I made sure he was took care of proper, though. He wasn't. . .Sarge was he family?"

"I ain't got no family, Jesse. You know that," Roland shook his head. "I found a bunch of kids holed up in a warehouse, living on garbage about three weeks ago. Been trying to figure a way to keep 'em alive, and get 'em out of the city. Somewhere safe, maybe."

"Ain't no such thing no more, bro," Jesse shook his head again. "Whole country, whole world, done lost its mind." Roland looked up at this old teammate.

"Jesse, it's good to see you," Roland shook his own head, smiling. "How long have I been here?"

"Four days," Jesse told him. "You was almost bled out, Ro'. Gran didn't know you was gonna make it or not."

"I told you it was up to the Good Lord's will did he live or not, Jesse Owens Fuller," a short, elderly and scratchy voiced woman corrected, walking into the room on a cane. "That ain't the same thing."

"Yes, Gran," Jesse rolled his eyes where only Roland could see them. The woman rapped Jesse on the back of his head with her cane without missing a step.

"Don't you roll your eyes at me, boy," she snapped. Jesse rubbed his head, but stayed quiet.

"Ma'am, I'm..."

"I know very well who you are Roland Stang," the woman groaned a little as she sat down. "Been knowing who you was since my sassy mouthed grandson brought you through my door."

"Yes, ma'am," Roland nodded. He didn't know what else to say.

"How you feelin'?" the woman asked. "'Spect you got a headache, and your arm is achin' something fierce by now," she added. Roland nodded.

"Yes, ma'am. And I'm..."

"Boy, go and get the man some water," the woman hit Jesse again with the cane. "Sit here slack-jawin' when a hurt man done been asleep four days and ain't had no water but what we could get down 'im. Get on!"

"I'm going!" Jesse snapped back, but waited until he was out of reach of the cane before doing so.

"Crack brained idjit," Roland heard the woman mutter. He decided to stay quiet.

"'Spect you've got a story to tell," the woman spoke. "Hush boy, 'fore you tear your throat lose tryin' to talk with a dry body!" the woman snapped as Roland opened his mouth. "I can talk for both of us."

"I heard you say you was protectin' a bunch o' children. Why? They yours?" Roland shook his head.

"Reckon a man such as you ain't got no children, do he?" the woman asked, her voice softer. Gentler. Roland shook his head again.

ROLAND

"You got a long, sad road ahead o' you Roland Stang," she said softly. "Lord have mercy on you boy, 'cause you done walked the Devil's Road, and now you got to make amends, ain't you?"

Roland looked at the woman wide-eyed, but nodded slowly.

"You won't save them all, boy," she continued. "Accept that now, so that you can keep goin' when things look bad. No matter what you do, or how well you do it, you won't save 'em all. Hush!" she slammed her cane on the floor. "I said you ain't to speak."

"You think you can atone, boy, for all the blood on your hands? Think you can wash all that away, by doin' this?" Roland looked at her angrily this time, and shook his head, no.

"Good, cause you can't," she nodded in approval. "Ain't nothin' but the blood o' Jesus can save you, child. You too far gone for anything else. That dark man inside you done been let out to play too many times." She leaned forward, working her way to her feet.

"You lay here and rest a while, Roland Stang. Where you're goin', you gon' sho' nuff need it." With that she hobbled out of the room, meeting Jesse at the door.

"Here's the water, Gran," he smiled, offering her the bottle.

"Well, give it to him, idjit! I look thirsty to you?" Jesse walked in and handed the water bottle to Roland, who almost drained it in one draught.

"Nice woman, your Grandmother," he gasped.

"You ain't got to lie, Ro," Jesse chuckled. "She's good as gold though. Took one look at you and started in fixin' you up." Jesse settled into his chair.

"So, feel like tellin' me what you been up to?"

~*~

"And that's when I found all them kids," Roland shrugged, leaning against his pillows. He had drunk three more glasses of water as he and Jesse caught up on old times, and new.

"Hell of a thing," Jesse shook his head. "Seen that too many times overseas. Never thought we'd see that day here in the World."

"Tell me about it," Roland nodded. "Anyway, me and Ralph, and W..." the name hung in his throat for a moment as he remembered once more that Willie was gone.

"Anyway," he forced himself to continue, "me, Ralph and Willie were looking for a truck to help us get away. Something heavy that I could beef up a little, in case we hit a roadblock. Only truck we could find, with all the fuel we could get, and now it's gone," Roland commented bitterly. "And on top of that, I let Willie get killed. All for nothin'," he almost spat out.

49

"Ro', I know you tried to save that boy," Jesse frowned. "How you figure you 'let' him get killed? I counted the bodies, Roland. Was twelve to one against you." He frowned a bit. "Couple of them was. . .I thought you was seein' a doctor about that, Ro'."

"I was," Roland admitted. "Til there wasn't no doctor. Things has gone to hell in the Army, too, Jess. I was the last man left in my platoon at Campbell."

"You discharge?"

"Nope, just walked off. Like most everyone else. Family people left first, I guess. Trying to protect their own. Then folks drifted away in two's and three's, going to see what was happening, I guess."

"Well, I guess that ain't a problem, way things are right now," Jesse shrugged. "And there sure ain't no authority left nowhere. Like you said, folks is tryin' to care for their own, now." He looked at Roland.

"How is it you got stuck with them kids?"

"I told you, they ain't got nobody to look after 'em no more. Parents are dead, or just plain up and left 'em behind. I guess they figured someone would step up."

"Looks like someone did," Jesse said seriously. "What do you aim to do, now you got 'em?"

"I haven't the slightest idea," Roland admitted. "I wanted to take them south, maybe to a state or county park, where they could be outside. Maybe raise a garden to keep 'em fed. Or if I could find a community that was still functioning that might take them in. They still need an education."

"That's a tall order, bro," Jesse observed. "Who else is involved?"

"It's just me and six. . .five other kids, now," Roland replied. "Three teen girls, and now two boys." He closed his eyes for a moment, thinking about how badly he had let Willie down.

"Roland, you got to forget that boy," Jesse said softly. "Wasn't your fault, and you can't bring 'im back."

"Of course it was my fault!" Roland shot back. "Wasn't for me, he wouldn't have been out there! Probably still be alive."

"Or not," Jesse replied evenly. "You said yourself that bunch in the warehouse was gettin' ready to trade 'em out. At least Willie had a chance because o' you. You could o' just left 'em there, and moved on. But you didn't. Give yourself a little credit, at least."

Roland turned his head, looking out the window. It was dark. Where had the day gone? And what time was it?

"I need to get back," he said suddenly. "I... they're probably scared stiff right now. I need to see if Ralph made it back, too."

ROLAND

"You can't go nowhere, shape you're in," Jesse said. "Rest tonight, then I'll help you tomorrow. We'll get you back there, and see what's what."

"I can't ask you to do that, Jesse," Roland shook his head. "Your Gran needs you here."

"You didn't ask," Jesse replied, standing and stretching. "Now rest. We'll get a start after light." With that Jesse left the room. Left Roland to rest.

If he could.

~*~

Roland awoke sometime during the night, needing to use the bathroom. This was the first time since he'd been awake that he'd had to. He wondered if he had been nearly dehydrated.

He slowly got to his feet, noticing he was still in his BDU pants, but shirtless.

"Your shirt's done for, I think, but it's wearable, 'til you can do better," Gran Fuller spoke from the shadows. "Bathroom through yonder," she pointed in the dim light of a single candle. "Get done, come to the porch and sit with me, Roland Stang." He watched her light another candle, leaving him the one now burning, and make her way out. He used the candle, finding the restroom. Out of habit he went to wash his hands, but found there was no water. He shook his head. He had known that.

He found the old woman in a rocker on the porch, first light still distant. He took a seat near her, downwind since he was pretty ripe, and breathed out a little heavy. Just the little movement he'd made had cost him a lot.

"You ain't fit to be up," she told him. "But 'spect you ain't got much choice."

"No ma'am."

"You want to know about what I said before." It was a statement, not a question.

"If you want to tell me, ma'am," Roland replied.

"I got the sight, boy," the old woman said after a few minutes. "Got it from my Grandmother, my momma said. Some says it's a blessin', but others tell of it as a curse."

"Which do you think it is?" Roland asked.

"Ain't never rightly decided," the old woman cackled with quiet laughter. "Truth be told, I ain't never thought on it over much." She sat forward, and even in the dark Roland could tell she was looking right at him.

"You got a dark cloud hangin' about you, boy," she said gently. "Ain't your doin', and you don't like it, but it's there, just the same. Like me, you ain't never took no thought about it, whether it's a gift or a curse." She sat back again,

"Knowed men like you a'fore, son," she went on. "Some good, some bad, and a few just plain indifferent. I 'spect you was one o' the indifferent kind, at least 'fore you found all the young'uns.

Yeah?"

"I guess so," Roland answered honestly. "Like you said, I never thought on it much."

"You like the violence, don't you boy?"

"I don't like having to be violent," Roland thought about his answer. "But once it's on, I..."

"You enjoy it," he could almost hear Gran nod. "There was a time when such men was needed, Roland Stang. And that time's comin' again. Already on us in some ways, but it will get worse. Don't expect to see it get any better in your time. This is bad, boy, but it ain't the end. Understand?"

"Yes. At least I think so."

"Then you listen to me, Roland Stang," Gran leaned forward again. "There's people you ain't met yet, that will influence and help you. And there's some that will do anything to stop you. You got to be watchin', boy, and be wary, like a lamb in the lion's den. You don't keep watch, you'll get et."

"I know all about how well you can take care o' yerself," the woman waved Roland's attempt to defend his abilities away. "But you're vulnerable now, Roland Stang. You got people to look after. That gonna influence your thinkin'. And your doin', too."

"Train the acolyte," she continued. "He's more like you than you know. One day he'll have to carry your burden. No, it ain't right, nor fair, but it is, that's all. Train him. You can't change his path, so make sure he can walk it, comes the time. Understand?"

"You mean James," Roland answered her.

"You know who I mean," Gran nodded. "You can trust him. Reckon he looks up to you. Somethin' to aspire to. And he's more like you than not. Understand?"

"You mean he's like me when I'm fighting," Roland replied.

"You know what I mean." She paused for a time, rocking in her chair. Roland stayed quiet, his mind reeling.

"Know you don't understand what all I'm sayin' now, boy, but reckon it'll come to you, when it's needed. You take heed. There'll be a woman with hair like the sun, and she'll lead you astray you ain't careful.

She'll look like a cool drink o' water on a hot summer day, but inside she's poison."

"There'll be a man with a heart of iron, and he'll stand by you 'til the end. You won't like him at first, but you will in time. He'll tell you you're crazy, with a busload o' kids that ain't your responsibility, but he'll be there when you need 'im."

"And there's a girl with hair like coal that'll watch you. Watch ever step you take. She's different from the others. Be mindful of her. She's your future, Roland Stang. If you've got one that's not covered in blood and misery, she's it." The old woman rose, a bit unsteady.

"I ain't long for this world, Roland Stang," she told him bluntly. "I done seen it. Jesse don't know it, and I ain't gonna tell'im. You ain't to tell 'im, neither. When I'm gone, he'll like as not seek you out. You watch over him, boy. He's as loyal as a sheep dog, and as true as clean water. You wait two weeks before you leave. Hear me? When you get back, you wait two weeks before you leave." She started inside.

"Think bigger," she said suddenly.

"Ma'am?"

"You need a truck," Gran reminded him. "Think bigger." She started to the door, but stopped before she opened it.

"There's a word for people like you, Roland Stang. A word from the old world, some would say. But it's a good word." She paused for a moment, as if sizing him up.

"Fare thee well, Paladin."

And then she was gone.

CHAPTER ELEVEN

"You up already?" Jesse asked, walking out onto the porch. Gran Fuller had been gone for half-an-hour, and Roland had simply sat, staring into the coming day, his mind a swirl of emotions.

"Yeah. Reckon four days is about all the sleep I can handle at one go," Roland joked.

"You up to makin' the trip then?" Jesse asked, concern for his old friend and teammate in his voice.

"Ain't got no choice but to be," Roland shrugged, standing. "Just need to get my pack. I didn't think to ask if you picked it up."

"And your rifle," Jesse nodded. "Wish I had my old M-4, nowadays," he said mournfully. "Could sure use it."

"We get where we're going', I'll fix you up," Roland promised. "I might have an extra laying around." Jesse's grin was wide enough to drive a car through.

"That sounds fine!" he drew out the words. "Let me get some gear, and pick up your stuff. Might as well get going. Most of the rowdy ones'll still be sleepin' it off this time of the mornin'."

"Sounds good," Roland nodded. "Need to say good-bye to your Gran, too."

"She's fast asleep, Ro'," Jesse shook his head. "I can tell'er you wanted to, but I'd appreciate you don't wake'er. She's out of her heart meds, and she ain't doing real well."

"That's fine," Roland nodded. "I wouldn't want to wake her. I appreciate all she's done. And you for saving my ass, too."

"Ain't like you never saved mine," Jesse reminded him. "Let's git."

~*~

ROLAND

Jesse knew the area well, being a native. He led Roland through a dizzying array of alleys and back streets as they made their way back to the warehouse.

"Let me lead when we get near," Roland cautioned. "There's a boy'll likely be on watch. No need to get hit with Blue." Jesse nodded.

It took four hours to make the journey with Roland in the shape he was in. They'd stopped to rest a couple times but Roland kept pushing. He needed to get back and see what was happening.

"Okay, Sarge, we're about a block away," Jesse told him. Roland nodded.

"Yeah, I've been seeing familiar things last few blocks."

"If you can make it alone, I can head back," Jesse suggested.

"No," Roland shook his head. "Need to get you outfitted. I got it to spare, promise. And I want to give you a ride back. No need for you to walk."

"Waste o' gas, Ro'," Jesse argued.

"Not to me. C'mon."

Roland took the lead, walking as upright as he was able. The walk had about done him in. He was still about a hundred feet from the door when someone called out:

"Stop!"

Roland stopped.

"It's me, Roland!" he called out. "James, is that you?"

"Roland?" James stuck his head over the tall roof, amazement in his voice. "Roland is that really you?"

"What's left of me," Roland nodded. "Everything okay?"

"Fine," James replied. "Who's that with you?"

"Believe it or not, just about my best friend, ever," Roland smiled. "He pulled me off the ground and nursed me back to health. We soldiered together."

"So we're cool?" James asked, his voice wary.

"Yeah, we're cool," Roland smiled. "Us foster boys got to stick together, right?"

"Right!" As Roland hoped, James remembered their conversation from before. No one else would know what they'd said to one another. It also let James know, more or less, that Roland was okay. James was quick on the uptake. Thinking that made Roland remember Gran Fuller's admonition to him. He made a mental note then and there to start teaching James everything he needed to know. Starting today.

The walk through door opened, and Maria looked out, tiny pistol in her hand. She saw Roland, and for a brief instant, relief shown on her haggard face. Then she smothered it.

"We thought you were dead," she said flatly.

"I can feel the remorse from here," Roland muttered, limping his way to the door. Jesse followed, hands clear.

"Who is he?" Maria demanded.

"Friend of mine that's responsible for me not being dead," Roland shot back. "Let us in." Maria frowned, but stepped back, opening the door wider. Roland managed to get inside and to a chair before he gave out.

"Home, sweet home," he whispered. James and Ralph came running to meet him.

"Mister Roland!" Ralph hugged him, making pain shoot through his arm. "I was. . .I was afraid you..." He stopped, unsure what to say.

"I'm okay, Ralph," Roland assured the boy. "I'm glad you got back safe. Have any trouble?"

"No, sir," Ralph shook his head. "Made it fine. I'm. . .I'm sorry 'bout the truck, Mister Roland," he added quietly. "And Willie. If I had..."

"Don't finish that," Roland said sternly. "I don't know how you kept that truck upright as long as you did, Ralph. That was some serious driving you did. They shot both the right rear tires off. You did great." The boy smiled slightly.

"And what happened to Willie wasn't your fault, either. Was mine. I didn't see him soon enough to stop him, that's all."

"But you told him not to go out the window, Mister Roland!" Ralph objected. "I heard you!"

"I wasn't fast enough," Roland shook his head. "Never think it was your fault, Ralph. Never. Hear me?"

"Yes, sir," the boy nodded, looking as if a giant weight had been taken from his shoulders.

"Would you get me and Jesse some water, please?" he asked. Ralph nodded eagerly, and ran off.

"Damn, Ro', you wasn't kiddin', was you?" Jesse whistled, looking around. "That's a passel o' young'uns, sure enough."

"James, looks like you did good," Roland smiled. "This is Jesse Fuller. Me and him been all over the world together, seems like."

"Mister Fuller," James nodded.

"Call me Jesse, James," Fuller smiled, then laughed at his pun. They all laughed at that.

"I'm pleased you can laugh, with Willie dead," Maria said scornfully, walking up unnoticed and unannounced.

"Maria, we aren't laughing about Willie," Roland sighed. "Jesse just made an almost joke. It was pretty bad, but funny at the same time. Give it a rest, will ya?"

"Were you joking around when Willie was shot?" Maria was relentless.

"No, I was killing the people who shot him," Roland snapped back. "And bleeding to death in the process. I'm sure you'd be much happier if I had bled out, but unfortunately for you, not everyone shares your hatred of white people just on general principles. Jesse found me. Saved my life. Hate him for a while, since it's his fault I'm still alive."

Maria turned in a huff and stalked away.

"Damn, Ro'," Jesse murmured. "Ease up, bro."

"She hates me cause I'm white," Roland shrugged. "Ain't like that's my fault or nothin'. And I ain't done one bad thing to her. Or said nothin' bad, either," he added.

"She gave Ralph hell for two days, when he came back alone," James said softly. "Had the poor kid thinking it was his fault. Kinda made it sound like he'd just ran off, and left you and Willie."

"Maybe I made up for that," Roland grimaced. "If she wasn't so good with these kids..."

"That's the only reason she's still alive," James said flatly. "Ralph cried for hours. And she never let up. If I thought we could have managed without her..."

"I get the picture," Roland held a hand up, forestalling any further comment from James. Jesse gave Roland the stink eye.

"Jesus, Ro', are you sure he ain't some kind o' kin o' yours?"

~*~

Things were tense, but there was work to be done. First, Roland walked over to his trailer and unlocked it. He began removing items from inside, handing them off to Jesse.

"Jeez, Roland, are you sure?" Jesse asked, seeing the gear being piled at his feet.

"Yep," Roland nodded. "I told you, I got it to spare. There was sort of a buyer's market when I left."

"What all you got in there?" Jesse asked.

"Little o' this, little o' that," Roland shrugged. "It's all good, Jesse. And you need the gear. Don't bother sayin' ya don't," he added. Jesse finally nodded, gratefully.

"Here," Roland said, thrusting a pack at his friend. "Half-dozen Ethiopian Rejects, water tabs, fuel tabs, mess kit, canteen, and M-9. Should be a set of web gear in there, too."

"Water purification is. . .man that's a godsend," Jesse replied. "Thanks Ro'."

"No problem my friend. Least I can do, considering. Think of anything else you might need? If I've got it, it's yours."

"No, this is awesome. Full load of ammo, too," he added. "I don't know what to say, Roland," Jesse said earnestly.

"Try 'Gee, thanks Roland'," came Roland's sarcastic reply, but he laughed as he said it.

"Gee, thanks Roland," Jesse grinned. "I hate to take and run, but I gotta head back. Things'l get active, soon."

"I'll get James to drive you back," Roland offered. "Him and Ralph."

"Nah, vehicle would just attract attention. And thanks to you I'm geared up good, now. I'll make it fine." Roland looked at him for a moment, then nodded. He reached back into the trailer, and removed a satellite phone.

"Take this, then," he offered. "I've got one, too. My contact is on the back. Get in a jam, call me. Battery's full up, so if you're conservative, you should be good for a while."

"Awesome," the former soldier smiled. He put the phone into the pack, and slung it on his shoulder.

"Roland, take care, okay? You need some rest 'fore you start into doing anything else for a while."

"I will. I think we'll hang here another two, maybe three weeks. After that, we'll start looking for a home. You decide you want to come see us, gimme a call."

"Roger that," Jesse nodded, and extended his hand. Roland took it, and the two friends drew each other into an embrace.

"Keep your feet and knees together," Roland smiled.

"Watch your six," Jesse replied. Roland watched him go, and then sat down heavily on the trailer's floor. It was harder than he had thought to see Jesse leave. But according to Gran, he'd see Jesse again soon enough. Meanwhile, he had other things to take care of.

"James, come on over here," Roland called out. "I need to talk to you, buddy."

ROLAND

CHAPTER TWELVE

Well, it's good to be home, I guess. I really miss Willie. Fifteen years old, his whole life ahead of him, and now he's gone. Just like that.

And it's my fault. Jesse can say anything he wants, but I know it's my fault. I should have done the job myself. I could have walked back and got the truck later instead of taking Ralph and Willie out there. I depended on the low life's laying up in the mornings since they were laying it on thick every night.

That was a mistake. I made the mistake but it was Willie who paid for it. Sometimes I think it would have been better if I had never walked out of that jungle alive. Everywhere I go, death follows.

Gran Fuller was right about that when she said it. Or words to those effect. Walking the Devil's Road. I really liked that old woman. I wish she would come here, and be with these kids. They could really benefit being around someone like her.

Then again, if she's right, then they would only have time to start getting attached before she was taken from them, and that might be worse for them in the long run. Like I would know, anyhow.

I've started teaching James, like she wanted. He's taken to it like a duck to water, and that really doesn't make me feel very good. It's like I'm taking his future away. Why am I putting so much faith in what she said anyway? For all I know she's a crackpot.

No, scratch that. She's definitely not a crackpot. I know why I'm putting faith in her, damn it. She reminds me of the Medicine Man. And damn him too, for me still being alive. Who asked him to 'intervene' as he called it? Did he 'intervene' just so I could be here, and get Willie killed?

Or maybe, just maybe, so that I could save at least some of the others? Gran says I can't, that I won't, save them all. To accept that now, so it's easier to keep going later.

N.C. REED

Just how in the hell do I do that? Will I have to choose who I can save, and who I can't? How does someone make that kind of choice? Any one of these kids could be key to our future. How do I know who that might be?

And even if I did know, what gives me the right to decide which child lives, and which dies? Nothing, that's what. They all deserve to live. To have a shot at some kind of future that doesn't revolve around being huddled in this damn warehouse, afraid to laugh and play for fear that it will attract attention to themselves. To scrape and scratch for enough to live. Never being happy, full, or content, just surviving, and that only barely.

Dear God, please help me. Not for me. I don't deserve it. But for them. Surely they do. Surely.

~*~

Maria barely speaks to me these days. It's been a week since I got back and she's never more than civil, and that only when the younger children are around. I hate her. I mean I really hate her. Ralph is still having nightmares about Willie, and there's not a doubt in my mind that she's at least partly to blame.

Damn her for tormenting him like that. I've never seen so much concentrated venom in one little woman. It's like she hates the whole world, and blames everyone she comes in contact with for her problems.

She's not the only one who's lost her family. These little kids, and the older ones, are all alone, save for each other. It sucks, and that's a fact, but for her to take it out on Ralph is beyond wrong.

As for me, I couldn't care less what she says to me, or thinks of me. If I could manage on my own, I'd give her food and water for a week or two, and she could step on out now. Arrogant bitch. I mean, I know she's been through a lot, but so has everyone else. I'm getting mad all over again just thinking about her flogging Ralph about Willie.

I don't think I've ever hated anyone the way I do her. Ever. And that's saying something.

~*~

The kids seem to feel the tension between us. I know that Deena and Terri are aware of it, though I don't think Maria is really speaking to them very much either. Ralph avoids her like the plague, and James watches her with hawk eyes. If she steps out of line again, he may decide he's had enough.

ROLAND

Hell of it is, I don't know whether to stop him, or help him. It's that bad.

We've been working on the bus, some, trying to get it beefed up a little. James suggested we dismantle some of the shelves in the warehouse, and use the material to cover the windows, tires, and sides. Not as good as real armor, but it might make the kids safer when we leave. I've emptied my Jerry cans into the bus, and now it's got almost a full tank. No idea how far that will carry us. For that matter, I still don't have any idea where for us to go. I've looked at the map until my eyes blur, but I just can't see it. I can't see the spot.

So, I've decided to head south. Even a hundred miles might mean warmer temperatures, and easier living. We need to be near a dependable water source. What I'd really love to find is an abandoned old school house, with a well. Plenty of room, maybe some playground equipment, and a gym. Room to grow some food. Fenced in area. And books, of course. Books for the kids to learn. And there might be a library.

Too bad there's no more internet. I could Google search schools, and see where they all are.

James helped me redress my arm earlier today. It's ugly, but there's plenty of scars on me, so one more won't matter. The important thing is that it's not red or swollen. I definitely got lucky. Meaty part of my arm, no bones broken, no veins or arteries damaged. It will heal, and not cost me any use in my arm.

I've stayed away from the younger kids, mostly because of Maria. I don't want me and her getting into an argument in front of the smaller children. They've got enough tension without that. I feel guilty about it for some reason, but I still think it's the best idea. Despite her hateful and ugly personality Maria really does take wonderful care of them.

I guess that gets her a pass where social skills on an adult level are concerned.

A few more days and we'll head out. I think I'll talk to James tomorrow. He seems to know the area pretty well. I want his input before I make any final decision about direction.

Who knows? He might just know where there's a school house we can use.

~*~

"Okay, James, how would you sign to me if there were five men out front, but also three more sneaking around the… south end of the building."

Roland had been teaching James all he could think of, including the hand signals that the Army used in the field when noise discipline was in effect. James had taken to all of these things easily, most on the first try. Signaling not so much. But he was working on it.

His hands began flashing signals, pausing occasionally as he worked out what he needed in his head. When he had finished, Roland flashed a series of instructions back to him. James watched, and then nodded.

"Okay, what did I say?" Roland asked.

"Observe the three moving along the south side, leave the front side to you," James replied at once.

"Good job," Roland praised. "I think you've got it. Keep practicing. Come at me now and then with a report, one you've made up. I'll repeat what you signal to me, and we'll see how accurate you are. Got it?"

"Got it," James smiled slightly.

"All right. Take a turn on the roof. Be sure and stay out of sight, and use the scope. Let me know if you see anything. After that, take a break, and get some chow."

"Yes, sir," James saluted slightly, and headed to the roof.

"You shouldn't be teaching him these things," Maria's voice ended Roland's good mood in an instant.

"And you should mind your own business," he snapped back. "What I teach James, or anyone else, is a great big barrel full of *none* of your business."

"And when he gets killed like Willie did?" Maria glowered back at him.

"Then he's dead," Roland said flatly. "And by the way, since you brought Willie up, if you ever, and I mean ever, make Ralph feel responsible for that again, I might just decide to see if I really can get by without you. Know what I mean?"

"That was pathetic, Maria," he continued, feeling his anger rising. "Ralph is fifteen years old. You had no business laying into him, blaming him for something that wasn't his fault."

Maria opened her mouth to object, but then closed it sullenly without speaking.

"Go ahead, Maria," Roland responded. "Try and justify what you did to him. See if you can come up with an adequate reason for making that kid feel like Willie's death was his fault." Maria remained silent.

"You really are pathetic," Roland told her flatly. "You carry all that hate and venom around, just waiting to unleash it on anyone you can. If I didn't despise you as much as I do, I'd probably feel sorry for you."

"You know nothing," Maria almost spat.

"I know plenty, Princess," Roland shot back. "You need to accept the fact that you aren't the only one who's lost something. Look at all these kids," he swept his arm around the room. "They don't have anything left either. And some of us never had anything to begin with. We made our own way because there wasn't anything else we could do."

"So spare me the attitude. You wanna go, go. But until you do, get off your high horse, and give Ralph a break. Give me one, too, while you're at it. I tried every way in the world to keep Willie alive. If it makes you feel better, I admit it was my fault. I should have done it alone. I only let him go because he wanted to so bad. That was my screw-up." Roland sighed, suddenly exhausted. This had been coming for a while, but he hadn't meant for it to be now. Reluctantly he sat down, wincing as pain shot through his arm.

"You are not healed enough to be up and around so much," Maria noted.

"Yeah, well, I don't have much choice. We're going to leave here soon. I need to be ready. I can't do that sitting around. I've been shot before. I'll deal."

"Where?" Maria asked.

"Where what?" Roland asked, eyes closed for a moment.

"Where were you shot?" she asked.

"Which time?"

"Any. All."

"First time was in Afghanistan," Roland spoke without thinking about it. "Took a round through the thigh trying to pull a friend of mine out of an ambush. Second time was in South America. A three round burst stitched me right up the middle. Should have killed me."

"Why didn't it?" Maria asked.

"A tribal Medicine Man whose tribe I was trying to help nursed me back to health. I had been reported MIA, suspected to be KIA. I reported back two months later, healed and ready to go."

"MIA?"

"Missing in action," Roland explained. "Assumed KIA, or Killed In Action. My unit reported me as likely to have died in combat."

"You have lived a violent life," Maria observed, though for once with no hostility.

"That's true," Roland didn't bother denying it. "You get good at something, people above you tend to send you on rough jobs. You get a reputation for getting things done, they want you to be the one with the hard-to-nearly impossible missions."

"That sounds very dangerous." Again her voice was absent its usual hostility.

"Can be, I guess," Roland shrugged, and regretted it instantly as a new spike of pain shot through his arm. "Lot of my friends and comrades didn't survive. I probably shouldn't have either. If I hadn't, Willie might still be alive." His voice was bitter, but he didn't notice. Maria did, however.

"And he might not," she said softly. "In fact, none of us would be, or if we were, we might be wishing for death. That is thanks to you." Roland's eyes shot open in surprise, looking at her.

"I am not so wrapped up in myself that I have not seen what you have done," she admitted. "None of us are. Perhaps that is why I was so hard on Ralph. He did not know where you were, or if you were even alive. All of us were afraid. Without you here, we were helpless." With that she walked away, before Roland could frame a reply.

He watched her go, confused. What was her deal, anyway?

~*~

"Roland, we got company," James' voice came through the radio very softly. "I…I think it's Jesse, but I'm not sure yet. He's alone, whoever it is."

"Keep an eye out," Roland ordered. "I'm headed for the door."

Twelve days since he'd spoken to Gran. Wait two weeks, she had said. Now, twelve days later...

He shook off that thought and walked to the door.

"Ro', it's me," Jesse called, his voice conversational. "Okay if I come in?"

"Sure," Roland agreed at once. "Good to see you, man. What brings you out here?" He noticed that the pack he'd given Jesse was bulging, and a bedroll was strapped beneath it. He was pulling a small wagon, too.

"Lookin' for a place to be," Jesse shrugged as he walked inside. "Gran passed yesterday morning. She was sick for a couple days, and then yesterday mornin' she didn't wake up," he relayed sadly.

"Jess, man, I'm so sorry," Roland told him, meaning every word. "I… I really like her."

"She did you too, Roland," Jesse nodded. "Told me a couple days ago that she was feelin' like it was her time. If it was, she said, I should come and help you. That she wanted me to help you if I could."

"You're always welcome at my fire, Jesse, you know that," Roland replied softly. "And if you want to help, that's fine by me. No one I'd rather have, to be honest."

"Thanks, bro," Jesse smiled weakly, and they hugged briefly. "Where can I put my stuff?"

"Anywhere you want, brother."

ROLAND

CHAPTER THIRTEEN

Gran was right almost to the day. That worries me. Because now I have to admit that everything else she said might be right, too. Now I have to be on the lookout for a woman with hair like the sun, and a heart of ir. . .no, poison. She's poison, and will lead me astray if I don't watch her.

It's a man with a heart of iron that I won't like at first, but he'll be a good friend. Okay, she didn't say he'd be a good friend. I don't think she did. Shit, why didn't I write all this down when I got back? He won't be a friend, maybe, but he'll be there when I need him. Yeah, that was it.

She was right about Jesse, too. But she kinda sand bagged that one, suggesting that he come help me if she passed. Still, he didn't have to do it. Without her, though, I suspect he didn't really have much else. No reason to stay, and nowhere to go.

Just like me.

What else was it? James would take my place, eventually. I'm seeing to him, every day. A girl with hair like coal, who watches me. She's my future, if I have one.

Well, that sounds pretty good, anyway. Hard to believe I might have a future of any kind, let alone one that's. . .well, maybe not happy. She didn't really say I'd be happy. Hell, I wouldn't know happy if I had it anyway.

Still, wonder when I'll meet her? I hope she's pretty.

~*~

"I think it's time to go over what we're gonna do," Roland said to the group he had assembled. Jesse, Maria, James, Ralph, Deena, and Terri.

"We need to find a better place than this," he said flatly. "We need a place with water, preferably a well, and some room to move around. We need to get some clothes for these kids, and some shoes. We need to get as much food as we possibly can."

"And we need to find a truck. A really big truck," Roland added, thinking about what Gran Fuller had said.

"We can try the warehouse foods place again," Deena spoke up. "It might still be good."

"That was what I was thinking," Roland admitted. "Best chance for us, I think."

"I got no idea where we can go," James shook head slowly. "Be cool if we could find an old school somewhere, though. Plenty of room, maybe some books and stuff. And most schools have a fence around them, too," he added. Roland looked at him for a moment, his face blank.

"What?" James asked. "Not a good idea?"

"No, it's a great idea," Roland told him. "One I'd thought about, too. Great minds, huh?" he grinned, and James grinned back at him.

"Which direction you planning on going?" Jesse asked.

"South," Roland replied. "Even a hundred miles, I think, would give us a little better weather that we'll get here, come winter."

"Plenty of places south of here," Jesse nodded. "Depending on how bad things got in rural areas, might find some civilization left, too. Course they might not be too happy to see us when we get there."

"If we find a place not in use, I don't care if the folks around are happy. We're not going to be a burden on anyone. We'll take care of ourselves, as best we can."

"Works for me," Jesse nodded.

"We have much work still to do in making preparations," Maria warned. "Finding clothing and shoes for everyone will probably be the hardest things. And the *ninios* are growing, even with the starving time we had."

"If we can get enough clothes, the smaller kids can use the hand-me-downs as they grow. We can try to get material and thread and what not to make better clothes for when they're grown," Terri offered one of her rare speaking engagements.

"Hey, that's a good idea," Deena nodded. "I know how to sew."

"So do I," Maria nodded. "We can do that, if we can find the things we need."

ROLAND

"All right, we're starting to have a plan," Roland nodded. "Let's keep at it. Deena, why don't you go get that phone book, and a pad and pencil. James get that map of the city streets if you will. We need to list all the places we want to try and visit, and then locate them on the map. We'll plan our route in a circle, and try to get everything at once."

~*~

The hardest thing was going to be locating a truck. The second hardest was fuel for the truck. No one doubted that. Working vehicles were difficult to locate anymore. The school bus, and the now wrecked U-Haul had been lucky finds. Luck only struck so often.

If the warehouse foods place hadn't been bothered, they could gain more than enough food, especially if they could find what they were looking for; a tractor trailer. A trailer loaded with basic food stuffs could keep them in fine shape for a long time. Roland didn't know exactly how long, but he figured several months. Maybe even a year.

Second hand clothing shops were numerous. The popular stores, often called 'dig stores' by many, could contain clothing of almost any size or style, so they would have to make do with what they could find.

Shoes were another problem all together, but there were two shoe stores within driving distance. If no one was there, then they'd just take what they needed. If someone was still trying to maintain a business, then Roland would use what silver he had to buy shoes for the children. Hopefully they would last long enough that the children could pass them on down as they outgrew them. At least for the time being there would be shoes for them, anyway.

Roland rubbed his temples as he felt a headache threatening. There was so much to do. Having Jesse here was a fantastic stroke, of luck, though the cost was too high in Roland's opinion. But there was still so much uncertainty. So much unknown.

"Okay, I think the first order of business has to be the truck," Roland declared. "Unless and until we know we have a truck to haul things in, there's not much point to gathering a whole lot, yeah?" Everyone agreed with a nod.

"Okay, the next thing is teams. We'll have James here for security of the building. If there's a problem he can't handle, he calls us, we come back as fast as we can." James nodded, his face expressionless. Roland knew the teen would rather be out with them, but he accepted that he was the best suited to defend the warehouse other than Roland or Jesse.

"So, Ralph and Deena will come with us. Maria and Terri, when, and as you have the time, keep studying the list. There's always going to be something we haven't thought of. The less we miss, the easier things will be on us when we get where we're going."

"Any questions?" he asked. "Or do we have a consensus?" No one spoke, although most nodded their heads.

"Okay, one last thing," Roland said gently. "We're in this together. I know that you're all young, and probably used to being treated like, well, teenagers. In the situation we're in now, you're pretty much grown. You've all been doing an adult's work for a while now. So when you have an idea, let's hear it. When you see a problem, point it out. No one else may think of what you do, or may notice what you see. We can't afford to make any mistakes if they're preventable. Understand?"

This time everyone nodded, almost eagerly. Well, except Maria, who Roland simply ignored.

"All right then, everyone has work to do, so let's get to it." The group broke apart, then. Roland called Deena and Ralph to wait.

"You two aren't going today. This is just a scout mission. We might get lucky and find a truck we can bring back, and if we can, we will. For the most part we're going to make the circle and see what's where. It'll limit our exposure later. So today, I want you two to take a look at the bus. We'll need to haul stuff on there as well as the kids."

"Here's what I want you to do. We need to carry some of everything on the bus. Food, water, medical supplies, you name it. So you two start working out what we can store, and how. We can use storage tubs, boxes, whatever we have or can scrounge."

"Why not just carry it all on the truck, Mister Roland?" Ralph asked, with Deena nodding her agreement.

"Because we might lose the truck," Jesse spoke up. "Never put all your eggs in one basket. If we lose the truck, then we've still got basic supplies to last for a little while, so we have time to recover." Both teens nodded, seeing the wisdom.

"But, what if we lose the bus?" Ralph asked, clearly not challenging, but curious. Willing to learn.

"Then we're screwed," Roland replied.

~*~

They had been moving for a while, Roland eyeing the fuel gauge almost as much as he was the road. The Hummer drank gas like a kid drank soda, but he couldn't see any other way to get everything else done. When it came to fuel, he was willing to abandon the Hummer if necessary to get the bus and whatever truck they could find to a place of relative safety.

That would be a last resort, since he firmly believed they needed the Humvee, but he would do it if he had to.

"You know," Jesse broke into his thoughts, "we could just add some storage to the top of the bus."

"I've thought about that," Roland nodded, "but I'm not sure we can attach it properly without tools we don't have, and power to run them. You got something in mind that might work?"

"No, hadn't thought about that," Jesse admitted. "I keep thinking like things are normal, even though I know they ain't. Habit, I guess."

"I know how that is," Roland sighed. "It's hard to adjust. Too used to having logistical support."

"Have you thought about checking the armory?" Jesse asked.

"What armory?" Roland asked, puzzled.

"The National Guard Armory, here in Nashville," Jesse replied. "They might just have some vehicles in storage still, you know. Might have fuel, too."

"No, I hadn't checked it, or even thought about it," Roland admitted. "It never even crossed my mind," he shook his head in wonder at his own shortsightedness.

"Well, it might be a bust," Jesse shrugged. "Might be somebody already took it over, or what's left of the Guard may have taken their families there for protection. There ain't really no way to know except go look, I guess."

Roland thought about that. He thought about a lot of things. What if the armory was deserted? Even if the equipment was gone, the place would make a good permanent home. There was room there for everyone, and there would probably be sufficient room to grow at least some food. The area would be protected by good fencing, and the facilities would be a great boon to them.

But they would still be in the city, where lawlessness ruled. They would be confined to the facility for the most part. No freedom of movement to amount to anything. He ran all of this through his mind, thinking furiously.

"Which way would we go from here to get to this armory?" he finally asked. Jesse grinned, and pointed.

"Turn right up here."

CHAPTER FOURTEEN

They sat, looking at the grounds. The place was larger than Roland had imagined, until he remembered that this would be the State Headquarters. Signs around the area had told them that both the Army and Air Guard called these grounds home.

"Well, it's intact, anyway," Jesse offered from the passenger seat.

"So it is," Roland agreed. Looks imposing, too. Larger than I had thought."

"You thinking what I'm thinking?" Jesse asked.

"Depends on what you're thinking, now don't it?" Roland smirked slightly. "But if you're thinking this just might be a good place to hole up, then yeah, I am."

"We're gonna have to see if anyone's home, I guess," Jesse sighed.

"Yep," Roland nodded, and put the Humvee into gear.

"We going now?" Jesse asked.

"No better time," Roland affirmed. "its broad daylight, we're in an official Army vehicle, and we're pretty much desperate."

"Well, when you put it that way," Jesse nodded, checking his rifle.

"Don't bother," Roland told him. "We're here to talk, if anyone's home. If no one is, and we can get in, we're heading straight back to get the kids."

"No harm in being prepared," Jesse observed.

Roland eased the Humvee up the drive, slow but steady. He didn't want anyone thinking he was being aggressive. This place would have the ordinance to split their Humvee in half, and leave nothing but a burnt husk, if that.

"There's a soldier on the gate," Jesse informed him, looking through binoculars at their destination. "He's armed. Looks like he's on the radio, too."

ROLAND

"Well, it's not empty, but it seems like they're on the ball, whoever is here. I'm assuming if they're still bothering with uniforms their discipline is intact." Roland tried to sound hopeful.

"Works for me," Jesse agreed. "He's definitely on the radio. I suggest we stop well short of the gate and walk up there."

"I'll walk up there, you stay with the truck," Roland shook his head. "I'm not going to carry my rifle, so you cover me. Something happens to me, you beat it."

"I'm not leaving you behind, Ro'," Jesse said quietly.

"Something happens to me, you're all those kids have, Jesse," Roland said firmly. "That means you git. Understand?"

"I understand," Jesse nodded. "I just don't like it."

"Since it means I'm probably dead, I don't much like it either," Roland chuckled darkly. "I still want it to happen that way. Okay?"

"You're the Sarge," Jesse nodded. "I'll do it however you want, Ro'."

"Good."

Roland stopped when he gauged he was still one hundred feet or so from the gate. The soldier manning the gate was not very animated, which Roland took to mean he was calm, and professional. It might also mean that this place hadn't had any trouble, at least lately. That was a guess, though. He stepped carefully out of the vehicle, hands clear. The guard watched him, but didn't challenge him. Hopefully another good sign.

Roland walked slowly but deliberately to within twenty feet of the gate, stopping before the soldier ordered him to.

"Help you, friend?" the soldier asked calmly.

"I hope so," Roland replied, keeping his voice conversational. "I need help, if you can spare it. I'm responsible for nearly thirty children who have been left alone. Their parents are either deceased, or have abandoned them. I'm trying to find a way to get them to a place of safety."

"Sounds like a rough time," the guard commented.

"You said a mouthful, brother," Roland nodded. "I need a truck to carry supplies for them, and fuel. I've got a working school bus for transport, but it can't carry enough supplies for all of them. Not for a substantial time, at least. I need to find something better. Preferably something heavy that can ram its way through a roadblock, or smash a technical if needed."

"Captain's on his way," the guard replied. "Don't know that we can help you, but he will."

"I'm mighty appreciative," Roland nodded. "I haven't heard much news of late. Anything you can tell me about the situation? Local or regional, hell national if you guys have heard anything."

"Things are a mess all over," the guard confirmed. "Coms are down most of the time, though we get some use once in a while. Brass are trying to hold things together, but there's no support for anyone anymore. Most of the riots have stopped from sheer hunger and lack of anyone to participate."

"I assume you know that there's armed gangs running lose all over the city, right?"

"Yeah, afraid I've met at least one of them," Roland nodded. "Not overly friendly. Or talkative for that matter. They generally just start shooting as soon as they see you."

"That's about the size of it," the guard nodded. "Things are pretty bad here, and just as bad nearly everywhere else. Now that the cities have been pretty much used up, a lot of the larger gangs are moving into more rural areas."

"I'm assuming that the casualty count is pretty high," Roland fished.

"You'd assume right," the guard nodded as a Humvee pulled up to his post. "That'll be the Captain. Might be he can help, I dunno."

"Thanks." Roland watched as a short, almost pudgy man exited the vehicle, walking to the gate. The man had a no-nonsense look about him.

"Who are you, and what do you want?" the man demanded gruffly.

"My name is Roland Stang, sir," Roland came to attention. "I have a group of twenty-eight children that have been left without parents. I'm working to get them to a place of safety, try to provide a decent place for them to live."

"I need a heavy truck, and some fuel, in order to do that. I was hoping you might be able to help me, or point me in the right direction to look for what I need."

"How'd you come to have all these children, Stang?" the Captain asked.

"Just luck of the draw, I guess, Captain," Roland shrugged helplessly. He'd asked himself that same question more than once after all. "Someone had to do it."

"You Army?"

"I was," Roland replied truthfully. "Last man left in my platoon. Most of the other guys left. To look after their families, I guess. I waited, but nothing was happening. So I finally left, too."

"Deserted?" the Captain's voice was contemptuous.

"They deserted me, really," Roland shrugged again. "I got tired of sitting in the barracks alone when things were falling apart all around us. So, I decided to try and do something about it. I admit that at the time I didn't know what I was getting into."

The Captain lost some of the starchiness at such direct answer. He sighed heavily.

"Well, at least you're honest. And still trying. Not many are, anymore." He looked at the guard, and nodded.

"Come on inside. We'll see if we can help you. You can bring your Humvee inside if you want. We won't take it from you, got plenty of our own." Roland grinned and turned to motion for Jesse to bring the vehicle in.

"You armed?" the Captain asked.

"Yes, sir," Roland replied.

"Be stupid if you weren't," the Captain nodded. "You can keep 'em, just don't shoot anybody."

"Thank you, sir," Roland nodded again.

~*~

Roland followed the Captain's Hummer to an office building, and he and Jesse exited their vehicle when the Captain got out of his.

"I'm Captain Jason Thomas, Headquarters Company for the 278th." He shook hands with Roland and Jesse. "There's not many men here, either, Stang. Just the few who wanted to stick, and some of their family members. That's why we're taking security precautions. Well, that and the supply dumps," he added. "What's your situation?"

"I have twenty-eight kids, ranging from four years to nineteen years, sir," Roland recited. "They have no one to care for them, and nowhere to go. My goal is to get them somewhere secure, with access to water, and some semblance of safety. I have a bus to transport them in, but very little room to move supplies. And very little fuel," he added. Thomas nodded his understanding.

"Things like that are getting hard to come by, that's for sure." Thomas considered for a moment.

"I'd invite you to come here, but we're short of water, and everything else, too. They would still be hungry. Do you have anywhere in mind to go?"

"I hope I can find a rural school building for them," Roland replied. "A place with room enough to spare, and with a fence, at least, to provide some added security. And books for them to learn from. It's a lot to figure out, sir," he admitted.

"I can imagine. What are you doing for food?"

"Well, we found a warehouse foods supplier. One of those companies that ship to grocery stores. It's abandoned, and still reasonably well stocked. We took some of that food to feed the kids with for now. My long term goal is to find a place where we can grow our own food, supplementing that with wild game. That's my hope, anyway."

"A whole warehouse, huh?" Thomas' eyes lit up at that. "Maybe we can work something out. You willing to share that food?"

"Of course," Roland blinked, surprised he hadn't thought of that. "We could never carry it all, even if we had a truck. Which we don't."

"Would a deuce-and-a-half work?" Thomas asked, his brow furrowing in thought. "Or even two? I could give you two, and fill all your tanks for you. Might even scratch up some Jerry cans, but I can't promise that. Does that sound like a plan you can get behind? We're running short on food stuffs ourselves. We've got plenty of MREs of course, and some field kitchen packs, but with the civilians here we need something better than that."

"Sir, that is absolutely a plan I can get behind," Roland agreed at once. "One hundred percent. With those trucks, I can hopefully scavenge some clothing and shoes for the children, and haul the supplies we need to set up shop somewhere until we can start producing food on our own."

"I might can spare some manpower for a day or so to help with that, too. It'd be worth it to lay our hands on a good supply of food," Thomas said. "Let's see what we can come up with, huh?"

ROLAND

CHAPTER FIFTEEN

I can't believe how lucky we've been the last two days. In just forty-eight hours, we've gone from hopeless to hopeful.

Captain Thomas has been great. He told us to go ahead and bring the kids to the base for the time being, since we had our own food, and had provided a place for him to get more palatable food for their own children and civilians. Their doctor even checked all the kids over for me. They had their first real bath in weeks, scrubbed clean and treated for any skin problems, while the medic showed Maria how to prevent problems like that in the future.

A convoy of trucks journeyed to the warehouse foods place yesterday, with myself and Deena along as guides. The place was stripped bare in just a few hours by eager and willing hands from the Armory. Two of those trucks, loaded evenly with everything Deena could think of and that was on the ever present list in her hands, are ours. Enough to keep us going for maybe three months, or even more.

Even better, one of the trucks has been fitted with a snow plow blade, courtesy of the Tennessee Department of Transportation. She'll ram through a road block now, without question.

This morning three people from the Armory accompanied us on our quest for clothes and shoes. They need the same things we do, so it's in their best interest, I guess, to help us while they help themselves. Maria is satisfied that we've got sufficient clothing and shoes and socks for the children for the immediate future. There are also several pairs of boots which we hope the smaller kids will grow into.

Deena and Terri found a small sewing center that was still standing, and managed to load up on some material, along with thread and needles and what not. They told me everything, but about all I know about sewing is I don't know how. I can usually put a button back on, or sew up a tear in my uniform if I'm in the field, and that's pretty much it.

N.C. REED

Terri, it turns out, likes to knit. She has grabbed every bundle of yarn she can find, and is still looking. She's promised to teach Deena, and some of the older girls how as well. I guess we'll have blankets by winter. Well, afghans maybe. Afgans? How do I spell. . .never mind.

There's a mechanic here, and he's fine tuning the bus, and my Humvee. He should be done this evening. We'll head out in the morning.

~*~

"Sergeant, I really appreciate whatever providence brought you our way," Captain Thomas said as he reclined with Roland and Jesse outside. "The help you've given us may be just what keeps us going. I am genuinely sorry that we can't offer you a place here with us."

"I'd say you've helped us more than we've helped you, Captain," Roland shrugged. "And while I can't deny it would be nice to stay here as part of a larger group, I do understand. Your resources are limited, and adding our group to it would simply mean you would exhaust them sooner."

"I really appreciate that," Thomas scowled. "Cause I feel like a cast-iron sum-bitch for turning you away. I'd give anything to be able to do more for you. But you've seen how tight things are for us here. Without the food you found, we couldn't have really maintained here more than another month. Whatever help we've given you pales in comparison to what you've given us. Hope."

"The help you gave us, letting the kids bathe and get medical attention, was. . .well, more than I could have hoped for, sir," Roland told him honestly. "One of the things I've worried about most, to be honest. Without access to medical care, almost any sickness will be harsh for us as a group."

"I'm relieved we could do it," Thomas admitted. "We're actually set pretty well for medical issues. I wish we were better off in other areas, especially water. Right now, we're dependent on the Cumberland for water, purifying it for drinking and cooking, and simply filtering it for bathing. If we didn't have that portable water plant from when we were in Iraq, we'd be screwed. Still will be when it goes down for the count."

"You should think about leaving here, sir," Roland told him. "Find a place outside the city with a clean well, perhaps. Somewhere you can be sustainable. You have enough manpower to make that happen."

"We have thought about it," Thomas admitted. "And may do it yet. To be honest, I'm waiting to see what happens. I keep hoping some semblance of society will return, but with each passing day that becomes less and less likely. I think our societal breakdown may be a long time correcting."

"If ever," Jesse nodded. "Do you have any idea of the casualties this has caused?"

"News reports are a thing of the past, I'm afraid," Thomas shook his head. "We have contact with the Army on occasion, but if they know anything they aren't sharing. The com situation is pretty bad at the moment. Folks may have working equipment, but no power. Or limited power through generators or solar cells, but neither of those are long term providers. And fuel is getting hard to come by in many places. We were just lucky. The fuel depot here is maintained because of the equipment storage and maintenance shops, or we'd be up the creek. Our tanks were topped off right before the wheels came off, so we're good for now."

"Ideally, I'd like to find some form of civilian law enforcement still in play, and assist them in getting some order restored. We can loan a squad to them, and our firepower would let them do their jobs without fear of reprisal. Trouble is..."

"Trouble is, there aren't many, if any, left," Roland nodded. "They're just like the rest of us, Captain. Looking after their own."

"All too true, I'm afraid. And you can't really blame them, either," Thomas shrugged. "I mean, we're all doing it. That's all we have left, it seems like."

"Is there any viable government left?" Roland asked.

"There's what claims to be a central government," Thomas raised his hands, palms up, "but I don't recognize a single name they use. Not one. And no one with the Army that we talk to will 'confirm or deny' anything. Honestly, I think there's a power struggle going on for what's left, and no one wants to take sides."

"Don't see what difference it can make," Jesse shrugged. "We're too far gone for any kind of central government control, these days."

"I'm afraid that's truer than any of us wants to admit," Thomas nodded his agreement. "If what's left of the Federal Government can simply protect our shores, then I think that's all we can hope for. Things in the interior will go back to how they used to be. Local and regional government. But right now, we don't even have that in a lot of places." He turned to Roland.

"I have no idea what you're going to find outside the city, Roland," he admitted. "We haven't had any real news in weeks. If we had a HAM, maybe we could find out something, but we don't. We can tune into what's being said, sometimes, with a receiver one of my people rigged up, but we can't ask anything. We just have to take what we get."

"Should be able to find HAM equipment at a Radio Shack, if there are any of them left intact," Jesse offered. Thomas looked at him, and blinked.

"What did you say?"

"Radio Shack," Jesse said again, cautiously. "They sold HAM stuff. Should be some of it left, maybe."

"Son, of, a, . . .I never even thought about that," Thomas leaned back in his chair. "I've been sitting here like a good little soldier, using what Uncle Sam provided for us, and never even thought about looking for civilian equipment. Some officer I am, huh."

"You've had a lot on your plate, sir," Roland pointed out. "And I hadn't thought of it, either. Good one, Jesse. If I had done that, I might know more about what we could expect out there."

"We can see about grabbing something on the way out," Jesse shrugged. "If it was just us, I'd say just roll the dice. Be like an adventure, you know? But with the kids, we really need to know what we're getting into. Or heading toward, at the least."

"I'll put Deena on it," Roland nodded. "If there's any place like that on our path, she'll sniff it out. Maybe we'll get lucky."

~*~

"There are three of the Radio Shack stores along or within a few blocks of our route out of Nashville," Deena told him later that evening. "Entirely possible that one or more of them are reasonably intact, they're so far outside the city proper. We may can find what we need in one of them."

"Thanks Deena," Roland smiled. "You're a godsend. Always finding stuff for us. Don't know what we'd do without you." The teenager blushed prettily at that, looking at her notebook to hide her face.

"All right everyone, are we set to go tomorrow?" he asked the assembled group.

"I do not understand why we cannot remain here," Maria said again. She was angry that they weren't allowed to stay in the relative safety of the Armory grounds.

"Because they don't have the resources, Maria," Jesse answered for him this time. "They used a whole lot of their fresh water to allow us to bathe the children, and then clean up ourselves. The only way for them to replenish that is draw it from the river, and filter it. It's hard to do, dangerous to be out there doing it, and the filter isn't an infinite resource. It will eventually break down or ruin the filter. Adding over thirty people on a permanent basis would just speed that up."

ROLAND

"And we'd have to leave then, anyway," Roland nodded. "This way, we're out and gone, and maybe have time to see about a garden wherever we end up."

"It is their responsibility to care for us," Maria argued. "They are supposed to be..."

"Maria, we can argue about this until we die of starvation, and the situation won't have changed," Roland cut her off, his voice taking on an edge. "If you want to ask them to let you stay, personally, go ahead. They might be able to take one person without any trouble. They simply don't have the resources to take care of us all. And they've already been a major help to us in more ways than one."

Maria grew quiet at that, and Roland didn't push the matter. He honestly hoped she would ask. They might just let her stay, after all. They needed her, but they could get by without her. And her attitude being gone would be a big plus, in his opinion.

"All right, I want everyone getting a good night's sleep," Roland continued after a moment. "The civilians here have offered to look after the children during the night, so none of us have any duties tonight. Everyone get some sleep, and rest up. Tomorrow might be rough, and you can bet the days after won't be any better." He stood.

"We'll leave in the morning."

CHAPTER SIXTEEN

Roland was surprised to see Captain Thomas waiting beside his Humvee when he went to stow his gear. They still hadn't worked out who was driving what, but they had just enough drivers for all four vehicles.

"Morning, Captain," Roland nodded, storing his sleeping gear. "You're just in time. We're getting ready to depart."

"So I see," Thomas nodded. "I have something for you on that subject. I'm sending a fire-team with you on an MRAP. To lead the way and provide some road security. They can't stay with you forever, but they can at least help you get to a place of safety." He waved to four fully outfitted soldiers, who walked over to him.

"This is Corporal Jenkins. Jenkins, this is Sergeant Stang. You'll be under his command, until you start your return trip. These are troopers Willis, Vaughan, and Mackey."

"Nice to meet you fellas," Roland nodded, and then shook hands with them. "Captain, I don't know what to say. This is really a boon to us."

"I hate not being able to let you stay," Thomas murmured, his voice full of self-loathing. "The least we can try to do is see you safely to a good spot. Jenkins and his team will stay with you until you're established. And the MRAP should make short work of any roadblocks or ambushes. All of these men have seen action, and are among the best troops in the outfit."

"Thank you, sir," Jenkins smiled. "We'll get it done."

"I know you will," Thomas smiled. "Load up and get ready to depart." He watched them go,

then turned back to Roland.

"Any room left in that trailer of yours?"

~*~

ROLAND

"Wow," Jesse breathed as he looked at Captain Thomas' 'care package'. Three cases of MREs, and field surgeon kit with field medicine guide, an ample first aid kit including anti-biotics, and even morphine. A dozen M-4's, five cases of ammo and mags, a SAW with three full mags, and three LAW tubes.

"That about says it all," Roland nodded, eyeing the case of frags and the other of smoke grenades.

"We'll have to dump a lot of stuff if we decide to leave here," Thomas shrugged. "I figured better for you to have it than for it to be blown up." There were also a dozen 92F's, with extra mags, and three cases of ammo. And a dozen complete sets of field gear. There's also a goodie box. If you find yourself in a jam, open it. Might help."

"We've got plenty of stuff, and nothing like enough people that we'll ever use it all. I figured you could make use of it, down the road," Thomas shrugged. "Good luck, fellas." They shook hands.

"Well, you better mount up," Thomas 'ordered'. "I suspect it's going to be a long day."

~*~

The little convoy left the grounds slowly, everyone getting the feel for their vehicles. Ralph was driving the bus, while James and Jesse each drove a truck. Roland brought up the rear with the Hummer, while Jenkins and his team led the way in the MRAP.

For the first time in two months, Roland felt hopeful, if not downright optimistic. They were much better off than they had been a week ago.

They just might make it.

~*~

Their first stop on the 'Radio Shack Tour' had produced handsomely. Roland had secured three two-meter band hand-held radios, a wider band base station, with coax and antenna. Jenkins had secured similar equipment for Thomas. Among the most wonderful things Roland had found were a pair roll-up solar chargers for small electronics, such as the radios. He packed them carefully before they got back on the road.

Roland had instructed Jenkins to head south. Ideally he would take I-65 if it wasn't blocked. He hadn't had the chance to see much in the last two months, and neither Jenkins nor any of his troops had been so far south. It was a gamble, but these days all life was.

"Looks okay from here, Sarge," Jenkins radioed. *"We're on the ramp, and while it's not clear, it's not jammed, either. Want to take it?"*

"Can your vehicle push the odd stalled car or truck out of our way, Corporal? Roland asked.

"Passenger vehicles, sure," Jenkins replied. *"Something bigger, probably not. The Deuce might, I don't know."*

"We won't be trying anything that might damage any of our vehicles," Roland instructed. "Including yours. Pick us a path, and we'll try it."

"Roger that," Jenkins called back. *"Moving."*

The little convoy followed dutifully, vehicles falling into line. Jesse's truck was second in line, then the bus, then James' truck, and finally Roland. Jesse stayed back about five car lengths from the MRAP. In an ambush, the MRAP could more than take care of itself. The truck was just a standard truck.

They traveled slowly but steadily, and made excellent time as far as Roland was concerned. The MRAP carried enough fuel to make a round trip of about three hundred fifty miles. The other vehicles were topped off, and Roland had managed to scrounge enough cans to add twenty-five gallons for each vehicle extra. Hopefully they wouldn't need it, and could save it for the Hummer and Jesse's truck, both of which might be useful even after they were settled somewhere.

They had covered almost forty miles when Jenkins radioed Roland.

"Looks like a roadblock ahead, Sarge," the trooper called. *"Too organized to have been a wreck, or just abandoned vehicles. I can't see any activity, but..."*

"But in a good ambush, you wouldn't," Roland finished for him. "Are there any vehicles sitting in line along the road?" he asked.

"Yeah, now that you mention it," Jenkins replied. *"Victims, maybe?"*

"Probably," Roland sighed. "Recommendations?"

"Well, it's three miles back to the nearest exit, which is. . .the 412. We can backtrack, and...stand by." Roland waited while Jenkins attended to whatever it was.

"Sarge, Trooper Mackey recommends backtracking to the 431, and then heading East to a place called Bethesda. There's a natural and recreation area there, and a small primary school that might be available for shelter. At the least, there's a place for the children to get some outdoor time, and a good place to make camp tonight. Assuming there's no more problems with the 431 than we've seen along 65, it would take about three hours from our present location, roughly."

Roland considered that. A recreation area? Primary school?

"Does Mackey know if there's a well there?" There was a pause.

"He believes so. He attended school there himself, Sarge. Building is for about two hundred students or so. Should be plenty of room if it's not in use."

ROLAND

"Let's try it, Corporal," Roland ordered finally. "If there's a chance we can inhabit the place, and that there's water there, it sounds like a plan to me."

"Roger that, Sarge. We'll be heading back. Recommend that the rest of you re-form now, and we'll pick you up on the way back."

"You copy that, Jesse?" Roland asked.

"Affirm. Turning now."

"James, Ralph, you two copy?"

"Yes, Mister Roland," Ralph replied.

"Copy," James answered, keeping his transmission short. Roland smiled in spite of the problems. James was coming along fine, he decided.

"All right then. I'll turn around here, and hold position. Re-form to my front. When Jenkins gets back, we'll head out in order, and try it again."

The MRAP made its way back, and stopped next to Roland's Hummer long enough for Vaughan to dismount carrying a SAW. He got in beside Roland as the MRAP carried on up the highway.

"What's up?" Roland asked, as the trooper made room to access the top hatch.

"Corporal Jenkins decided someone should be with you, since whoever set up that road block might pursue. You have to drive, so I'm your shooter," he grinned. "I can probably convince 'em to leave us be, was that to happen."

"Probably," Roland grinned. "Good idea. And thanks."

"No problem," Vaughan smiled. "It's a good thing you're doin'. We're glad to help."

~*~

The trip took almost five hours, since the roads weren't completely clear. Roland was amazed they hadn't met any resistance. They hadn't seen a single person, either. Of course, this did look like a military convoy, and with all the stories about how rogue elements would act in a post economic collapse, most people would want to go undetected.

There were bodies, though. They had become accustomed to seeing dead bodies, though. While not packed like cord-wood, the sight wasn't at all uncommon. People dead from violence, from dirty water, from starvation.

From hopelessness.

"We're here, Sarge," Jenkins called suddenly. *"Let us check things out, and we'll get right back to you."*

"Copy that," Roland replied. "Everyone hold position, and be alert."

"We always need more 'lerts," Jesse replied, laughing.

"Smart ass," Roland muttered with a grin, while Vaughan laughed outright.

"You know you're crazy, right?" Vaughan asked, once his laughter had subsided. "I mean, trekking around all over with a load of children and two adults. What can possibly go wrong?"

"Ain't got a lot o' choice," Roland shrugged. "I can't just leave'em."

"Be surprised at how many would do just that," Vaughan replied.

"Yeah, well, I can't," Roland told him.

"No, I don't imagine you could," Vaughan's voice was low, almost admiring. "Still, you got to admit, it's a little crazy."

"I do admit it," Roland chuckled darkly. "I am the *last* person who needs to be in charge of a group of little kids, I assure you."

"Seems like you done okay, so far," Vaughan shrugged.

"Place is clear, Sarge," Jenkins called. *"Come on in. We've checked the building, and it's clear. Undamaged. And they have water from somewhere,"* he added.

"You heard the man," Roland radioed the group. "Jesse, lead off."

Five minutes later, they were sitting in front of their new home.

ROLAND

CHAPTER SEVENTEEN

This place is pretty good for what we need. We found the well, and the greatest thing was that it runs on a solar pump. I guess the electrical demand on a pump for so many kids was pretty costly, so they installed a solar pump. That's luck all out of proportion compared to what we're used to.

The children are still quiet and huddled together. They've seen so much, endured so much in the last little while I think they've developed a pack mentality. They don't feel safe if they're not all together. I wish I could find everyone responsible for what these kids have been through and destroy them root and branch.

Over a three or four-day period.

I've got to stop thinking like that. I can't let my anger get to me. There's too much to do, and these kids deserve better than to see me mad all the time. Or at all.

Jenkins and his team pitched right in, and with their help we unloaded everything and got it stored securely. The central office area is a pretty good set up, with a connecting hallway to the mess hall...er, cafeteria. We'll let the kids bunk together in there for the time being. It's large enough, and easy to secure. Jenkins and his team have set a watch schedule for tonight, allowing us all the chance to get some sleep.

They're really good guys.

Maria is still mumbling about not being allowed to stay at the armory, but the more she inspects the school, the less she mutters. We're much better off here, in my opinion, other than the fact that there's so few people able to defend the place, or do manual labor.

Tomorrow we'll pick out a spot for our garden. Thankfully, there's plenty of ground inside the fence for that. It'll be easier to protect the food from critters. Four legged critters, anyway.

We'll see what happens with the two-legged kind.

~*~

They had a small mulching tiller they had taken from Maria's father's shop. Roland had complained about it at the time, but as he watched Mackey till the ground easily using the small machine, he was glad he'd lost that argument. It was ridiculous how much easier this was than using a rake and hoe.

"I wanted to make sure you guys were off to a good start," Jenkins had explained when Roland had emerged from the building to find the four soldiers already working on the garden. "We're sorry you couldn't stay with us," he added, shamefaced. "But I have to say, Sarge, you guys are better off than we are. Especially with the well."

"It's a godsend, that's for sure," Roland nodded. All of the smaller children had drank greedily once they realized they weren't rationed for the first time in recent memory. He was glad to see them be able to slake their thirst.

"The Captain wanted us to scout around some, and report back on what we found while we were out here," Jenkins continued. "I think he's still thinking on the fact that we can't stay where we are forever."

"Always welcome here," Roland shrugged. "I'd say there's enough room. Might get on each other's nerves a little, but hell, we'd do that anyway."

"I hear ya," Jenkins grinned. "Truth to tell, I wouldn't mind being a part of a set up like this. I wonder how the locals will respond, though."

"That's on my mind as well," Roland nodded. "Just have to wait and see, I suppose. That's all I know to do."

The work continued until almost dark, with a short stop for lunch. Under Maria's supervision, they managed to plant almost two acres total in row crops, root crops, and berries. It was amazing what a few grown adults could accomplish in just one good day.

Everyone was tired that evening. Terri and Deena had watched over the children, allowing them outside to play on the playground equipment for a time, before taking them back inside for nap time. Even the tweens were still weak from malnutrition, and rest was stressed by the medical staff at the armory. The two teens had then prepared a simple but filling meal for the workers.

The cooking equipment in the kitchen ran off propane. Roland had checked the large tank in back, and found it about three quarters full. It would go a long way, but wouldn't last forever. But for a week or so he'd let them prepare hearty meals from the stocks they had with them and what they had found still in the school. There had been a lot of number ten cans of veggies still in the kitchen. There had also been some very ripe meat in the cooler that no longer cooled. James and Ralph had volunteered to clean that out, and had taken the mess almost a mile from the school before dumping it.

Roland leaned back, resting his aching back, and watching the goings on around him. The children were actually talking happily, still excited over their afternoon in the sun playing. That warmed his heart more than anything else.

"You look tired," he heard Maria's voice, and fought a sigh. Could she not let him have just a little peace?

"I am tired," he nodded, trying to be nice. "Long day, and a lot of sleepless nights. Catching up to me, I guess."

"We have all gone too far without proper rest or nutrition," she agreed, sitting down beside him, which made Roland have to fight not to stir. She looked at him.

"I want to apologize for my complaints about not staying where we were," she said firmly. "You were right. This is much better than staying with the others."

"Well, it's better from some standpoints," he agreed. "I wasn't knocking your desire to stay, Maria," he decided to try and make peace. Again. "I would much rather be in a larger group, with more adults to assist. With safety, security, and especially with the children. I know the three of you are being worn to a frazzle. Maybe now, when we're able to let them go out some, and talk freely, and play without worrying about someone hearing them, they'll be easier to manage."

"You should spend time with them," Maria suggested. "They are not exactly afraid of you, but you are unknown to them. They should feel more comfortable around you."

"I know," Roland sighed. "I hope now, since we're somewhere that might be safer, I'll have that chance. Before it was just too much, all the time. There just wasn't any opportunity for that sort of thing. Maybe now it'll be different."

"Are the soldiers staying?" Maria asked.

"Only for a couple days, to make sure we're set up good," Roland replied. "They have orders to scout around some before heading back. I think Jenkins'l use our place here as a base while they do that. I also told him that anyone from the armory would be welcome here, if they decided they wanted to move."

"You would offer them a place here, even when they cast us out?" Maria asked, an edge to her voice. "Why would you help them?" she demanded.

"Because they helped us." Roland pointed out. "We're two trucks better off. The kids had good baths and a medical exam. They sent Jenkins and his men to escort us until we found a place to call home. They provided us with medicine, and with first aid equipment. Do I need to go on?"

"Maria, there's more to helping than just giving someone a place to stay. Did you notice how they were keeping a guard post around the clock? They're still taking fire from the gangs inside the city. They're low on water, and it's getting worse. The food they got when we led them to the warehouse was the best meal they've had in two months."

"Here, at least for now, we're safe, and we've got plenty of good, clean water. That's a miracle right there. We're actually better off than they are, except in numbers. That's what I wanted. Safety in numbers," he sat back again. Maria studied him quietly for a time.

"I did not consider all that," she admitted. "The government has a responsibility to care for us, and they are government soldiers. That is as far as I thought."

"I know," Roland sighed again. "People like you that think like that, you want to depend on the government for everything. No matter what it is. That's the wrong mindset to have, Maria. You don't ever want to be totally dependent on something as fickle as a government. You see how well that's turned out so far, right?"

"Thing is, government 'control' is an illusion," Roland went on. "The reason that two thousand cops can keep order in a city of a million is because for the most part, people respect that authority. They know and obey the laws. They don't cause problems. If a judge orders something, they do it, or they appeal."

"But when society breaks down, there's very little the government can do. There aren't enough people in uniform to keep the wheels on when they're determined to come off. And that's why you never want to be totally dependent on any type of government, anywhere, for your survival."

Maria listened to all of this quietly, nodding occasionally. Finally, she spoke again.

"I see the wisdom in that," she said slowly. "Unfortunately, I would not have before things happened the way they did. Experience is the best teacher for this, no matter how bitter the lesson may be, I think." She rose suddenly.

"It's time to for me to start getting the younger children to bed. Good night, Roland."

"Night, Maria," Roland nodded, watching as she went to take care of the children. Maybe she was growing up a little, he decided, before settling back in, trying to get comfortable again.

Stranger things had happened, he figured.

ROLAND

~*~

"Can I borrow your Humvee?"

Roland looked at Jenkins as if he'd grown a second head. They had been here two days. In that time the gardens were planted, the children were settled into rooms, and a schedule of sorts had been established. The children were looking healthier, and were laughing now and again.

"Sure, I guess," he shrugged. "Why'd you want a Hummer when you got a MRAP, though?"

"It's less intimidating," Jenkins shrugged. "It's just an armored truck, but it looks like something more. Your Humvee is up-armored, so it's good protection but we don't look so aggressive in it."

"Makes sense," Roland nodded. "I guess with you guys being a Guard unit, they train you about that kind of thing. I never had to worry about it much."

"Well, MRAPs aren't the kind of thing you use on civilian work or emergency mobilization," the Corporal agreed. "I want to scout around some, and see what I can see. That Humvee won't be nearly as intimidating to the locals as my MRAP."

"Where you going'?" Roland asked, curious.

"Today we're gonna just look around here," Jenkins admitted. "I want to make sure there aren't any trouble spots nearby. I'd like to leave you guys in good shape."

"Works for me," Roland smiled. "You guys be careful."

"I'll leave Vaughan here with you," Jenkins informed him. "Just in case."

"You might need him worse than us," Roland shook his head. "If we get into a jam, we'll call you right off."

"Okay, then," Jenkins nodded. "We're off."

Roland watched as the fire team left on its patrol. While it would have been nice to have Vaughan to help with security, Roland didn't want to get spoiled. When the Guard soldiers left it would be him, Jesse, and James left to stand guard. They needed to get used to that.

Thinking along those lines, he gathered the other two with him out front.

"Okay, the Guard guys are starting their scouting mission," he informed them. "They're gonna spend today just looking around our immediate AO, and making sure there's nothing around here that might be a threat to us."

"Today is a good day for us to settle into a watch. When they're gone, it'll just be us three. That means we're gonna have to tighten up some. Suggestions?"

"We spend today looking over the ground, and making defensive plans," Jesse said at once. "We need contingencies for action against the school. And it wouldn't be a bad idea to start teaching those three girls how to handle a rifle and handgun. If someone makes it past us, they need to be able to defend themselves."

"Good idea," James nodded.

"All right. We'll start with their lessons later in the day. For now, I agree. We need to establish the ground, and see about firming up our defense. The school building looks pretty strong, but we still need to re-enforce weak points like doors and windows. Almost makes me wish it was two story. We could fortify the downstairs, and use the upstairs for the kids. But, we work with what we've got."

"There are several ways we can close off the doors," James mused aloud. "But we may need the use of the doors at some point. We'll have to be creative."

"Hey, we're all about creative," Jesse grinned.

"Well, let's creatively look over the grounds, first," Roland chuckled. "We need to see if we can anticipate how someone would attack, and then design plans to defeat it."

They set off to do just that.

~*~

"I wish we had some wheat to plant," Maria said as she and Terri worked to prepare lunch for the children. "We could make our own flour from the wheat to make bread. Once this flour is gone, there won't be anymore."

"Well, at least there's a lot of it," Terri shrugged. "That gives us time to come up with something."

"I do not like not having a way to do things," Maria said sourly.

"I don't either," Terri replied. "That doesn't change the facts. We're lucky to be as well off as we are. Considering where we could be, without Roland and the others, I'll take this and be happy."

"Do you ever wonder why Roland does these things?" Maria asked.

"What do you mean?" Terri frowned.

"I mean, what is his motivation for all this?" Maria pressed. "Why take such an interest in us?"

"Well, some guys are just like that, I guess," Terri replied. "I mean, not every man is a bastard like Wright was. Roland took care of him, too," she added firmly. "Some men have a natural instinct to protect the weak, or so. . .so my momma said," she finished, pained at the memory of her mother, now dead.

ROLAND

"I would like to believe that," Maria said quietly. "I hope it to be true. But Roland is a violent man. I am not sure we can trust him."

"Well, I'm sure," Terri stated flatly. "He hasn't said a thing out of the way to any of us, and he doesn't try to undress us with his eyes the way Wright and his cronies did. He's been a gentleman the whole time."

Maria thought back to the scene in front of her house just days ago, and wondered. Her fear was rational, she told herself. The man was dangerous, and unpredictable. And very violent.

"We shall see," she settled for saying. "We shall see."

CHAPTER EIGHTEEN

Roland and Jesse were going over some of the decisions they'd made about their defense when the Humvee returned, followed by a pick-up truck. Roland was unhappy to see that truck, but also curious as to what Jenkins had found. And why he'd brought them back with him.

Jenkins and his team dismounted, Jenkins himself waving the truck in beside the Humvee. A tall, older man got out of the vehicle, while a woman stayed inside. Jenkins motioned for the man to join him as Roland walked up.

"What's the deal?" Roland asked, trying to keep his voice friendly.

"Well, there's a little community up the road a ways," Jenkins told him, pointing it out on his map. "This fella here is Derrick Turnbow. He's the local leader, and a preacher. He wanted to meet you, and see how things were going." Turnbow approached them just then.

"Mister Turnbow, this here is Roland Stang. He's in charge around here."

"Well, that remains to be seen, doesn't it?" Turnbow replied. Roland immediately didn't like him.

"No, sir, it doesn't," Jenkins answered the man before Roland could speak. "As I told you, Roland has worked hard to help keep these children safe and secure. He's kept them fed, clothed and safe. Captain Thomas made no bones about who was in charge."

"Yes, but your Captain Thomas has no authority here," Turnbow said, his voice calm, but unyielding. "And our community may yet need this building."

"You're welcome to any part of it we're not using," Roland told him flatly. "We're only using a few rooms, and the playground when the weather is okay. There's plenty of room left."

ROLAND

"This is our school, young man," Turnbow replied. "And we decide who uses it, and for what."

"You know, I was prepared to like you," Jenkins cut in. "You pretty much lied to me, didn't you? Saying you wanted to see how things were set-up. All you really wanted to do was come in here throwin' your weight around."

"I am the community leader," Turnbow nodded. "And this is community property."

"I'm not figurin' it is," Roland answered this time. "I figure its county property. Property of the school board, to be exact. How far away is it you live, Mister Turnbow?"

"That's hardly the issue, Stang."

"I'm makin' it the 'issue', Turnbow," Roland shot back. He could be rude, too. Enjoyed it sometimes, in fact.

"They're about ten miles away, Roland," Jenkins provided, red faced. "He's a two face, lying ass wipe, is what he is. Led me to believe that he and his 'people' would be willing' to help you with the kids. I'm sorry."

"Don't be," Roland smiled. "We needed to know where the assholes lived, and now we do." He looked at Turnbow.

"Let me set you straight, Mister Turnbow. We're living here now. This place has become an orphanage. We're self-sufficient, and a burden to no one. We'll keep it that way, too. You folks just stay on up there in your 'community', and we'll just stay on right here, and leave you be. And that's a courtesy I expect to be returned, now I'm thinking on it. We got an understanding, Mister Turnbow?"

The community leader was red faced by the time Roland was finished speaking. He sputtered and carried on some before getting a coherent sentence out.

"I'll have the Sheriff on you before the day's out, and you will be gone!"

"I'll be here waitin', jackass," Roland smiled. And it wasn't a pleasant smile. "Meantime, you've overstayed your welcome. Got no time for liars. Git."

"Yeah, about time you went," Jenkins agreed, and motioned to Vaughan and Mackey.

"Make sure Mister Turnbow here makes it back to the intersection and heads for home, boys. Turns out he's a snake in the grass."

Turnbow wanted to argue, but two soldiers in full battle dress were a bit intimidating. So, he went. Muttering threats all the time, but went just the same.

"Dammit, Roland I'm sorry," Jenkins muttered as his men 'escorted' Turnbow away. "I bit his tale hook, line, and sinker," he sighed heavily.

"I told you, don't worry about it," Roland said earnestly. "I was serious. We need to know where the assholes are. And he definitely qualifies."

"Think he'll really get the Sheriff?" Jenkins asked, worriedly.

"Don't really care," Roland shrugged. "We're staying' right here. Period. Sheriff gets to be a problem; I'll take care of it."

"That might not be the best idea," Jenkins warned. "Local civil authority is about all there is left. They pretty much rule everywhere, these days."

"Not where I am," Roland shrugged. "I hate bullies. I don't care what shape or size they come in, or what kind of title they wear. We're not hurting anything. They really needed this place, they'd have had it already." He thought about what Jenkins had said.

"He really told you they'd be willing to help with the kids?" he asked.

"Well, yeah," Jenkins nodded. "Help you all, maybe even take some of 'em into their homes, adopted like."

"Did he now," Roland said, far too calmly for Jenkins' liking.

"You think he had some other motive in mind?" he asked.

"I'm thinking just that," Roland nodded firmly. "This is farm country. And there ain't much fuel left, I reckon. Ever study history much, Jenkins?"

"In school, sure."

"Ever read up on why families were so big back before the industrial revolution? Why they had so many kids?" Roland's eyes were still on the road, where Turnbow's truck was finally out of sight.

"No, not really," Jenkins shook his head. "Why?"

"They had so many kids so they would have plenty of farm hands," Roland finally turned to look at him. "They needed the young'uns to help tend the farm. You see many young people in this community o' his?"

"Now that you mention it, no. I didn't." Jenkins frowned suddenly, getting Roland's drift.

"You don't think..."

"I sure do," Roland nodded. "Orphans have always been victims of society. Always. Even in modern times, when things like that weren't supposed to happen. By now, Turnbow and his bunch have realized that they've got nothing but hard work ahead of 'em. A nice, fresh batch of orphan kids with no one to look after 'em would sound like just the thing for a community that don't have fuel to power their farm machinery anymore. Wouldn't it." Not a question. A statement.

"Son-of-a-bitch," Jenkins growled. "Maybe I should have the boys make sure..."

ROLAND

"No," Roland cut him off with a shake of his head. "Won't help, or I would have done it already. I don't want you guys gettin' into trouble like that. Make your job harder, once word got out."

"No, I'll deal with Mister Turnbow myself, if the need arises. No problem at all." He looked at Jenkins again.

"Turnbow look hungry to you?" he asked suddenly.

"No, he didn't," the soldier shook his head.

"What about the others? You see anyone else in town, or whatever?" Roland pressed.

"Well, there were a few out and about," Jenkins got a faraway look in his eyes, trying to recall everything he'd seen. "Some looked fit as a fiddle, to be honest. But. . .yeah, some of 'em looked peckish. Wearing clothes that fit a little to lose, maybe. Maybe Turnbow and some of the rest were better prepared for something like this."

"Possible," Roland nodded, clearly thinking about that. "Still, him being a preacher an' all, wouldn't he be of a mind to help out his fellow man?"

"Just cause a man's a preacher don't mean nothin'," Jenkins almost spat. "I've known more'n one 'holy man' wasn't all that holy. Or much of a man, neither, now I think about it."

"Exactly," Roland nodded as if his point had been made. "There's a bit more to Mister Turnbow than meets the eyes, I'm thinking. We already know he's a lying snake, and power hungry. Wonder what else there is to know about him?"

~*~

Turnbow was true to his word. A car bearing the title 'Sheriff's Patrol', pulled up in front of the school later that day. Two men got out, one carrying a shotgun. The driver was a tall man, dressed in jeans, a button down shirt, and wearing a Stetson of all things. His boots were some kind of lizard, with golden covers on the tips.

The second man was shorter, wearing a uniform. He was slightly overweight, and about the same age as the taller man appeared to be. He was also the one carrying the shotgun.

Roland watched the men approach, sitting casually in a chair he'd brought out front. The MRAP was behind the building, out of sight. Only the Hummer was in view, along with one of the trucks.

"Afternoon," Roland nodded as the two men walked up. "Help you fellas?"

"Are you Stang?" the taller one demanded. Roland nodded.

"I'm Sheriff Tom Wilson. You got exactly fifteen minutes to load up and get out of here. Whatever you can't load, you'll have to leave behind."

"That a fact?" Roland replied easily. "Well, Sheriff, that's not going to happen. I got twenty-eight kids living here, and already got a garden planted to feed 'em. Used all our seed to do it, too. So we'll be staying on, at least until the garden's in. Anything else you boys need today? Ain't got no coffee, but I can offer you a drink o' water."

"I don't think you understand the situation, soldier boy," Wilson ground out. "You aren't staying here. Period. We don't want nor need your kind in our community, or near our kids. You are leaving, and you've got thirteen minutes left."

"My kind?" Roland asked, voice dangerously soft. "What kind would that be, law man? I would be mighty interested to know that."

"Listen you," the uniformed deputy started, but the Sheriff stopped him with a raised hand.

"You come in here, carrying all these children, threatening locals, seizing government property, that's what kind, Stang. We don't aim to stand for it."

"Threatening locals?" Roland asked, his voice puzzled. "Sheriff, we ain't seen any locals. Ain't seen but one soul at all since we've been here, and he ain't really local. Lives ten or so miles up the road a ways. Least that's what he said."

Wilson frowned at that. This wasn't going the way he'd had in mind.

"Let me do some explaining to you, Sheriff Wilson," Roland said softly. "I fought gangs, murderers, pedophiles, and other kinds of predators to protect these children, and keep them safe, fed, and reasonably healthy. I lost one of them to a gang, shot him to pieces, just 'cause. Mister Turnbow came down here today throwin' his weight around, making noises about who was in charge, and hinting that he and his might just be taking these young'uns." Roland stood suddenly, and both men backed away. The deputy started to raise his shotgun, but the bolt going home on an M-4 stopped him.

Both men turned to see a teenager covering them with a military rifle, his eyes cold as a winter morning. He didn't say a word. He didn't have to.

"Let me make things clear to you, Sheriff," Roland continued. "We haven't harmed or accosted a single person. This school wasn't in use, and I figure it ain't likely to be in the near future, right? It's obvious no one around here really needs this place, or they'd already be using it."

"I got a pretty good idea what Mister Turnbow had in mind for my kids. And I'm telling you, right now, straight up. Anyone who so much as looks at one of these kids the wrong way won't live to brag on it. And I don't care *who* it is, Sheriff. Get me?"

ROLAND

"All I want to do is provide a safe place for these kids. They got no one else to see to them. Abandoned, left orphaned, and preyed upon by all kinds. I won't see that happen. No one else will, either. Are we clear? Sheriff?"

"What claim do you have on these kids, anyway?" Wilson shot back.

"I don't 'claim' anything," Roland shrugged. "They're under my protection."

"I may have to get the State involved. And the judge," Wilson threatened.

"You can get the President involved if you can find him," Roland shrugged. "Won't change anything. You're welcome to drop by any time you want, Sheriff. So long as you come peaceable. If you've got anything else on your mind, I'd rethink it. Hard. No one is going to take advantage of these kids. No one."

"You seem so sure that someone is aiming to take advantage, how do we know you ain't taking advantage of them?"

"He isn't," Maria's voice cut through the tension. Roland didn't turn to look at her, but it took willpower. He had no idea she was even around.

"Who are you?" Wilson demanded.

"My name is Maria Consuelo Tomas," she said with a regal dignity that Roland found interesting. He'd never heard her speak that way before. "I am the caretaker for the smaller children. I see to their welfare. Roland sees to their safety, and to their needs. They have no one else."

"You illegal?" the deputy almost sneered.

"I am a third generation American citizen," Maria said proudly. "Not that this should concern you," she added tartly.

"We been runnin' illegals out from around here," the deputy grinned. "Can you prove you ain't illegal?"

"Can you prove I am?" Maria countered. "I am an American citizen. As such I have to prove nothing. It is you who must prove your accusations. And you cannot." She turned her gaze back the Sheriff, as if bothering with the deputy anymore was beneath her.

"As I said, Roland is not in any way taking advantage of anyone or anything. I do not especially like Roland, nor he me, but we have managed to work together to provide some semblance of normalcy for the children."

Wilson scratched his neck, at a loss for how to proceed. He normally wouldn't have done anything for Turnbow if it meant hell fire raining on Main Street. But the man had convinced him something was wrong here.

Now he was having second thoughts. Trouble was, he had burst in here like gangbusters, and now he needed a way to retreat gracefully. One that hopefully didn't include getting shot by a dead-eyed teenager.

"It's beginning to look like I was fed some false information," he settled for admitting. "And yeah, it was Turnbow who notified me. He made it sound like you were a bunch o' gypsies, takin' up residence here. And that really and honestly is something we just don't need."

"Gypsies?" Roland blurted, surprised. "Seriously? I mean real gypsies?"

"Yeah," Wilson nodded. "We get 'em about three, maybe four times a year. Steal anything that ain't tied down. Cut loose some stuff that is tied down. That's why I came out here like I did. The best way to deal with them is start out hard and stay that way."

"Huh," Roland scratched his head. "Who would of thought?"

"I know it sounds crazy, but almost every area has trouble one time or another," Wilson nodded. "Anyway, you for sure ain't gypsies. And it looks like you ain't some kind of criminal, either. You military?"

"I was," Roland nodded. "I came upon the kids by accident. Literally looking to get out of the rain. Walked into a hornet's nest. Well, a viper's nest is more like it."

"Well, I wish I could help you, but we're stretched thin all over," Wilson told him. "Normally there'd be Child Services to call on, but not anymore."

"I know," Roland nodded. "We're fine on our own. Won't deny another adult or two would be welcome, but we manage. From your tone, can I assume we can stay on here, peaceably?"

"I don't see why not," Wilson shrugged. "I would like to see these children for myself. So I can say I know they're safe and cared for."

"That's agreeable," Roland nodded. "C'mon with me and Maria. We'll give you the grand tour."

"Wait here, Tony," Wilson told the deputy. "Won't be long."

"You shouldn't go in there alone," 'Tony' objected. "No tellin' what might happen."

"Well, you ain't going in there with that scatter-gun," Roland said firmly.

"You're carrying a rifle," Tony pointed out.

"I trust me," was Roland's only reply. Wilson chuckled at that.

"Wait at the car," he ordered. "I'll be along." Tony looked reluctant, but followed his orders. Wilson didn't miss the way James watched the deputy all the way back to the car. Or the way he *kept* watching him.

"You can relax, son," Wilson told him. "Tony's got a lot of bark, but not much bite."

"I'm always relaxed," James said calmly, never taking his eyes off the deputy. Tony was lounging on the car, still carrying the shotgun.

"C'mon, Sheriff, and see for yourself what we're trying to do," Roland suggested.

ROLAND

Twenty minutes later, Wilson was back outside with Roland. What he had seen had convinced him Roland was on the level in more ways than one.

"I gotta hand it to you, Roland," Wilson shook his head. "You've done a hell of a job getting this far."

"Wasn't just me," Roland replied. "Maria has been a godsend. If not for her, and James, and Ralph, Deena and Terri, we wouldn't have made it. They've all worked long hours and done without to keep the others fed, and safe. Willie died working to keep them safe. He was just a kid. Bravest little fella you ever seen, though." Roland's voice caught a bit, but he stayed firm.

"Well, far as I'm concerned, you're fine here. And you're right, there like as not won't be no more school here. There's no one to pay the teachers, and no fuel to run the buses, either. Probably won't be for some time. We're short on everything except problems."

"Anything we can help with?" Roland asked.

"Not unless there's more of you than I've seen here," Wilson shook his head. "We're starting to get some violent types through here. Home invasions, raiding parties, that kinda thing. Better keep that rifle handy," he nodded to Roland's M-4. "Wish I had one myself," he laughed. "Come in handy if I could ever catch up to the bastards."

"Wait here," Roland said, and walked back inside. When he emerged he was carrying two M-4's, a dozen mags, and three hundred rounds of ammunition.

"Here," he said, offering the package to the Sheriff. "Hope it helps."

Wilson took the offered gifts, stunned.

"Are you sure you can spare these?" he asked. "I mean, you might need 'em yourself."

"These were extra," Roland shrugged. "We don't need them. I still have one extra, for the girls to keep inside." That was the truth, in as far as it went. He did have one extra. He also had more extra. He figured the Sheriff didn't need to know that.

"Roland, I don't know what to say," Wilson admitted.

"Say we're friends, Tom," Roland shrugged. "Or at least friendly. That'll do for me."

"I can safely say we're friendly, Roland," Wilson smiled. "We're using HAM and CB radios to communicate with outlying areas. You have one?" Roland nodded. Wilson scribbled in a pocket notebook, tearing the page out and handing it to Roland.

"There are the frequencies we're using. If something happens, give us a call."

"We'll do that," Roland nodded, pocketing the paper. "Same here. If you're out this way and need a hand, let us know. We'll try to be listening."

"Well, I need to go. I'll swing through and have a word with Turnbow. You watch out for him, Roland. He's an odd duck for all that he's a preacher. And he's spiteful. He won't like that you've gotten the best of him."

"I'm sure that'll keep me up nights."

ROLAND

CHAPTER NINETEEN

Jenkins and his team left this morning, headed back to Nashville. I was sorry to see them go. Having them nearby was a nice security blanket. I'm pretty sure they all wanted to stay, but they feel obligated to Thomas. I don't blame them. He's a good man. Combat forges a bond between soldiers like no other.

It's been three days since my discussion with the Sheriff. I half expected to see Turnbow down here that night with torches lit, pitchfork in hand. Haven't seen hide or hair of him, though, nor anyone else for that matter.

Had a gentle rain last night. Perfect thing for the garden. I could see sprouts this morning. Lord willing, we'll be able to feed the kids this winter.

I sent a list with Jenkins of stuff we could still use, including some stuff Maria wanted. Jenkins promised if he could locate the items, he'd ask Captain Thomas for permission to make another run down this way with them. He's a good man, and so are his team. The kind of guys you'd be glad to have at your back in combat.

Things aren't going too bad, at the moment. I mean, there's still plenty to worry over, but we're so much better off than we were two weeks ago it's ridiculous.

Of course, all that does is make me think something is bound to go wrong.

~*~

"Roland, have you been outside?" Jesse asked, his face creased with a frown.

"Not this morning," Roland shook his head, looking up from where he'd been writing. "What's wrong?"

"Sky looks a little stormy."

Roland got up and followed Jesse back outside. James was outside as well, rifle in hand, looking back toward the west.

"That looks bad," he commented, never taking his eyes from the clouds.

"That is bad," Roland sighed. "James, go and tell Maria to gather the children in the inner hallway. You and Ralph gather cushions and blankets for them there, please. And you may want to hurry."

"Yes, sir," James nodded, taking off at a run.

"You think it's gonna come a blow?" Jesse asked, concern in his voice.

"I'm almost sure of it," Roland nodded. "This school's built pretty well, but this time of year, with the weather swinging back and forth, we're as likely to have a tornado as we are a snow storm."

"You got that right," Jesse agreed. "The vehicles are all behind the building. Think they're all right there?"

"They'll have to be," Roland shrugged. "We got nowhere else to put 'em. They're all empty, right?"

"All but the emergency, 'get out of dodge stuff'," Jesse nodded. "We might have time to unload..."

"No, that's what they're for," Roland shook his head, cutting Jesse off. "Leave them there. We can't go running every time a cloud comes up and unload. We'll wear that stuff out. Let's check the windows and doors. Make sure they're all secure."

"I'll take the west," Jesse nodded, already moving. "I'd say we'd better..." Even as he spoke, Roland saw the line of fast moving clouds swirl, rise sharply, and then start back down.

"Twister coming down!" Roland shouted. "Get inside! We'll have to trust that the building is shut." The two raced inside, stopping to secure the front doors. They moved to the interior hallway, where Maria and the others were doing a frantic head count.

"What's wrong?" Roland asked, seeing the look of fear on her face.

"We're missing two children!" she almost screamed. "We were on the playground when James came to warn us! They must have ran away when we were trying to get everyone inside!"

ROLAND

Roland didn't wait to hear anymore. He was already moving toward the rear of the building where the playground was located.

"Stay here!" he ordered when Maria moved to follow. "They need you here with them! Jesse stay with them." She reluctantly stayed behind, her face a mask of sheer terror. Roland ran on, knowing that he didn't have much time.

He hit the rear doors without slowing, bursting out the back at a dead run. He stopped as he hit the yard, looking frantically around for the two missing children. A gust of wind hit him suddenly, died just as quickly, then returned with greater force to stay. Roland had to struggle to stay on his feet.

He looked back toward the rapidly approaching clouds, and was shocked to see the now fully formed twister was already on the ground, and grinding steadily toward the school.

"Kids, where are you?!" he shouted, desperate to get them under cover. He didn't know if he was looking for boys or girls, or even what their names might be.

"Cassandra! Todd!" he heard James' voice, and turned to find the teen behind him, shouting names.

"Get back inside!" he ordered. James shook his head.

"You need help," he yelled back over the wind. "We've got to hurry!" he added. "Cassandra! Todd!" he yelled again. Roland picked up the call.

The two separated somewhat, going in different directions. Roland kept calling the two names James had used, working his way east while James took the west. Roland saw a flash of color behind an outcropping of bricks and ran toward it.

A boy of about seven years old was huddled behind the flange of brick, hugging the wall with strength born of desperation. Without even thinking Roland scooped the child into his arms and ran. Todd clung to him tightly, shaking with fear.

Roland could see debris in the air as the storm grew closer, and felt stinging pelts of rain hitting him in the face. Seconds later he realized he felt stings because it wasn't rain, but hail. Small stones of ice about the size of a pea.

Covering the boy's head with his hand, Roland bent his head into the increasing wind, and managed to straggle to the door. When he opened it, the wind jerked it out of his hand. Struggling to contain the door with only one free hand, Roland wound up stumbling into the building, and felt himself falling. Twisting his body, he managed to land with the boy atop him rather than beneath and felt his back contort in pain. The jolt of pain was strong enough that Roland lost his breath and gasped in reaction to it.

He struggled to stand, helping the boy get to his feet. Todd promptly took off running again but at least this time he was inside. And running in the right direction. Roland let him go, trying to get to his feet to go and look for James and Cassandra. He gasped aloud again as pain shot through his back once more.

"Roland!" he heard Jesse shout. "Are you okay?" The other man was next to him seconds later, trying to assess Roland for injuries.

"Get me up!" he ordered, and Jesse complied, pulling his friend carefully to his feet.

"I've got to. . .got to look for James and the girl!" he gasped out.

"You can't!" Jesse shook his head, and Roland was mindful that Jesse was having to shout to be heard. He followed Jesse's pointing finger to the windows of the doorway, to see debris rolling past, whipped into a hail of metal and wood by the winds of the tornado.

"Twister's on us, Ro'," Jesse shouted about the din. "We got to get undercover!" Jesse dragged a protesting Roland toward the inner hallway, where Maria ran to meet him.

"What happened?" she asked, moving to his side opposite from Jesse, slipping her arm around his waist, taking his arm over her shoulder. Together the two managed to get him seated on the floor, and then Jesse forced Roland to lie down.

"Boy. . .make it in okay?" Roland gasped out. Damn, but his back hurt.

"Yes," Maria nodded, looking him over for injury. "Did you find Cassie?" she asked, once satisfied that Roland was at least not bleeding.

"James is still out there, looking for her!" Roland struggled to get up. "I've got to go help..."

"It is too late, Roland," Maria shook her head, pointing to the roof. "Listen."

Pouring, pounding rain was beating down on the roof of the building now, so loud it was nearly deafening. The children were huddled into a group surrounding Terri and Deena, who were trying valiantly to hide their own fears, and reassure the terrified children that all would be okay.

"James and the girl are still out there!" Roland tried again to get up. This time he was stopped by another jolt of pain through his back.

"Roland you're hurt, bro," Jesse shouted to be heard over the driving rain. "Roland!" Jesse shouted again, getting his struggling friend's attention.

"You can't go out there, man!" he said firmly. "None of us can. Not until the storm blows past." He leaned down, placing his face right in Roland's own.

"I know you want to, but we can't risk it. There are still twenty-six kids in here, Roland. Someone has to be here with them. You go and get killed, who takes care of them? I can't. Wouldn't know what to do. So stop struggling and lie back. I think your back is strained. At the least a pulled muscle. You can't operate like that."

Roland finally ceased to struggle, looking up at both Jesse and Maria with a horrified look on his face.

"Oh, my God," he moaned. "I've lost them."

~*~

James had been far to the west side of the doors when he realized the storm was on him. His frantic search for Cassandra Dodds became instead a struggle for survival. There was no way back into the building near him, and nowhere to take cover except one place.

He ran the two dozen feet to the deuce-and-a-half truck he had driven to the school, and dived beneath it. He knew that if the twister hit the truck directly, or even sideswiped it, the truck could literally be pulled off of him, but there was simply nowhere else to go.

Pulling himself underneath the center of the truck, he watched as flying debris roared past. Realizing that he might still be hit by the storm's wind generated debris field, James crawled to a spot behind the dual axle rear tires, taking cover behind them. There was nothing else to do but wait.

The debris was past, finally, and then came the rain. Hard, driving, deafening rain. Heavy rain the likes of which was only seen in the midst of a driving thunderstorm, or a tornado. James could literally see drops of rain bounce up again as they slammed into the pavement and concrete around him with startling force. In a minute, water was rushing through the small parking area, and run off began to fill ditches and streams all around the school.

As he lay there, watching, he saw something out of place in the low lying grass behind the

school area. A splash of white.

"Oh, no," he mouthed in despair. Despite the storm raging around him, James crawled from underneath the truck, and ran toward the drainage ditch behind the school yard. Twice he slipped, falling once into the now soft, muddy ground. Yet even as he struggled to regain his feet, he never took his eyes from that little patch of color. Afraid that if he looked away, even for a second, he might never find it again.

Rain beat at him, whipped into a fury by driving winds, but he ignored everything save that little splash of color in front of him. He slowed as he finally reached the spot, falling to his knees, unaware and uncaring of how wet, muddy, and miserable he was.

Lying in that drainage ditch, face down, was the body of little Cassandra Dodds. Age eight. Parents unknown, but presumed dead. Drowned in a pool of rain water.

James lifted his eyes skyward, ignoring the sting of wind and rain on his face. For the first time since his parents had died so many years before, James Henry Golden cried. He cried for a very long time as the rain washed down his face, carrying away his tears.

Finally, when he could cry no longer, when he had exhausted all the rage and frustration and self-loathing and despair that had closed in around him, James tenderly lifted the little body from the water, cradling her in his arms. He stayed that way for a long time, ignoring the rain and the wind. Finally, he slowly stood up and started for the school building.

As he walked his heart began to harden. By the time he reached the doors it had become stone. Hard, unbending, unforgiving.

I won't let this happen again.

~*~

"Oh, no," Roland heard Maria almost whisper. "Jesse, look," she hissed. Roland lifted himself from where he was lying, and felt utter despair.

James, muddy and soaking wet, stood in the entrance to the hallway, a small body cradled in his arms.

"I found her," James said simply. "I found her and brought her back."

ROLAND

CHAPTER TWENTY

I've lost another child. Gran warned me, but I had convinced myself that she was wrong, just this once. That she might be wrong. We came so far, through so much, and I thought we were safe.

Safe. Every time I say, think, or hear that word, it's like a terrible, haunting joke of cruelty. There is no safe. Not anymore.

The children are in shock, seems like. I don't know what else to call it. I wish we had someone who was better able to deal with their emotional needs. Maria, Deena and Terri do their best, but they're just teens themselves, and suffering through their own version of pain and loss.

James is. . .James is just flat-lined. I've seen it before, when the horrors of combat hit a young, idealistic soldier. When he realizes that it's not the glory filled, music backed thrill a minute his recruiter told him he'd see.

The pain, the loss, the shock of seeing innocents caught in the crossfire. Dying and dead and maimed because they had the misfortune to be born in an area that two or more groups of violent people wanted for themselves. Their homes caught in a war they know nothing about. Fighting between two groups of people who want to rule over their lives.

I'm worried about him, but he's got nothing to say. He was quiet before, but now he's simply turned to stone. He's as sharp and aware as he ever was, but there's even more hardness about him than before. It's plain to us all that he blames himself for little Cassandra's death, but it's not his fault. It's mine. I should have planned better. I should have thought about this possibility. We always have weather like this in the spring time. Why, why, why didn't I think about it?

The others are quiet, going about their own tasks. Maria likewise blames herself, and is pushing herself even harder now. She's not to blame either. If I had thought about the possibility, like I should have, then we would have already trained the kids on what to do if a storm blew up.

N.C. REED

But because I didn't, Cassandra, and Todd, had no idea what to do. When they got scared, they did what children always do. They hid. Cassandra hid in the wrong place. Ralph found one of her shoes lodged in a tangle of roots and branches where James found her body. The water poured in around her, and her little foot got stuck. As the water rose, she was trapped beneath it, and drowned.

Oh my God in heaven, how she must have struggled. How scared she must have been. Child I am so sorry. I'm sorry I didn't protect you better. Sorry I didn't tell you what to do. Sorry I didn't know you.

So very sorry...

~*~

It was a somber affair. James had dug the small grave himself, insisting that no one help. Roland hadn't argued, knowing that this might be the best therapy for the boy. The older children gathered around for a small service. Roland, laid up with his back, stayed with the younger kids inside.

As James placed Cassandra's sheet wrapped little body into the grave, Jesse stepped forward, bible in his hands.

"Almighty God, we here today commit to your care the spirit of Cassandra Dodds. An innocent child of no sin and no stain. We failed her, Lord, in allowing her to perish from this earth, and for that we are sorry, and beg forgiveness."

"Yet we know, Lord, that she is now with you, and is far better off than we who are left here on earth, poorer for her absence. We pray Father that she be nestled in your arms, now in your care and beyond our own."

"Strengthen us, Father, in this loss, that we may continue on without her. That we may find comfort in knowing she has gone to a better place, where one day we might re-join her in Thy Presence." He looked down at the bible in his hands.

"Your Word tells us that there is a better place, and that your Son had gone before us to prepare for us a place with Thee. We pray, Lord, that we may someday be re-united, together, in this place called Heaven."

"Amen."

"Amen," the others repeated, tears in nearly every eye. Everyone stepped forward, one at a time, and gathered a handful of soil, which they dropped atop the little bundle. Jesse was last, tears running freely down his face. He looked up at James.

"I'll help you," he offered. James shook his head.

"For me to do," he replied. "I'll take care of it." Jesse nodded at that, and walked back toward the building behind the others. Ralph was waiting a short distance away.

"C'mon, Ralph," Jesse said softly, but the teen shook his head, watching his friend.

"He might need me," was all he said. Jesse nodded again, a small smile on his face. He silently damned the people responsible for children such as these having to assume such a difficult role. It wasn't right, and it wasn't fair. But then Gran had always said life was neither.

"Rain falls on the just and the unjust, boy," he could hear her voice. *"Don't worry 'bout that child, she's in God's hands, now, and the better for it. It's the rest of you what's in a pickle."*

Nodding his agreement with the silent proclamation, Jesse went inside.

Ralph watched silently, ready to help his friend however he had to.

~*~

The rest of the day was very subdued. Jesse checked the building and the vehicles, finding no real damage anywhere. Not that the loss of Cassandra wasn't damage enough. Still, they had been lucky, considering. The storm had brushed by them, doing no more than uprooting a few trees.

Roland was morose. Forced to inactivity due to his sprained back, he could only recline in pain and face his own private demons. Maria wasn't any better, but she had the advantage of working, which distracted her somewhat from the guilt that wracked her.

Deena and Terri went about their work in silence, speaking softly on occasion to the children, still reeling from their fear of the storm, and the loss of one of their own. They huddled in groups, taking comfort in the presence of others.

Ralph watched as James finished his self-appointed task, packing the dirt down tightly, and covering the grave with rocks gathered from around the school. Finally satisfied with his work, the older boy then went and retrieved a hand saw from the room where their tools were stored, and walked slowly down to the place he'd found Cassandra. Ralph followed at a respectful distance, stopping well away, but where he could keep an eye on his friend.

James waded into the water with the saw, and began to cut the roots and bushes that had trapped Cassandra. He worked steady, taking his anger and despair out on the job he had taken for himself. Ralph watched him struggle with the brush for a moment, and then joined him. Without a word Ralph waded in beside James and began to help drag the brush out of the water.

James nodded his thanks, returning to the saw. Ralph continued to pull the cut brush from the water, piling it high on the ground behind them. Finally satisfied, James left the water, shivering slightly in the cool wind. He gathered a handful of the brush and began pulling it toward the small grave.

Ralph helped quietly, no words passing between the two. Ten minutes later both stood in silence, looking at the small brush arbor that now covered Cassandra's final resting place. With a nod to one another, the boys slowly made their way back inside.

Behind them, the small brush covered mound sat alone in silence.

~*~

Supper was a subdued affair. No one spoke other than what speech was necessary for meal preparation, and serving. When supper was finished, most of the smaller children went to bed unasked, exhausted from the trials of the day, their little bodies worn out from fear and loss.

Roland watched them with a heavy heart, afraid of what this might do. They had made so much progress in the last week, and this could undo everything.

He also watched James, who sat alone, cleaning his gear. The teen had taken the loss personally, as a personal failure. Roland would have to talk to him about that, and soon, but for now he thought it best to let the boy grieve.

Maria was a broken shell of the confident young woman she had been just this morning. She, too, felt the loss was a personal failure since she had been the one to carry the children outside. It was the same routine they had been following since their arrival. But she had lost sight of the two children and blamed herself for it. Roland knew he'd have to talk to her as well, but was more hesitant. Maria didn't care for him much, so he'd have to approach her a bit differently.

"Mister Roland," Ralph's hesitant voice broke into his thinking. "There's someone outside." Roland looked up sharply.

"Know who it is?" he asked, rising, reaching for his rifle.

"No, sir," Ralph shook his head. "It's a woman, with a little boy, and a baby." Frowning, Roland moved toward the door.

A ragged looking woman with filthy, tangled, dirty blonde hair was standing at the entrance to the school. She held an infant in her left arm, and carried a trash bag in her right. There was a boy of about four standing beside her, with a smaller bag. Both looked exhausted. Roland opened the door, leaving his rifle inside.

ROLAND

"Ma'am, are you okay?" he asked gently. The woman looked at him in alarm until Ralph walked out to stand beside him.

"We. . .I was hoping to stay here overnight," she told him hesitantly. "Our. . .our house was. . .it's gone," she stammered dejectedly. "The storm got it."

"Please, come inside," Roland offered, reaching out to take the bag from her hands. "We've got supper ready. We've already eaten but there's still plenty. You can get cleaned up, and eat, and get warm."

The woman reluctantly released the bag, then wrapped her now free arm around her baby. Ralph took the smaller bag from the little boy and laid a gentle arm on his shoulder.

"C'mon, sport," he smiled slightly. "Want something to eat?" The boy nodded, his eyes sunken and dark.

"Please, Ma'am," Roland said gently. "Let us get you out of the weather. It's safe here. We've made this a safe haven for several children. You're most welcome to join us."

"Thank you," she almost whispered. "We've. . .we've been walking all day," she admitted.

"Come inside, and rest," Roland urged. "There's time enough tomorrow to think on that."

She hesitantly followed him inside, along with the little boy, Ralph bringing up the rear. Deena met them when they entered the cafeteria.

"Hello, I'm Deena," she said to the woman, and then to the little boy. "Are you hungry? Supper is still warm."

"Ralph, go and turn the hot water heater on," Roland ordered. "They need a warm shower, and you, James and I need to get cleaned up anyway." Ralph hurried on his way to comply. They only used the hot water heater rarely to save the propane used to heat the water for showers. Roland decided that tonight was a good night to use it.

He made his way over to James.

"Water's heating," he said simply. "Take a good, warm shower, and get some clean clothes on. Make you feel better and help you sleep." James nodded, and went to do as Roland had ordered. Roland winced as his back reminded him it was still hurt. Rubbing the offending area lightly, he made his way to his own bunk, gathering clean BDUs and skivvies. He saw Deena and waved her over.

"James and I are gonna hit the shower," he told her. "Once they've eaten, you or Terri can help them into the girl's shower and let them get cleaned up, too." He handed her a clean BDU set. "Let the woman wear these, if she needs them. Be a little large, but the waist can be cinched and the top will button. I don't imagine she's got any clean clothes. Okay?"

"Sure, Roland," Deena nodded. "We'll take care of it. How's your back?" she asked.

"Hurts like he. . .heck," he told her, and she laughed.

"I have heard the word before, you know," she told him.

"Not from me, though," he shook his head. He walked over to where Jesse was reclining at a table, watching the woman and boy eat hungrily.

"I'll be in the shower, Jesse," he said softly. "Deena will look after them. Just keep an eye on things."

"How's your back?" Jesse asked, nodding his agreement.

"Hurt's like a sum-bitch," Roland admitted. "I'm hoping the hot water will help."

"Might do," Jesse nodded again. "Don't fall."

"I'll try not to."

~*~

Roland stood under the hot water for a long time. It was a decadence in their situation, but Jesse was right. He wasn't able to operate like this. He had allowed himself one morphine ampule from the well-stocked bag given them by the medics at the armory, and that had taken the edge off his pain. He wanted to get clean and lie down before it wore off, because he wouldn't allow himself another.

James had showered and left, never saying a word. Roland hadn't tried to get him to talk. Not tonight when the pain was still fresh. He'd try tomorrow, if James was open to it. Forcing him to talk wasn't an option Roland knew from firsthand experience. People had tried to make him talk. All it had done was make him irritable, and then angry.

His thoughts turned to the woman who'd arrived earlier. He realized he didn't even know her name. To be fair, getting some food into her and her children had seemed more important than social pleasantries at the time. It was clear that they had been traumatized. He wondered absently if they had been in the house when the tornado destroyed it. Probably not, he decided. Most places in this part of the country had storm shelters for days like today.

He wondered if she had anyone to take her in. Odds were she had family somewhere around, but you never knew. If she didn't, well, she could always stay here, he figured. Homeless was homeless, no matter what your age.

Homeless. That word bounced around in his head for a long time. Roland himself was homeless, unless you counted this place. He'd never had a real home, anyway. The Army had been his home.

Funny, he thought. *If I had stayed, I'd be in pretty good shape, probably. Three hots and a cot, and all that. But if I had, where would these kids be? Would anyone else have stood up for them?*

ROLAND

Probably not. He might have let down his First Sergeant when he left, but surely the old soldier would look at what he'd done since and be proud. He was protecting innocent civilians. Wasn't that what the Army was all about? Protecting Americans?

Probably couldn't tell that in recent years, of course. It was difficult to see how what he'd been doing the last seven years had anything to do with protecting Americans. But he was now.

Roland shut the water off reluctantly. His back was about as good as it was going to get, now. His reluctance wasn't the loss of the steaming hot water. It was the realization that he would have to go back out into the school. For a few precious minutes of introspection, he hadn't had to focus on his troubles.

It was a rude awakening to realize they were still there. He was still here. Drying off, he dressed quickly, shivering slightly now that the effect of the hot water was wearing off. He headed back to the cafeteria to see if the woman was out of the shower. Might be a good time to talk to her, and see what her story was.

When he entered, the only person there was Maria. She was sitting at a table, nursing a hot cup of something. That made Roland wish he had a cup of coffee, or even better, hot chocolate. He didn't, so he shrugged it off and went to sit down opposite the young woman.

"How you doing, Maria?" he asked softly.

"I am well," she shrugged, looking up at him. "How is your back?" she asked, eyes showing her concern.

"it's better," Roland lied. "Hot water helped. Where's our guests?"

"They have turned in for the evening," she replied, taking a sip from her cup. "Her name is Andrea Turner," she provided. "Son's name is Bryan, and infant daughter Alyssa. Their home was completely destroyed by the storm today. Those two bags were all they could salvage alone. Clothes, a few toys and pictures, and a handful of diapers."

"Wow," Roland murmured. "That's rough."

"We do not have diapers," Maria told him. "I do not know how to get any, either. Perhaps we can make some?"

"Do you know how?" Roland asked. This was about the nicest conversation the two of them had ever had. Roland found himself enjoying her company for the first time since. . .well, ever.

"I believe there are a few sheets the Army gave us that would be heavy enough. But we will need safety pins for them, and I have none." Roland nodded, thinking about that.

"Could we sew buttons on them?" he asked. "I mean could you. I don't know if that would work, but..."

"Perhaps," Maria nodded, clearly thinking about it. "It would not be perfect, but it would work, perhaps. Excellent suggestion, Roland," she smiled. Roland realized with a start that Maria was actually very pretty. Especially when she smiled. He'd never noticed that before.

"Well, I have to do something to earn my keep," he shrugged, smiling back.

"You have done far more than that," Maria told him softly. "I owe you an apology, Roland Stang. And I am sorry."

"For what?" Roland asked, genuinely puzzled.

"I have doubted you from the start. Not just because you were gringo. That was a convenient excuse, and true as far as it went. But. . .you frighten me, sometimes. You are a very violent man, Roland, and in my doubt and fear, I worried that you might be so with us. I also could not understand why a man such as you, one who could clearly survive in this time of trouble, would burden himself with such responsibility. I looked for an ulterior motive in all that you did, wondering what your plan really was."

"Yet, this morning, you never hesitated to risk your life for Todd and Cassie. You didn't know them, they weren't your family, and you had no obligation to look for or protect them, other than the one you placed upon yourself. But you did it anyway. Without a thought to your own safety." She reached across the table hesitantly, and placed one small hand on his much larger one.

"Thank you," she said simply. "I hope you can forgive me." He squeezed her hand slightly before letting it go.

"Maria, I told you. I'm not really a good man. I haven't been in a long time. Maybe I never was. I was still working through that when things went to hell." Roland paused, making sure he worded this right. "All of you are my family now, Maria. I've never had one before, I told you. Maybe the Army, in a brotherhood kind of way, but never a real family. I can't remember my parents; I was so young when they died. My earliest memories are of foster care, and that was no picnic. People take in foster children for many reasons. Some genuinely love children, and want to help them any way they can."

"Others, they want the money the state gives them for taking care of us. Money that should be, is *supposed* to be, spent on the children in their care. That doesn't always happen. And you're a scared kid, with no one to look out for you, so you don't say anything. You get by as best you can, waiting for a chance to get away."

"When I realized what was going on in that warehouse, I had to do something. Had to try, anyway. All of you dependent on those scum bags, basically at their mercy, made me think of the times when I was in a bad home. No one was there for me. I... I couldn't let the same thing happen to all of you." He looked at her.

ROLAND

"And you didn't have to be there either," he said softly. "You could have left at any time, made your own way. But you stayed for the rest of them, didn't you?"

"Yes," she almost whispered. "I had nowhere to go, and they needed someone. I know that some of the parents died while looking for food and water for the children. I am not certain, but I think Wright may have killed some of them, especially the women."

"Some of the parents, though, I think just left," she continued sadly. "They were without hope, for themselves or their children. And some of them didn't really seem to care. As if the children were a burden they could no longer support. Or no longer had to support," she added with a tinge of bitterness. "They just left them. I have often wondered how it was that so many children were gathered in such a place. I suppose the warehouse was out of the way, and therefore seemed safe, but I do not know. Some were found on the streets and brought there by people trying to help, even when they couldn't seem to help themselves. Some, like James, Deena, and the others, made their way on their own from wherever they had been when things turned bad. I do not know how they found the place, they just did," she shrugged.

"Well, however it happened, we're all here, safe and sound, at least for now," Roland said. Maria looked up sharply at him.

"I know, we lost Cassandra," Roland held his hands up. "That was no one's fault but mine, either. It never even occurred to me to plan for what to do during a storm like that. And it should have. I lived in this area, well all over it, really, until I joined the Army. First thing you learn around here is watch the sky." He sighed, dejected again.

"I should have made a plan for that. We should have drilled the kids on what to do, and where to go. And we will, now, because this could easily happen again. We can't. . .can't bring Cassandra back," his voice broke a bit. "But we can make sure we don't lose anyone else in the same way. It's all I know to do," he admitted sadly. "I messed up, and I can't fix it. All I can do is make sure it don't happen again."

"You are no more to blame that I," Maria said mournfully. "I should have kept up with them better. I should have counted them as we came inside. Tomorrow I will have the children select play buddies. In an emergency such as today's, they will all find their play buddy. When I see someone alone, I will know someone else is missing, and who it is. As you say, it will not bring Cassie back, but it will, perhaps, prevent another loss like hers." She paused, and then laid her hand on his once again.

"You did save Todd, Roland," she told him softly. "And that is not nothing. It is very much something, in fact. We could have lost two children today, if not for you."

"James was there, too," Roland shook his head. "He blames himself for what happened to Cassandra. He was out there, in the middle of the tornado, looking for her. What more he could have done I just don't know."

"There was nothing more," Maria said simply. "I have not said anything to him, but I plan to tell him so tomorrow. He was very brave to do what he did. He deserves to be commended for that, rather than berated for her loss. He has much courage, that one," she said firmly.

"Yeah, he does," Roland agreed. "I think that's a good idea, Maria," he added. "I planned on speaking to him too. Maybe between the two of us, we can convince him."

"We do make a formidable team," she smiled wanly.

"Well, I'm off to bed, I think, before the hot water wears off completely. Have Ralph turn off the hot water heater before he turns in. Jesse on watch?"

"Yes, and James will relieve him, and then wake me for breakfast. You are to rest. We cannot be without you, Roland Stang."

"Why, Maria, you almost sounded like you meant that!" Roland joked, grinning at her.

"I almost did," she replied dead pan, and then laughed.

"Good night, Maria."

"Sleep well, Roland."

ROLAND

CHAPTER TWENTY-ONE

The next morning was beautiful. As was usually the case, the storm front had moved on through, leaving clean, crisp air and clear blue skies behind it. It was cool but not cold, and the day promised to be a pretty one.

There was still a dark mood around the school building after yesterday's emotional events, but at least the children were talking as they filed into the cafeteria for breakfast.

Roland eased into a chair at the side of the room, observing but not intruding. He hadn't been there long before Maria was in front of him, a bowl of oatmeal in hand.

"Good morning, Roland," she smiled down at him, setting the bowl before him. "I hope you still like oatmeal."

"Love oatmeal," Roland nodded. "You didn't have to do this, Maria, but I really do appreciate it."

"You are quite welcome," she smiled again, before heading back to the kitchen. Roland watched her go, realizing again just how pretty she was, then dug in. Jesse was probably still asleep, and James might be, he hadn't checked. Things were quiet this morning, and so Roland decided to just go with the flow.

He was about half way through with his oatmeal when Andrea Turner walked in, her baby in her arms, and son by her side. She looked around in dull shock, her eyes finally coming to rest on him. She walked over to where he sat.

"May we join you?" she asked hesitantly.

"Sure," Roland replied, gesturing to the seats opposite him. The woman sat down tiredly, the boy sitting beside her.

"I wanted to thank you," Turner said at once. "I was so tired last night, we all three were, that as soon as we ate and got cleaned up we were asleep. Sorry."

"Nothing to be sorry for," Roland assured her. "I went to clean up, and pretty much did the same thing. How are you this mornin'?"

"I. . .I'm in shock, I guess," she sighed. "Still sinking in. We're lucky to be alive, so it's hard to be angry. But we didn't have much to begin with, and now it's gone."

"We can head over there sometime today, and see if we can salvage anything, if you want. I can understand either way."

"I don't think there's any point," she sighed. "I looked for a long time to get what we did. Like I said, we're lucky to even be here." She suddenly looked down at Bryan. "Honey, would you like to go sit with the other children?" A resounding shake of the head was the boy's only answer. She sighed again, and looked back up at Roland.

"Will it be okay if we stay here another day?" she asked hesitantly. "I don't know if I can find..." she stopped as Roland held up his hand.

"You can stay as long as you like, so long as you're peaceable and willing to work. We put a large garden in, if you know anything about gardening."

"Oh, we've always raised our own food," Andrea replied. "Sure, I know how to do that. And to can, and preserve if you have the equipment."

"I doubt we do, but maybe we can come up with something," Roland replied. There was something they could sorely use. "Maria is trying to come up with something to make cloth diapers out of."

"She is?" Turner looked surprised. "I… I don't know what to say! All of you have been so good to us."

"Well, we're good people," Roland smiled.

"You sure are," she smiled back. "Well, I guess I need to get these two monkeys fed, and then see what I can do to be useful." She stood.

"Thanks again."

"No problem," Roland answered as she headed for the kitchen. Roland was suddenly wary, for no reason he could fathom. It bothered him, but he didn't know why, and that bothered him worse.

He was still working on it when he finished his breakfast.

~*~

Roland decided to sit outside, lounging in a chair, and soak in the sunshine. He hated to admit it, but his back was hurting like hell. He'd taken some Extra Strength Tylenol earlier and that was helping, but it still hurt.

He could tell that it was strain rather than a more serious injury by the way his muscles tensed. He was grateful despite the pain. Getting something like a serious back injury fixed now days would be dicey at best. And he'd be out of action for a long time. Maybe permanently. He had too many to look after for that to be the case.

So deep in his own thoughts, Roland was uncertain of when James had decided to join him. The teen was deadly quiet when he wanted to be. He saw him out of the corner of his eye.

"Mornin', James," he said calmly.

"Morning, Sir. Roland," he corrected, and that brought a grin to Roland's face.

"How you feelin' today, kid?" he asked.

James seemed to think about that for a moment before answering.

"I don't really know," he finally admitted. "I've never been responsible for someone dying before. Not like this." Roland caught the inflection, but pretended not to. There was a lot lying under the surface of this kid.

More like you than you know, he heard Gran Fuller's words in his head.

"You weren't responsible for Cassandra dying, James," Roland said gently, but firmly none the less. "I was. I knew what happened yesterday could happen, and I didn't do a damn thing to plan for it. That's no one's fault but mine."

"I was hiding under a truck while she was drowning," James said bitterly.

"So? There was a *tornado,* James. Hiding under the truck while it passed over was the smart thing to do. Showed good sense on your part. I'm proud of you for thinking so smart." James looked up at him.

"But I failed," he protested quietly. "How can you be proud of me when I failed?"

"How, exactly did you fail here, James?" Roland asked him. "How is it that you're responsible when there are adults all around you supposedly smarter and knowing better? You ran into a storm to search for her. That's not failing, James." He paused for a moment, gathering his thoughts. This had to be done just so.

"Sometimes things are just beyond our control, James," he said finally. "It doesn't matter what we do, how well we do it, nothing. We still lose. That's life, kid, and it ain't fair. I shouldn't have to explain that to you."

"When I was nineteen, I was in a firefight in Afghanistan. It was tough going, and a buddy of mine took a round in the belly. I patched him up, just like I learned in class, got the bleeding stopped. He was talking to me, the whole time, telling me how he was going to enjoy being out of the desert for a while, looking at pretty nurses and getting sponge baths while I was still getting shot at in the heat and the dust."

"I slung him and started for the aid station and he's still talking away. He got quieter as we got near the medic station and I figured the pain was finally hitting him, so he was trying to be still." Roland looked at something in distance, remembering.

"When I got him there, the medic took a look, and shook his head at me, just like they do in the movies. I asked him what he meant, since the guy had been okay just a few minutes before."

"Turns out I may have stopped the external bleeding, but all the while I was carrying him he was bleeding out on the inside. The medic told me I did everything just right, exactly the way I was supposed to. So I asked him, if I did so much right, how come he died?" Roland turned to look at James then.

"He told me that sometimes it's just your time. That no matter what you do, it's never enough. I did everything I'd been trained to do, James. I did it exactly like I had been taught. And it didn't mean a damn thing. He still died."

"Sometimes, no matter what you do, it will never be enough," he finished quietly, leaning back. "You showed real courage yesterday, James. Courage that many a grown man twice your age wouldn't have had in the same situation. That's not failure. That's *never* failure." Roland grew quiet then, not knowing if he'd helped or hurt. Finally, James spoke again.

"I just feel so. . .useless," he admitted. "There should have been something I could have done differently. Maybe stayed to help them get the children inside."

"I told you to get Ralph and gather blankets and cushions in the inner hallway," Roland pointed out. "Did you do it?"

"Yes," James nodded.

"Then how could you have done all that and still helped Maria?" Roland asked. "I should have told you to help her. I didn't. I was trying to cover everything at once, and if I had planned for emergencies like yesterday I wouldn't have needed to. Everyone would have known where to go, and what to do."

"That failure rests with me, James," he said forcefully. "I'm the one who failed. I let her down. I let you down. I let everyone down. I can't fix what happened yesterday, but I promise that I'll do my best never to let it happen again."

"I'll help," James nodded. Roland smiled, and laid a hand on the boy's shoulder.

"I know you will. And that's part of what keeps me going. Knowing that you, Maria, Ralph, the girls, are all willing to help. I couldn't have done any of this without you, James. Without you watching over them while I was out gathering stuff, I couldn't have left them alone for that long."

"So don't feel like a failure, James. Feel proud of what you've accomplished. You've done a man's work and make no mistake of that. You're a man, now, no matter how old you are. And I'm proud to know you." James' face grew red at that, but his eyes seemed to have recaptured some of the light that Roland had always seen there.

"Thanks, Roland," he nodded.

"Thank you, James."

The two sat together in companionable silence after that. No more words were needed.

~*~

Roland was working on organizing their little 'armory' room when Maria tracked him down.

"Roland, have you spoken with Andrea?" she asked, frowning.

"Briefly, this morning," Roland replied, taking the chance to sit down on an ammo crate. His back was killing him. "Well, I spoke to her a few minutes when she got here, too. Why?"

"She said you had offered to let her stay here so long as she worked. Is that true?"

"Yeah," Roland nodded. "I mean if they need to. But we don't have any room for dead beats. Every one of us is working. She wants to stay, she works. I mean, that's okay with you, isn't it? That she earns her way?"

"Of course," Maria nodded. "But. . .is she in charge now?"

"In charge of what?" Roland asked, puzzled.

"She is in the kitchen giving orders like she's our new boss," Maria explained, frowning. "It's not. . .I mean, Deena, Terri and I have been doing this a while. We really don't need her help. Or her supervision. And she's using too much food."

"I don't understand," Roland shook his head. "Too much food for what?"

"We have things figured pretty well," Maria explained. "We have very little left over each night, and that's on purpose. We plan our meals days in advance, and figure down to almost the exact amount of everything. We can't afford to be wasteful, you know. Andrea is cooking, or wants us to cook, far more than we normally do. There will be waste, and we cannot afford to waste anything."

Roland sighed, standing up. He winced sharply, and Maria noticed.

"You lied to me," she accused. "You said your back was better."

"It is better," Roland insisted. "It's just not well. Still hurts, and probably will for a few days. And whether it hurts or not, I got work to do too. Which at the moment seems to be straightening Andrea out. You go on back, and I'll just sorta amble in about five minutes from now and casually ask why you're cooking so much."

"That'll keep her from thinking you're telling on her," he added with a wink. Maria flushed at that, and started to object.

"Maria, you're in charge," Roland said bluntly, cutting her off. "Period. You have been doing an excellent job and I don't intend for that to change. I told her she'd have to work, *not* take charge. I'll take care of it such a way that it keeps you clear of things. I want you to be able to focus on the kids, and keeping things running. There's no one I trust more with their welfare than you."

Blushing slightly at his praise, Maria nodded, her objection forgotten. After a brief smile, she went on her way.

Roland sighed again, wondering why he couldn't seem to catch a break. He was almost out the door when Gran's warning came back to him.

Was Andrea the blonde woman he had to look out for? She didn't really fit the description, he decided, after considering for a moment. Andrea wasn't ugly, but she wasn't all that attractive, either. And her hair, while sort of dishwater blonde, certainly wouldn't qualify as 'sunny'.

No, he decided, Andrea was just another person in the mix of things. And right now, she was mixing things up. That had to stop.

He limped toward the kitchen, muttering to himself the whole way.

~*~

Things were tense in the kitchen to say the least.

"I told you to put more flour in there, Terri," Andrea ordered. "Why didn't you?"

"Because this is how we always do it," Terri replied, fighting to keep her composure. "We don't have a lot of food, Andrea. We have to stretch what we do have until our garden starts producing."

"We figure the food based on how many people we are feeding," Maria explained again, sighing. "So much of each item, times the mouths we have eating. It has worked very well for us these past weeks. Please just let us do our job."

"If I'm going to run things around here, we're going to do them my way," Andrea shot back. "Understand?"

"Who said you were running things, anyway?" Deena asked, seeing Roland appear in the door behind her.

"Roland did, that's who," Andrea smirked.

ROLAND

"He did?" Roland asked from behind her. The smirk died on her lips as she whirled around.

"Roland, you startled me!" she exclaimed, smiling. "How is your back?"

"My back is fine," Roland told her flatly. "Let's get back to the part where I put you in charge. I'm a little fuzzy on that part." Roland had meant to just ease in, say a few choice words, and then let things work out on their own. Catching Andrea in a lie changed that.

"Well, I assumed that's what you meant," Andrea smiled at him. "I mean; these girls are just..."

"Doing a damn fine job," Roland finished, frowning. "I think, if you'll recall our conversation, I said you'd have to work. Not supervise. None of these girls need supervision. They've kept us fed when all there was to eat was oatmeal and junk food, and when we didn't have enough water to wet our mouths. They can handle things here just fine. If you really want to help, and I assure you, you do, then go and watch the children for them. Ralph is watching them now, so all you have to do is help him."

Andrea started to object, but Roland cut her off.

"I really, *really* don't want to hear you talk for a while, lady," he said darkly. "You've already told one lie, and that's all you get with me. Now you can either get with the program or see your way down the road. Be glad to give you food and water for three days, and a ride anywhere you want to go. You decide. Matter of fact, I just decided for you. Be thinking about where you want to go. We'll leave right after lunch."

"Oh, and Ralph can watch the children just fine. All you have to do is see to your own children. Now go do that, and leave these ladies to their work."

Andrea's face lost her smile, and suddenly she looked venomous. Without a word she stalked out of the room, leaving them in peace. Roland watched her go, shaking his head.

"Sorry about that, ladies," he apologized. "I didn't tell her she was in charge of anything. I more or less told her she'd be working in the garden, and she agreed."

"Thank you Roland!" Deena and Terri said together. Roland laughed at that.

"*Gracias*, Roland," Maria nodded her agreement. "But beware. You have made an enemy of that one."

"Story of my life," Roland shrugged. "Women just naturally hate me."

"Not me!" Deena and Terri chorused again, making Roland laugh again. This time he stopped short, wincing in pain.

"Don't make me laugh girls, it hurts," he grinned, albeit painfully.

"Sorry," both girls said at once, and then giggled. Roland left before he hurt himself again. Once out of the kitchen, he had a thought he didn't like. He used his radio to call James.

"James, where are you, bud?"

"I'm on the roof, Roland," James replied.

"Okay, keep an eye out. If Andrea goes out to the garden, call me at once."

"Will do."

"Jesse, you up?"

"Right here, boss man," Jesse replied. *"I'll keep an eye on her,"* he continued, reading Roland's mind.

"You do that. Her and her young'uns are leavin' right after lunch. I'll explain later."

"Copy that," Jesse replied.

Feeling slightly better, Roland started back to the armory. He realized he'd left the door open. That was careless, something he never was. His back was hurting, and he was frustrated by what Maria had told him. That was still no excuse.

He reached the open door to find Andrea inside, trying to load a rifle. Roland drew his pistol, and aimed it right at her.

"Mind telling me what you're doing? And for your sake, it had better be *awfully* good."

ROLAND

CHAPTER TWENTY-TWO

Andrea froze, seeing the pistol aimed at her.

"Now would be a good time to start explaining," Roland warned.

"You wouldn't believe me anyway," she said dejectedly and tossed the rifle down onto a duffle bag.

"Probably not, but you can try me," Roland told her. His pistol never wavered.

"Can we do this somewhere sitting down?" she asked.

"We can do it right here, or I can shoot you," Roland shook his head. "And just so you know, I'm leaning *real* hard toward shooting you. You try to stir up trouble, you try to turn us against each other, and all when we've been nothing but nice to you. We buried a child yesterday that we lost in the storm, so when you and your two kids showed up, it hit a soft spot."

"They aren't my kids," Andrea told him flatly. "I don't have any children. I have a sister, named Megan. And right now, the Reverend Turnbow is. . .*entertaining* her at his home, waiting for me to wreak havoc on your little commune, here. I either do what he wants, or my sister is in dire trouble. It isn't personal."

"I *assure* you its personal," Roland seethed. "If you had just asked for help, we'd have given it to you, just like when we did when you fed us that cock and bull story about the storm. If those kids aren't yours then whose are they?"

"How do I know?" Andrea sighed. "He just gave 'em to me, and told me to pretend they were mine. Since he's literally holding a gun to my sister's head, I didn't bother to ask," she finished bitterly. "So go ahead and shoot me. At least if you shoot me, maybe he'll let her go. Or at least not send her away to somebody he wants to impress."

Roland was at a loss. He wanted to feel sorry for her, in a way, but flatly refused to do so. She had betrayed their trust.

"So what were you going to do with that rifle?" he asked.

"Go get my sister," was the surprising reply. "I knew I'd screwed up already, and I knew Turnbow would know before long, so I thought maybe if I just took one of your guns and shot his ass I could get her back." She looked at him a moment, and then abruptly sat down on the floor.

"I'm exhausted," she shrugged. "I haven't slept in three days to amount to anything. And I'm sure you don't care. But whatever reserves I had are gone. I've got to sit down."

"Not in here you don't," Roland shook his head. "Get up and come out of there. And do it slow, because I'm prone to scaring easy. I might do something you'll regret." The woman did so, moving slowly. She doubted Roland had ever been afraid in his life, but she took his meaning.

Roland pushed her down the hallway to an empty room, and forced her inside. Taking a seat, he sat near the door, indicating she could take a seat anywhere else. He reached for his radio.

"Jesse, you up?"

"You bet," Jesse answered. *"Say, I can't find ..."*

"Don't worry about it," Roland cut him off. "Just go get Maria and meet me in room one-oh-seven. And get a move on."

"Roger that." Jesse didn't ask questions. Roland released his radio, and looked at Andrea, if that was her name, again.

"Now. What do I do with you?"

ROLAND

~*~

Andrea was safely locked away in her new 'room', with James on guard duty. Andrea had taken one look at the dead-eyed teenager and knew he'd kill her without a thought. He might be a kid but the eyes didn't lie.

Meanwhile Jesse, Roland and Maria were having a meeting.

"You believe her?" Jesse asked.

"I don't know," Roland shrugged. "She sounded truthful, but then she sounded truthful yesterday, too."

"I believe it is *possible* she is being truthful," Maria offered. She had been silent until now.

"Mind sharin' why?" Jesse asked, interested.

"She was in a hurry," Maria explained. "If her intention was to create a place for herself here, she should have taken more time. One cannot step into a situation such as ours and expect to be accepted right away. Not well enough to try what she did, anyway. This one is smarter than she lets on. She would know how to create a rift between us, and do so over time, unless she was pressured."

"Well, that does make sense, of a sort," Jesse nodded, looking back to Roland. "So what do we do with her? Or about her?"

"I don't know," Roland admitted. "I need to know what Turnbow's endgame is. And I don't. Does he even have the girl? No way to verify that. What does he expect to gain from getting us into some kinda uproar around here? Can't know that either. There's just too much we don't know," he shook his head.

"She has admitted the children aren't hers," Maria pointed out. "If we force her out, then we should allow them to stay with us."

"We will, but be prepared for Turnbow to use that against us," Roland warned. "He'll try and make it look like we stole her kids, and probably stole the others, too. To use 'em, or make money off 'em." Maria's face furrowed in disgust.

"I know, I know," Roland held off her retort. "I'm just tellin' you what he's likely to do, that's all. That man does have a power fixation like I ain't never seen in a man claimin' to be a preacher. I don't know what he's got in mind, but I don't aim to let him get it. Period. Not when it comes to these kids, anyway."

"But that still leaves the question what do we do," he finished lamely. "All I can think of to do is try to sneak into this town of theirs and see if the girl's really there. If she is, maybe we can spring her."

"No," Jesse shook his head adamantly. "No way. For any number of reasons. First, you ain't a hundred percent. Second, this might just be the play all along, gettin' you to come ridin' in playing hero, and wind up ambushed. Third, this ain't our problem, it's hers. Like you said, if she had

127

just asked for help, explained the situation, then maybe we could have helped."

"Ro', we can't trust that woman, or nothing she says. You know it as well as I do," he finished.

"I don't want to set idle by and see her sister wind up in Turnbow's tender care. Or someone else's, for that matter. Andrea said something about Turnbow shipping her off. I don't like the sound of that at all. Not even a little."

"Nor do I," Maria agreed. "But Jesse is correct, Roland. We cannot risk it. Any of us in Turnbow's hands is a lever to use against the rest. And we can't afford to lose even one person. You know that."

Roland weighed their words, finally nodding.

"I think you're right," he sighed. "Much as I want to help, I don't see how we can. And I don't know what to do about her, either. I mean we could kill'er, I guess, but that seems harsh considering the circumstances. Provided she ain't lying again, of course," he added.

"You know, maybe that ain't a bad idea," Jesse mused. "No, I mean. . .I mean I *don't* mean actually killing her," he held up his hands to stave off protests. "I meant just act like we had. But that won't help her sister any, if we do that."

"So what, then?" Roland asked. "Let her stay on here, acting like she's still doing the job he wants her to do? That could backfire, big time."

"Why do we not call the Sheriff?" Maria asked. "We should let him handle this. It is his job, after all. He was quick enough to come here when he thought things were out of hand."

"Now that's the first *good* idea any of us has had today," Jesse nodded firmly. "Call Wilson and turn the whole thing over to him. Let him deal."

It was a sign of how things had been that Roland hadn't even thought of that. And why not call him? Maria was right, and so was Jesse. This was a law enforcement problem.

"Okay, I'll try and raise him on the radio. Tell him we're making a special dinner for him that our friends up the road wouldn't want him to miss. Maybe that'll get him out here without everyone knowing what's going on."

"Sounds like a plan, my man!" Jesse clapped his hands together. Maria merely nodded.

"Call him," was all she said.

ROLAND

CHAPTER TWENTY-THREE

Wilson listened to the story without interruption, nodding on occasion as Roland related the entire event in detail, with supplements from Maria. When Roland stopped, Wilson scratched his head for a minute, grimacing.

"What is it you want me to do?" he asked finally.

"Don't care what you do," Roland shrugged. "I want her outta here, and she says the Right Reverend Turnbow has got her sister held hostage. You're the law. Your problem, I guess. I got no authority, real or imagined, to get involved in all this."

"Let me talk to her," Wilson said. "I don't recognize that name, to be honest. Did you ask her if she was from around here?"

"Didn't think of it after I found her messing with my rifle," Roland admitted.

"Can't blame you for that," Wilson nodded. He followed Roland down the hall to where James was still standing guard.

"Open up, James," Roland ordered. The teen did so, taking a step back from the door. Wilson nodded in approval at his actions. He looked in the room and saw a young woman he didn't recognize sitting in a desk chair, half asleep.

"I'm Sheriff Wilson," he introduced himself. "I understand you're a bit sideways with Roland and his people. Care to enlighten me as to why?"

"I'm Andrea Turner," she said dully, apparently exhausted. "My sister Megan and I were traveling through, trying to reach our uncle's place in Franklin. He had told us to come there if things got rough. I figured this qualified."

"Imagine so," Wilson nodded.

"We were walking through a little redneck commune when the Sheriff there arrested us for 'trespassing'. Seems they've decided they own the road coming through their hillbilly heaven, and no one passes unless they pay." She looked down.

"We didn't have anything to pay with except. . .well, anyway. Their preacher, he's the one really in charge, he decides to make me an offer I can't refuse. I can take two kids he's got from somewhere, and come here and try to make trouble for Roland, or he can just sell us to the highest bidder. He kept Megan as 'insurance', as he called it."

"And here I am," she shrugged. "I'm not an actress, and I'm not real big on crime, either, but he's got my sister, and she's all the family I have left, save for our uncle. And we don't really know if he's alive anymore."

"And you say Turnbow is the one who put you up to this?" Wilson asked.

"He didn't 'put me up to it', Sheriff, he threatened to sell my sister into a life of sexual slavery. That was if he didn't decide to keep her for himself." She looked at Wilson.

"Are you going to help me? Or just take me to jail?"

"Well, that depends," Wilson replied calmly. "Why don't you tell me everything you can remember about this 'Hillbilly Heaven', and the people you met while you were there. Don't leave out anything, no matter how simple it may seem."

Andrea sat there for a moment, looking at him.

Then she started talking.

~*~

"Everything she said is accurate," Wilson informed Roland. They were once more sitting in the office of the school, Andrea Turner securely behind her locked door. "Right down to the color of the buildings. I've just about got to believe she's telling the truth."

"Turnbow the kind to do something like this?" Roland was skeptical. "And does he have that kind of influence over the people around him?"

"Well, I once would have said no, to the first," Wilson scratched his jaw. "Thing is, it's a big ole 'yes' to the second. And Turnbow and his bunch do follow an odd kinda religion. Don't cotton to outsiders much. And they got some peculiar ideas. About women folk, and such. That bunch has been squirrely since things got bad." He rubbed a hand over his face.

"I've got to think on this a bit," he admitted finally. "I flat don't have the manpower to challenge him out in the open. Every breathing body in that whole community'l back Turnbow to the hilt, bar none. I've only got three deputies left, and they ain't the kind to stack up against a crowd like that. This is gonna take some careful handlin'."

"What about these children?" Roland asked. "Any idea where he got them?"

ROLAND

"Never seen 'em before," Wilson shook his head. "And that bothers me more than the Turner girl. I can't see someone giving up their kids peaceable like."

"You'd be surprised," Roland sighed. "Several of these kids here? Their folks just drifted away from the pack and left."

"Well, reckon you can take care of 'em," Wilson patted Roland's knee.

"We got more'n we can say grace over now!" Roland protested. "And one of them is an infant. We are not set up to care for an infant."

"I'm sure you'll figure something out," Wilson smiled. "Meantime, I gotta get back."

"What about her?" Roland asked. "Ain't you takin' her with you?"

"Nah," Wilson shook his head. "'Til I can figure what's up, need you to keep her under lock and key. Outta sight. Only way to keep her sister safe."

"You're enjoying this a bit too much, Tom," Roland groused.

"I really ain't," Wilson shrugged. "I just don't have a better idea. I've got to see about gettin' a posse together, I reckon. And I'll have to be careful doing it. Until I know what I can call on, just lay low and let things flow, so to speak."

"Thanks for nothin'," Roland muttered as Wilson left. He turned around to see Jesse and Maria standing behind him.

"You heard?" he asked. Both nodded.

"This sucks," Jesse almost spat. "This ain't our job."

"Tell me about it," Roland growled. "Well, we're stuck with it for now. Guess we better lay down some ground rules."

"Let her stew for tonight," Jesse replied.

"I agree," Maria nodded. "Let her contemplate things over night. I suggest moving her to a room with no windows, however. And she will need access to the restroom."

"Put her in the janitor's closet, and give'er a bucket," Jesse grumped.

"We'll see what we can come up with," Roland sighed.

~*~

"You're kidding, right?"

Andrea Turner stood with arms crossed, one hip shot out, foot tapping the floor as she surveyed her 'room'.

"Do I look like I'm kidding?" Roland growled. "This may not be homey, but considering that I was thinking about just putting a bullet in your head and dumping you in a hole out back, I'm sure you'll agree it's cozy."

They had, in fact, put her in the janitor's closet. It was also the janitor's work room, locker room, and break room, so it had a bathroom, and a sink. Two blankets had been tossed inside as well. A plate from supper was sitting on the table, along with three bottles of water.

"This is ridiculous," she fumed. "All I was trying to do was save my sister!"

"And you went about it the wrong way," Roland shrugged. "I'm sorry about your sister, I really am. But the fact is I can't trust you. You came here to do malice, whatever the reason. You're a threat to these kids, far as I'm concerned, and I've worked too hard and killed too many people trying to keep them safe. I won't hesitate to kill *you*, either, the minute I think you're a danger. Understand?"

"I wouldn't hurt a child!" she retorted. "For God's sake, what do you take me for?"

"Someone who admitted she came here to cause trouble for me and my kids," Roland said firmly. "And that's really all I care about when you get right down to it. So do yourself, and your sister, a favor, and don't give me any more reason to think my best move is to bury you quiet and deep and forget I ever saw you. Get me?"

"I get you," Andrea snorted. "This is grossly unfair. No matter where we turn, we're victims."

"You weren't a victim here," Roland reminded her. "We were doing our best to make you feel at home, and help you care for the children you lied about being yours. From my perspective, that makes us the victims. You think about that while you enjoy your stay here at Club Mop and Broom."

He slammed the door before she could say anything else, fuming at her callousness. It was all about her and her sister. The woman truly didn't see where she'd done anything wrong in trying to set them up for a fall for the Right Reverend Turnbow. If she was telling the truth about that, anyway. Roland wasn't sure she was.

He secured the door, locking the dead bolt, and then padlocking it as well. She kicked the door a few times in anger, but had stopped by the time he was a few feet down the hall.

Roland decided that if she tried to raise any hell, and keep the children awake, she'd spend the night tied to the shelving, and uncomfortable. He was clear out of patience where she was concerned.

ROLAND

CHAPTER TWENTY-FOUR

I am at my wits end. Why is it that so many people harbor ill will towards us? All I'm trying to do is keep these kids safe, and taken care of. And I'm getting very tired of people getting in the way of that.

Very. Tired.

~*~

The next day brought a surprise for Roland. For once it was a happy surprise.

"Roland, there's a convoy approaching," James called from his self-appointed exile on the rooftop. *"It might be Jenkins from the look of it."*

"Well, that wouldn't be bad news at all, now would it?" Roland answered. "I'll go meet 'em. Jesse you up?"

"Yeah, I'm on my way."

Roland stepped outside to see an MRAP coming down the road, leading two trucks and a bus, with a Humvee following.

"Well, that looks familiar," Roland thought, smiling. He waited patiently as the MRAP pulled into the drive out front, followed by the others. Roland could see several people on the bus, but couldn't make out faces. As he looked on, sure enough, Jenkins climbed down from the MRAP.

Sergeant Jenkins.

"Well, somebody gotta 'attaboy', didn't they?" Roland grinned, shaking hands with the newly promoted Jenkins.

"Things have changed, of late," Jenkins nodded. "How are you Roland?"

"We're hanging in there," Roland sighed. "How's things up your way?"

"Better, actually," Jenkins grinned. "You gave the Captain a lot of ideas, Roland. Once we got back, he sort of went on the offensive. There were a few cops still trying to do what they could, and we formed up with them and started running the gangs to heel. Lost a few men and women along the way, but we made a lot of progress."

"Man, that is good news," Roland agreed. "What brings you down this way?"

"Well, there's a bit of a story to that," Jenkins admitted. "This place will hold more than just you guys. Are you willing to take in more people?"

"If they're willing to work, and if we can feed 'em, sure. But the penalty for trouble making is pretty severe."

"Shouldn't be any, probably," Jenkins shook his head. "Most of these folks have been with us for a while. Plus, Vaughan and Mackey will be staying on to supplement your security. And we brought two trucks loaded with supplies. Turns out there are several warehouses in the city that were storing dry goods. Canned stuff, flour, meal, oats, that kind of thing. We're still doing inventory, but it's enough to keep us going for a while. And, like you, we're raising food now ourselves."

"But we're still short of water," he admitted, quieter. "There just aren't many wells in a place like Nashville. Our filtration unit can only deal with so much a day. We've been on the radio looking for another one, but so far no luck. I know there were a few more in-state, but we haven't made contact with anyone that's got one so far."

"Any luck getting the city's plants up and running?" Roland asked.

"No power," Jenkins shook his head. "And that's going to be the key. There's just not enough power to run something like that. We're hoping to be able to actually build something ourselves out of what we found at the city's water plants, but right now we're at a loss as to how to power it effectively."

"Might try a water wheel, just on a big scale," Roland offered. "I've seen villages in Africa and South America using them to power their villages."

"I'll pass that along," Jenkins nodded, scribbling a note in his note book. "You still having issues with Turnbow?"

"And then some," Roland nodded, explaining the events up to that point.

"Dammit," Jenkins growled. "We'd gotten some rumors about trafficking like that, but I was hoping it wasn't true. We've seen it in the city, though," he added grimly.

"May not be," Roland shrugged. "Couldn't trust that woman far as I could throw her."

ROLAND

"Well, I'll contact the Sheriff while we're here," Jenkins offered. "We can provide the extra manpower if he wants to clean that nest out. Until then, you want to talk things over with the others? About the new folks? And then meet 'em?"

"Yeah, that's be a good idea," Roland nodded. "I've got to stop making all these unilateral decisions."

~*~

"How many people?" Maria asked, looking skeptical. "Our food reserves are already stretched thin."

"Brought two trucks worth of supplies with us, ma'am," Jenkins promised. "And there's no dead weight on that bus. Fourteen in all, all good folks. One's a paramedic, too. She's not a doctor, but she's very smart. That's got to help."

"It does," Roland said quietly. Everyone was thinking about Cassandra.

"What about the others?" Maria asked.

"Well, there's two teens, boy of fifteen and girl of eighteen. Brother and sister. No idea on their parents. Mackey's girlfriend, she's the para. In fact she's service, a combat medic. After them, there's two married couples. The Roberts' and the Williams'. Nice folks, middle-aged-ish. Three younger men, in their twenties, and four younger women, also in their twenties except for one, who I think is just turned thirty."

"None of them have been any trouble at all, and all of them have worked hard to help keep things going at the Armory. And, they all agreed to help with the children. Captain insisted that anyone who came here would agree to that."

"Well, that's good to know," Roland actually smiled. "Maria, we have room for them, right?"

"Si," Maria nodded, lost in thought. "I mean, yes, we do. We can give the older couple's two smaller classrooms, to allow them some privacy. We can use two of the larger rooms as dormitory style rooms for the singles. Similar to what we do for ourselves, in fact. We can easily manage that many."

"Mackey and Angie are gonna want one of the small rooms, I imagine," Jenkins nodded. "They're all but married. Have been for over three years. One reason he's here. Angie wanted to be here to help with the children, and no way was Mackey gonna be separated from her. And I'm not sure, but I think Vaughan's got something going with the older single woman. You didn't hear that from me," he winked, and the others laughed.

"Seriously, though, you think you can handle that?" he asked. "I don't want you guys to feel obligated. Cap'n said to make sure you knew that, too. He thought these folks would be a help to you, and it gets some of the people out of town and off the water ration."

"Water actually hasn't been a problem so far," Roland nodded, knocking on the wooden table he leaned against. "You guys want a hot shower while you're here, you can get it. We just have to turn on the hot water heater a little bit before you go."

"A *cold* shower seems like a treat," Jenkins shrugged. "I'm sure everyone will take you up on that. We were going to overnight here, if that's okay."

"How many of you are there?" Roland asked. "Going back, I mean?"

"Two fire teams," Jenkins replied. "If you can get hold of that Sheriff, we can offer to back him up if he wants to go after that girl. I think we can intimidate any opposition to his performing his duties. Captain broke out the heavy hardware when the clean-up started. I've got a Deuce on the Hummer, and an Mk19 on the MRAP."

"That's serious firepower," Jesse whistled softly.

"It's been that kind of month," Jenkins shrugged again. "I mean it when I say that just clearing the area around the Armory was hard, tough work. As bad as anything we saw in Iraq."

"I don't doubt it," Roland nodded. "I'll see if I can get Wilson on the horn. He probably won't want to come out here again so soon. He hasn't got a lot of fuel left."

"Brought you one hundred fifty gallons," Jenkins informed him. "Three drums. You can offer him a fill up."

"That just might do the trick," Roland nodded.

~*~

"What now?" Wilson demanded as he climbed out of his car. "I told you I'd get back to you. . .hey, who are. . .what is all this?"

"Sheriff, I'm Sergeant Gerald Jenkins, 278th Cav. I understand you need some reliable firepower to end a situation. I've got eight men and two armored vehicles I'm willing to put at your disposal."

"You do? You are?" Wilson looked a little confused. "What about. . .I mean, I thought you guys needed the governor's permission..."

"We haven't had contact with the Governor for several weeks," Jenkins shrugged. "Last I had any word, he was sick, but recovering. His people are doing what they can with what they have, but. . .well, you know how it is, I'm sure. There are a lot of fires to put out, and not enough firemen. Our last orders were to assist locals in maintaining order."

ROLAND

"I *do* know how that is," Wilson nodded. "I actually had a pretty sneaky idea about this, but I was still looking for manpower. If you're willing to help then I think my idea might work."

"Why don't you tell us about it while one of my men fills your car up with fuel?" Jenkins offered. Wilson brightened at that.

"Really? That's great!"

"C'mon inside and let's hear this sneaky plot of yours, Tom."

~*~

"That is the craziest thing I've ever heard," Roland shook his head in awe.

"You don't think it'll work?" Wilson asked.

"Oh, it'll work," Jenkins nodded, grinning. "Roland was just expressing his admiration for how your mind works."

"Something like that," Roland nodded his agreement, chuckling. "Jenkins and his boys will have to head back tomorrow," he turned the discussion back to the plan.

"We can head up there right now, far as we're concerned," Gerald offered. Wilson rubbed his chin, clearly weighing his options.

"You know what, why don't we do just that," he said suddenly. "Don't make no mention of you boys leaving tomorrow, by the way," he added. "If they think you'll be around somewhere, or even here, most of the time, that's a tiny club I can use to defuse something later, if something was to need a good. . .well, defusing."

"No problem," Gerald laughed. "And I can't promise how often, but we will be around on occasion. We're trying to work with any and all local law enforcement to knock down the raiders and gangs that have popped up since things fell apart."

"Sounds good," Wilson nodded. "We definitely need the help. That stuff is getting larger than small departments like mine can handle."

"Well, let's clear this first hurdle, and then we'll see what we can see," Gerald offered. "Parker!" A young corporal snapped to.

"Yes Sergeant!"

"Gather the crews. We're about to assist the Sheriff here with some anti-slavery work." Parker's eyes grew very hard, suddenly.

"Right away, Sergeant," he nodded, and scurried off.

"We found. . .well, things were pretty bad in places," Gerald explained to the questioning looks. "Parker and the others have all seen some rough shit. Stuff they never expected to see here at home. I think it reminds them a little too much of the kind of things we saw overseas."

"They won't, uh, you know..." Wilson asked.

"No," Gerald shook his head. "They're solid men. All of them. But for their sake, I hope your little community up there minds their manners. I won't lie to you, if they look like a threat, they'll probably get dead. Quick."

"I can live with that," Wilson shook his head. "You ride with me. Here's how I want to work this when we get there."

Thirty minutes later, a tiny convoy of three vehicles started off down the road. Roland watched them go, and hoped everything worked out.

And reminded himself that if it did or didn't, Andrea was leaving with Jenkins tomorrow. One way or another.

ROLAND

CHAPTER TWENTY-FIVE

Wilson had led the way so that everyone would realize he was the one in charge. They parked in the middle of the road, dead center of town. Wilson got out, taking his time, squaring his hat on his head, giving him a chance to look around.

People were out working, either on gardens or other projects. A few of the elderly people were gathered on benches around town, each surrounded by a few children or even younger adults, teaching old skills to willing hands.

Wilson frowned slightly. This wasn't the scene of a town under a theocratic dictator.

As if summoned by the thought, Turnbow showed up just then.

"Mornin' Sheriff," he smiled. "I see you've got some friends along," he nodded to where three men from each vehicle had dismounted. Jenkins walked up alongside Wilson, and Turnbow lost his smile.

"Hello again, Mister Turnbow," Jenkins said calmly.

"You," Turnbow almost spat. "What in tarnation do you want now?" he demanded.

"He's looking for a murder suspect," Wilson said smoothly. "Woman named Megan Turner. Had a report she was hid out in this area. Woman's dangerous, Reverend. I mean the real deal dangerous. You had any new folks in town of recent?"

"Might be out there with that bunch o' gyps," Turnbow growled.

"They aren't gypsies, Reverend," Wilson sighed. "It's orphans for the most part. Two former soldiers trying to protect a few older teens that are helping them, and a lot of little ones. Kids that's already been preyed upon more than once. They aren't bothering anyone. Besides, we already searched the school, and she's not there," he added. "That was the first place we looked." Wasn't really a lie, Wilson decided, since he had looked around some.

Turnbow looked surprised at that.

"Why'd you look there?"

"Cause I don't know them," Wilson explained. "Strangers in town, first place I look is places where I don't know everyone. She ain't there. Only other settlement anywhere around is here. Now, have you seen anyone like that?" Wilson described the girl again. Turnbow looked thoughtful, then shook his head.

"I can't say I have, but I don't see everything," he admitted. "Let's ask around. If she's been through, someone probably saw her."

Jenkins and Wilson exchanged a look. Something wasn't adding up. They dutifully followed Turnbow around, questioning everyone. Wilson noted that no one looked to Turnbow before answering. They simply replied that no, they hadn't seen any strangers in several days. Weeks, more like, most agreed.

"Do you get the feeling we're being hosed, here?" Jenkins asked softly, when he and Wilson were alone.

"One way or another," Wilson nodded. "I think that woman's lying. Again. I'm going to lay my cards on the table and see what happens." He walked toward Turnbow, catching the older man off to himself.

"Reverend, I'm going to level with you," he said gently. "We were told by a woman claiming to be this Megan person's sister that she was being held against her will, by you specifically."

"What?" Turnbow spluttered. "Again. . .what kind of blather is that?"

"Just like I said," Wilson shrugged. "Let me search your home," Wilson urged. "If you will, then I can go back and arrest this woman for lying. More than that, I can see why she's doing it. Something isn't right, here, Mister Turnbow. I'm starting to think this woman is setting us up for something."

"Search my house?" Turnbow turned red in the face. "Why would I let you search my home?"

"To let me prove this woman's a liar," Wilson said flatly. "I need to find out what game she's playing. It's possible that she's trying to get us fighting among ourselves, softening us up for a raid of some kind."

"There's a lot of that going on, sir," Jenkins offered. "We've been fighting them for several weeks now. We've had some success up in Nashville, and now we're trying to move out into the rural areas. We suspect that many of those we didn't catch actually in the city are basing in areas just like this one. If she's part of one, and we can get her talking, we may can wrap up the whole bunch."

Turnbow looked at both men for a long time, clearly warring with his own rage. Finally, he nodded.

ROLAND

"Fine, search ahead. I've certainly got nothing to hide. But I don't appreciate being treated like a criminal."

"I'm not treating you like a criminal, Reverend," Wilson corrected him. "If I were, I'd just search, permission or no. But I won't force someone to let me search otherwise. That's why I asked your permission. And if you want to take it back, then we won't search." Turnbow studied Wilson for a moment, before nodding again.

"Well, that's fair enough," he sighed. "And we can't afford any kind of trouble. Feel free."

"Would you go with us, sir?" Jenkins asked politely. "I'd feel better if you could watch us while we look." Surprised again, Turnbow nodded.

"I may have misjudged you, young man," he told Jenkins, almost grudgingly.

"Well, you wouldn't be the first, sir," Jenkins smiled widely.

~*~

Roland paced along the front of the building again, agitated. He wanted this done, and over with. Something was nagging at him about all this, and he couldn't quite put his finger on it. He couldn't even satisfy himself about why he was feeling on edge, and that bothered him even more. Usually he could figure things out, but not today.

What was wrong?

"Roland, that woman wants to speak to you," Maria's voice cut into his thinking. He turned to see the petite woman standing at the front door, agitation on her face.

"What does she want?" he asked.

"She will not tell me," Maria shrugged. "She just insists that you come talk to her. That it's in your best interest."

"Is that right?" Roland mused. "Well, I'll get around to her, sometime. Maybe. Meanwhile, how's everything else going?"

"We're doing fine, so far," Maria smiled. "All of the new people are settled in and getting acquainted. I admit, I was not sure this would work, but they all seem willing to work and everyone is willing to help with the children. We will be stronger, now, I think, and that can only be good. And with so many more adults, what happened to Cas. . .what happened before is unlikely to happen again."

"Good," Roland nodded. "I wasn't sure of it myself, but I'm glad to hear things are working out. And it's nice to have some more adults around. We might even get some rest, once in a while," he smiled.

"*Si,* that would be good," she smiled again. Roland noticed again how pretty she was when she smiled.

"Are any of them working in the kitchen?" he asked.

"Yes. We have organized three shifts. One each led by myself, Terri, and Deena. One team will cook each day, allowing the others time to do other things."

"That's a good idea," Roland nodded. "Yours?"

"*Si,* I mean yes," Maria nodded. "All of us are working today, to give everyone a chance to see how we do things."

"Good deal," Roland nodded again. "That reminds me," he added, lifting his radio.

"Vaughan, are you up?"

"*Right here, boss,*" the soldier replied at once.

"Come down to the front entrance please," he asked. "I need to speak to you."

"*On the way.*" Roland looked at Maria.

ROLAND

"I think it's time everyone learned to shoot, Maria. I don't like what's happening."

"I think that is an excellent idea."

~*~

"Can you organize and teach a class on firearms safety and marksmanship?" Roland asked the younger man.

"Sure," Vaughan nodded eagerly. "We were already doing that back at the Armory, so most everyone in the group knows the basics. And everyone is already armed and equipped," he added.

"That's great," Roland was pleased. "Start today, then. Break everyone into groups and get started with one of them today. If I have time I'll help too."

"You worried?" Vaughan asked.

"I'm always worried," Roland admitted. "But right now I'm really worried. Something ain't right, but I can't put my finger on it. It's right there in my mind, but always just out of reach. I think we're being played by that woman, only I can't figure out how. Not yet."

"Well, if she's lying, then at the least she might get something stirred up between us and that bunch down yonder," Vaughan nodded. "Anyway, I'll get started."

"I want you to let James assist you," Roland added. "It's time he took on a more advanced role. I want him learning responsibility. He'll need it one day."

"He's a good kid," Vaughan nodded. "I'll get him and get started."

"Thanks Vaughan," Roland nodded. "I really appreciate it. I'm glad to have you and Mack joining us, too. I couldn't ask for better help."

"Hey, we volunteered," Vaughan grinned. "We wanted to be here." With that, he wheeled sharply and went to collect his first class. Roland watched him go, pleased with Vaughan's words. He appreciated them almost as much as he appreciated them being here.

~*~

"Well, she ain't here," Wilson sighed. "And that leaves us with another problem."

"It sure does," Jenkins nodded. "Reverend, have you had any kind of trouble lately? Or any suspicious behavior? Maybe someone lurking around, watching you folks?"

"Well," Turnbow rubbed the back of his neck, "now that you mention it, we've heard a lot of motorcycles in the distance, last few days," he admitted. "Jonah, he caught sight of a couple of them, and the riders were decked out in leather, kinda like motorcycle gangs wear. We hadn't thought too much on it, but *have* tried to keep watch because of it."

"That's what I figured," Jenkins sighed. "Look Mister Turnbow. I don't know that I'm right, but I got a feeling that this Turner woman was trying to cause problems between you and Roland. Have any of your people gone missing of late? Or would any of them give information about you to potential raiders?"

"Well, we've had folks leave, of course," Turnbow shrugged. "Some going to try and find family, or find a better place to live. By better, I mean a place where you don't have to work sun-up to sun-down. This kind of life ain't for everyone."

"Do you know if any of them might have joined a group of raiders?" Wilson asked.

"Well, maybe," Turnbow shrugged. "You remember Marty Roy, don't you? He left a couple weeks ago, in a huff. He and Mary got into it, and she pretty well told him she didn't ever want to see him again. He was pretty mad."

"And he's about as big a waste o' skin as we got around here," Wilson sighed again.

"I hate to agree, but he is pretty much a lost cause," Turnbow echoed his sigh. "I tried to work with him, Tom, but he was just too angry and bitter about. . .well, pretty much everything. He always did feel like he was owed something."

"A free ride," Wilson nodded. "Derrick, this might be a bad thing. If someone's deliberately trying to set your group and Roland's against each other, then there's got to be a reason for it."

"Well, it's common knowledge that we don't get along," Turnbow mused. "And that's my fault more'n his," the man admitted. "I didn't trust the look of that outfit. I really thought they were gonna be like gypsies. Using them kids to prey on us and anyone else around. I see now that I was wrong, but what's said can't be unsaid. In the time they been here, they ain't really caused no problems I'm aware of, and Stang's been true to his word. They ain't been about, and they ain't asked for anything."

"I told you, his primary concern is for those children," Jenkins nodded. "Every one of them is an orphan. Some of their parents were killed, others just plain walked off and deserted them. Roland's trying to look after them, and make sure they can at least grow up safe and be prepared to live in what's left of the world. I promise you Mister Turnbow, if you're friendly to him, Roland'l be friendly to you."

"I've about figured that out," Turnbow admitted. "Tom here is hard to fool, and he said the same thing. I was just mad, and worried about what they might do. None of us are really young, for the most part. And we're not the violent sort. I've tried to keep things calm here, and pray and hope for the best. But I'm not foolish enough to think there aren't bad people about that would love to take advantage of a bunch of old farmers and planters."

"There's things you can do to help make yourselves more secure," Jenkins replied, looking carefully around at the small community. "My men and I will be glad to help you get started. We can stay a day, and work with you."

"I... I'd be much obliged by that, young man," Turnbow looked surprised. "Much obliged indeed."

"No problem," Jenkins smiled. "I'll get my guys, and we'll get started."

"I'll head back to the school and deal with the Turner woman," Wilson said grimly.

"How?" Jenkins asked.

"No idea."

CHAPTER TWENTY-SIX

"Well, I can't say I'm surprised," Roland sighed. "This bitch is weaving lies inside of lies. What a piece o' work."

"Yeah," Wilson sighed. "I know. Thing is, we don't know where she's coming from, who she's working for, nothing." He removed his Stetson and scratched his head.

"I gotta admit, Roland, I'm not sure just what to do next."

"I got an idea, but I don't know how far it'll run," Roland mused after a moment of thought. "We can try to run a game on her. See what she does, or how she acts. Beats nothing, I guess."

"What kinda game?" Wilson asked, as Roland got up from his chair.

"I'm gonna tell her that we found her sister," he grinned maliciously.

~*~

Andrea Turner looked up from where she sat as Roland and Wilson walked into her 'room'.

"What is it now?" she sighed, getting to her feet.

"Just wanted to tell you we found your sister," Tom smiled his best 'vote for me' smile. "Looks like she's just fine. Doc's checking her out now."

"Wh… tha. . .that's great!" she stammered. "Did she say anything? Was she injured?"

"Like I said, she seems fine. Medic is checking her out, just to be safe, but she's walking and talking. She asked about you, worried you'd been hurt. We told her she'd see you soon, and you're fine," Roland answered. "She'll stay here with you until the Guard leaves. They'll carry you to Nashville to see your uncle."

"They will?" Turner seemed surprised.

ROLAND

"Sure," Wilson nodded. "Going that way anyhow. Won't be a problem."

"I don't know what to say," Turner almost muttered. "I didn't really think she'd still be there." She sat down on the bed, hands folded in front of her. "How do I know it's really her?" she demanded suddenly. "I should see her. Take me to her!"

"That ain't gonna happen," Roland shook his head. "You ain't gettin' outta here until they're ready to take you on away from here. Regardless of your reasons, you still caused a lot of trouble here, and then tried to steal a rifle. So you stay right here until you leave."

"Sheriff, I demand to be taken to my sister!" Turner exclaimed, her voice tinged with desperation.

"Sorry Miss Turner, but I have to side with Roland on this," Wilson shook his head. "You might have had reason, but you caused him a good bit of trouble. He's within his rights not to allow you free reign of his home. Just sit here and be patient. We'll bring your sister along as soon as the medic is done, and she's had something to eat."

"No!" Turner shouted, jumping to her feet. "I want to see her *now!*"

"Not an option." Roland's face was a mask. "Sit down, and be patient. She'll be here shortly."

"You're lying!" Turner exclaimed.

"And so are you," Roland shrugged. "You ain't even got a sister, do you?"

Turner stopped dead in her tracks, mouth open for a retort, when Roland's calm words penetrated. Suddenly her eyes darted around the room, like a lion in a cage.

"Don't even think it," Roland warned, his pistol appearing in his hand like magic. "I got no problem shooting you where you stand and burying you out behind the school."

"You can't do that with Howdy Doody standing there," Turner almost snarled. The change in her was almost instantaneous.

"I can always bury him too," Roland replied flatly. "It's nothin' I ain't done before, I promise."

"Hey, I bet my coffee is ready," Wilson said suddenly. "I better just go and check on that."

"You can't leave me here with him!" Turner cried, suddenly showing fear.

"Sure I can," Wilson nodded. "And I will if you don't start talking. Right now."

"If you want to live out the next five minutes," Roland's voice was like ice, "then here's your chance. I won't give you another."

~*~

Thirty minutes later, Roland and Wilson were in the office, still reeling from Turner's 'talk'.

"What are we going to do?" Wilson asked, more to himself than Roland.

"I'm going to defend this school, and my kids," Roland said flatly. He didn't even realize he said 'his' kids. He couldn't have told anyone when they became 'his' kids, either. They just had.

"I'd love to be able to help, Roland, but. . .I've got the rest of the county to worry about too."

"We can take care of ourselves," Roland shook his head. "We've got some extra manpower now, with so many new faces. You need to get yourself a posse organized, though. I'll check with Jenkins when he returns, and see if he can help you any. Even if they can't stay, they might have some hardware you can use."

"That would help," Wilson nodded. "There's a few vets around here that could make use of military style hardware. I've got to start talking to them right now." He looked at Roland.

"I don't know what to expect these next few days, Roland."

"Expect war," Roland shrugged, his voice flat. "Cause that's what it'll be. Take care, Tom," he extended his hand. "You get into a bind, you can always come here."

"Thank you, Roland," Wilson nodded gratefully, taking the proffered hand. "I hope it won't come to that. I have to get going." Roland watched the Sheriff leave, his face hardening.

He had things to do.

~*~

Turner was afraid. For the first time since her arrival here, she was truly afraid.

"What are you going to do?" she demanded. Hands cuffed behind her, barefoot, she was walking into a field near the school, being prodded forward by the barrel of Roland's rifle. "If something happens to me, it'll go badly for you when they get here," she warned.

"As opposed to how it's going to be anyway?" Roland scoffed, giving her a not too gentle shove. "That's not much of a threat, now is it?"

"I can help you," Turner promised, her voice edged with fear.

"You already helped me," Roland assured her. "Stop right here," he ordered. "Stay real still, so you don't scare me." Turner froze, fighting to stay perfectly still as Roland freed her from the cuffs.

"Start running," he ordered suddenly.

"Wh… what?" Turner stammered, almost turning to look at him before catching herself.

"You heard me," Roland's voice was flat. Devoid of any emotion. "Start running."

"Why?"

"I'm giving you a chance," Roland replied. "More than you would have given us. So start running."

"Please don't do this," Turner whimpered. "I didn't have any choice! I was forced to..."

"Stop it," Roland's voice still had no emotion. "You're lying. Every word you've spoken since you got here was a lie. Got no interest in nothing you got to say. Time's running, by the way."

"Roland, please," she tried again. "This isn't. . .you don't have to..."

The gunshot echoed across the field, scaring nearby birds into flight. The only sound after that was Turner's lifeless body hitting the muddy ground.

"Told you time was runnin' out," Roland said calmly. He started back to the school, without bothering to bury the body.

He still had work to do today.

~*~

"Where is that woman?" Maria asked carefully. Roland's face was a mask. She had seen the look before, but it was still. . .unsettling.

"She ran away," was all he said, never slowing. Maria hustled to follow him down the hallway.

"Roland, what is happening?" she asked.

"We're going to be attacked," Roland said simply. "Might be tomorrow, might be a week from now, but its coming. We have to be ready. There's work to do."

"What. . .what kind of work?" Maria stammered. "How many are attacking? What are we going to do?"

"We have to get this place ready for a fight," Roland told her. "I don't have the exact number, but figure a lot. As for what we're going to do?" He stopped suddenly, and looked her right in the eye. Despite knowing that Roland would never harm her, Maria still took a step back. It seemed as if the temperature had fallen ten degrees in just that second.

"We're going to kill them all."

CHAPTER TWENTY-SEVEN

"And that's the way it is," Roland finished, standing before the assembled group of residents at the school. The children were in the cafeteria with the older children.

"We have to go back," one of the women said suddenly, breaking into the silence. "We have to go back to Nashville, where it's safe!"

"I'm not going back," one of the men spoke firmly. "There's no way I'm leaving all these kids here defenseless against something like that." He looked at Roland.

"I'm not a soldier, but I do know how to shoot. Been shootin' all my life. I'll do whatever it takes, sir." Roland nodded at him, smiling slightly.

"Thanks. If any of the rest of you want to go, then you need to let Jenkins know as soon as he gets back. I expect he'll come on in soon, once he gets this information." Wilson had promised that would be his first stop, to warn both Turnbow and Jenkins. "No hard feeling for anyone who wants to go. Just don't come back. We don't need people who want to just sit back and enjoy what other people are willing to bleed and die for."

Several that had been thinking of leaving winced at that.

"For those of you who are willing to stay, Vaughan will get you armed and checked out on weapons. No heroics," Roland warned. "I don't need dead heroes. I need live helpers. Once this is over, there'll be plenty of work to do, and we'll need your help to get it done."

Two of the single women, and the oldest of the two couples stayed put. They looked on shame
faced as the rest followed Vaughan out of the room.

"You can help watch the children while Maria and the others get ready," Roland told them flatly. "You can go as soon as Jenkins gets back. Don't bother coming back."

ROLAND

He left them sitting there, walking out of the room. He had too many other things to do to dwell on people who weren't willing to fight to survive.

~*~

Jenkins rolled in two hours later.

"Roland, we need to evacuate this place," he said at once.

"No." The answer was flat and final.

"There's no other choice!" Jenkins demanded.

"We're staying," Roland shook his head. "We've got too much hard work invested here. If we run this time, we'll just face something like this again. Someone has to start standing up. Fighting back." He turned to face the soldier.

"I would like you to take the children," he said, his voice softer. "They'll be safer with you until we can beat this off."

"Roland, you aren't being reasonable," Jenkins was almost pleading. "There's no reason to defend this place!"

"There's every reason!" Roland was almost yelling. He stopped short, visibly calming himself. "This is our home," he continued, calmer. "More than that, this is still America. I know it's just a shadow of what it was, but it's still here. And I'm not going to allow anyone else to take it away." He looked away for a minute, collecting his thoughts.

"I've been all over the world, fighting for other people. I know you and most of your guys have been to Iraq at the least. Some of you may have been other places. If we can fight for others, then we can damn sure fight for our own. I'm going to fight for what's mine, what's ours, and I'll kill anyone who tries to take it away or hurt my kids. *Anyone.* "

"Roland, we can't help you," Jenkins looked pale. "We have to go back. I'll try to get the..."

"I don't need your help," Roland said firmly. "You've done more than enough. You can protect my kids. Take them with you and get the hell out of here. Take anyone else who wants to go. I don't need them in the way if they're not going to help."

Jenkins fell silent at that. He managed to nod his agreement, face still drawn. Realizing that he wasn't going to change Roland's mind, he headed to find his men. They had work to do.

~*~

"Okay, we need to get these bags filled, and get them on the roof!" Jesse called. Everyone that wasn't working elsewhere was filling bags with dirt. Sandbags from the county's flood stores had been brought to the school by one of the few county workers still on the job. He had dropped them off as he made the rounds to other places, including Turnbow's group.

They didn't have sand but they had plenty of dirt. They were using a front-end loader attached to the small tractor that the grounds keeper had used to tend the yard. Digging into the soft dirt from the field next door, the bags were filled by hand, then hoisted onto the roof by rope.

The work was exhausting, and Maria, Deena and Terri kept a steady stream of cold water coming for the workers as well as helping fill bags in the interim. One of Jenkins' fire teams was assisting, while the other was providing security. Jenkins and his men would leave in the morning, but they were working as hard as they could to help secure the school beforehand.

Roland was grateful for their help but he wasn't depending on their defenses. He wasn't thinking about placing the school in the center of a firefight.

He wasn't even thinking about allowing the fight to reach the school. He was following an old piece of advice given to him long ago.

When you don't like the game, change the rules.

ROLAND

The next day came early, with everyone up at dawn. Breakfast was already cooked, the girls and their new helpers having risen just after four to start cooking.

Afterward the children were quietly loaded onto the bus, all curious as to why. The adults all smiled and told them they were going on a field trip to see a new place and they'd be back in a few days. Roland watched as Maria, Deena and Terri said their goodbyes. He'd asked them to go with the children but all had refused. This was now their home, and they intended to stay there. Roland decided not to argue. They had as much right to stay as he did.

Jenkins broke into Roland's reverie.

"We're loaded and ready to go," he announced. "Where's that Turner woman? I'm sure you want her out of your hair."

"She escaped," Roland replied, looking straight into his eyes. "Two days ago. Probably back with her group by now."

"Why didn't you tell me!" Jenkins was astonished. "Roland she'll have told them everything!"

"Most likely," Roland nodded calmly. "No help for it now. At least the children won't be here." He offered his hand.

"Thanks for that, by the way." He smiled.

"Roland, please, come with us," Jenkins asked once more. "We can easily get you back to Nashville. We'll find you another place. A better one!"

"No," Roland shook his head. "If we abandon this place, then it'll just go harder for the others. We'll stick it out here. That bunch won't wait very long. They'll make their move, soon. When they do, we'll get'em."

"Fine, I give up," Jenkins threw his hands up. "I hope you know what you're doing. I really do."

"Either way, it'll be over soon."

Jenkins sat in the passenger seat of his Humvee as the small convoy left the school. As he looked to his right, he saw vultures circling in a field, and others on the ground.

"Ran away, huh," he said to himself.

Then he looked forward and kept moving.

CHAPTER TWENTY-EIGHT

Two days passed. Work continued at a frenzied pace as the school took on the look of a fortified castle. Look out posts were erected on the roof, and surrounded with sandbags. Logs and concrete rails were placed before all weak spots to prevent vehicles from being able to ram at full speed. Sandbags were used inside to strengthen the walls against any incoming fire, and windows were covered with scraps of steel to prevent entry while allowing those inside to return fire.

A jury-rigged water tank was placed on the roof and tied into the sprinkler system and the school's fire hose system. Fed by gravity, these additions would be important if a fire broke out during the fighting. Everyone took the time to learn how to turn the system on and use the equipment. Fire extinguishers were placed ready to use at each window that wasn't covered completely.

On the second day Roland opened the 'goody' box that had been given to him when the group departed Nashville. He hadn't known what to expect and he was pleasantly surprised.

Inside were three cases of Claymore mines, six mines to the case. Beside them was a box containing an Mk 19 grenade launcher with three boxes of ammunition. Jesse whistled silently as he viewed the contents of the box.

"Wow," he finally said. "That's some goody box."

"Ain't it though," Roland breathed. He hadn't thought about the box a single time since they had arrived here, and had no idea that it contained so much firepower.

"Remind me to kiss the Captain, next time we see him," Jesse chuckled. Roland nodded.

"No doubt."

ROLAND

~*~

Vaughan and MacKey weren't really surprised at the contents. They'd helped pack it.

"Should be a little C-4 in there, too," Vaughan added, pulling the panel from the top of the case. Sure enough, eight sticks of the composite explosive were nestled into the box, with the detonators in a separate box beneath the Mk19.

"Damn," was all Roland could say, shaking his head.

"Nashville has the state armory," MacKey shrugged. "No one really knew, other than the brass I mean, what all was in there until things went to hell. I mean, we knew that we were supposed to have everything we needed to deploy, but. . .anyway. Here it is."

"There it is," Jesse grinned. "What you want to do, Roland?"

"You three take two cases of the Claymores, and the -19, and decide where to set them. Leave me one box. I got something in mind for them. You guys get things set up."

"And just what is it you're gonna do?" Jesse asked.

"I got some thinkin' to do."

~*~

"You sent for me, Roland?" James asked. Roland looked up from where he was sitting.

"Yeah, I did, James. C'mon in and take a seat." James sat down on an ammo crate in Roland's makeshift armory, taking the opportunity to open a jar of ice water Maria had given him when she found him. He drank half of it in one drought.

"You know what we're facing," Roland said, rather than asking.

"Yes, sir," James nodded.

"Well, I had me an extra little talk with Turner, 'fore she left."

"You mean before you killed her?" James asked, never batting an eye.

"How would you know that?" Roland demanded.

"It's what I would of done," the boy shrugged easily. "Can't let'er go, can't keep'er. Ain't much else to do."

"How does that make you feel?" Roland asked warily.

"Like I said," James shrugged again, "I'd o' done it." Roland thought about that for a minute, then nodded. He was more certain than ever, now, that he was making the right choice.

"I don't want to let these people just attack the school, and us defend," Roland said finally. "I want to take the fight to them."

"Ain't really got enough people, do we?" James asked, leaning forward.

155

"I was thinking about just you and me," Roland admitted, eyeing the teen carefully. James' eyes lit up at that.

"Sort of whittle them down, is that it?" he asked.

"Or get rid of them completely," Roland nodded. "Would you be interested in something like that? I need someone to watch my back, and I need someone who won't have a problem shooting. Is that you?"

"Sure is," James replied at once. "When do we leave?"

"This isn't a game, James," Roland emphasized. "You could get hurt, or killed. You have to do what I say, when I say, or we could *both* get killed. Are you sure?"

"I'll do whatever you tell me to, Roland," James said seriously. "And us orphans, we gotta stick together, right?"

"Right," Roland grinned. He spread a map before them.

"All right. This is where they're supposedly laid up..."

~*~

"When do we leave?" James asked, as Roland finished.

"Tonight, right after dark," Roland informed him. "We can't wait any longer. If they decide to move, then we'll be away from here when they strike, and we can't have that. We can't take the Hummer, either. One, they might need it here. Two, this bunch may see it or hear it coming. We'll have to go on foot. Or we might find some bikes or something along the way."

"Long way," James noted.

"That's why we're leaving early," Roland nodded. "If this outfit is like most others, then they'll be up late, which means they'll sleep late. I want to be in place long before daylight, if we can."

"We'll have trouble seeing," James rubbed his neck. "Using a light won't be much good, we want to stay hid."

"I got that covered," Roland smiled. "Nice shiny NVGs. One apiece."

"Well then," James stood. "I think I'll get some rest, and get my bag packed."

"I'll call you when its time."

~*~

"Where are you going, Roland?"

Roland turned at the question and saw Maria looking at him, eyes slightly narrowed, arms crossed beneath her breasts, and hips shot out to one side. That was a look that could only mean trouble.

"I'm taking a little walk, that's all," he said calmly, hoisting his pack onto his shoulder.

"In the middle of all this, you want to go for a walk?" she asked, clearly suspicious.

"Yep," Roland nodded. "Be gone a day or two, I'd say. Just gonna take a look about, that's all. See what's what, and where."

"And you were just going to leave, and tell no one?" Maria pressed.

"Jess," was his only reply.

"Is 'Jess' the only one deserving enough to be allowed to know what you're doing?" Her calm, steady questions were starting to get on his nerves.

"Maria, what are you getting at, exactly?" he asked. "Think I'm running out on you?"

"Of course not!" Maria stomped her foot on the floor. "I think you're about to do something incredibly stupid. There's no other reason for you to have to sneak away alone in the dark of night!"

"I'm not sneaking away, and for your..."

"Yo, Roland, I'm ready to go!" James' voice preceded him into the room. Maria's eyes narrowed further. James realized at once that he had walked into an 'issue', and tried to extricate himself at once.

"Hold it right there!" Maria's voice cracked across the room. "So it's a conspiracy, is it?" she demanded.

"A what?" James asked, trying, and failing, to act innocent.

"It's not a conspiracy, Maria," Roland rolled his eyes. "It's a recon. That's all. James and I are going to try and find this bunch, and maybe slow them down. That's all."

"So the two of you are going to just go out and find them, all by yourselves, and take care of things? Is that it?"

"Right!" James nodded firmly.

"Not at all!" Roland said at the same time, then glared at his apprentice.

"So which is it?" Maria demanded.

"Uh, what Roland said," James replied. "I'll just. . .uh. . .yeah, that. I'll go and do that," he nodded again. "Be right outside, Roland." Without another word, and before either could stop him, James was gone.

"Pansy," Roland muttered under his breath.

"Roland, I can't believe you're doing this," Maria said softly.

"It needs to be done," Roland shrugged.

"I mean taking James!" she all but shouted. "He's just a -"

"He's a grown man, as far as I'm concerned," Roland's flat voice cut across her's. "You need to realize that he's the future, just like you are. And that means he has to know what. . .he has to learn to..." Roland sighed, trailing off.

"Learn to be like you?" Maria asked quietly.

"Yes," Roland agreed. "He's already more like me than you know. But he has to learn what that means. He has to be ready. Prepared."

"For what?"

"For when I'm not around, anymore," Roland said simply. "Like I said, he's the future. Now as much as I'd love to keep debating this with you, I got to go. We got a long ways to go."

"Please don't," she asked.

"Got to. Can't be helped."

"There has to be another way."

"There may be, but I can't find it."

"Have you looked?" Maria asked, a demanding tone easing into her voice again.

"Yes, I have," Roland assured her. "This is what we've got. I don't like it, but that's how it is."

"You're a liar," Maria sighed. "You not only like it, you live for it. Please, don't deny it," she held her hand up to silence his objection. "I'm not a fool."

"Never said you were," Roland nodded. Maria took the three steps that separated them before Roland could react, and grabbed his face with both hands. Without a word she pulled his face to hers, and kissed him on the lips. Hard.

She broke the kiss as abruptly as she began it, and then spun on her heels, walking quickly away. Before she'd taken five steps she whirled again, facing a stunned Roland.

"Please come back safely," she said simply.

And then she was gone.

Roland stared after her for several seconds, no words coming to mind. Then he slung his pack, and headed outside.

He had work to do.

ROLAND

CHAPTER TWENTY-NINE

The two men walked quietly, constantly scanning their surroundings. It had taken James a few minutes to adjust to using the night vision, but once he had he didn't slow Roland down. If anything, James was doing better than Roland on the road.

The two covered ground quickly in spite of the dark and the fact they were walking. Roland estimated they had covered almost eight miles by the time dawn approached. He indicated for James to halt and the two moved off to the side of the road.

"We're pretty close, I think," he whispered harshly in the still dark of the morning, unfolding a map. He pointed to a spot circled in red.

"This is where they're supposed to be," he told the teen, "and this," he stabbed another spot close by, "is about where we are. There's a ridge that runs from here to right up overlooking the place they've taken up in. We should be there not long after full light, I think, but we're leaving the road here. Too much chance of being spotted." He put the map away and looked closely at James.

"From here on out, we're in enemy territory, kid. Be silent. Think like the bushes, the trees, even the ground. When you go to ground, mimic the movement of the wind in the bush, see what I mean? Never move against the wind, it's a dead giveaway to a trained spotter or good woodsman. Understand?"

"Got it," James whispered. Roland nodded.

"We need to get into position as soon as we can," Roland continued. "We want to be able to observe them for a while, take a look at their actions. We want to get a good head count too. We gotta know what we're up against. Keep an eye on their weapons. If we know how they're armed, then we'll know what kind of resistance they can put up. And what kind of attack they can unleash on the school. Get me?"

"Got you," James nodded.

"Let's go."

The two moved cautiously up the hillside, angling for their objective. Today might be a long day.

~*~

Maria was sitting outside, watching the road in the direction that Roland and James had taken. She wouldn't admit to anyone how worried she was.

"Watching won't help," Jesse said from behind her, causing her to start slightly.

"It won't hurt anything, either," she shrugged.

"That's true enough," he admitted, taking a seat beside her. "You really like Ro' don't you?" he asked. She turned then to look at him.

"What?"

"You got a serious case on Roland," Jesse grinned slightly. "Ain't no point it denying it, girl. And I ain't makin' no fun, either. Ro's a good man, best there is. You couldn't do much better in the world we're livin' in nowadays."

"What's that mean?" Maria asked, not quite as sharply as she once might have.

"Roland's a warrior, Maria," Jesse said quietly. "Not just a soldier. He's a good soldier, don't get me wrong, but a soldier has to be able to take orders, act in a group. Roland's good at that, but he don't like it."

"He prefers to go out and work alone. No one to depend on but himself."

"He's not alone. James is with him," Maria pointed out.

"And that says a lot about James," Jesse nodded. "Roland just ain't the trusting sort, ya know? Takes a while to get to know him, and longer for him to trust you. James must be pretty good or Roland wouldn't of taken him along." He frowned.

"You ain't pining for James are you?" he asked suddenly, unwilling to believe he'd read the situation that wrong.

"I'm not *pining*, as you put it, for anyone," Maria almost huffed. "I'm simply concerned that two of our best men are away at a time when we may need them to help defend this place."

"So it is Roland, then," Jesse smiled. It wasn't an ugly smile in any way, just a friendly one, like someone who was tickled.

"No!" Maria snapped, turning away.

"Like I said, Maria, it's okay if it is. Roland's one of a kind. Just don't expect that you can tame him, that's all. He's as wild as the wind, and has been ever since I've known him. Just accept him like he is, and work with it, ya know?"

"I'm not. . .I don't. . .It's not like that," Maria sputtered slightly.

"Well, I never said I was perfect, so sometimes I guess wrong," Jesse shrugged lightly. "Anyway, you ain't got to worry about Roland, one way or another. And if he trusted James enough to take him along, then you probably ain't got to worry 'bout him, neither."

"Why didn't he take you, instead?" Maria asked suddenly. "Does he not trust you?"

"Trusts me enough to leave me here to look after you," Jesse grinned. "Which, according to Roland, is more important than what James is doing." Maria's face went red at that, and she could feel the heat emanating from her blush.

"Anyway, I got work to do," Jesse stood. "See you later."

Maria watched him go, but then returned her attention to the road.

~*~

"Well, I'd say we found it," Roland said softly as the two pulled the sage and bushes apart enough to look down into the valley. A large two story house sat there, surrounded by motorcycles and other vehicles. Two barns lay in view, with other vehicles around them as well.

There was no movement around the house except for one man who appeared to be on guard. There was movement around the barns, however, as several figures appeared to be doing chores. Roland had no idea if they were prisoners or belonged to the gang. That was one reason they were going to be watching.

Roland and James worked swiftly but carefully establishing their observation post. A pup tent frame strung with camo netting gave them a place to work without obstructing their visibility. They crawled slowly around their area removing sticks and rocks and other obstructions that might hurt them or give them away.

Fishing line created tangle-foot around them, which would hopefully trip up anyone who came near and give them some alarm, as the lines were attached to sticks that would move quietly when they were hit. Finally, Roland took a separate bag with two days of MRE's, back up weapons, and water, and hid it well about a mile behind them while James started the work of examining the farm itself. Using a small waterproof notebook, he took notes on everyone he saw, what time, and what they were doing.

He also started a list of descriptions, along with nicknames for each. Lastly, he created a rough sketch of the farm and its outbuilding. By the time Roland returned, James had managed to have their 'system' up and running and had already started recording his observations.

Roland looked it over, nodding his approval, and then settled in beside the teen.

Now, they would wait and watch.

~*~

"Be dark soon," James mentioned softly. Roland nodded, gauging the sun.

"When it gets toward dusk, we'll slip down to the road," he said. Road was really a misnomer, as it was the only way in or out of the small valley the farm occupied, making it more of a driveway than anything else.

"What are we doing?" James asked.

"We're gonna leave a nasty little surprise for when our friends start heading for the school," was all Roland said.

The two waited in silence until the light began to wane, then silently bellied their way down the hillside. Once there, James took up a lookout position while Roland went to work.

He carefully removed the Claymore mines from the bag he had used to carry them, and laid them out on the ground, along with their electronic detonation circuits. Working slowly but steadily, he readied each one. Satisfied with his work, he signaled to James, and left his hiding spot.

One by one he placed the mines, staggering them along each side of the narrow road. It was nearing full dark before he was finished, forcing him to use his night vision. As he placed each mine he attached a tiny piece of reflective tape to the back. In the event they didn't use them, the mines could be recovered later on.

Done, he made his way to where James was still keeping watch, now wearing his own night vision gear. Using only hand signals to communicate, the two made their way back to their OP. Settling in once more, James looked at Roland.

"I can take first watch," he mouthed. Roland nodded, and settled in to rest.

James took their scope and began once more to survey the house below. There were lights on, now, which meant the gang using the house had at least one generator, and enough fuel to use it. He checked his watch, and made a notation in their notebook.

They would stand four hour watches from now on, allowing each man to be at least partially rested at all times. Not knowing when the group would make their move, it was important that the two of them be rested enough to react.

But for now, there was only the waiting.

ROLAND

CHAPTER THIRTY

For two days they watched. It was hot. It was cramped. It was uncomfortable. Neither complained nor commented on it. Roland nodded to himself in approval of James' actions. He had taken careful notes, used the laser rangefinder to map ranges to various points on the farm, and accounted for many of the descriptions in their book.

On the morning of the third day Roland awoke to gentle pressure on his shoulder. He was alert and oriented in seconds, turning to look down at the farmhouse.

"Lotta movement this morning, Roland," James murmured softly. "Lot more than usual. Way too many people up and about compared to what we been seeing. And they're fueling the vehicles, too."

"All of them?" Roland asked, using the scope to see the action for himself.

"Most," James replied. "And all the motorcycles, too," he added. "I think they're planning on moving out in a big way."

"Might just be," Roland mused. "Any sign of BD?" he asked, their nickname for the one they had decided was the leader.

"He was out about thirty minutes ago, yelling orders at several people. Went back inside after they all got started working. Ain't seen him since, though."

"What about Foo and Ponytail?" These were the two that seemed to be BD's main lieutenants.

"They're supervising," James informed him. "Foo is watching over the fueling, Ponytail's making the rounds to the outbuildings and shaking everyone out."

"Interesting," Roland said, more to himself than James, but the teen nodded.

"We'll give'em a little bit, and see what they do."

~*~

"Look Roland," James slowly pointed. Following that point, Roland was able to see movement, and aimed the scope that way. As the scope came into focus, he could see a line of prisoners, mostly women but including a few men and children, being herded toward the larger barn, guarded by four very unsavory men and two equally unsightly women. Everyone was attached to a long chain by a collar. That was how so few guards could watch over thirty prisoners. Well, that and guns.

Looking back to the vehicles, Roland studied the movement around them. He was certain the group was preparing a sortie. Everyone was armed, and a few were checking over their weapons in a manner that suggested at least these members of the group knew what they were doing. That wasn't so good.

What to do, what to do. While Roland didn't want to leave the prisoners, his first duty was to

his own people. He and James had counted at least forty-seven people in this group, gang, whatever, that were definitely not prisoners. That was a lot of people. Enough to possibly overwhelm the school, even with the defensive preparations and the heavy weapons they had.

Roland needed to whittle those numbers down some. At the very least, it might help the defenders of the school hold against the attack. There was also the possibility that if they hurt them bad enough, the 'gang' would call off the attack altogether. Roland sighed, rubbing his eyes.

"I'll free the prisoners," James said softly. Roland looked at him.

"I can do it," James nodded in assurance. "If they only leave those six, I'll have the advantage."

"How do you figure one against six to your advantage?" Roland asked. He actually didn't doubt the determined teenager, he just wanted to hear what James had in mind.

"They'll probably leave one, or even two, outside," James mused, his eye once more on the scope, watching the prisoners being herded into the barn. "I can take them with the suppressed rifle from cover. If they're rotating the guards, then I'll just wait for their relief, and do the same thing to them. That would only leave two. I can take two."

James wasn't bragging, and it wasn't bravado. He was simply stating facts, and Roland knew he was right.

"Once you free them, what then?" Roland asked.

"I'll take them into the wood-line, and start making our way back to the school," James said at once. "We can keep hidden. If this bunch," he waved at the assembling gang members, "still manages to attack the school after your surprise party, then I can help from the outside." He turned to look at Roland, and smiled.

"Easy."

Roland had to choke off a laugh at that.

"You got sand, kid," he said after he was sure his laughing fit was under control. "Okay, this is what we'll do, then."

~*~

"We better get set," Roland whispered. James nodded beside him. Their blind was gone now, used to cover whatever they weren't taking with them. Each man had stripped down to just the equipment he would need to get the job done.

"Whatever happens, we meet back at the school, no later than tomorrow, right?" Roland was looking at James intently.

"Got it," James nodded, grinning. "We can do it."

"Well, reckon we better get ready," Roland said. His job wasn't going to be easy, either. He would ambush the 'convoy' with the mines, allowing himself to be seen after the smoke cleared, shooting at whoever was still moving. The plan was that the survivors might pursue him.

Not exactly the ideal situation, but then two against fifty or so never was.

James started off to the left, having already located a good place to slide down off their hill. Roland watched him go, sparing one more glance at the assembled gang below. They were mounting up.

Time to go.

~*~

James slid down the hill on his belly, low crawling around trees and tall bushes. Nothing gave away his position. Once on the floor of the valley he spared a glance through his rifle scope at the barn. No movement. He had been right; two men were posted outside on guard. Good.

He began to work his way into position. He would take these two down the minute Roland touched off the mines. He'd have to wait, then, and see if anyone came back or if the others inside the barn would come running out to see what had happened.

Funny, everything had seemed so simple when they were talking it out. Now it seemed almost impossible that this could work out. What the hell had he been thinking? Easy? Sure, for the Army.

Shaking the thought away, James settled into position, rifle at the ready. He didn't have time for doubts now. He had work to do.

~*~

Roland was having similar thoughts as he hid in the sage above the roadway, waiting for the thugs he knew were coming.

The longer he had to think about their idea, the more he came to doubt it. Like James, Roland had thought it was a good plan when they were talking it over. Now, however... Now it seemed just one rung above suicide. He shook his head. Too late now. He could hear them coming.

They were committed.

~*~

The man James and Roland had dubbed 'BD' led them out. Six cycles in front, followed by the two vans, then the rest of the cycles. This was how they rode. All the men on cycles were armed, while the vans carried men without 'rides' and their heavier weapons.

They had been a small though ruthless gang before everything went to hell. Their numbers had increased of late as people realized that the 'law' was pretty much gone anymore. So far they had run over anything that got in their way. BD didn't intend for today to be any different.

There had been a lot of discussion over which target they would hit next. Many favored the small community next door, but others, mostly the men without old ladies, wanted to hit the school. There were several women there, and that's what they wanted most of all at the moment.

In the end, the vote hadn't really been close. The school was the next target. BD hadn't heard from his old lady in several days, not since she's gone inside to scope out the school. He was anxious to see her and so he didn't have a problem with taking the school first. The old people weren't going anywhere, and he was ready for some quality time with her.

He was still dreaming about the reunion when the explosions started.

ROLAND

CHAPTER THIRTY-ONE

Roland had a two channel detonator. He had staggered the mines down the road over a fifty yard spread, on both sides of the road. As the small convoy passed him he waited until the front cycles were past the far mine, and then triggered the string on the far side of the road from him.

The result was satisfactory to say the least. Three Claymores spewed a total of eighteen hundred ball bearings across the road way. It was a broad pattern, but very effective.

The rear cyclists on the far side of the road were shredded, the last mine on that side hitting them broadside. Two of the cycles caught the worst of the blast, and were literally lifted off the ground and slammed into other bikes next to them. Almost every bike went down, either from the blast, or from the blind panic the attack caused.

The vans were hit as well, the second one getting the worst of it, but the other taking a solid hit. As the sound from the explosion faded, Roland watched to see how long it would take them to try and reorganize.

Both van's doors burst open, their stunned occupants exiting onto the roadway. Some were still clutching their weapon; others were just trying to get out of the damaged vehicles. The rear bikers were getting to their feet, at least the ones that weren't killed or crippled in the blast.

Roland looked to where the lead cycles had stopped, and saw them dismounting, coming cautiously back to the rest of the little convoy. Glancing again at the mess on the roadway, Roland realized that many of the men in the vans, and even a large number of the rear bikers had escaped with minor injuries, or none at all.

He smiled grimly, and flipped a switch on the detonator.

Time to fix that.

~*~

BD was still trying to assess the situation when the second blast happened. Two of his men, further ahead than the rest of the vanguard, were shredded right in front of him, their blood and body parts coating him and the others.

But the men still with the vehicles...

Even as the sound of the second blast died away, the screams of his men reached his shattered hearing. His men, dead, dying, writhing in pain. Blood was everywhere, soaking into the dusty roadway. Body parts littered the area as well.

BD went from stunned, to shocked, to furious in less than a minute. Even as he started forward to help he saw a man rise up on the small ridge to his left, aim a rifle, and start shooting.

"Get that sumbitch!" he almost screamed. The men with him grabbed for their weapons and tried to do just that, but in another instant their attacker was gone, having walked his rifle's thirty round magazine down the length of devastation. BD turned to the nearest man and grabbed him by his colors.

"Get back to the farm!" he shouted. "Bring everyone who's left, and get the dogs! I want that bastard dead!"

The frightened man nodded, and almost tripped over his own feet trying to get on his way.

"I'll kill you!" BD shouted with impotent rage. "You hear me! *I'll kill you!*"

~*~

James had waited until he heard the first explosion before shooting. There were two men outside, one near the door and another taking a walk around the barn. James took down the man standing at the door with one well-placed shot. The suppressed rifle made a soft crack as opposed to its normal loud report.

While a suppressor wouldn't make the rifle 'silent', it would muffle the sound and make it difficult to tell where the shot came from.

Exercising patience that was rare for one so young. James waited for the walking guard to return. Alerted because of the distant explosion, the target came running back to the front only to see his comrade on the ground.

The man lifted his rifle, looking around him. Too late.

James squeezed the trigger gently and the second guard's head exploded in a mist. Two down.

James settled in to wait. He had intended to move closer after taking the second man, but hadn't factored in the sound of the mines going off.

ROLAND

I didn't plan this very well, he thought to himself. *Too late now, though. Just gotta run with it.*

Sure enough, the barn door opened and another man stepped outside followed by one of the women. He watched briefly through the scope as the two had an animated conversation. He couldn't hear what was being said, but he could see they were both worked up. Not good.

James targeted the woman first, believing that the man would look for him before ducking inside. If he took the man first then the woman would be more likely to turn back into the barn, and safety.

Not wanting to take a chance, James aimed for the woman's chest and touched off another shot. Bulls- eye. She looked stunned, or dazed maybe, as she slid to the ground. The man looked around wildly, just as James had hoped he would. Mistake.

Another shot and this man crumpled to the ground as well, his life's blood leaking onto the valley floor.

Counting to ten, James waited. No one else came to the door. He could hear shouting inside the barn, but there was no way to make out what was being said. He didn't hear any shots coming from there, so he hoped for the best. Cradling his rifle across both arms, James started crawling to his next position.

He had gone about ten feet when the second blast went off.

Sounds like Roland's having a good time.

~*~

Roland was *not,* in fact, having a good time. He had counted on the mines taking out nearly all of the bikers at once. And several *were* taken out.

Just not nearly as many as he'd hoped.

There had been thirty men in total in the group. Seventeen of them were either killed or wounded to one degree or another by his ambush. That left more than enough to come after him as he high tailed it out of the area.

Eleven men hit the slopes coming after him. Roland had hoped for no more than six. Six were manageable. Eleven were a problem.

Too late for that now, he thought, running through the brush.

He had made time to create one booby trap before he had to get ready for the attack. Just one. His hope was that if one man got caught, then the others would slow down, fearful of more.

Right now that hope was pretty weak.

Nothing goes like it ought to, he thought as he ran through the scrub brush.

~*~

James was about to move toward the barn when a motorcycle came roaring up the drive causing him to freeze in place. This wasn't part of the plan.

Like that'll make it all better, he snorted to himself.

He watched as the man practically leaped off the bike, yelling at the top of his lungs. Men and women came running from all over the place, responding to his outcry.

Holy shit, where the hell did they all come from? James wondered. He counted at least eighteen people swarming around the yelling biker. He couldn't hear what was said, it was just too far, but he could tell that the guy was pretty worked up.

Once he was finished, the rest jumped. Grabbing weapons, the entire bunch headed up the road in three pickup trucks, following the motorcycle. James had seen four dogs loaded into the truck. That was bad. Very, very bad. James watched them go, his heart beating a mile a minute.

I would have walked right into a hornet's nest; he shook his head in wonder. *Thank goodness Roland's ambush drew them off. But they've got dogs. That's going to make Roland's escape a lot harder. Still easier for him than for me and those people in the barn. I gotta get clear of here, and quick.*

Taking a deep breath, James counted to ten, and then repeated it. Satisfied that they were gone, he returned his attention to the barn. There was still one man and one woman on guard there.

Time to get things back on track.

~*~

Roland was glad he'd always kept in shape. If he hadn't he'd be dead by now. For a bunch of biker trash that supposedly lay around drinking beer all day, these guys could run. He was keeping ahead of them, but he wasn't gaining much.

And he'd get tired eventually.

He flinched involuntarily as a bullet clipped a nearby tree.

Damn, not only can they run, but they can run and shoot at the same time! he thought to himself. *That ain't fair!*

That's when he heard the first braying hound.

Are you kidding me?

If he got out of this, he was going to have to seriously reconsider how he and James made their plans.

ROLAND

CHAPTER THIRTY-TWO

Roland heard a scream from behind him, and smiled grimly as he ran. Someone had found his booby trap. It was a simple sapling spring trap, made and hidden in a hurry. Stakes tied to the sapling had probably hit someone's leg. If he was lucky, at least one more of his pursuers might pause to help their injured comrade, but he didn't count on it.

As if to re-enforce that thought, another bullet snapped a limb above him as he dove through the bush.

Oh, well, you can't have everything, he thought philosophically. He continued to run, but was watching for a good place to lay an ambush. He might take one or two down and force the others to seek cover. If he did, then he'd try to slip away again.

And I gotta do something about them dogs, he reminded himself. He hated to shoot the dogs, but he really didn't have much of a choice. Getting away from these idiots might not be too difficult, except for them.

Another bullet hit a tree to his left.

Okay, that's about enough of this shit.

He turned, firing as he did so.

~*~

James lay beside the barn, watching the door. He knew there were still at least two targets inside, one man and one woman. He needed to get somewhere he could see inside. There. About half-way down the barn's wall, there was a broken board, with the bottom third exposed. Not enough room to get inside, or to get out either, but still enough, maybe, for him to get a look inside.

He slow crawled, using his elbows and knees, toward the hole, still stopping every five seconds or so to just listen. He needed to hurry, but he needed to be cautious, too. He wouldn't be able to do the prisoners any good if he was caught. Or shot.

Coming to a rest near the broken board, James paused to catch his breath. He could hear an occasional shot in the distance, but they were growing fainter. He could also still hear the dogs once in a while, but again fainter each time.

Roland was running for his life, buying James time to free these people. He had to get it done, and soon.

Levering his way to where he could see inside, he cautiously eased around, looking through the barn at each stop, slowly moving to where he could see the entire interior of the old building.

The prisoners were all gathered together in the center, on their knees. They were ragged, haggard, and had a look of hopelessness that James didn't think he'd ever seen. His anger only grew as he noted that several of the women bore signs of being attacked. One woman he could see clearly was holding a tattered dress together in front with both hands, sobbing quietly.

"Shut it, bitch," the male guard came into view, and slapped her face. The woman fell over, and the man kicked her for good measure. James could almost hear her rib breaking.

Enough of this shit, he decided. He removed his pistol, suppressor already attached, and angled it through the hole. He waited until the man presented his back, then fired three times, stitching the rounds up his spine. He groaned and fell where he was.

The woman guard heard him fall and came running, lifting her gun as she did so.

"Who did that?" she screamed, sliding to a halt. James swore silently, realizing the woman had stopped in just the right spot. A beam kept him from getting a clean shot.

"I said who did that!" the woman screamed again, and lifted the pistol. When no one answered, she fired randomly into the group, striking a teenage girl in the chest.

"NO!" James yelled, horrified at what he'd seen. Before he could act, the woman fired again, and again, this time hitting a man sitting near the first victim, and then another woman, sitting near the front.

Hearing him yell, the woman turned in his direction, a look of malicious glee on her face.

The look disappeared when three rounds fired from James' pistol struck her in the chest. When the woman turned, she had moved away from the beam's protection. Now she paid for it.

James was on his feet in a flash, running to the front door of the barn, only to find it bolted from the inside. He kicked it in frustration.

"Somebody open the door!" he yelled. "Hurry!" He could hear movement inside, but couldn't see what was happening. He could hear muffled exclamations, and a few words of conversation. Finally, just as James was about to kick the door again, he heard the bolt slide. He opened the door to see one of the male prisoners pointing the woman's pistol at him.

"I'm not your enemy, man," James said calmly. "Case you missed it, I just shot that bitch that was shooting you. I'm trying to get you people outta here and somewhere safe."

"Who are you?" the man demanded.

"Just a friendly neighbor," James shrugged. "Now listen. We're on borrowed time. My friend is leading that bunch through the woods away from here right now, being chased by no telling how many, and a bunch of dogs. He's buying this time. We have to go, and go now."

"Why should we go with you?" a woman asked, looking up from one of the dead biker woman's victims.

"Well, you ain't got to," James replied. "I just figured you might want outta here and away from these people." *What the hell is wrong with them,* James thought.

"Who says you're any better than they are?" the man with the pistol demanded.

"I ain't got time for this," James snapped, his patience at an end. "Any of you wanna come with me? I can get you somewhere safe, with food and water, and a medic. All I can offer."

"I want to go," the woman holding her dress together raised a hand. "Please, please get me out of this," she held up the collar. James started toward her, only to have the man block his way.

"You just hold it right the..." He didn't finish as the butt of James' rifle smashed him in the mouth, sending the man to the ground and the gun flying.

"Had just about enough from you," James muttered. "Either of these murdering skunks have the keys to these locks?" he asked the group.

"She does," a man pointed to the woman James had shot earlier.

"Get'em, and start freeing yourselves," James ordered. "Any of you know how to shoot?" several hands came up, including the woman who had asked to go with him. He picked up the discarded pistol and handed it to her.

"One of you grab his guns, too," he pointed to the dead biker. "Least wise you can protect yourselves after I'm gone. Now. . ." he paused as the man who had taken the keys started releasing the others.

"Now, does anybody else want to go? Last chance." Several hands went up this time, but not all, much to James' amazement.

"All right then, start gathering up over here as you get free." He walked to where one of the women was kneeling over the teen girl.

"Ma'am, is she alive?" he asked gently. The woman shook her head.

"No, she's gone. All three of them are," she added, rising. "I'm. . .well, I was a nurse. There was nothing to be done," she said tearfully.

"I'm sorry, ma'am," James said softly.

"I want to go with you," she said firmly. "Any of these sheep that want to stay here are welcome to, far as I'm concerned."

"Suits me," James nodded. They walked back to where eleven others had gathered together.

"Anyone else?" James asked. He shook his head sadly when no one else came forward.

"I don't know when they'll be back," he warned. "Last chance." No one moved, or spoke.

"Good luck to you, then," James said sadly. He turned to those who wanted to follow him out.

"Let's move."

~*~

Roland had selected full auto on his M-4, and when he turned he emptied the entire magazine back in the direction he'd just come. It wasn't good tactical shooting, but he wasn't looking for tactical. He wanted to give his pursuers something to think about.

He heard a startled yelp and realized he'd hit at least one of the men following him. He turned swiftly, picking up his pace again, changing the mag out in the rifle as he ran. He could still hear startled shouts behind him, and there was random firing, but this time nothing came his way. He smiled grimly.

This rabbit's got teeth, boys. As he ran, another thought hit him. *Wonder how James is makin' out?*

~*~

James was angry. He was working hard on *not* being angry, because he needed to be focused entirely on getting clear of this farm and then heading back toward the school. The people he was escorting were in bad shape, though, and he knew they wouldn't make good time. Once they were in the woods that would be okay. He wished he had some food to give them, but the only thing he had were two MREs and that wasn't much for so many. They also couldn't be eaten on the run very well.

ROLAND

He decided that at the first stop he'd give them the MREs and his water.

He wasn't mad about the people with him not being able to go faster. No, his anger was reserved for the idiots that had stayed behind. What on earth were they thinking? Did they like being held prisoner?

Another thing was eating at him, too. The death of those three people were direct consequences of his actions, and that hurt the teenager more than anything else he'd been through. And that was saying something.

"What's wrong?" the nurse asked him, as they entered the tree line. James had stopped to check behind them as everyone found a place to rest for a few minutes.

"What?" James turned to her.

"I asked what was wrong," she repeated. "Name's Melissa, by the way. Melissa Andrews." She held out her hand.

"James," he replied. "There's nothing wrong," he shook his head. "Just checking our back trail, that's all. I don't think anyone's left there to give chase, but there's no harm in being cautious."

"That's true," she nodded. "Thanks, by the way," she added. "We were in a bad way, James. I'm sure you saw that."

"Welcome," he nodded. Suddenly he blurted out, "What the hell was wrong with the others? Why would they stay?"

"They're beaten," she replied sadly. "Given up. It's been rough, James. Some made it better than others."

"I can't imagine not taking any chance at freedom I had," James shook his head. "I just can't."

"Neither can I," Melissa shrugged. "But not everyone's made that way. I'm used to a hard life, I guess. Worked my way through nursing school, and then worked three doubles a week to get my student aid paid off. Had I known this was coming, I'd have let it go," she laughed. It was infectious, and James grinned.

"Know what you mean," he nodded. "Well, we need to get moving. We've got a ways to paddle, and we won't get there today unless we can find some transport."

"You won't be able to push too hard," she warned. "Some of us. . .well, some were there longer than others."

"I won't," he promised. "Just until we get clear of this place, and somewhere I can defend for the night. If I get lucky, my radio might reach far enough to get some help, but I can't count on it. We're looking at a ten mile hike, minimum."

"We'll make it," Melissa said confidently. "We'll just have to take it slow, that's all."

"Let's get to it, then."

~*~

Roland had gained some ground at last. The running was starting to take a toll on the beer and cigarette crowd behind him. The dogs were still there, but whoever was using them was smart enough to know if he let them go, Roland would shoot them.

There were a couple of guys that seemed to be out in front, and Roland decided they were probably the better woodsmen of the group. From what little he'd seen of them, they moved well, and didn't waste that movement.

The rest were just typical thugs, as far as he could see. That meant the two in front had to go.

Never stand out, fellas, he thought to himself. *It's the nail that sticks up that gets hammered.*

Roland checked the sun. He still had a good bit of light left. More than enough to put some serious hurt on his pursuers, and gain some more ground on them. He eased his suppressor out, and attached it to the M-4. No sense advertising his presence more than necessary.

He picked a good spot and settled in. He had to do this quick, since the rest of the group was still coming as well. He hated the thought of giving back the lead he'd built up over the last hour but it had to be done. He couldn't risk these two following him on into the night.

There. Just a flash of the wrong color. Roland put his scope on the area, and started searching centimeter by centimeter. Suddenly, there was an eye, looking back at him. He squeezed the trigger without thinking.

He put the scope back on the area as soon as he had the recoil under control. It was only a second, but the bullet had already gone home by then.

Nothing. He searched for fifteen seconds, all the time he could allow. Still nothing. Had he missed? He didn't think so, but...

It didn't matter. He had to move. The sound of the others tramping through the bush was getting closer. He moved carefully out of the brush, as started moving again.

He had been moving less than a minute when he heard the screaming.

~*~

BD stood looking down at his younger brother. He could tell it was him because of the clothes. His brother's head was pretty much gone. After a moment of just staring, BD tilted his head back and let out an animal like scream that echoed through the woods around them. His men, having never seen this kind of behavior from their leader, hesitated, not knowing what to do.

When he was done, BD knelt by the body, carefully straightening his brother's arms, then his legs, laying the body out as if on view. He removed his own leather vest and gently covered his brother's ruined head with it. Sobbing softly for a moment, he looked up.

"Carry him back," he ordered.

"What about the guy, boss?" one of them asked. "Do we..."

"Carry him back," BD repeated. "We'll get him, but first we bury my brother. And the others. See to the hurt. I know where that guy's goin'," he added. "We'll get him. We'll make him pay. All of them pay."

Nodding, the group set off back the way they came. They would bury their dead, tend their hurts, and then start again.

~*~

Roland stopped to check his back trail, and get his breath. He hadn't heard anything in a while, and wondered if their leader was finally wising up.

Roland was positive he'd gained some ground and decided to risk some of it to check behind him. Using his rifle scope, and then his binoculars, he scanned behind him.

"That's odd," he murmured. "There ought to be something."

But there wasn't. No one was following. No dogs braying. His trail was clear.

"Well, no point in looking a gift horse in the mouth," he decided. "Time to go home."

CHAPTER THIRTY-THREE

James looked at the group worriedly. They weren't in the best of shape, just as Melissa had warned. He'd known that, of course. He just hadn't factored that into the trip.

Why does this shit look so much easier in the movies? he wondered, snorting mentally. He and Roland really had to re-evaluate their decision making paradigm. To be fair though, these people had thrown a monkey wrench into their scheme.

The two of them had been intent on an ambush and nothing more. They had literally derailed their own plan when they decided to try and help the prisoners. Considering all that, he couldn't be too unhappy with the way things were going and that buoyed his spirits somewhat.

Besides, they'd make it. Just had to be careful, that's all.

He had led them a good mile into the woods before turning for home. He figured it was roughly a twelve-mile hike as the crow flies, but wasn't anticipating it being that easy. There were more than a few rough spots between where he was and where he wanted to be, and these folks would need more rest than he would.

And some of the obstacles would have to be gone around. There just wasn't any way that the people he was leading could make those climbs or hump deep brush in their weakened condition.

James was breaking trail and suddenly stepped into a small clearing. The ground was level, and the woods surrounding it were thick. He made a decision to stop for the night. He estimated there was about two hours left until dark, and he wanted their camp to be set up by then.

"We'll stop here," he ordered. "You folks take it easy." He shrugged out of his pack, and set it on the ground.

There were eleven people in all, including two men, and a boy of about fourteen, James guessed. Six women, including Melissa and the woman in the tattered dress, and two girls, tweens it looked like. Maybe even sisters.

James dug into his pack, pulling out a clean shirt that he had left and a pair of sweats. He took them over to the woman still holding her clothes together by hand, and knelt down.

"Ma'am, this isn't much, and they won't fit good and proper, but you take 'em, okay?" he held out the clothes. She looked up at him, tears in her eyes, and tried to smile.

"Thank you, so very much," she whispered.

"It's no trouble, ma'am," James assured her. He motioned for Melissa to come over, and returned to his pack, pulling out his first aid kit.

"You don't mind, how about going with her, and letting her change. You'll know more what she might need, and how to use this," he handed her the kit.

"All right," she nodded. She helped the woman to her feet, and the two slipped into the trees on the far side of the clearing. James watched them go, and then turned to the others. He reached into his pack again and produced the two MREs. He looked at them pitifully, shaking his head. It was all he had, so it had to do.

"These aren't much, but it's all I have," he told them. "You'll have to share, and I mean share," he stressed. "I'll try and find you something else as we move, but all of you need food and these are pretty high calorie." He opened them both, and started passing the contents out, setting aside some for Melissa and the woman he'd given the clothes to.

The two men refused anything, insisting that the others take their share. James nodded his understanding, and allowed the three younger members of the party to share the men's portions. One of the women frowned at him over it, and James glared at her until she went back to her own.

Melissa and the other woman returned, and James gave them their share. Both took it gratefully, and sat down near him to eat. Melissa noted he wasn't eating.

"Don't you need some of this?" she asked.

"I've eaten since you have," James shook his head. "I'll be fine. Eat up," he encouraged. She smiled at him, and he couldn't help but notice how pretty she was, even in the state she was in.

"We'll rest here tonight," he told them all. "Start again tomorrow at first light. We'll try to move as quick as we can, but when you need a break, tell me. We'll stop as we have to, but remember that until we get where we're going, we're in danger."

"Where are we goin'?" one of the men asked. His tone wasn't unfriendly, or demanding, just curious.

"Place called Bethesda School," he replied, and the man nodded, as did several others in the group.

"Know where that is," the man replied. "Name's Mackey, by the way. Tom Mackey. I'm right beholden to ya son, for rescuin' us."

"Mackey?" James looked at him closer. "Any relation to a soldier named Mackey?"

"I got a nephew in the Guard," Mackey nodded. "What's his given name?" James thought about that for a minute.

"You know, I don't think I've ever heard it," he admitted finally. He described the man he knew as Mackey, and Tom Mackey nodded.

"My sister's boy," he said. "He's a good boy."

"He is," James agreed. "He and his girlfriend are staying at the school as well. With luck, you'll see him tomorrow. Day after at the latest," he added.

"Well I'll be. That's right good news, son. Thank you." James nodded, then stood.

"You folks rest up. We don't have any blankets and a fire's a bad idea, so it's liable to get cold before morning. Best make some sleeping arrangements that let folks use each other's body heat."

"We'll see what we can do," Mackey nodded.

"I'm gonna take a look around us, make sure we're clear," James told him. "Make sure everyone keeps the noise down. Last thing we need is them on us."

"Maybe we better keep movin'," Mackey suggested, but James shook his head.

"That's no good, sir," he replied. "Too many of you are give out. You need rest tonight, and a chance to recover. We'll move out at first light." The same woman that had frowned when James had given the men's portion of the food to the teens, looked up at that.

"You can't expect us to walk all that way," she objected. "Send for a vehicle to carry us."

"I have no way to do that, ma'am," James told her. "We'll have to do the best we can on foot." The woman sulked, but said nothing else. James was starting not to like her. At all.

He drifted into the woods, traveling roughly one hundred yards out before starting his circle around the camp site. To say he was nervous would be an understatement. They were exposed here and James could count only on himself to defend the camp. If they were attacked in force, he knew that he wouldn't be able to do much.

Once he had circled the camp, he returned only to see the other man stacking wood for a fire.

"I said no fire," James reminded him.

"Women and kids need to get warm," the man replied. "We're makin' a fire."

"No, we're not," James told him, and kicked the wood pile apart. "That fire could be seen for miles. Smell of smoke could lead them right to us. Tonight is a cold camp, mister."

"Who the hell put you in charge, anyway?" the woman who had complained earlier demanded.

"I did," James told her simply. "You want a fire? The two of you? Then you head on off somewhere and have one. There won't be a fire *here* tonight."

"I'm not gonna be told what to do by some kid," the man said quietly.

"Then it's time you went," James replied coldly. "You will not put the rest of these people at risk for personal comfort. That's not open for discussion. Anyone who tries to start one, leaves. One way or another." He looked the man straight in the eyes, and the older man broke eye contact first, muttering under his breath.

"Now everyone try and get some rest," James ordered. "I'll stand the watch."

The sullen pair glared at him hatefully, but obeyed. James shook his head. Why would they deliberately want to draw attention to themselves? Asking that question made him think of an answer he didn't care for.

He resolved to watch the two very closely from now on.

~*~

Roland halted after perhaps another mile, and rested briefly. He consumed an MRE and drank nearly a quart of water, knowing he needed it. By his estimate, he was anywhere from eight to ten miles from the school.

The sudden halt to the pursuit worried him. Had they discovered James had freed the prisoners? Had they decided to go ahead and attack the school? Not knowing the answers left him concerned, but there was little he could do. Trying to find James was useless. He didn't know which exact direction the teen had taken; how many people were with him or what shape they were in. He had no way to estimate how long it would take them to cover the distance to the school.

He stood, policing the area, and prepared to move out. With no way to help James, his best bet was to make it back to the school as quickly as possible. With that in mind, he set off at a ground eating jog, careful to keep his eyes moving.

There was still danger out here.

~*~

Melissa dropped to the ground next to James, smiling slightly.

"You handled that well," she complimented. James shrugged.

"How old are you?" she asked, and he looked over at her.

"Why?" he asked, surprised by the question.

"Just curious," she shrugged in reply. "You look like a teenager, but you handled that like an older man would have."

"Eighteen," James answered. "I'm eighteen."

"Thought so," Melissa nodded. "I'm twenty-one, myself," she offered. "What's your last name?" she asked. He looked at her again, puzzled, though not allowing it to show.

"James Henry Golden, at your service," he grinned tiredly. "Pleasure to meet you, Miss Andrews."

"It was certainly mine," Melissa smiled, and James felt a blush spreading across his cheeks. "You saved us from a terrible fate, James. I can't thank you enough for that."

"No need," James shook his head, resuming his scan of the area around them. "We couldn't leave you there. Not without trying to get you free."

"Who is 'we'?" Melissa asked. "You said back at the barn that your friend was buying you time to get us free. Who's he?"

"A friend," James repeated. "You'll meet him, soon enough. If he's alive," he added, almost against his will.

"You think he's not?" she asked. She drew her knees up to her chest, and wrapped her arms around them. James realized that she was cold, and stripped off his jacket, wrapping around her. She looked startled for a moment, then drew the jacket around her tighter.

"Thank you," she murmured, blushing.

"Welcome," James nodded, getting to his feet. "Try and get some rest," he ordered, slipping on his night vision gear. "I'm gonna take a look around. I'll be nearby if you need anything." With that he disappeared into the growing darkness. Melissa strained to hear him in the trees, but couldn't.

She pulled the jacket tighter, and leaned back against the tree James had been using for a back rest. She was very tired...

ROLAND

James made another circuit of the camp, trying to keep his mind on what he was doing. Melissa seemed awfully interesting, and that was distracting him, which he couldn't have. He had to stay on top of things. He had not one, but two troublemakers, nine others who were weak and injured, not to mention terrified, and a long way between him and home. And help.

He paused in the woods, sighing deeply. He was tired. He'd been up since before daylight, and the prospect of getting any sleep tonight wasn't looking good. He fortified himself with the idea that once he was back at the school, he could hand these people, and the problems of having them, off on someone else.

Realizing he was day dreaming, James shook himself, and started another round. This was going to be a long night.

It was approaching dawn when Roland came into sight of the school. He exhaled sharply seeing it still looking ship shape. His worst fear had been to return and see either a pitched battle in progress, or the signs of one in the recent past.

He pulled his radio out, switched it on, and called the school.

"Guard post, this is Roland, please reply."

"Ro'?" Jesse's voice came back at once. *"Damn it's good to hear your voice. Where ya at?"*

"I'm lookin' at you," Roland grinned into the radio. "I'll be there in a couple minutes. I don't suppose someone could fix me somthin' warm to eat, could they?"

"I know someone that'll be glad to," Jesse chuckled. *"C'mon in, bro."*

"On the way." Roland put the radio away and started toward the school.

It was good to be home.

CHAPTER THIRTY-FOUR

James got to his feet as the first light of dawn appeared in the eastern sky. It wouldn't be full daylight for a while yet, but they had a long way to go and they were way too exposed. He figured these people were good for about one day's travel and that was it. He had no more food to give them, and unless they found something somewhere along the way their best bet was to cover the ground between here and the school today, if possible. Even if they couldn't get it all, maybe they could get close enough for his radio to reach someone.

He bent down and gently shook Melissa's shoulder. Sometime during the night the woman he had lent his clothing to had snuggled under his jacket with the young nurse for warmth. James was very careful not to touch her as he woke them.

"Wake up, sunshine," he said softly. "We gotta get moving." Melissa's eyes shot open, and James raised his hands when he saw the wild look in her eyes.

"Easy, now," he told her calmly. "Think about where you are." She blinked at him a few times, and then smiled slowly.

"I was afraid it was a dream," she admitted, raising up on her elbows. "What time us it?" she asked.

"Daytime," James told her. "See that light in the sky? Now get up and get the blood moving. We got a long ways to go, today." She nodded, rubbing her face with both hands, and then turning to her companion.

"Wake up, Susan," she prodded the other woman gently. James nodded at that. Now he knew the other woman's name. 'Susan' jolted awake, clawing at the air in front of her.

"Take it easy," Melissa soothed. "It's all right. Look around you, and remember what happened yesterday." Slowly Susan returned to something resembling aware, and blushed.

"I'm sorry," she said softly.

"Don't be," James said at once. She looked at him and smiled faintly. James grinned in return, then started moving to wake the others, choosing Mister Mackey first.

"Sir, it's time for us to be going," he said gently, and Mackey surprised him by opening his eyes.

"I been awake a little while," he admitted, sitting up smoothly. "Tend to wake early on a farm, son," he smiled.

"I imagine," James nodded. "If we can make it to the school today, then we can all sleep in tomorrow."

"You think we can?" Mackey asked.

"I hope so," James sighed. "Thing is, if we can just get close enough for my radio to reach, then I may can call some help. Get us a ride."

"That would be nice," Mackey grunted, getting to his feet. "I feel my years today, that's for sure. Let's get this bunch on their feet then." Between them, it took only a minute or two to get everyone awake.

Getting them on their feet was another matter.

"We can't possibly walk that far until we've had something to eat," groused the woman who had complained last night.

"I don't have anything to eat, ma'am," James replied patiently. "We get where we're going, there'll be food and water, and a chance to clean up. Until then we just have to tighten our belts and make do."

"I can't believe you didn't bring food with you," she grumbled. "How much planning did you put into this 'rescue'?"

"We didn't plan a rescue," James informed her. *Again.* "We saw you were prisoners, and *changed* our plans to try and get you free. Sorry if we're a little low on amenities." He wasn't that patient.

"Don't you sass me..." the woman started, and James patience reached its limit.

"Lady, I'm walking outta here in ten minutes. You wanna come along, then get on your feet and get ready. You don't, then just wait here and those nice gentlemen you seem to miss so much will likely be along shortly and take you back where you'll be more comfortable." Having said his last word on the matter, James started to walk away, only to have the woman's cohort grab his arm.

"You listen here, boy," the older man growled. "You don't talk to her like th..." Which was where he got to before James hit him with his rifle stock.

"Don't ever touch me," James looked down at the man, now laying on the ground, holding his jaw. "Not ever. You got something to say to me, you say it, but you do it without laying hands on me. I won't tell you again." His voice was as cold as his eyes as he looked at the man.

"You understand me?" he asked. The man glared up at him.

"I asked you a question, mister," James' voice dropped to nearly a whisper. "Do. You. Understand?"

It began to dawn on the man that the 'boy' he so casually dismissed might not be someone to mess with. He nodded slowly, still holding his jaw.

"Then get up and get ready, if you're going." With that James stalked away. Mackey chuckled as he looked down.

"Bob, you better watch yourself. That 'boy' might not be so gentle, next time."

~*~

BD looked at the body of his brother, and of twelve more of his men, with cold raging hatred in his heart. He was beyond furious, having reached that point where everything was simply. . .dead. Just like his little brother.

It never occurred to BD that he and his men had asked for it. No, that kind of thing never occurred to him, or men like him. All he could see was that someone had killed his brother, as well as some of his friends, and they had to pay.

He had returned yesterday to find six more people dead, and all but one of the prisoners gone. Three dead prisoners were still in the barn with the man BD called Raggedy. The man was more than a little off, and the group had teased him without mercy for over a month, but the little man had been eating, and sleeping inside, even if it was a barn, and he had stayed, unwilling to travel with no food and no shelter again.

Raggedy had told BD everything that had happened, and even showed him where the others had gone. Oddly enough, that had touched BD somewhere inside him and the gang leader had been oddly kind to the train wreck of a man since then.

BD looked over at his lieutenant, the man Roland and James knew as 'Foo', due to his Fu Manchu facial hair, and nodded. The man nodded back, and tossed the burning torch onto the pile of bodies, already soaked in kerosene. The bodies caught fire, and the bikers cheered for their lost brothers, a ritual that no one knew the origin of.

BD watched the flames for a few minutes, then assembled his people.

"Manny," he ordered 'Fu', "take two men, saddle up, and head over to Murfreesboro. I want Lincoln here no later than tomorrow night, and I want every swinging dick and every piece o' hardware he's got here with 'im. If he tries to buck, shoot him, and lead the rest here yourself. Got it?"

"Got it, Boss," Manny nodded. He pointed to two men and motioned for them to follow.

ROLAND

"Brick," he spoke next to Ponytail. "Take ten men, and get after the group that left with that kid. Get the prisoners back if you can, especially the women, and kill that kid. I expect you back tonight, hear?"

"We're on it, Boss," Brick nodded. He also selected his men, and headed out. BD looked at the rest.

"We'll go after the largest other group. Get ready. We head out in ten minutes."

BD watched them all go to prepare, and then turned back one last time to the pyre, still burning.

"Raggedy," he spoke softly to the little man still standing there. "You keep an eye on this, and don't let it spread. Let it burn, but don't let it spread. And you show some respect," he added, looking at him. "That's my baby brother, right there."

"'ight Boss!" Raggedy nodded, trying to be as serious as the others. "Raggedy do it."

"I know you will," BD smiled slightly. "Keep an eye on the place for me, okay? We'll be back."

"Eye on," Raggedy nodded again. "Got it, Boss." BD left him standing there, heading back to the house.

He had work to do and plans to make.

And someone to make suffer.

~*~

Despite his best efforts, it was thirty minutes before James as able to lead the group away from the small clearing. The people were just too weak, some of them, to be rushed. Calls of nature had to be obeyed, and some of them required more than five or so minutes to simply get loosened up enough to walk. He hated every second of lost time but couldn't begrudge them too much. They'd had a hard road for a long time.

He had taken the time to dig out a map and his compass. There hadn't been time yesterday, and he had the area around the farm committed to memory, anyway. Now, he took the time to orient himself.

He also removed his back-up pistol and two extra magazines from the pack. When he had the chance to do so privately, he had taken Mackey aside, and handed him the items.

"Know how to use this, I imagine," James had said, offering the older man the gun. Mackey nodded, accepting both.

"Keep it to yourself," James warned. "I don't trust that man, or that woman," he indicated the two he'd had trouble with.

"Well, Bob's all right, other than bein' an asshole," Mackey had chuckled. "Shirley, though, she's a bitch clear through, and mean as a rattle snake. You're smart to pick up on that."

"Well, she's about one rung off being left behind," James told him, and the older man nodded.

"That might be the best thing," he admitted. "I hate to say it, but it might. I'll leave that to you. You're the one runnin' this show."

"I'm just trying to get back," James shook his head.

"You call it, and I'll back you," Tom Mackey promised. "I'm ready when you are." James nodded his thanks, and then walked over to Melissa Andrews. He pulled her aside, out of ear shot.

"You know anything about guns?" he asked, and she nodded.

"I learned to shoot when I was eleven," she informed him. He held out a small automatic, and a spare magazine.

"Can you work with this? It's all I've got to spare at the moment."

"Wow, a Sig .380, that's nice," she almost whistled. "Yeah, I can work with it."

"Hide it away and keep it to yourself," he told her. "That ain't for you to fight with, it's to defend yourself. Understand?"

Melissa looked into his eyes, and almost gasped at the seriousness she saw lurking there. Unable to speak, she nodded.

"Good. Now, let's get ready to move."

~*~

"Where's the boy?" Jesse asked, as he shoulder bumped Roland.

"I was hopin' he'd made it back, but I managed to make pretty good time," Roland sighed. He gratefully accepted a canteen and took a deep drink.

"We had to kinda alter our original plan," he said, once his throat was wet. He explained the situation briefly, Jesse nodding on occasion.

"Anyway, for some reason, they let off trailing me," Roland finished. "We hurt 'em, and bad, but. . .I don't like the way they left off following me. Their head guy was some kinda mad at me. Whatever happened, it must have been a big deal."

"Maybe they left off to chase James?" Jesse asked, concern etched on his face.

"Could be," Roland nodded. "Honestly, I'm too tired to give it a lot of thought. And too hungry," he admitted. "I don't suppose..."

"Roland?" He turned at the sound of Maria's voice, just in time to prevent her from bowling him over as she ran over to him, throwing her arms around him.

"I'm so glad you're back!" she exclaimed. "Are you all right? Are you hurt?"

ROLAND

"I'll just go and check on. . .that thing. You know, over there, somewhere," Jesse grinned, and made his way over to. . .that. Over there. Maria blushed furiously at the implication, but didn't let go of Roland.

"I'm fine," Roland assured her. "No harm, no foul. Hungry, though," he admitted.

"I'll fix you something. Come in and rest while I cook you breakfast," she took him by the hand, leading him into the school.

"Where's James?" she asked, realizing that the teen wasn't with him.

"He's on his way, I imagine," Roland replied, worry in his voice. Again he briefly detailed the change in their plans, and James' roll in the new one.

"Do you. . .do you think he's okay?" she asked, worry in her own voice.

"I'd lay odds on it," Roland nodded. "He's smart, and he's tough. Only problems he'll have are the people with him. Some of'em looked to be in pretty bad shape," he admitted.

"How many people?" Maria asked.

"At least thirty, if they all made it," Roland said. She nodded.

"Once you've eaten, I want you to get cleaned up, and rest. I'll make sure we're prepared for the others when they arrive."

"Yes, ma'am," Roland had to smile, and Maria blushed again, but smiled back. She still hadn't let go of his hand.

~*~

It was just after noon when James heard the dogs. He stopped, turning his head and cupping his ear. Yep, dogs. They weren't close yet, but they were moving. His best guess was that they had covered maybe four miles since daylight. And that was generous. Weak from near starvation and mistreatment, most of the people he was leading simply weren't able to keep pace.

"We're gonna have to pick up the pace," he said to Tom Mackey. "They got dogs trailing us." Tom nodded, understanding the danger. 'Shirley' on the other hand, overheard.

"We can't go any faster!" she snapped.

"Gonna have to, ma'am," James managed not to snarl, but it took effort. "Someone's on our trail, and they're using dogs to track us, sounds like."

"Can't you shoot the dogs?" the woman shot back. "You certainly didn't mind shooting people!"

"Ma'am, it ain't the dogs that bother me, it's the people with'em," James told her, gritting his teeth. "Now you need to hush up and get moving. Talking just makes it harder to get your breath."

"Why you little..."

"You're welcome to stay behind," James finally snapped. "I'm sick of listening to you, lady. You could have stayed behind. Everybody listen up," he turned to the rest. "I know you're tired, and hurting, but someone's following us. We've got to go faster. Everyone pick up the pace!" He kept his voice low. No sense in giving their pursuers any freebies. He turned again to Tom Mackey.

"I'm guessing you know this country pretty well," he asked.

"I do."

"You take the lead, then. If you know of any place along the way we can hole up, let me know. If they're closing, it might be our only option." Tom nodded, and took the lead. James stayed where he was, waiting as the group passed him by, and then taking the trail position.

He hadn't been overly worried before, but things had changed. He hadn't expected the dogs. The gang had taken them to pursue Roland and James had counted on them to keep after him. For some reason, they hadn't.

James figured the people following were not going to be very happy with him if they caught up.

ROLAND

CHAPTER THIRTY-FIVE

Jesse found Roland in his small office/armory, looking at a topographical map of the area around the school.

"Thinkin' about the boy?" he asked, sitting down on an ammo crate.

"Tryin' to think *like* him would be more accurate," Roland sighed wearily. "We didn't have much time to plan anything, and did most of this on the fly. We made a general plan, but I got no way of knowing if James was able to stick to it or not." He pointed to the map.

"His original plan was to get into this area, in the woods, and make his way back here generally along this route. If he managed to do that, then he would be somewhere along here," he motioned along the map, "assuming everything went well."

"Which we know nothing ever does," Jesse snorted, to which Roland nodded his agreement.

"Which presents me with a problem," Roland sighed. "There's still quite a few of those thugs out there. The Claymores worked great, but even they only do so much, and a lot of the damage was absorbed by vehicles. There were at least eleven chasing after me, and maybe more."

"Which brings us to the reason they stopped chasing after you," Jesse observed, and again Roland nodded.

"That worries me," he admitted. "They were staying with me, pretty much. I didn't think they'd be able to, but they did. I gained on them every so often, but it was slow, and small. Every time I stopped, they gained. And the dogs. They were using dogs to keep on my trail. So why quit? What changed?"

"They maybe found out that James had the prisoners and was gone," Jesse finished for him.

"Right," Roland nodded. "Now, here's an additional problem. My little mission to even the odds wasn't a complete success. There's still too many of them. And that's even assuming everyone was in the convoy, which they probably weren't."

"We can't leave this place unprotected to mount an effective search for James and the others. Not without risking them coming straight here and attacking."

"Plus, any patrol we send out has less than a fifty percent chance to actually come across James," Jesse sighed, reluctance in his voice. "Best we can do is wait and see if he tries to make radio contact."

"Which will be hard to do," Roland rubbed his face, trying to scrub away his fatigue. "But it's not impossible. We need to have someone monitoring the radio all the time. Preferably on the roof. The GRMS freqs will give him more range, but we've got to be listening."

"Look, Ro', I'll take care of that," Jesse promised. "Dude, you have *got* to get some rest. If we find James, you need to be able to stand a post, or join the rescue. And right now, you ain't in no shape for either. Get. Some. Rest."

"All right," Roland didn't argue, which made Jesse's eyebrows shoot skyward.

"I'm really bushed," he admitted. He went over to his sleeping bag and laid down.

"All right, then," Jesse stood. "I'm gonna go put someone on radio watch."

Roland didn't reply. He was already asleep.

~*~

James tried to stay calm, but it was getting more difficult by the minute. The group was struggling now, with weaker members starting to lag further and further behind. There was no point in chastising them. They were doing the best they could.

He had tried his radio, but so far nothing. He was sure Jesse was listening, or if not then he had someone else doing it. The radio just wasn't strong enough to make it.

He'd lost track of how far they might have traveled, and didn't honestly have time to try and work it out so he didn't bother. Regardless of how far they had come, or how far they had to go, they weren't going to make it before their pursuers caught up to them.

That only left him one choice, and it was the one he really, *really* didn't want to have to make. Not that it mattered. It had already been made for him. He made his way up the tiny 'column' to where Tom Mackey was leading the group through the bush.

"Take five minutes," he ordered the group. "Don't leave the trail, though. Just rest in place. We're back moving in five minutes, no exceptions." He took Tom's arm and led him away from the group.

"We're not going to make it, Mister Mackey," the teen said simply. "They're gaining with every step. I'm pretty sure I heard a shout a few minutes ago, which means they're closer than I had figured."

"We can't go any faster, son," Mackey sighed. "We just ain't able. Maybe. . .maybe you ought to leave us," he said. "You've tried your best, and I'm eternally grateful to you. You can make it, on your own."

"I am leaving the group," James nodded, and Mackey's eyes registered surprise. Clearly he hadn't expected to hear that.

"I'm staying here," James told him. "You're going on. You know where you are, and where the school is. You can lead the way and make sure everyone stays together."

"What are you plannin' on doin'?" the older man asked, though he was pretty sure he already knew.

"I'm going to make sure you have the time you need to get there," James told him softly.

"Son, that's -"

"Our only option," James cut him off. "And I don't have time to debate it. I got work to do, and not much time to do it. Get them on their feet, and get on your way. Take this," he thrust his radio into the older man's hands. "Won't do me any good, way out here," he explained. "But you may be able to call for help, once you get closer. I know they'll be listening, I just don't know how far the radio will carry in this terrain. There's no repeater, so it's short range at best."

"James, this. . .you shouldn't do this," Tom said flatly. "I'm an old man. Let me -"

"No," James reply was flat. "You're not in good shape yourself. This is mine to do. Do me a favor and keep Melissa, and Susan too, I guess, close to you. Now, time's up. Get going, and try not to stop for anything. It's the only way you'll be safe. Tell Roland..." James trailed off at that, seeming to be at a loss for words.

What message did he send his mentor? What to say? Thanks? So long? See you around?

"Tell Roland this was the only way," he settled for saying. "He'll understand. Tell him it was my choice. And... tell him thanks for bringing me along. He'll know what I mean." He sniffed slightly, and hardened himself.

"Now, it's time you went." With that James started back the way they had come. Melissa Andrews grabbed his arm as he passed.

"James, where are you going?" she asked, concern in her voice.

"Just going to check our back trail," he lied smoothly. "I want to see how many there are, and how close they're getting. If they keep gaining, we'll need to find a place to hole up. Tom's going to work on that as he leads the group toward the school. Stay close to him," he said finally. With that he continued on his way.

"I can come with you," she called after him.

"No, you can't," he called back, never turning. "Go on now."

She watched him go, butterflies in her stomach. For some reason, she was scared for him. It seemed silly, but. . .she liked him. She was older than he was but...

"Miss, let's get started," Tom said softly, breaking into her thoughts. "Keep an eye out for people struggling, if you will. We need to move quickly as we can."

"He's not coming back, is he?" Melissa asked.

"He'll catch up, soon as he sees what's behind us," Tom assured her, unknowingly saying just the right thing. "He's worried they're gaining on us."

"All right," she nodded, and helped Susan to her feet. "Let's get going."

Behind them James continued walking back the way they had come.

~*~

James eased himself into a small clump of trees and brush, behind a large tree that had fallen during some past storm. It was still solid, and would provide at least some cover.

Cover and concealment, Roland had told him. *Not the same things, but both important. When engaging a superior force, use stealth, ambush, move and repeat. Keep moving, always keep moving. If you stop moving the enemy has a chance to zero in on you. Once that happens, you're finished.*

No mercy. Never give an enemy a break. There is no honor on a battlefield, that's for stories, for children, for writers and dreamers and poets. On the battlefield there's only life and death. Live or die.

James settled himself, waiting. He could hear the dogs plainly now, and could hear distant voices as well. He couldn't yet make out what the pursuing men were saying, but their voices were becoming clearer by the minute.

He removed the magazine from his rifle, more from impatience than need, and checked it. It was full so he slammed it back home. He repeated the action with his pistol, and then checked his gear to make sure that spare magazines were where they were supposed to be.

ROLAND

His hands roamed by feel to his knives, checking that they were secure, and then to the tomahawk. He'd learned to use one a while back, and liked the ancient weapon. It just felt. . .*right*, in his hands.

James licked his lips and found them dry, as was his mouth. He took a drink from his canteen, swishing the water in his mouth, making the most of the single mouthful of water he allowed himself. This might be a long day, and most of his water had gone to the people he'd rescued.

He could hear them now. Shouting directions to each other. Laying his rifle along the tree trunk in front of him, James dialed the selector switch to semi- and waited. He didn't have long to wait.

A bloodhound burst from the woods, sniffing the ground in front of him. He was followed shortly by a Doberman, following his lead. His eyes sad at the thought of what he had to do, James took careful aim and squeezed the trigger.

The suppressed rifle made a flat crack and the bloodhound fell dead. Another shot took the Doberman before the large predator dog could react. James looked intently around the edge of the woods, knowing there should be at least one more dog. He was sure he'd heard three distinct dog 'voices'.

Sure enough, just seconds after he'd killed the first two a chocolate colored Lab followed them. She was hardly out of puppy hood, tail wagging, and tongue out from exertion. James could have cried as he took aim once again. Just as he was about to pull the trigger, the dog raised her head, looking right at him, and wagged her tail.

He stopped.

I'm not shooting that dog unless it attacks me, he thought to himself. The voices were still behind, and no motion was visible through the trees. James made a quick, risky decision, and whistled softly.

The Lab responded at once, galloping in his direction. Working through his small hiding place, the dog came to his side and sat down. James hesitantly reached out and stroked the dog's side, getting a lick to his hand for his efforts.

James smiled suddenly, and ruffed the dog's head. For just a minute, a brief, wonderful, carefree minute, he was a teenager again. Just a boy with a dog.

Then he turned his attention back to the wood line. There were many voices now that the dogs had gone silent. Questioning. Concerned. Worried.

But still coming. James closed his eyes for just a second, breathing deeply. When he opened them, he could see the first of them working toward the small clearing.

He waited until four of them were visible before he opened fire.

~*~

"Roof reports distant gunfire," Maria informed Jesse as the older man was eating lunch. "It's the right direction to be James, perhaps," she added. Jesse nodded, standing.

"Do me a favor, please, and fill two of the two quart canteens," he asked. Maria nodded. "I need four MRE's too," he added.

"You are going after him." It was a statement, not a question.

"Don't know what you mean," Jesse said casually. "Just gonna see if all this shootin' is something we need to worry about, that's all."

"I see," Maria managed to keep a straight face. "Will you need anything else on this. . .sight seeing trip?" she asked.

"First aid kit," he said calmly. "I'll be by to collect them in a minute."

ROLAND

CHAPTER THIRTY-SIX

James shot three of the pursuing thugs before they could comprehend they were under fire. The others scattered, running and hopping in a way that would have been funny had it not been so deadly.

As soon as he had shot the third man, James himself was moving to his next spot. He had picked four places, including the first one, that he felt were the best available for both cover and concealment, and to escape if the numbers were too great. If they pursued him so much the better, since he would lead them away from the former prisoners.

If they didn't? Then he'd just have to hunt *them*.

The remaining pursuers were returning fire now, but wildly, simply spraying the woods around them. James smiled as he could almost hear Roland snorting, *amateurs*.

But even spraying fire wildly someone could get lucky, and James buried his head under yet another fallen tree, this one not quite as large but solid none-the-less. He felt the impact of more than one round striking the old tree trunk but there was no way to tell if it was on purpose or not.

The fire slackened, and he could hear one of them yelling at the rest to stop firing. Taking a chance, he raised his head to take a peek over the log.

~*~

"Stop shootin' dammit!" Brick yelled again. "Did anyone *see* anything?" A few more sporadic shots were heard, and then the firing died down.

"Dammit, did you see him or not?" Brick demanded.

~*~

James could see a large man with dirty blonde hair, beard, and a leather vest bellowing at the rest. He didn't recognize him as Ponytail, but ...

He must be the leader, James thought to himself. *I take him out, might keep the rest of 'em off kilter.* He raised his rifle, but before he could take a shot, the big man moved, and James couldn't get a shot.

~*~

"See about them," Brick ordered, pointing to the rest. "Tommy, did you see anyone?"

"No, Brick," Tommy admitted, looking around them. "I didn't. Didn't hear the shots, neither."

~*~

James couldn't see the leader anymore, but he could see the man the leader was talking to. Adjusting his aim, he squeezed the trigger.

~*~

"I was shootin' at places I thought he could be hid," Tommy was saying. "Anywhere there was cov..." a hole appeared in Tommy's forehead, cutting his statement off. Tommy looked confused for a second, and then fell to the ground.

Brick was still standing there, stunned, when the others opened fire again.

~*~

James ducked behind his tree as the woods around him once more exploded with gunfire. Again he felt rounds hitting his tree, but not in any concentrated force. They were just spraying the woods again, hoping for a hit.

Time to move, he thought to himself. *Let them get comfortable, and then hit'em again.* He looked at the Lab, cowered slightly by the gunfire.

Oh, man, he thought. *I hope she don't panic.*

"C'mon, girl," he said softly. "We gotta run." He rose into a crouch and took off into the woods.

A hail of gunfire sounded behind him.

~*~

Jesse had taken the Humvee. He didn't mind walking, but if James was hurt he'd need to get him back as soon as possible. Plus, there were the people he was supposed to free. Some of them might need help, too.

Jesse stopped five miles from the school, pulling well off the road, and hitting the kill switch Roland had installed. He stood near the front of the vehicle for a while, listening. By his estimation, there was no way James and any people he had with him could have gotten further than this, and likely hadn't made it this far.

Jesse studied the map, eyeing the route that Roland had showed him. If James had been able to stick to his plan, then he'd be somewhere along. . .*here.*

Folding the map, Jesse shouldered his pack, and set off in that direction.

~*~

Brick yelled yet again as Wilbur, one of the dumber guys in the group, (and boy wasn't *that* saying something!) ripped off half a mag from his rifle into the woods.

"Dammit, Wilbur, you moron!" he screamed. "Stop shootin' at shadows!"

"I seen somethin'," Wilbur said firmly. "Color o' some kind, right over there!" he pointed, never taking his eyes off the spot. Brick thought about that, and nodded.

"All right," he said finally. "Lead us over there, Wilbur," Brick ordered. "Jack, you come with me. Rest of you, see about Greg and Johnny." There was no helping Tommy, nor the other man. Both were shot in the head.

The three of them walked over to the spot Wilbur had indicated, near a fallen log. Brick pointed Jack around the left, and eased to the right, leaving Wilbur to the front of the tree.

There was no one there, Brick discovered, but someone *had* been there. The grass was still flattened in places, and he could see where the toes of the man's boots had dug into the softer ground where moss was growing. He smiled when he saw something else.

"Good eye, Wilbur," Brick complimented. "And looks like you got him, too," he added, pointing to a spot a few feet further on. A spot now wet with blood.

"We'll send two men back with our wounded, and the rest of us will go on," Brick ordered. "Whoever this is, he's wounded, now. Game's changed."

"We'll git'im."

~*~

James stopped as soon as he felt it was safe to do so. He found another clump of bushes, just off the path the others had followed, and hid inside. As he sat down he felt something wet on his leg and looked down to see his right pants leg soaked in blood.

"I got shot?" he said aloud, surprised. He hadn't even felt it.

And then, suddenly, he *could* feel it. He hissed in pain, pulling the leg of his pants up to see an angry hole on the outside of his thigh. The bullet had gone through the meaty part of his leg, the entrance hole much smaller than the exit.

"Son of a *bitch*, that hurts!" he exclaimed aloud, then looked around to make sure he hadn't been heard.

I gotta fix this, he thought to himself. He quickly shucked off his shirt, and then his tee. He used his knife to cut the tee's lower half into strips, then cut the front and back of the upper half of his shirt into two large patches. He folded each one twice, and placed them to the exit wound, and then the entrance. He used the strips to bind the makeshift bandages into place, tying them tightly, and hissing in pain once more as he did so.

All the while the Lab sat watching him intently, though looking back the way they had come every few seconds.

"I know, they're probably coming," he whispered to the dog, and she wagged her tail at him. Once finished James stood, placing his weight on the leg experimentally.

"I think my running game is gonna be off, girl," he said softly. The leg hurt, but it would hold, at least for now. He put his shirt back on, and hastily buttoned it up. As he was doing so, he happened to glance at the ground, and was shocked to see blood on the leaves.

I'm leaving them a trail, he thought. *I've got to move.*

That galvanized him into action. Grabbing his pack and his rifle, he was on the move again. He had gone less than a dozen steps when he stopped cold, his eyes narrowing.

He could use that.

CHAPTER THIRTY-SEVEN

Jesse kept up a steady pace, though he was cautious. Today of all days there was no telling who he might find out here. Roland and James had stirred up a hornet's nest to be sure. Every so often Jesse would stop and just listen for a minute. He'd learned long ago that silence and stillness would often pay big dividends.

Today was no different. He'd been walking steadily toward the area he thought James and his charges might be in. He came to a lightly wooded area and stopped near a large oak tree, using some scrub brush to conceal himself. He leaned against the tree, resting his back on the trunk, closed his eyes, and listened.

To voices. Several voices, at that. Growing nearer.

"For the love of God, *shut up!*" he heard a woman say. "You have done nothing but complain the entire time. There's nothing anyone can do to improve our situation until we get to the school, so just *shut up!*"

"You little *witch!*" an older woman's voice by the sound, retorted. "Just because you..."

"Shut it!" a man's voice hissed. "Or stay here! I'm sick o' listenin' to ya! Keep your mouth shut and keep movin'! No matter how good James does back there, we gotta keep going, and you're wastin' energy runnin' that mouth o' yours."

James, huh? Jesse thought to himself. *Back there* didn't sound good, though. Jesse decided it was time for him to make his presence known.

"Hold it right there, all of you," he said firmly, his quiet voice carrying. Everyone froze, and the man in front raised a pistol.

"No need for that," Jesse called from cover. "Are you friends of James'?" he asked.

"You know James?" the woman he'd first heard speaking asked.

ROLAND

"I do," Jesse replied. "Friend of mine, in fact, and I'm looking for him. I'm coming out, so let's all be friendly." Jesse walked out into the open, surprising them all.

"Name's Jesse," he told them. "James and I work together for a man named Roland. Where is James?"

"Reckon we need to talk," the man with the pistol said evenly. "I got a message from James for Roland. Reckon I can give it to you." Jesse nodded, and motioned for the man to follow him. They walked a short ways off.

"Name's Tom Mackey," the man told him. Jesse's eyes widened slightly.

"You ain't kin to..." Jesse started.

"Yeah, I am," Tom nodded. "James asked me about that too, so I reckon you're on the up and up. Look, we're in a bad way, folks ain't able to move much faster, if any. James, he decided to go back, try and buy us some time. We've heard a hellacious amount o' shootin' behind us, but James has got one o' them suppressors on his rifle, like yours," he pointed. "So I figure it's gotta be them that's following."

"How long since he left you?" Jesse asked.

"At least three hours," Tom guessed. "I'd guess we've covered maybe three miles in that time, tops. And that's bein' generous."

"You know where the school is?" Jesse asked. Tom nodded.

"I have to go find James," Jesse told him. "Keep going, best you can. I'm going to. . .hold on," he ordered, and shook off his pack, removing the sat phone Roland had given him. He dialed the connection for the phone that Roland had placed in the radio room, waiting for the call to connect.

"Mackey," he heard after about two minutes.

"Just the man I needed to talk to," Jesse said. "I'm about five miles due east of the school, parked along Wadel road. I got a man named Tom Mackey here, claims he knows ya."

"Uncle Tommy!" Mackey exclaimed. "Man, I been lookin' for him for weeks!"

"Well, here's your chance to talk to him. Send a truck to give these folks a lift back to the school. Hold on," he looked at Tom. "Your nephew's on the phone. Where's a good place for him to meet up with you that ya'll won't miss each other."

"Ask him if he remembers Widow Mason's farm," Tom said.

"I sure do," Mackey replied, having heard the question. "Tell him I'll be there in thirty minutes or so."

"Take them longer but he's nodding," Jesse replied. "I'm heading further in. James was dealing with some pursuers. I'm going to extract him."

"Roger that," Mackey's voice became crisp. "We'll monitor. If you need assistance, Vaughan will be on deck."

"Thanks. Fuller, clear." Jesse put the phone away, and shouldered his pack.

"You know where you're going, Mister Mackey," Jesse said. "I'm going to look for James. Stay hid best you can, and your nephew'l be along."

"You boys have been a sure enough Godsend, Jesse," Tom Mackey told him. "That James has got balls he needs a wheel barrow to cart around."

"That he does," Jesse chuckled. "I better get movin'. You folks be careful." With that Jesse started back the way the group had come.

"Where are you going?" the older woman demanded. "Why aren't you helping us?"

"Already helped you," Jesse told her, never slowing. "Ride coming to meet you soon enough. Just follow Mister Mackey, he's in charge."

"And what if we get attacked?" she demanded. "You should be protecting us!"

"Dog eat dog world now, lady," Jesse snorted. "I'm going to help my friend, who helped *you*. 'Bout all the help you can count on today. Now, keep your teeth together and listen to Mister Mackey. He knows where you're going."

He ignored the woman's jabbering after that, studying the ground in front of him. This bunch had left a trail a blind man could follow. Even someone who knew nothing about bushcraft could follow it. A thought came to his mind just then.

Maybe he could use that.

~*~

James had limped, hopped and crawled his way to the stop of small rise about fifty yards on from where he'd bandaged his leg. He was very careful not to leave a trail, whether in blood stains or disturbed earth. The Lab had stayed with him the entire way, and James was starting to think of her as 'his'. He wished he had something she could eat, since she looked hungry.

Come to think of it, so was he.

"Sorry, girl," he whispered, giving her a brief hug. "I'm hungry too. Once we get clear of all this, I promise I'll get ya something." The dog wagged her tail licking his face in reply.

Gotta think of a name for her, James decided. Her collar didn't have tag, so whatever name she once had was lost forever.

ROLAND

He found a good spot in a wallow left by a long ago uprooted tree, and used leaves and small branches to hide himself. He had left the dog several feet back, instructing her to 'stay', and she had done so. Whoever had owned her before the collapse had definitely trained her well.

Nestling his rifle in his arm, James watched his back trail, working on a plan. The men following would know he was wounded. Thinking of that made him realize how much he was hurt, his leg throbbing in case he was to forget. Getting shot sucked, he decided.

His focus was drawn to voices coming from the direction of his pursuers. His breathing a little rapid now, James settled lower to the ground, waiting.

~*~

Brick led the way, mostly because he didn't really trust the rest to do it. He didn't like being out front, not with the way this guy could shoot, but was comforted by the fact that he was injured and had lost a good bit of blood.

That didn't mean he was out, though. Brick had seen men wounded in Afghanistan and Iraq keep fighting with their back to the wall. The man they were following was tough and resourceful, and that meant you couldn't *count* him out until you *laid* him out.

He had six men, counting himself. Two of his original ten were dead, and two more wounded, once pretty serious. One man had remained to get the wounded back to the house where Doc could have a look-see. Six was probably enough to finish this, if he was cautious. And four men down made a man cautious all on its own.

Brick stopped, examining the ground in front of him. There were still blood stains on the ground, so they were still on the trail. At first the man they were following hadn't been concerned with leaving a sign behind, but as he'd gotten further along, he'd taken more precautions about disturbing the ground. Smart.

But he couldn't hide the blood. Or hadn't. At least not yet. Brick found himself wondering if the man was even aware he'd been hit. Sometimes adrenaline would keep the pain at bay for a while. If he wasn't, then he might just pass out from blood loss.

Brick waved the rest forward as he followed the trail. Some of them made so much noise that he winced when they took a step, but there was no help for it. They just weren't made for this kind of work.

The others had spread out on either side of him, lagging a few steps behind to keep him in sight. Suddenly, one of them hissed at him, waving him over. Brick joined him in a small stand of scrub.

"Looks like he patched himself up," the man said, pointing to a blood stained patch on the ground, and strip of Tee shirt. Brick nodded.

"He's lost a lot of blood," the leader said more to himself than anyone else. "And he's got to be hurtin'," he added. His thoughts turned to the man they were following. What would he do now, since getting away probably wouldn't work...

"Get down!" he yelled.

Just too late.

~*~

James noted that the party was smaller, and suspected they had left at least one man with their wounded. His eyes narrowed at that. Maybe he could use that, too.

He took aim at the most exposed member of the group, and lowered his scope to the man's right leg. He squeezed the trigger gently, and was rewarded with the sight of the man grabbing his leg as he dropped his rifle, crying out as he crashed to the ground.

"Get down!" he heard from his right, and swung his rifle that way. The blond man, again, the leader. *Well, well, my old friend Ponytail,* James thought. He snapped off a shot at the diving man, but had no idea if he'd hit him or not. He heard a yelp of surprise, though, so he must have been close.

One of the men on the left showed himself to return fire, and James nailed him chest high, knocking the man back. Two down, he thought to himself. At least four left. At *least* four, he reminded himself again.

"Stay under cover!" he heard Ponytail yell. Gauging where he thought the shout had come from, James placed two three-round bursts into the brush, again getting a yelp of surprise, but not able to see if he had struck a target.

A man near the middle of the line took that chance to try and move to better cover, and James rattled off another pair of bursts at the running man. His target flinched once and seemed to favor his left leg as he went back into cover, but James didn't count on that. He hadn't seen it, so it didn't count.

James felt the need to move, but fought it down. He was in a good position and there was no sign that he'd been discovered yet. His mobility was hampered by his leg and he would certainly give away his position if he went staggering off. Suddenly, he smiled.

He wouldn't go staggering off. He'd *crawl* away. He'd stay here for a while, since by just staying here he was doing his job, buying time for the others. He'd shoot once in a while, letting them know he was still here, and then he'd just fade away. They might lay there fifteen minutes or longer, thinking he was still watching.

Roland would like that, he thought to himself, ignoring the slight dizziness he felt at nodding his head.

CHAPTER THIRTY-EIGHT

Jesse heard gunfire from up ahead and instantly stepped off the trail he was following into deeper brush. The gunfire wasn't too close, but that didn't mean enemies weren't closer.

The gunfire *did* mean that James was still taking it to his pursuers, however, Jesse grinned thinly.

That boy is a pure caution, he thought to himself.

He stepped back out onto the trail after a couple of minutes and continued on his way, angling toward the sound of the gunfire.

~*~

James had finally realized he was in trouble. He was lightheaded now, and felt weaker. If he stayed here much longer he feared he'd stay here forever.

Snapping a fresh magazine into his rifle, he looked carefully through the scope at the places he had seen the men following him take cover. Anything that looked like a patch of color earned a three round burst. Every time he fired he risked giving away his position, but he had to do something.

Exhausting the new mag, he changed again quickly, and started backing out of his wallow. The effort made him light headed again, and his eyes swam.

Not good, he thought. *Not so good at all.*

He'd had no idea he was that weak. His great idea was turning into a colossal mistake, it seemed like. Yet, having started, there was no choice other than to finish.

He reached the spot where he'd left the Lab, finding her waiting patiently despite the gunfire. He patted her head, which set her tail to wagging, and then started crawling toward the back of the rise he was on. He needed to get down unseen, and take off before that bunch realized he was gone.

It was his only chance.

~*~

Brick hugged the ground, silently cursing. Twice they had walked right into an ambush. There was one guy out there, and he had taken down five of Brick's men, dead or wounded. He still wasn't sure about Clay, and didn't dare yell across the distance to ask.

Brick checked his watch. No firing for at least five minutes. Was the shooter conserving his ammo? Was he out? Had blood loss finally taken its toll? He had no way to answer any of those questions. Well, he had *one* way, but since it could end with a bullet in his head Brick was less than enthusiastic about that one.

He decided to wait fifteen minutes. If there hadn't been anymore firing after that, he was going to make a rush for the high ground. Even if the shooter wasn't there, it might give him a small advantage if he could get there.

If he could get there.

~*~

James was on his feet now, off the hill, but by now he was nearly dragging his leg behind him, and making enough noise to wake the dead. But he couldn't see any other options. Not now. He had to get somewhere that he could make a real stand and have some chance of survival. He needed water for sure, having exhausted what little he'd had left earlier in the day.

Some food wouldn't hurt anything, either. He hadn't eaten since breakfast the day before, and his stomach was letting him know it, too. His hunger probably wasn't helping with the dizziness, either, which was getting worse all the time. His head was fairly spinning now, and it was all he could do to stay on his feet. He was reduced to hopping from tree to tree, using them to maintain his balance.

The Lab stayed right with him, walking alongside him.

If I don't die, I really gotta think of a name for this dog, he thought numbly.

~*~

Brick looked at his watch one last time, took a deep breath, and got to his feet.

"Follow me!" he yelled, and ran for the hill to his front. He didn't bother looking behind him. They'd either follow, or they wouldn't.

Brick charged up the hill, breathing hard from exertion and fear. Every step he took he expected to feel a bullet impacting him. No bullet came, however, and sooner than he would have thought he was standing atop the hill.

There was no one there.

"Son-of-bitch!" Brick hissed quietly. "No tellin' how long he's been gone!"

"There's a trail, Brick," Wilbur called gently from where he was studying the ground. "Looks like this is where he was holed up," he pointed. "Little pool o' blood here, too. And look here. Lot o' disturbed ground, leadin' off this way."

"All right, listen up," Brick told his remaining men. "This guy's probably hurt bad, but he's smart, and he's sneaky. We know roughly which way he's headed, but he may double back or hole up again and try to ambush us like the last two times."

"We're gonna split up," he told them. "Me and Wilbur will stay on his tail. Clay, can you walk on that leg?" he asked.

"Just a crease," the biker nodded. "I can hack it."

"Then you and Tim take the right, about seventy-five yards out. Move quiet. If we run into an ambush," he indicated himself and Wilbur, "that should put you two in a place to flank him. Hoss, you take the same on the left, and we'll get him in a pincer. Use the ear buds on the radios and call in anything, no matter how little it might seem, okay? I don't want anyone else gettin' hit."

"Once we've got this guy, we can concentrate on gettin' the women back. Clear?" Heads nodded all around.

"Then let's get to it."

~*~

James staggered slightly, missing the tree he had aimed for and falling to the ground. He managed to bite off a scream of pain as his injured leg hit the ground. He lay there for a minute gasping for air, trying to force the pain down.

The Lab lay down beside him and licked his face, forcing him to stay awake.

"Okay, girl, I get it," he whispered hoarsely. "I'm gettin' up." He managed to lever himself onto his stomach, then used his rifle as a crutch to get to his feet. He wobbled for a minute trying to overcome the wave of nausea that assaulted him, and barely kept from vomiting.

I'm not gonna make it, he decided grimly. *I can't go much further, not like this. I'm gonna pass out. I need to find a hide, and either ambush these guys, or let them pass by.*

That *sounded* simple, but in his condition James knew better. He hobbled to a nearby tree and leaned against it, working to steady his breathing while looking around him. There wasn't much of a place to choose from within view. He had a choice to make. Either find a place here, or risk moving further on hoping for a good hide up ahead.

He listened for a minute, trying to force his heart to stop hammering in his chest. He couldn't hear any indication of a pursuit yet but by now his pursuers would be more cautious, so the quiet wasn't a guarantee that they weren't close behind him.

Still, the choices here were slim at best. He decided his best bet was to push on a little further, and see if he couldn't find a better place to defend.

Five minutes, he told himself. *I'll go five more minutes, and then I'll take whatever I can find.*

As he hobbled off, he wondered if Mackey and the rest were making good time. He hoped so, because he was about at the end of his rope. He'd done all he could. He could buy them a little more time, with some luck, but not much.

He smiled slightly as he thought about Melissa Andrews. She was pretty hot. And a nurse, too. He wished he was a little older. Maybe he would have a chance with her, then. He snorted at that.

I'll be dead in a few minutes, he thought sarcastically. *Even if I was older, that wouldn't happen.*

With that less than inspiring insight James abandoned that train of thought completely, concentrating instead on finding a way to make his enemies wish they'd never met him.

~*~

At that very moment Melissa Andrews was thinking about James Henry Golden. Not only did she think he was cute, and interesting, thinking about him allowed her to ignore Shirley's incessant grumbling.

It was probably not a good idea to be thinking along those lines, she knew, but she found her thoughts wandering back to him as she walked along. He was far more interesting that any man she'd known her own age. And it wasn't like she was old, anyway. She was only three years older than he was, and with the world like it was now that really didn't mean anything.

Melissa was smart. Both academically and in common sense. She knew that the world had changed dramatically in the last few months. It would be a long time righting itself, and whatever recovery happened might or might not restore the world they had once known.

Life would be difficult and dangerous for some time to come. As a nurse, she knew that poor hygiene and medical care would lead to disease and sickness, possibly even epidemics of no small proportions. Medicines that might once have stopped, or at least slowed such outbreaks, would no longer be readily available, at least for the time being. She had seen that before during the last days of the hospital she was working in, as doctors were forced to ration medicines due to shortages.

As she thought about the courage and skill that James had exhibited, she found herself comparing him to men she had dated in her life. She had always been discriminating in her taste, but most of the men she'd dated had been academics. She didn't know what had become of them since society had crumbled but she doubted they had fared well in the new normal. That wasn't a judgment of their personalities, just simple facts. None of them, or many others she had known, had the ability to survive in this kind of dog-eat-dog world that James had.

In these new times it wasn't going to be the men who could provide a fancy car or a fancy house that made the best mates. It would be the men who could provide protection, food, and shelter.

She blushed at the thought of the word 'mate', chiding herself for thinking such a thing about a man she barely knew. Yes, he'd rescued her, and yes he was fighting for her and the others even now. But she couldn't allow herself to be carried away by that.

Then again, she mused, what was wrong with a little forethought and planning? He was cute, after all. And strong. Courteous, and brave, and behaved like a gentleman.

So yeah, she would indulge in a little innocent day dreaming. It distracted her from Shirley, from hunger, from her aching feet.

And from wondering what was happening to James.

~*~

Roland awoke all at once, sitting straight up when he did. He looked around him wildly for several seconds until he remembered where he was. He had been sleeping outdoors for several days, and waking inside was a shock to his system.

Must have been more tired than I thought, he mused to himself. Wondering how long he'd been asleep, he looked at his watch.

Four hours.

ROLAND

He scrubbed his hands down his face, and then got stiffly to his feet. He realized that all the water he'd drank before sleeping was now ready to leave his body, and hurried to the bathroom. Once finished, he wandered toward the kitchen, hoping to find some lunch and see James.

Maria saw him coming and smiled prettily, walking to him.

"How are you feeling?" she asked.

"I'm stiff, sore, and hungry," he admitted, smiling in reply. "James get in yet?"

"No, he has not," Maria shook her head. "Jesse has gone to look for him, and found the people James freed from the bikers. Mackey has gone to pick up those people, one of whom is his uncle."

"Jesse is continuing to look for James, who left the group to hold off pursuit by the bikers. That is all that I know at the moment."

"Jesse left without telling me?" Roland asked, shocked.

"His exact words were you were at the end of your rope, whatever that means," Maria told him. "If it means you were beyond your limits, then he was correct. Roland, you could not go further without sleep. Jesse is able. Allow him to help."

"James is my responsibility," Roland shook his head. "I have to go…"

"We are *all* your responsibility," Maria interrupted, taking his hand. "Roland, we need you. You can't go out there without food and rest. And we may still be facing an attack, you said so yourself. James, Mackey and Jesse are all out. You cannot leave us even more shorthanded. Let. Jesse. Handle it."

Roland looked at Maria, and realized that she was concerned about him. Personally. When had that happened?

"Maria, are you. . .are you worried about me?" he asked, too surprised to hide it.

"I am," Maria replied directly, her face darkening in a blush that made her look adorable. "I. . .I have feelings for you, Roland," she admitted softly. "I don't even know when they began. I do not want you to take chances, please. At least no more than necessary," she added. "I know there are risks, but please, I ask you, do not add to them. Please," she repeated.

"I… I don't know what to say," Roland admitted. "I thought. . .well, it's not like you and I really got along before. I mean, you're really pretty…"

Did I just say that? Roland wondered. Maria's renewed blushing answered that.

"Thank you," she murmured, eyes down cast.

"Well, it's true," Roland told her, grinning slightly. "I… I guess you're right," he said. "I can't just run off. And I am hungry," he admitted. "I don't suppose there's any lunch left?"

"I will make you whatever you want," Maria promised, beaming at him.

"Well, that's an offer I can't really refuse, now is it?" he laughed. "Have you eaten?"

"Not as yet, no," Maria admitted.

"Then make enough for two and have lunch with me," he said. She beamed even brighter if that was possible.

"I would like that very much."

"Well, I'll check in with Vaughan, and then meet you in the cafeteria. I don't suppose we have the makings for a tuna salad do we? Pickles and onions only?"

"We do," Maria nodded. "One tuna salad coming up, with fresh homemade bread."

"Sounds like a date," Roland smiled. Maria blushed again, and hurried away toward the kitchen.

"Well if that don't beat all," Roland shook his head, walking off to find Vaughan and get an update. He had taken three steps when it hit him.

Hair like coal, Roland Stang. If you got a future that ain't covered in blood, she's it.

ROLAND

CHAPTER THIRTY-NINE

James struggled to stay conscious. He had found a good place to hide, in a small circle of cedar/fir trees. In a part of his pain and blood-loss addled mind he remembered that the trees most people referred to as 'cedar' were actually not real cedars, but a type of fir tree. Sage grass growing in and around the small copse of trees provided additional concealment for him.

The Lab lay on the ground next to him, head on her front paws. He reached out absently and stroked her head, earning a lick on his hand and a wagging tail. He smiled weakly and rubbed her head a little more vigorously.

Lying next to him were two full magazines for his rifle. He had already checked his pistol, and his knives. He doubted he'd be able to physically confront any of the enemy that managed to get to him, but it cost him nothing to be prepared.

He relaxed against one of the trees, trying to steady his breathing. His leg hurt worse now, the pain approaching the worst he'd ever felt, including a kidney stone he had endured at the age of twelve. His foster parents at the time hadn't really been too concerned about his wellbeing, and had refused to take him to the doctor. He had eventually passed out at school and the administrator had called an ambulance.

The resulting investigation had seen him moved to a new foster family after surgery, and his former foster parents going to jail for three years. His last view of the man in the courtroom had been one of his former foster father promising retribution someday.

With time off for good behavior the man had been released after eighteen months, and had made good on his promise. Or tried to.

James' deepest, darkest secret rested with the man in a shallow, unmarked grave in one of Nashville's many small parks. The disgraced and exposed foster father had caught up to James leaving school one day, and had bitten off more than he could chew. Not even Roland knew that.

He never would, now.

James didn't regret killing the man. He'd been a pig even on his best days, and he hadn't had many of those. James was certain that the man had been molesting his foster sisters, and wasn't sure the woman hadn't been as well. The woman had been smart enough not to look James up after prison, though.

The events had hardened James, forging him into the iron willed teen he now was. The teen that had killed at least ten men in the last two days was not wasting a single second of regret on any of them.

James closes his eyes, using his breathing to try and ease the pain. He was starting to regret leaving his first aid kit with Melissa. He would keep a smaller kit on him from now on, he resolved, forgetting for a moment that he wasn't likely to have a 'later on'. He didn't know why he hadn't thought of that before.

Suddenly his eyes shot open, and he looked around him. He'd almost gone to sleep. That would be certain death. He had to stay awake. He rolled his head side to side, trying to loosen up, and found that to be a mistake, as it made his head swim much worse. A wave of nausea swept over him and he went still.

Better not do that again, he thought to himself.

Beside him the Lab's head came up sharply. Seeing her reaction, James readied his rifle.

~*~

Brick knew he was making too much noise, but he couldn't seem to be any quieter. Focusing on what was in front of him kept him from looking for obstacles in his path that made noise when stepped on.

He'd never have admitted it to anyone but himself, but Brick was scared. This was supposed to be a kid. Easy meat.

But that 'kid' had already killed six people the day before, and now at least three more today. Whoever the boy was, someone had trained him well.

Through the trees he could see part of a small clearing up ahead, and he slowed without thinking. He was starting to understand how this kid thought. How he made his decisions. This was a good place for an ambush and Brick doubted the boy would pass up the chance to take out another of his men.

ROLAND

He held up a hand to slow Wilbur and reached for his radio bud. Softly he warned the others, waiting for their hushed replies before slowly moving forward.

He wouldn't be fooled again.

~*~

Jesse was in stalking mode now. While he still didn't know where James was, or his pursuers were, the back of his neck was itching, always a bad sign. While he wanted to find James as quickly as possible, rushing into the situation and getting himself killed wouldn't do the boy, or him, any good. The plan was to extract James from the trouble he was in and get the both of them safely away. Roland would need them both if the gang was able to follow through with its planned attack.

That didn't make it any less frustrating, however. Jesse felt the pressure of getting to James as quick as possible, and of securing the rear area of the fleeing group of former captives. Allowing the gang members to get past him and return to their pursuit of the group was unacceptable. In their weakened condition, the prisoners might never be able to get to the rendezvous point before being overtaken and either killed or recaptured.

Jesse stopped short as he heard the deep growl of a dog up ahead. Stepping into cover, he lifted his rifle.

~*~

James reached out to still the Lab as she growled deep in her chest. She looked at him, ears up, alert for anything. He gently shushed her, rubbing her ears. The dog licked his hand again, but returned her attention to the area before them, still alert.

James didn't know what she would do when the shooting started, but hoped she'd run away. The men following would probably kill her if she stayed around. He didn't want that. He had tried to send her away, but the dog would have none of it, remaining stubbornly at his side.

James stiffened slightly as the leader came slowly into view. He smirked slightly, noting the caution the man was using. They had started out the day cocky, but James had taken that away from them he was happy to see.

But it had come at a cost. The pain in his leg was almost unbearable now, and blood loss was threatening to send him into unconsciousness. Before that happened, he had something to finish. Lifting his rifle slowly to his shoulder, he breathed deep and slow to steady himself, and laid the rifle barrel on the branch he'd chosen to help him.

He would finish his job.

~*~

Jesse heard the crack of a suppressed rifle, close by. Right to his front he was almost sure. He managed not to move, despite being startled.

That had to be James, didn't it? He waited.

~*~

"Brick's down!" Wilbur shouted into his radio, too startled to realize that he was giving away his own position. Without thinking, he ran toward his friend and leader.

He almost made it to his side.

Almost.

~*~

James waited for sign of the others, eyeing the two to his front. He'd taken the leader, and the louder one as well, both with head shots. They wouldn't be getting back up. By his count, there were at least three left. He hadn't been sure of one guy in the last ambush, and was counting him as being part of the group, just in case. Even if his shot had put that man down, there were still at least two.

With the leader down, what might the rest do now? Would they cut their losses and run? Would they re-double their efforts to finish him off? *That wouldn't take much,* he snorted mentally. Still, he had to stay alert. Moving was out of the question, so if his two shots had given away his position then he was done for. At this point, he doubted he could get to his feet again.

Since his decisions were already made for him, he just sat as patiently as he could.

Waiting.

~*~

Jesse was almost certain that James was just a few yards to his front. He'd heard the one man yell about someone being down. That meant, he hoped, that James was alive and alert and had taken down one of his pursuers.

But, unable to pinpoint the exact place the shot had come from, Jesse was helpless to act yet. If it wasn't James, then whoever it was would simply think him another enemy if they saw him and shoot at him. If it was James, he didn't want to get shot by accident. James was in combat and had no idea he had a friend closer than the school. There was no reason not to shoot at anything that moved near him.

Frustration threatening to overwhelm his common sense, Jesse forced himself to wait.

There was really nothing else he could do.

~*~

Not realizing that help was literally steps away, James sat completely still, trying to imitate a tree branch.

~*~

The three men conferred softly via radio. All determined to continue. Closing in from each side, the three of them moved slowly, carefully, and above all, quietly. It was in each man's mind that one of them would eventually draw fire, giving the remaining two a chance to take the shooter out.

Each was equally certain that he wouldn't be the one to draw fire.

All were wrong.

~*~

It was the one called Hoss that came into James' view first. He was moving so slow that James didn't actually see him enter the clearing. Suddenly, he was just *there*. Even the Lab had missed him.

As soon as James saw him he shifted his rifle toward the new target, then held his fire, thinking. If this guy was a decoy then firing might give away his position to the others. On the other hand, the man was walking straight toward him. Shrugging mentally, James lined up his shot.

~*~

The man known as Clay heard the flat crack of the shooter's rifle followed by something hitting the ground, and was almost certain that Hoss was down. Tim tried twice to contact him on the radio before Clay could stop him.

Clay had *heard* the muffled crack of a suppressed rifle ahead, but wasn't exactly sure *where* it was. He had a pretty good direction for it though, and motioned Tim to follow.

The two moved forward slowly, making very little noise. At this point, neither wanted to return and inform the Boss that not only had they failed to carry out his orders, but almost every man in the detail was either dead, or wounded.

Clay stopped short. He could see that damned Lab, lying in the woods in front of him. Lifting his rifle before he thought, he was about to shoot when he saw a hand reach out of the grass and pet the dog on the head. Smiling grimly, he took a step to the side, then another. There he was.

Clay motioned to Tim that he had located the shooter, and Tim nodded, moving carefully to Clay's far side. They were intent on their mission. So intent that they failed to realize that as they stalked their target, someone else was stalking them.

~*~

Jesse couldn't wait. The two men he was watching could see James he was almost sure, judging from their hand signals. That made them unfriendly and that was really all that mattered.

Snapping his rifle up, Jesse opened fire, his suppressor reducing the sound of multiple shots to a muffled cracking sound.

Clay and Tim died in a hail of silent gunfire.

~*~

"Wha -" James' head snapped around at the sound. He hadn't been able to pinpoint where it had come from, but could see at least one man down from where he sat. He recognized the clothing as the man he'd snapped a shot at in the last ambush.

Well, at least I was counting him in the group, he thought drunkenly.

"James, can you hear me?" Jesse's soft words traveled to him. James just sat there, sure he was hallucinating.

"James, dammit, answer me!" Jesse's voice took on an urgent note. Maybe he wasn't imagining it.

"Jesse?" he risked calling out, keeping his voice low.

"Thank God," he heard the relief in Jesse's voice. "Hold your fire, James, I'm coming to you." Seconds later Jesse entered the small copse of trees where James was hidden.

"Jesus," Jesse hissed, seeing the shape James was in. The Lab stood, growling.

"Easy girl," James tugged her tail to get her attention. "Friend." The Lab turned to him, as if she recognized the word.

"Friend," James repeated, and the Lab wagged her tail.

"Smart dog," Jesse commented, kneeling beside his young friend. "Damn fool kid," he muttered. "What did you think you were doing?"

"Had to buy some t…time," James managed to gasp out as Jesse slit the pants leg to examine the leg wound.

"Dammit, James, where's your first aid kit?" Jesse demanded, shrugging off his pack and digging out his own.

"Gave it to the nurse," James replied. "Needed it more than me, back then."

"Well you sure as hell need it now," Jesse didn't quite snarl. "Are there any more of them?" he asked, pulling an ampule of morphine out and jabbing it into James' leg, causing James to hiss slightly. That faded as the morphine went to work and the teen's body started to relax.

"Nah, think I got 'em all," James told him. "Took me a while though. But hey! You got a couple of 'em, didn' ya?" Jesse almost smiled at the drunken like behavior as he quickly cleaned the wound, and dusted it with blood clotting agent. Taking a trauma bandage from his kit, Jesse slapped it over the wound and bound it tight. James makeshift bandage hadn't held, and he had lost a lot of blood. The only good thing that Jesse could see was an exit wound.

"Yeah, I got a couple," Jesse replied. "Got a count?" he asked, not really expecting one.

"Sure," James nodded, or thought he did. He wasn't sure. "Lezz see. Kilt six, or was it seven? Anyway, that was yesterday. I think it was yesterday. Yeah, pretty sure it was. Then killed me about, hmmm," he paused, clearly thinking.

"Let's get you on your feet, soldier," Jesse said, meaning every word. He tugged the boy to his feet, slinging James' rifle over his shoulder first. He gathered their gear, and then slung James into a fireman's carry.

"I need to start workin' out more," Jesse grunted. This was a load.

"Five," James said suddenly.

"What?" Jesse grunted, moving back along the trail, the Lab following close behind.

"I killeded fives today. Well, maybe six, but one I wanded purpose, so 'nother take care o' 'im." Jesse chuckled at James' drunken, slurred speech. Fatigue, blood loss, and morphine were taking their toll.

"You knows, this first I'm ain't hurted all days," James informed him. "Tha' some goood shiiit."

"Yeah, it is," Jesse agreed. "You did good kid," he added.

"I gots shot," James informed him. "You knowed dat? I got shotted?"

"Yeah, I know," Jesse grunted. "You'll be okay, kiddo."

"I got shot'm gon' die," James said sadly. "S'to bad, too. Goooood lookin' nurse in'at bunch. I thin' she liked me. Ever boy wans date a hot nurses," James rambled.

"You're *not* gonna die, James," Jesse promised him. "You'll be down for a while, but you'll be fine."

"S'ok, Jesse, I alreadys figger it out," James told him. "I knowned I wa'nt gon' make it. Bu's ok cause. . .cause. . .well, don' 'member why s'ok, but is. 'm good."

"You're not gonna die, kid," Jesse stressed, picking up the pace as well as he could. It was still a long way to the Hummer.

"m'kay, you says so," James mumbled. "Seepy," he mumbled into Jesse's shoulder.

"Sleep then," Jesse told him. "I'll wake you when we get home."

"Hm. Home."

Jesse kept up the killer pace he had set for himself as James fell into unconsciousness. His legs burned in protest, but he ignored it. He couldn't let up.

"You'll get a chance to see that nurse, James," Jesse promised him. "You earned it."

ROLAND

CHAPTER FORTY

Jesse's legs burned.

He was humping as hard as he could, considering he was carrying two men's gear, and had the near two hundred pounds of James' weight across his shoulders.

"Got to. . .get to the gym. . .more. . .often," Jesse gasped out, then realized he was just wasting air. He shook his head at his own foolishness, then concentrated on the job at hand.

His heart was pumping fast enough and hard enough that it was a wonder it didn't burst from his chest. His legs were wobbly and felt as though they were on fire. His back just plain hurt, as did his shoulders.

Need a training regimen, he thought. *We've gotten soft, and we can't afford that. Not in days like these.*

He resolved to start one the very minute he got back to the school. As soon as he'd rested, eaten, and got a shower.

And slept for a week.

Very. First. Thing.

Meanwhile, his aching legs continued to eat up the distance to the Humvee.

~*~

As the group topped a small rise the Widow Mason's farm, Tom Mackey could see a large army truck sitting in front of the house. He held up a hand, stopping the group.

"What is it now?" Shirley grumped.

"You mind if I make sure that's my nephew 'fore we go bustin' down there and mebbe get shot?" Tom's voice was acidic. Shirley scowled but said nothing.

"I can't see anyone," Melissa admitted.

"Neither can I, but he's a smart boy. Wouldn't be just sittin' out in the wide open," Tom nodded. "Reckon I'll head down and make sure it's him. I'll sound the horn twice if it's him. If it blows a third time, it ain't, so take into runnin'. Reckon you can find the school on your own?"

"I. . .I guess," Melissa nodded. "But. . .we should all go."

"And risk gettin' caught or killed?" Tom looked at her, eyebrows raised.

"If James..." she stopped short, about to say the one thing she refused to even think. "If any of them got past James, then we risk getting caught or killed anyway," she reasoned. "I'm going with you," she said suddenly, her voice firm. "I don't want to stay here."

"Well, if that's what you want," Tom nodded. He looked at the others.

"Melissa and me are gonna go make sure that's our ride. Rest o' ya stay put, and keep a look out. We'll honk the horn happen it's my nephew, and ya'll can come on down."

"Why is *she* going?" Shirley growled.

"'Cause she wants to," Tom shrugged. "Reckon you want to risk it, you can too." Shirley scowled at that, but said nothing else.

"I'm going," Susan said, her voice more firm than Melissa had heard it since they had met in that awful barn.

"All right," Melissa replied softly. Tom just nodded.

"Well, let's head on out, then."

~*~

Mackey and his girlfriend, Angelina Martens, were hidden along the eves of the house, watching the roadway and the woods through binoculars. Not only were they looking for Mackey's uncle, they were also keeping any eye out for Jesse, or James, or both, and for trouble. Trouble seemed to be on the menu today. Well, the last several days.

"We didn't work this hard in Iraq," Angie snorted, lowering her binoculars long enough to pull her flowing ebony hair behind her neck and secure it with an OD bandanna.

"Tell me about it," Mackey snorted, scanning the trees. "I'll say this much, though. When this outfit decides to do something, they dig right in, root hog or die."

"Jerome, you know I have no idea what that means," the pretty Puerto Rican woman replied, rolling her eyes.

"And you know I don't like that name," Mackey spat back, disgusted by merely the sound of his given name.

"Jerome is a very pleasant sounding name," she told him patiently. "It is the name your mother gave you. I like it."

"And you're the *only* one I let use it," he pointed out, taking the time to smile briefly at her before going back to the binoculars.

"Well, anyway, 'Mack'," she ribbed back, "if you mean they go all in, then I agree. I like them. Only good people would willingly take on the responsibility of so many children when none of them are their own."

"What I figured, too," Mack nodded. "That's why I agreed so fast when you asked to come here. I'm glad to be helpin' out."

"Helping," Angie corrected. "Not 'helpin'. Use your gee's *mi vida.*"

"Yes, Miss Martens," Mack shot back. "You missed your callin', darlin', when you. . .hey, I got something. Three people at about. . .seventy meters, comin' outta the brush."

"Coming out of the brush," she chided gently, taking a look. "I see one male, two females. Not as many as I thought," she mused aloud.

"That's Tom," Mack told her. "I'd bet he's left the rest hid out. He's cagey. No idea how they managed to take him the first time."

"Cagey?" Angie asked.

"Smart, cautious, tough, all rolled into one," Mack told her. "I'm gonna wave at him. Let him know it's us. How 'bout you stay here, cover me."

"Roger that," Angie nodded, all business now. She hefted her rifle, allowing the binoculars to fall on their strap. Mack stepped out into the sun, lifting his right arm high, hat in hand. He waved it right to left, making a circle. Tom stopped short, then waved in return. He turned back the way they had come, and waved. Tom saw several more people, counting eleven in all, start his way.

"There's the rest," he said over his shoulder.

"I see them," Angie risked a quick look, then resumed her job as lookout.

It took nearly ten minutes for the group to make it that far, and Mack's impatience bled away as he noted how tired and run down the group looked. There were a couple kids in there too, he noted, and one woman who looked like she'd been put through the ringer.

And Shirley Pippins. He couldn't help snort in disgust. Of *course* she'd be one of the ones to make it.

"Good to see you, boy," Tom grinned, hugging his nephew and only remaining family tightly.

"You too, Uncle Tom," Mack grinned as he stepped back from the hug. "You look rode hard and put up wet."

"Feel that way, too," Tom nodded.

"Can we get something to eat, here, or is this reunion gonna take all day?" Shirley snarled.

"Reckon you can make it a few more minutes," Mack bit back. "And if you can't, well. . .you'll still have to," he chuckled.

"Jerome," Angie chided.

"You let her call you...?" Tom's eyebrows rose in surprise.

"I don't *let* her, she just *does* it," Mack sighed. "Tell you later. Let's get everybody into the truck and get out o' here. Once we get back to base, we'll get ya'll a hot meal and you can get cleaned up."

"So there's no food here?" Shirley asked.

"Shirley, you know where Bethesda school is from here?" Mack asked politely.

"Of course I do!" she snapped back. "Don't be stupid!"

"You want to ride, or walk?" Mack asked, still polite. Her face purpled in rage, but she said nothing else.

"Shirley, I asked you a question," Mack said. "If I don't get an answer, I'll assume you wanna walk. Right?"

"Ride!" she snapped.

"Then how 'bout you keep your cake hole closed from now 'til we get there," Mack ordered. "Won't bother me a bit to stop and put you out, you can't. Got it?"

The woman nodded, his face even more mottled in rage. Mack decided to accept the nod this time. Much as he wanted to keep sticking it to the ornery woman, he had to make tracks.

"All right, folks, let's get ya'll situated and get moving."

Ten minutes later the truck was on the road. Mack wouldn't feel safe until they were back behind the fence with this group. He doubted they could make another mile.

~*~

"We should have heard something by now," Roland said, pacing.

"Jesse said it would take a while for them to walk that far, in the shape they were in," Vaughan reminded him.

"It's been nearly four hours!" Roland exclaimed, pacing faster. "And we haven't heard from Jesse, or from James!" he added, just for good measure.

"I don't expect to hear from Jesse until he's got something to report," Vaughan shrugged. "He knows he's beyond our help, Roland. And he's a pro. Let him deal."

Whatever Roland was going to say was cut off when the CB radio squawked.

"Base, this is Tango One. Pickup made, on route," Angie's voice came over the speaker.

"Roger that Tango One," Vaughan replied. "Any casualties?"

ROLAND

"Negative, but they are dehydrated, malnourished, and weak from it. They will need showers, clothing, and food, in that order. Suggest having bottled water standing by."

"Roger that, wilco. ETA?"

"Thirty mikes."

"Roger that. We'll be waitin'. Base out."

"Roger. Tango One clear."

"Well, now we know," Vaughan said, getting to his feet. "I'll go alert Maria."

"Fine," Roland nodded. Still pacing. Vaughan just shook his head as he left the room.

~*~

Jesse was sure his lungs were going to explode. Anytime now. Kill him for sure.

Unless his legs gave out first, of course. Then he would probably survive, lying on the ground until he could move again. Say. . .day after tomorrow.

But James would die. Knowing that kept Jesse moving long beyond what he really felt he was capable of. The last thing he wanted was for this boy, *no*, he corrected himself, this *man*, to die because he gave up.

He wasn't going to give up.

But he *was* slowing down, and nothing he could do could change that. He was carrying over three hundred pounds of man and gear, and it was starting to show. He legs wanted desperately to stop and let him collapse to the ground. He kept them going by sheer force of will.

His back ached so much that it had become a focal point of pain. No matter what he thought of, his back was in the forefront of his thinking.

And his lungs were sure to pop any minute. Just burst open, and not work anymore. They now burned as much as his legs did, and his breathing was labored.

On top of that, this couldn't be doing James any good. Jesse could feel something sticky seeping into his shirt along the shoulder, and knew that his field dressing had either come undone, or was soaked through. But there was no way he could stop to check it. If he did, he'd never find the strength to get James back on his shoulder. Or even get himself off the ground.

Despair was slowly creeping into him now. He wasn't going to make it in time. All of this would be for nothing. A young, promising life, wasted. Jesse thought about what James had said. He had known he was going to die and he was okay with it. No one his age should ever have to think like that.

Jesse hated the world he lived in because of it. Because there were people who would shoot children as easily as they would a dog. Because there were people who would imprison innocents for their own amusement.

Because he couldn't *kill them all.*

He didn't realize how long he'd been thinking about that when he noticed he was out of the brush, and had been for at least a full minute. There in front of him, *such a beautiful sight,* was a battle scared, ugly-ass OD Humvee. Jesse's anger had fueled his final burst of energy, and there he was.

By the time he reached the vehicle that energy was gone. Opening the passenger door, Jesse managed to lever James into the seat without banging him around too much. He checked the wound, and saw that the bandage had indeed slipped. He put it back in place, and retied it as tightly as he dared, then checked James' pulse.

Nothing.

Panicked, Jesse felt frantically for anything. Finally, at the edge of desperation, he felt it. Weak, a bit unsteady, but still there.

Strapping him in, Jesse tossed their gear into the back, except for his rifle. He turned away to close the door only to see the Lab sitting on the ground, watching him.

"You're going you better get in," Jesse ordered, pointing to the open back door. In a flash the dog was inside, sitting behind James. Jesse slammed the door and climbed wearily into the driver's seat. As he threw the Hummer into gear, he reached for the radio. One thing was certain.

James was going to need medical help sooner rather than later.

ROLAND

CHAPTER FORTY-ONE

"Jesse to Base, anyone listening?"

Roland almost leaped at the radio.

"This is Roland, Jess. What's the story?"

"I've got James, but he's bad off, Ro'," Jesse's voice was strained. *"He took one in the leg sometime this morning, maybe, and he's lost a lot of blood. Angie needs to be ready the minute we roll in, and I. . .I'll need help standing by to get him out."*

"You okay, Jesse?" Roland asked, suddenly worried.

"I'm just wore out, brother," Jesse replied. *"I don't know how far I carried him, and I'm about done."*

"We'll be ready."

"There's a nurse in that bunch that James rescued. If they're there, might have her be ready to help, too."

"They'll be here any minute," Roland assured him. "I'll get on it right now. Also, I'll contact Tom, see if there's a doctor around."

"That might be a good idea," Jesse agreed. *"I'll be there as fast as this thing will travel."*

"Blow it up if you have to," Roland told him. "I'll steal another one."

~*~

"Tango One, you up?" Angie took the call.

"Tango One," she replied.

"Expedite," Roland's voice was tense. *"Jesse is on his way in with James. Kid took a round to the leg and lost a lot of blood. We'll need you here when he arrives."*

"Roger that," Angie replied, already going over in her mind what she might need. "You know his blood type?"

"Negative," Roland replied.

"Ask around for O-Negative blood type," she ordered. "Have Maria boil water for me, and make sure the clinic room is cleared for action. We're. . ." she looked at Mack, who flashed five fingers twice, "ten minutes out."

"Roger that. Jesse says there's a nurse in the group you're transporting. Any idea if she's in any shape to help?"

"Negative, but we'll check," Angie promised.

"Base clear," Roland called.

"Tango One, clear," Angie replied. She looked at Mack.

"Fast as we can safely go," she ordered. "I need to be there ahead of him, if possible."

"You got it."

~*~

"What's wrong, Roland?" Maria asked as soon as she saw the look on his face.

"James is hurt, pretty bad," he told her. "Jesse's bringing him in right now, and Angie is on her way, and there might be a nurse in the group James found that can help. Angie needs you to get some water boiling, I guess for sterilizing stuff. I need to get her clinic room ready. Oh, and get one of the others to see if anyone's got O-Negative blood and are willing to donate. Mine's O-Positive, or..."

"I understand," Maria interrupted him. "You care for him deeply. And I do as well," she admitted. "He no longer seems. . .creepy," she smiled slightly. "He is a good man, and he has had a good teacher."

"Thanks," Roland murmured. "Well, let's get to it. We don't have much time."

~*~

Roland checked the clinic and found it squared away. Angie was very meticulous about it, anyway. With that done, he ran back to the radio room and called Tom Wilson.

"What's up, Roland?" Tom answered right away, thankfully.

"We've got a gunshot wound on the way in, Tom," Roland replied. "Is there a doctor anywhere close by that we might get to come see us? I mean, we'll provide transport and all, but one of my boys is hurt bad."

"Doctor Kingston is still around somewhere in town, last I saw her," Tom came back. *"I'm in town now, so I'll see if I can round her up. I'm sure she'll be glad to help, if I can find her. I'll bring her out myself, since it sounds like we need to talk."*

ROLAND

"Sooner would be helpful," Roland told him. "Tell her I'll do whatever I can for her, in return."

"I'll get back to you," the Sheriff promised. Roland sat back for a second, sighing. He'd done all he could...

He shot up as he heard the sound of the deuce-and-a-half returning. They would need to see to the people that the truck was bringing, and find that nurse.

~*~

"Who's the nurse?" Angie demanded as she and Mack helped the people in back unload.

"I am," Melissa said. "Why?"

"Come with me, please, if you can," Angie said in way of reply. "We're expecting a wounded man, soon. I'm a combat para, but a real nurse would be a great help."

"Is...is it James?" Melissa asked, hurrying after the female soldier.

"I forgot you'd know him, wouldn't you," Angie sighed. "I'm sorry. Yes, it is James. He took a round to the leg, and has lost a lot of blood. We're asking for O-Negative donors, since we don't know his blood type."

"I'm O Negative!" Tom Mackey shouted from behind them.

"You're too..." Mack started.

"I'm as healthy as a horse!" Tom shouted him down. "And I owe that kid my life, just like everyone else here." With that he took off following the two women.

"Mack, get them inside since we've had a change of plans," Roland ordered. "We'll get them something to eat, and let them get cleaned up. I think we can round up some clothes for 'em, even if it's just BDUs for now. We'll try and do better for them later on, if we can."

"I need someone to check my feet," an older woman informed him.

"What's wrong with them?" Roland asked before Mack could intervene.

"They're sore, that's what!" Shirley Pippins exclaimed. "I need something for them."

"You'll be fine with some rest, I'm sure," Roland managed to reply politely. "Meantime, our medical person is prepping to treat someone, so they can check you over once they have time."

"Aren't you supposed to be helping us?" Shirley demanded.

"What do you mean?" Roland asked, trying valiantly to keep his temper.

"You're from the government, right?" she almost snarled. "Well, I'm a taxpayer!"

231

"When's the last time you paid any taxes?" Roland snarled back, furious. "And no, we *ain't* from the government. We're helping you outta the goodness of our hearts, which you are *straining* at the moment. Now shut up and do as you're told, or start walking outta here on your tired, sore feet. We've got a man incoming who's been shot. Same one that helped you out, in fact. And your feet can *rot off* as far as I'm concerned, until that boy is out of danger." He leaned in closer.

"I'm off my meds, lady," he whispered. "You really don't want to push me. Understand?"

For once, Shirley Pippin thought before she opened her mouth. The look in Roland's eyes was murderous to say the very least. It slowly began to dawn on her that this man might just rather kill her than put up with her crap.

"I understand," she replied softly. "I'm sorry about the boy. I hope he's all right."

"So do I," Roland sighed, easing out of his mad spell. "Now, we can get you some hot food, and then you can get a shower and some fresh clothes. Food's plain, but it's hot, and filling. Any of you need medical attention, I promise you'll get it as soon as we can." He looked at Mack.

"Find Deena, and you two can handle this." Mack nodded, and waved for the group to follow him. Roland stayed outside, waiting on Jesse. He didn't have long to wait. No sooner had the group entered the building than Roland heard the Humvee coming up the road, engine wound tight.

As he watched, Jesse came roaring around the corner, maybe a quarter mile down the road, almost on two wheels. The Humvee went into a slide as Jesse applied just enough brake to be able to turn into the school without tipping over and then slid to a stop just outside the front door, less than five feet from where Roland stood.

Roland had the passenger door open before Jesse could shut off the engine. James was pale, sweaty, and for a second Roland couldn't tell he was breathing. James took a ragged breath, finally, and Roland felt relief flood through him. James was still alive, for now.

Reaching into the vehicle, Roland hoisted the boy into his arms, careful of the wounded leg. James actually regained consciousness for a few seconds. He looked up at Roland and grinned.

"Hey, Roland!" he smiled. "Whaz happeninin?" he slurred.

"Morphine," Jesse told him, crawling out of the Humvee and almost falling with the effort.

Roland nodded, and then ran for the door. He nodded to whoever was holding it open, not bothering to see who, and shot down the hallway to the room Angie Martens used as a clinic. She and Melissa were waiting.

"On the table!" Angie ordered. Roland complied.

ROLAND

"Out!" Angie ordered. "I'll call if we need anything. Melissa is Tom ready to go?"

"Yes," the nurse replied.

"Let's get started then. Prep James' arm, and start giving him blood, while I see to the wound. We have to get him stabilized as soon as possible. Why are you still here?" she demanded, and Roland realized with a start that the question was aimed at him.

"Sheriff said there was a doctor still in town," he told the paramedic. "He's looking for her, and if he finds her, will bring her out."

"Good. Now wait outside," Angie ordered. "We've got to have room to work. Stay close, or have someone else do it. And find out if there are any other possible donors."

"Yes, ma'am," Roland didn't think of arguing and departed.

"Oh, James," Melissa said softly, inserting the needle for the transfusion. "Why didn't you just stay with us?"

"No time for that now!" Angie insisted, already working on the wound. "Keep your head in the game, and worry about those things later. When he can answer you."

Melissa nodded, and turned to Tom Mackey.

"Ready?"

"You bet."

~*~

Roland figured Sheriff Wilson had come close to destroying the engine in his police car as he came sliding into the lot fifteen minutes later, a very scared dark skinned woman in the passenger seat.

"You *idiot!*" she shouted, desperately grabbing anything she could to remain upright. "I have to be alive to help him!"

"Sorry," Wilson muttered. "Anyway, we're here."

"Thanks be to *God* for that," the woman shot back, getting out. "Where is he?" she demanded of Roland.

"This way," he replied, leading her inside. When they arrived, Angelina was already debriding the wound, irrigating it with saline.

"What do we have?" Kingston demanded. "I'm Jennifer Kingston, by the way," she added.

"Angie Martens," the paramedic replied. "GSW to the lower right extremity, outside thigh area. No apparent bone damage, clean exit wound, primary problem at this point is loss of blood. Patient has received one pint of O-Neg blood, and we're prepping another donor."

"How long since his wound?" Kingston asked, looking.

"Unknown, but probably before noon," Angie replied. "He was alone, covering a group of people rescued from a biker gang."

"I see," Kingston hummed. "I see no major blood vessel damage. I assume no sign of any arterial bleed, considering the timing."

"None," Angie confirmed. "We're giving him fluids in addition to the blood, and I've started an IV drip of Levaquin at three per. I was completing the debride when you entered."

"Good work," Kingston remarked. "All right, let's take a look at the wound. Continue the fluids for now, and the antibiotic was an excellent call, especially considering the time passed and the condition of his skin and clothes. Do we have any more donors lined up?"

"Two more, Doctor," Melissa replied.

"Hello, Melissa," Kingston smiled briefly. "I didn't realize it was you."

"I'm one of the people he saved," the nurse nodded. "I'm sure I don't look like I normally do," she added dryly.

"None of us do, lately," Kingston nodded, working on James' leg. "All right, not knowing how much blood he's lost, we'll have to proceed carefully. I wish we knew his type, but I don't have the equipment with me to check it." She looked at Roland.

"I don't suppose you know, do you?"

"No, ma'am, I don't," Roland admitted. "For any of the kids, for that matter," he added. "They aren't here at the moment."

"I see," Kingston hummed again. "All right, ladies, let's be about it then. You can go now," she added, and Roland realized this was for him.

"I'll be right outside."

He stepped out into the hallway, almost tripping over something. Looking down, he saw a chocolate Lab sitting by the door, looking into the room.

"Where the hell did this dog come from?"

~*~

"So, how did all this come about?" Wilson asked as he and Roland sat in the mess.

"Well, I decided to be pro-active and see if I couldn't cut this bunch off at the knees," Roland admitted. "I had another, more private chat with that Turner woman, after you left. She let go of where they were, so me and James set out to kinda get a look at 'em."

"Where is Turner?" Wilson asked.

"She ran off," Roland said flatly. Wilson looked at him for a minute, then nodded.

"They'll do that," he said finally. "Anyway."

"Anyway," Roland got back to his story. "When we got there we realized they were holding several people prisoners. That kinda threw a monkey wrench into our plans and we had to improvise a bit. James hid out and waited while I sprung the ambush on the bikers. They were loaded for bear, too. Likely headed here, or maybe up toward Turnbow's folks."

"I got several of 'em, but not like I should have. I set the mines wrong, not realizing..."

"Mines?" Wilson blurted.

"Claymores," Roland nodded. "Anyway, I had them set up to catch a bunch o' bikers. You know, on bikes. Well they had bikes, but they also had three vans full o' people and hardware. The mines took out all but one of the vans, but the other two absorbed a lot of the firepower. I think I wrecked more bikes than bikers, to be honest."

"So I shot a few of 'em, let 'em see me, then took off into the bush. A bunch of 'em chased me, using dogs to keep to my trail. I left a few dirty tricks for 'em and stung 'em a bit, but they kept coming."

"Finally I laid an ambush, and I think I got one of their trackers. Whatever happened, they left off trailing me and I guess went back to their camp."

"I can only assume what James did, since I haven't talked to him. For that matter, I haven't had time to talk to the people he rescued. Guess you might want to do that."

"I will," Tom nodded. "Well, it sounds like you stirred up a hornet's nest, Roland. Any idea how many are left?"

"No idea at this point," Roland shook his head. "Our count had to be off, I think. Just seems like there were too many of them compared to what we expected. For all I know, some of 'em weren't even there."

"You know you've made sure that you'll be the next target, don't you?" Tom asked quietly.

"We were the next target anyway," Roland shrugged. "At least now, there's less of them."

~*~

BD watched as the rest of his crew motored into their compound. His chief lieutenant dismounted, walking up to his boss.

"I notice Linc isn't here," BD commented. Manny shrugged.

"He didn't wanna come," the biker said.

"I see," BD sighed. "Well, that's too bad. He was pretty good at salvage work."

"His second, Hube, is just as good," Manny shrugged again. "And he don't buck the Boss."

"Good point," BD allowed. "Brick hasn't come back," he added softly. "We got a few back, all wounded but one. This kid laid an ambush for 'em, apparently. Brick went on, but since we ain't heard from him, I'm forced to assume that he ain't comin' back."

"We did get most of the prisoners back," he continued. "Over half. Had to shoot a few of them, but you know what they say. No omelet without a few broken eggs." Manny just nodded. The Boss didn't wax philosophical often, and when he did it was a bad sign.

It was also a good idea to listen patiently.

"We'll let them get settled. We plan, we watch, and when they're not expecting it, we strike back. Hard, and permanent."

ROLAND

CHAPTER FORTY-TWO

Things are tense. I was looking through my things and found this stupid journal, and realized I haven't updated it in a long time. I never seem to finish what I start.

James is still in 'surgery'. No one reading this will know why, I guess, but short story, he and I rescued some people, and James got shot protecting them, while I thought I was leading all the bad guys away. Turns out there were more bad guys than we thought.

There's a doctor from town who's patching him up. Seems like a good woman. I might see if she wants to join our group, if she doesn't have one of her own. Be nice to have a doc around. There's a nurse, too, that was in the group James led away from the bikers. She's been a big help. Seems to like James, too. We'll see, I hope.

Wilson is talking to the others, getting their story. I really don't know anything about them except that one man is Mack's Uncle, Tom. He's a tough old man, I know that. Good fella to have around, I'd say.

We could be attacked at any time. We're a man down, now, and that's bad. I wish we had just a

few more guys, but we don't, so ...we don't. That's just how it is.

Maria and I seem to have reached some kind of understanding. She just out and declares she has feelings for me and floored me. It wasn't until after she had gone that I remembered Gran Fuller's statement about the girl with coal black hair. Her description fits Maria to a tee. I still don't believe it. And even if it is, so what?

I'm not a good man. I try to be, but ...but I'm not, that's all. She has to see that, and when she does, she'll get over this. . .thing, and forget it.

I hope that we'll still be friends when that happens. I do enjoy not having to worry about her knifing me in the back-

Where in the hell did that dog come from...?

~*~

"Who's damn *dog* is this!" Roland shouted, as the Lab roamed the halls. No one answered, though a few people did come to see what the shouting was about.

"I haven't seen a dog," Terri shrugged. "Sorry."

"Me neither," Deena repeated the motion. "Maybe Ralph found him?"

"Where is Ralph?" Roland asked. "Why haven't I seen him today? Or for a while, in fact," he added, trying to remember the last time he'd seen the kid.

"He's probably in his 'lab'," Terri rolled her eyes. "He's set up shop in one of those buildings out back, always running off there, usually carrying something that he hides from everyone else, like he's a mad scientist or something."

"It is a little weird," Deena agreed, though she didn't sound quite as condemning.

"I'm gonna have a look at that," Roland murmured. "One of you find out where that damn dog came from!"

"Haven't seen it," the two replied in unison, then giggled. Roland looked at them for a second, and then just walked away. The two teens looked at each other, shrugged, and returned to whatever chores they had been doing.

Roland slipped out back, and took a look around. He hadn't been out here in several days to amount to anything, since he'd been gone. Nothing seemed out of the...

Ralph came running out of one of the outbuildings, legs pumping as hard as they would travel.

"Duck Mister Roland!" he called, and then hit the ground. Seeing that, Roland dropped to the pavement just as the roof of the small building tore apart, smoke billowing from the hole.

"What in the hell?" Roland got to his feet. "Ralph, what the hell are you doing?"

"Uh, sorry 'bout that," the teenager got to his feet, dusting himself off. He avoided looking Roland in the eye.

"That doesn't answer my question."

"Um. . .well, see. . .it's a surprise. Yeah! That's it! A surprise!" Ralph's comments seemed to gain steam as he convinced himself.

"Well, it worked," Roland told him flatly. "What, *exactly*, are you doing?"

ROLAND

"I'm tryin' to help," Ralph sighed. "Might's well show you, I guess," he sounded dejected. Waving for Roland to follow, he led him to another shed nearby.

"Shouldn't we put out that fire?" Roland asked.

"Nah, it'll be okay," Ralph shook his head. "Ain't really no fire, no way. Just smoke and whatnot. Ain't nothin' in there to burn."

"The shed might burn," Roland replied, voice heavy with sarcasm.

"Nah," Ralph repeated. "I always soak the wood with water before I try anything new. Will have to patch that roof, though," he said seriously. He opened the door to the other shack, and led Roland inside.

"What is all this?" Roland asked, looking at the various jugs, buckets and barrels scattered around the small building.

"Bombs," the boy replied calmly, walking through the maze.

"Bo. . .*what?!*" Roland screeched.

"Relax, they ain't armed," Ralph told him. "They're just mixed is all."

"Ralph, tell me, *right now*, what you're doing," Roland said, his patience at an end.

"Told ya, I'm tryin' to help," Ralph answered. "These here is for when the bad guys come."

"Wher. . .*how*, did you learn to do this?" Roland demanded.

"Oh, my grandpa taught me," Ralph waved the question away. "We made homemade stuff all the time for beaver dams, stumps, that kinda thing. It's pretty easy."

Roland rubbed a hand down his face, trying to square away 'it's pretty easy' and 'homemade' in his mind.

It didn't work.

"What have you done?" he demanded again.

"They're fuel oil and 'monia," Ralph told him. "See, you take some fertilizer and mix that real careful like with..."

"I know how to make ANFO!" Roland almost roared. "How do you know how?"

"Oh, well if I'd known that, I'da asked you to help me," Ralph grinned. "I never thought about that. As to how, I just told ya. My grandpa taught me."

"Good old grandpa," Roland sighed. "He teach you anything else that. . .my God, what am I *saying?*" he asked no one. "I'm losing my mind."

"Anything what?" Ralph asked.

"Never mind," Roland almost shuddered. "This is. . .more than. . .what did you think you were going to do with these?"

"Well, I'm gonna set 'em up 'round the school, cover 'em with rocks and broken glass, and other odds n' ends, then when the bad guys get here, and get close to one, I'll blow 'em up!" Ralph's enthusiasm was disturbing.

Very. Disturbing.

"What made you think of this?" Roland asked. "And why not tell someone. . .*ask*, someone, before you started it?"

"Well, ever' one was busy, and I really didn't have that much to do, and I wanted to help, but I ain't really able to help like James does 'cause I'm still just a kid, and so I got to thinkin' how I could help, but then..."

"Jesus, Ralph, the *short* version," Roland begged, rubbing his temples.

"Oh, well, the only thing I could think of was this, that I knowed how to do. So, I did it."

"You sure did," Roland sighed. "Do you have any idea how dangerous this is?"

"Oh, it ain't that bad," the youngster waved the comment away. "Took me a while to get the ratio just right, but she's perfect, now."

"Took you..." Roland stopped. No sense in asking something he might not want to hear, anyway.

"Well, you know, if you want it stronger, you kinda got to..." Ralph started.

"No, don't tell me," Roland held up a hand, forestalling the explanation. "I may not can take it," he sighed. "Ralph, you could have been killed, or killed someone else, doing this. It's incredibly dangerous."

"Wasn't no danger o' that," Ralph insisted. "I been doin' this since I was a kid, I told ya. Long as you're careful, and don't get into a hurry, its fine. So anyway, there was a torch in the maintenance shed, and I been usin' it to cut up them old cars that we pushed away. I used the pieces to make some ugly lookin' spikes to tape to the outside of the bombs. I figured out I can put the spikes and other shrapnel on the bombs in a two hundred seventy-degree arc, and that gives me a directional mine so to speak. I leave the empty arc aimed in our direction so we don't get hurt when we set 'em off."

"Now, about settin' 'em off," Ralph went on. "I stripped the electrical wirin' from them cars, and spliced that together, but it wasn't enough. I found a roll of thermostat wire in the janitor's storage though, and that's even better, but it still left me short. So when I came across two rolls o' speaker wire I got to wonderin' if that would carry enough charge to set things off, so I was runnin' an experiment with that when ...well, I kinda used more magnesium than I really needed for that, and I had a small charge set up to see if it would ignite, but really it was a little too much, the way I mixed it, and, well, that's what happened when you was on your way out here," the boy finished.

ROLAND

"But it worked!" he started again before Roland could say anything. "So now I got enough wire to lay all the charges but now I got another problem, 'cause I need to disguise 'em somehow. I was plannin' on paintin 'em, and hidin 'em as sort of a landscaping kinda thing, only, well, I ain't got enough paint in the right colors, and I didn't figure a purple bomb would really hide all that well, so now I got to figure somethin' else out."

Finally, *mercifully*, he stopped.

"Where did you get magnesium?" was the safest thing Roland could think of to ask.

"Oh, them two cars I used had mag wheels," Ralph replied. "I used a hacksaw to cut 'em up, and boy wasn't that a job! and then used a grindin' wheel to real careful scrape the pieces into dust, and I put that in the bottom of all the containers I used to make the bombs. The electric spark lights the magnesium, and then the magnesium sets off..."

"I get it," Roland held up his hand again. "I get it," he repeated, almost as if trying to convince himself. "Ralph, I..." Roland stopped. He really didn't know what to say.

"So, Mister Roland, since you're here, can you mebbe help me figure a way to hide these things so's the bad guys won't see 'em. I'd like to *really* surprise 'em!"

Roland looked at the teen, fighting to keep a look of incredulity off his face. Ralph apparently realized exactly how dangerous his project was, which no doubt explained his reluctance to allow anyone to see or know what he was doing. And, it seemed, he had done his work well.

It scared Roland that Ralph had managed to accomplish all this without adult supervision, or without him, Roland, knowing it.

On the other hand, Ralph had done something that none of the adults had thought of. And in doing so had demonstrated that he knew how serious their situation was and had the intelligence to take on something like this on his own. And get it done.

Was this the shape of the world to come? he wondered. Kids having to grow up so fast, so violently? Having to do things like this to survive?

There was no help for it, he decided. He'd seen this in many a third world country. He'd never thought to see it here at home, where things were supposed to be different. But here it was and there was nothing for it. Not anymore.

"Sure, Ralph," he managed to smile. "I guess I can help you do that."

The joyous look on Ralph's face made Roland both sad, and happy.

And he didn't know which was worse.

~*~

Doctor Kingston stood back from the table, stretching. They were finally finished.

James had taken three pints of blood. She wasn't sure that he didn't need more, but his color had returned, so she had stopped. The only way to give him more would have been to know his blood type. She was grateful, and amazed, that there had been three people in such a small group with O-Negative blood, and all had given him a pint of blood and perhaps a little more.

It would be enough, she thought. James' wound hadn't been that serious. Painful, it would be sore for days, maybe a week. Had he not lost so much blood he would already be limping around.

The blood loss was much more serious. That kind of loss placed an enormous strain on the body's system. James was still out, but he wasn't in a coma and that was an excellent sign. With the physical strain he had been under, and the morphine, his sleep was completely normal. His breathing was normal now and his pulse was strong again. All signs were very good and she was confident that he would be on his feet soon.

"Ladies, I think we can deem James done," she smiled. She noted that Melissa looked extremely relieved, but didn't comment on it. Melissa also looked exhausted.

"Melissa, time for you to look after yourself for a while," Kingston ordered. "Get some food, get a shower, and get some rest. Don't argue," Kingston cut the other woman's apparent objection. "You're at the edge of exhaustion. All you're going to do is make yourself sick, and this young man will need you to look after him as he heals."

Melissa blushed at that and Kingston fought off a smile. She had meant that he would need Melissa's nursing skills, but. . .whatever made people happy.

"We can recruit someone to sit with him around the clock," Angie promised. "I'll see to it at once, in fact. All of us need a break." With that she stepped outside, returning with Terri.

"Hi," the teen smiled at the older women. "Is James gonna be okay?" she asked.

"Yes, dear, he is," Kingston smiled. "But we need to have someone monitoring him until he comes around. Would you mind?"

"Not at all," Terri shook her head. "James is a great guy, and he's risked his life to protect us more than once. He's. . .well, he's our big brother," she grinned. "Always hanging around, standing guard, protecting us. It'll be nice to do something like that for him for once."

"Thank you," Angie grinned, then turned to Melissa. "Come on," she ordered. "I'll show you to the showers, get you some clothes, and find you something to eat. Then you can rest."

ROLAND

"All right," Melissa nodded dully. She realized now, as the adrenaline wore off, that she had about gone her distance.

"I'll see about checking over the others," Kingston informed Angie. "I might as well give everyone at least a brief physical while I'm here. Maybe we can get someone to start collecting medical background, too."

"Oh, Deena would be perfect for that!" Terri informed them. "She's like an organizational genius!"

"Deena it is, then," Angie agreed. "I'll find her while Melissa showers.

Kingston left the room as the others decided how to proceed. She would check the others, but first she wanted to stretch her limbs, and see some more of this place.

~*~

Jesse woke up groggy. He looked at his watch from habit, and realized he'd slept for almost three hours. He jumped up.

Or at least he started to. His legs complained so loudly that his 'jump' turned into a desperate struggle to gain his feet. Legs that were still very rubbery carried him shakily toward the cafeteria. It was coming on to dusk, so he figured there would be something eat.

As he staggered toward the mess, a voice behind him spoke.

"Are you all right?" the woman's voice came to him over his shoulder.

"Fine," Jesse nodded, without looking. He didn't recognize the voice, but there were a lot of new people in here today. "Just a little sore."

"Do you need any help?" the silky smooth voice asked. Jesse turned, about to tell whoever it was that he was good, thanks, and go away. Politely of course.

Whatever he would have said died on his lips, however, as he got his first look at Doctor Jennifer Kingston.

Kingston was tall and athletic with long hair, and beautiful gray-green eyes. Very wonderful eyes, Jesse decided. Kingston's full lips parted in a smile.

"I'm Jennifer Kingston," she held out her hand. "Nice to meet you, Mister...?"

"Fuller, ma'am," Jesse was suddenly on his best behavior. His *very* best behavior. "Jesse Owens Fuller, at your service," he said, and lifted her hand to his lips briefly. She blushed at bit at that, but didn't take her hand back.

"I'm a doctor," she told him. "Sheriff Wilson brought me here to see to James, the boy who got shot."

"Then I'm in your debt, Doctor," Jesse said firmly. "And I assure you, James is a man from head to foot. He did a soldier's work today, all on his own."

"I see," Kingston nodded. "And what happened to you?" she asked.

"I, uh. . .well, I'm the one who found him, ma'am," Jesse explained. "I ran with him over my shoulder for a good while, and my legs, they don't like that very much, so they're complaining. Loudly."

"Better get those stretched out, then," she advised, smiling again.

"I intend to, as soon as I've eaten," Jesse smiled in return. "Speaking of which, can I offer you dinner for saving James?" He held out his arm to her.

"Why not?" she replied, and took his arm. "It'll give you someone to lean on, at least, won't it?"

~*~

"We can cover them with grass," Roland suggested, looking at the various sized jugs.

"Won't work," Ralph shook his head. "Thought about that, but the grass'l die in a few days. What happens they don't show up soon enough? For that matter, we need to disguise 'em 'fore we set 'em out, case they're watchin' us."

Stunned, Roland looked at Ralph, wondering again how old Ralph really was. Of all the...

"That's a very good point, Ralph," he said in reply. "And that means I need to go and check on something. Keep thinking about how to disguise your mines, okay. Oh, and no more experimenting without telling me first, either."

"Okay, Mister Roland," Ralph nodded seriously. "I'll figure it out."

"I'm sure you will Ralph," Roland smiled, and left the boy to his work.

He needed to check on something. He, too, had things to figure out.

ROLAND

CHAPTER FORTY-THREE

Roland went up to the roof of the school with his night vision binoculars. Ralph's statement had hit him where he lived, and he didn't like that.

Sure, they'd kept a good watch. Of course they had worked to be careful, establishing protocols to protect themselves, to prevent mistakes. How, then, with all the combined experience present in this group, had they not thought about surveillance?

Were the bikers watching them right now? If so, from where? How long had they been there, if they were there at all?

Questions like this assaulted him as Roland looked around the grounds in every direction. He scoured every foot of ground within view, painstakingly examining any and every place that might provide a concealed observation point.

He and James had executed an almost perfect hide and watch against the gang, so why in the world didn't it occur to him that the enemy could do the same thing?

He didn't know how long he stood there, looking, but he didn't stop until he was certain there was nothing else to be seen. Sighing, he lowered the glasses and started back down. Tomorrow, early, he would hit the woods, and do a complete recon. And he'd have someone watching around the clock from now on.

When did this get so complicated?

~*~

James came awake slowly, fighting into consciousness from what seemed like a great long distance. As he swam up into a full waking state, he opened his eyes, closing them again immediately, and groaning in pain.

"James?"

He heard the voice, sounding like it was far away, and opened his eyes again, slowly this time. It took him a moment to focus, as he was still a little loopy. Well, a lot loopy. When his vision finally centered for him, he was looking into the face of a very worried Melissa Andrews.

"M'lissa?" he mumbled, confused.

"Yes, it's me," she smiled, a single tear falling down her cheek. "I wanted to sit with you for a while. I didn't expect you to wake up so soon."

"Wake up?" James repeated.

"You've been out for a while," Melissa explained. "Let me get you some water. You have to be really dried out by now." She turned to get the water bottle from the table next to her, and lifted it to his lips. Slowly at first, then faster as his thirst hit him, James drank until the bottle was empty. He lay back, licking his dry lips.

"Thanks," he rasped. "I don't know how long since I had a drink," he admitted.

"Probably several hours," Melissa told him. "How do you feel?" she asked.

"Alive," he shrugged slightly. "More'n I expected." James still sounded surprised. Suddenly he remembered.

"Jesse! Is Jesse okay?" he asked. "What about all of you? Everyone make it okay?" Melissa felt her heart warm. Despite his injury and near death, James was asking about everyone else.

"Jesse's fine, though a little worn out from carrying you out of the woods," she smiled again. "We're all fine, too. The doctor looked us all over, and pronounced us malnourished, slightly dehydrated, but otherwise in reasonably good health. Susan, of course is a little different, after. . .well, after," Melissa shrugged. "But she's doing okay, considering."

"Doctor?" James asked. "When did we get a doctor?"

"She's from town," Melissa replied. "The Sheriff brought her after Roland called."

"Roland!" James started. He'd forgotten. "So he made it back okay?"

"Yes, and has been terribly worried about you," the nurse assured him. "Let me go and get him, he wanted to know when you were awake. After that, I'll try and bring you up to date."

"Okay."

~*~

"Well, well, well," Roland smiled, walking into James' room. "Look who's finally up and awake!"

"Hey, Roland," James smiled. "How you doing?"

"I'm fine," Roland assured him. "It's you that got shot. How do you feel?"

"Like I got shot, I guess," James told him. "I'm sore as all get out, I know that," he added.

"You had quite the adventure," Roland nodded. "You did a good job, James," he added, quietly. Proudly. "I'm proud of you."

"Thanks, Roland," James might have blushed a bit. "I just tried to do what you would do. What you taught me to do."

"And you did," Roland nodded. "You didn't try, you did. Jesse was very impressed."

"Reckon I owe Jesse a big one in return," James replied, laying back. "Wasn't for him, I'd be gone, I imagine."

"That's what friends do, James," Roland shrugged. "That's what team-mates do. Jesse thinks of you as a soldier. A comrade. We do all we can for our comrades-in-arms, little brother." James flushed again in pleasure at that.

"Well, I'll leave you to rest," Roland smiled, standing. "Need anything?"

"Did Jesse manage to get my gear?" James asked, hopeful.

"He did," Roland nodded. "Want it?" he asked, voice filled with understanding.

"Ain't too much trouble," James replied.

"I'll see to it," Roland promised. "Get some rest. Need you back on your feet soon as possible."

"I'll be up and around tomorrow," James assured him.

"We'll see," Roland smiled. "Rest tonight, anyway." He left, leaving James and Melissa alone.

"You most certainly will *not* be up and around tomorrow!" Melissa scolded once Roland was gone.

"Yes, I will," James told her. "I heal quickly, and I have a high pain tolerance. And I ain't got time to be laying around, neither," he added.

"You need rest," Melissa insisted, fussing with the bed. "You lost too much blood to be trying to get on your feet so fast."

"We'll see," James shrugged. He didn't much care for laying abed. Never had.

"You look better," he mentioned, and Melissa stopped.

"You look like you got something to eat, and a chance to clean up and rest," James clarified. "BDUs suit you," he added with a wink, and Melissa found herself blushing.

"Thanks. I do feel better," she admitted.

"How's Mister Mackey?" he asked.

"He's resting," Melissa told him. "He was one of your blood donors," she added.

"That old fella's tough as iron, I reckon," James shook his head, chuckling. "Everyone else okay?"

"Pretty much," Melissa nodded, sitting down. "Susan is. . .well, you know she..."

"I know," James told her softly. "I'm sorry I wasn't there sooner."

"I would probably have been next," Melissa admitted, her fear showing for the first time since he'd met her. "I... James, if you hadn't..." she stopped, not knowing what to say. After a few seconds, she began to sob, dropping her face into her hands as the stress and strain finally caught up to her.

"It's okay," James soothed. He reached out and rubbed his palm against the side of her head, stroking her hair.

Suddenly she leapt to him, hugging him tightly and bawling into his shoulder. Not knowing what else to do, James held her, stroking her hair, rubbing her back, and whispering encouragement to her.

When Roland came back later with James' gear, the two were sound asleep, wrapped in an embrace in the small hospital bed. He grinned, shaking his head as he set James' equipment nearby, laying the teen's pistol where he could reach it.

He turned the light out as he went.

~*~

Dawn seemed to come too early for some, and not fast enough for others. Such was the way of days filled with danger and tension.

Roland was outside at first light, already in the bush around the school grounds. He stalked quietly and painstakingly, looking for any sign of an observation post. It was slow and deliberate work, but it had to be done.

Maria was called to service in helping Ralph with his paint problem. She had scoured the school

kitchen and found some food coloring. It wouldn't help with the purple paint, but the schools other color was white, and the walls in all the rooms were white. As a result, there was a good deal of white paint on hand.

The food coloring probably wouldn't last as long as the paint, she decided, so she and Ralph had hit upon another idea. They would paint all the various devices with the white paint, and then line them with the purple. A little bit of landscaping would transform them into simple garden objects, ostensibly created by the students over the years. A close inspection would reveal the truth, of course, but anyone close enough to one of Ralph's inventions would have far more to worry about than fresh paint.

ROLAND

Jesse awoke humming, despite the pain in his legs. He spent over an hour stretching, well before the sun was up, so that he was loose and relatively pain free in plenty of time to shower and dress, and get to the mess hall just in time to join Doctor Jennifer Kingston for breakfast. Sheriff Wilson had departed the night before, the doctor wanting to stay at least overnight in the event that James needed her attention. She thought it unlikely, but the decision also gave her a little extra time to get know Jesse Owens Fuller a bit better. Something that was high on her list of priorities.

She had not really been surprised to enter James' room and find Melissa Andrews asleep in the teenager's arms. She had checked James' vitals without waking either one, and then eased out of the room. Both of them needed rest more than anything else, and she left them to it.

Susan Powers was another story.

The young woman had been frightfully abused by her captors, and she was fragile both mentally and physically. Jennifer had checked her thoroughly the night before, but she couldn't answer Susan's most important questions; had she been given an STD, and was she pregnant. Both required tests that Jennifer couldn't run with what she had with her. She had tried to comfort the girl as best she could, but knew that wasn't much.

Jennifer had given her the doctor's equivalent of a 'mickey', dosing her with a sedative at the same time she'd administered a healthy dose of antibiotics, which she promised would cure her of any normal STDs she might have been exposed to. She didn't need to add that it would do nothing to stop an HIV or other, similar, infection. Hopefully a good night's sleep would help her. It was all Jennifer could offer right now.

The doctor had explained quietly to Deena that James and Melissa would need to have breakfast set aside for them, and Deena had grinned knowingly and went about gathering the required meals.

Tom Mackey had breakfast with his nephew and his girlfriend, approving completely of his sister's son's choice in female companionship. Angelina Martens was pretty, tough, and smart as a whip. Tom Mackey figured a man simply couldn't ask for more than that out of life.

Shirley Pippins groused under her breath at everyone around her, but didn't speak her complaints loud enough to be made out. She would have died before admitting it, but that man, that Roland, had unnerved her the day before. She was genuinely afraid of him and thus decided she needed to be on her best behavior. She had missed the Sheriff being here or would have demanded transportation somewhere else. For some reason, Tom Wilson had decided he didn't need to interview her. Probably didn't want to upset her, she decided, ignoring the possibility that Wilson simply didn't feel like putting up with her.

Trooper Jarrod Vaughan stood the watch that morning, leaving the radio room every thirty minutes or so just to amble around, checking the doors, looking around the building. He kept a radio at his side, knowing that Roland was out in the woods.

Worries about reprisal ebbed as the day grew on into full morning with no sign of an impending attack. By lunch time the mood around the school was much lighter, for the most part.

~*~

Roland made it back inside just in time for lunch. He was dirty, tired, and bleeding from more than a few cuts, and had pulled at least ten thorns from his torn skin. He showered, doctored his cuts, and headed for the mess.

He sat down heavily at the table, and a tuna sandwich and glass of water appeared in front of him as if by magic. He looked up to see a smiling Maria looking down at him.

"How are you, Roland?" she asked, almost shyly.

"I'm tired," he admitted. "There's some really thick brush around here." He took a healthy bite from his sandwich. He'd miss tuna when it ran out. "How are you?"

"I, too, am tired," she admitted, sitting down across from him. "But you will be pleased to know that Ralph and I have painted all of his…devices."

"Good deal," Roland nodded. "How'd you do it?"

"Purple and white," she shrugged. "White body with purple highlights. It should look like school decorations created by the students."

"Hey, that's a good idea," Roland approved. "Your idea?"

"Yes," she blushed slightly. "It was the best we could come up with."

"Sounds like a winner to me," Roland assured her. "Everything going okay today?" he waved at the organized confusion around him.

"Si. I mean yes. Everyone is. . .well, not everyone," she suddenly looked downcast. "That young woman, Susan, is. . .she is damaged," Maria said softly. "I fear for her."

"You mean because of what happened?" Roland asked.

"Yes. She is very fragile at the moment. She is afraid, and she is hurting. Not just physically, but. . .here," she pointed to her own temple. "She needs something to do. Something that will empower her, and make her feel less vulnerable. Do you understand what I mean?"

ROLAND

"I think so," Roland nodded. "And I think I got just the thing, too. You busy?"

"No, today is my day off from the kitchen," Maria shook her head. "With no children, I am somewhat at loose ends."

"Well, then, let's you and I go and visit Miss Susan, and see if she feels like getting some of her own back."

~*~

"I don't understand," Susan looked from Roland to Maria, and then back again. "Why would I need to learn to shoot with so many here carrying guns?"

"You don't have to," Roland assured her. "I just thought you might like to be able to defend yourself, rather than depend on someone else to do it for you." His voice was soft. Gentle. Understanding.

Susan considered those words, thinking. She had never fired a gun. She had carried one with her away from the barn, and still had it, but she had taken it initially intending to use it on herself if it looked like she would be retaken. The idea of defending herself hadn't really entered her mind.

"I. . .I've never done anything like that," she said finally. "I have no idea how long it would take me to learn."

"All the more reason to get started now," Roland smiled at her. "We can have you shooting by the end of the day. I'll get you a pistol, and a holster, and you can carry it on you all the time, so you'll have it. Once you've got that down, we'll train you to use a rifle, too."

"All of us know how, Susan," Maria told her. She turned, lifting her shirt so that Susan could see the pistol tucked into the back of her jeans. Roland tried very hard not to admire the curve of those jeans from that angle, but failed. He did manage to look away before Maria caught him.

He thought. Inwardly Maria smiled as Roland jerked his gaze away from her rear. It was obvious he liked what he saw.

"It's not that I find the idea unappealing," Susan said. "I just don't know that I have the confidence to carry it off."

"Confidence comes with practice," Roland said easily. "No one knows how to do anything until they're taught. We'll teach you," he indicated himself and Maria. "It won't happen overnight, but I can practically guarantee that by sundown, you'll know enough to defend yourself. You'll only get better in the days to come."

"We need good people, Susan," he continued. "People who aren't afraid to stand their ground, and who aren't afraid to work to survive. I think you're good people. So does Maria. We want you to stay with us, if *you* want to. There's plenty of room, and when the kids get back there'll be a lot more work to do."

"But if you stay here, you need to know how to defend yourself. It's not that you'll be outside, fighting, but you'll need to be able to defend yourself, the kids, and the school."

Susan thought about that. It honestly hadn't surprised her that the men who had risked so much to help her and the others would have taken on responsibility for so many children. They were just that kind of people. Good, hard working people, trying to survive and help others along the way in a world gone mad.

Suddenly, Susan powers wanted to be one of those people. Wanted it very much, in fact. Something had been taken from her, and she could never get it back. But she could work to make sure it didn't happen to anyone else. She would work hard, too. Her eyes narrowed with determination as she saw her future play out before her eyes. She would work very hard, indeed. She nodded firmly.

"I'd like that very much," she said finally, her voice firm and strong. "And I'd like to get started right away."

ROLAND

CHAPTER FORTY-FOUR

"WHOSE DAMN DOG IS THIS!!!!"

Roland's yell could be heard all over the school building. Heads came up at first, then went back to what they had been doing as they realized it wasn't important. At least not to them.

Maria went to where Roland was standing in a hallway just off the school office.

Alone.

"Roland, what are you yelling about?" she demanded.

"This dog!" he pointed. "Where did it come from?"

"I see no dog," Maria shrugged.

"Are you blind?" he demanded. "it's right he..." Roland turned his head to look at the dog, then turned back to Maria. Then did a double take. There was no dog.

"Where did it go?" he asked the air around him.

"Roland, do you feel all right?" Maria asked.

"I'm fine!" Roland insisted. "I'm tellin' ya, there's a dog in here!"

"Where?" she asked, calmly.

"I swear it was right here," Roland told her, bewildered.

"Why don't you let me get you a cup of coffee," Maria soothed, taking his arm. "You aren't getting enough rest, Roland, and that can..."

"Don't gas light me!" Roland shot back, but allowed her to lead him toward the kitchen. "I *know* I saw a dog!"

"What kind of dog?"

"It looked like a chocolate Lab," Roland told her.

"I see," Maria nodded, and Roland flushed a bit.

"I'm telling you, there's a dog around here," he ground out.

"We'll find him, dear," Maria smiled, patting his arm. "I promise."

"You don't believe me, do you?"

"Of course I do," Maria smiled. "A dog made of chocolate. I'll ask everyone to be watching for him."

"It's a female," Roland almost sulked. "Her, not a him."

"I see," Maria said again, steering him to a table. "Wait right here while I get you some coffee and something to eat."

"I'm not a baby, you know," Roland told her, sitting down.

"I know, dear," Maria patted his shoulder, then headed for the kitchen proper. "I'll just be a minute."

Roland sat there, looking around him as others who were eating hastily went back to doing so.

"I'm telling you..."

~*~

James was on his feet when Melissa entered his room, followed by Doctor Kingston.

"What are you doing up?" she demanded, seeing James almost completely dressed.

"Uh, getting dressed," he replied.

"You should still be in bed!" the nurse insisted as she arrived at his side.

"I'm fine," James told her. "Too much to do for me to be laying around."

"Would you mind if I take a look at that leg first?" Kingston asked, smiling.

"Doc, I'm fine," James repeated. "Really."

"Please?" Melissa asked. He looked at her puppy eyes, and sighed.

"Fine," he grumped, and sat down on the bed.

"Pants off, youngster," Kingston demanded. Glowering, James stood up again, and pulled his pants off, sitting back down in a sulk.

Kingston looked at the wound, clucking on occasion as she did so. Finally, she stood back.

"Hurts plenty, I imagine," she told him.

"Some," James admitted. Reluctantly.

"Probably will for several days," she nodded. "But the wound looks like it's wanting to heal already. Stitches are holding, but I want you to take it easy, understand? That's some mighty fine knitting I did there, and I don't want it ruined."

"I can stand the radio watch," James nodded. "That'll free up someone who can do something I can't."

"I can agree to that," Jennifer nodded in reply. "I want you doing that at least three days. After that, if there's no seepage or swelling, then you can do what you can do. But James, when it starts hurting, sit down for a while. You'll have to ease your way back into fighting trim, understand?"

"I get it," James agreed.

"Okay, then, you can get dressed," the doctor agreed. James put his pants on once again, and then gathered the rest of his gear. He turned suddenly, looking at the two women.

"Hey, do you guys know if Jesse brought my dog with us?"

"What dog?"

~*~

"Dog?" Jesse frowned, then lightened. "Oh, yeah! The Lab! Yeah, she made the trip."

"Great!" James grinned ear to ear. "Where is she?"

"Uh. . .well, I don't. . .see I didn't. . .I mean that is. . .hell, I don't know," Jesse finally settled for saying. "I wasn't paying attention when we got here so I don't know where she got off to, but she came with us, I know that."

"Thanks, Jesse!" James smiled widely. "I'll just go see if I can find her."

We'll go see if we can find her," Melissa countered, her voice firm. "You'll be where I can keep an eye on you while you're healing."

"I can live with that," James gave her another grin, and Melissa blushed in spite of herself. The two set off, arm in arm, to search. Leaving Jennifer and Jesse alone.

"So how is your day going, Doctor?" Jesse asked. Jennifer looked at him, fighting off a smirk.

"My day is just fine, soldier boy," she replied smoothly. "How are you feeling? Still sore?"

"A little, maybe, but nothing like yesterday morning. A good stretch this morning helped a lot. I'm gonna go for a run here in a bit," he added, standing. "Work out the rest of the kinks that way."

"Running, huh?" Kingston's voice was non-committal. "Where do you run?"

"Track outside," Jesse nodded his head toward the back of the school. "Not a professional track, but it's comfortable to run on."

"I might just join you," the young doctor's silky voice told him. "It would be nice to have a relatively safe place to run, for once."

"Why not just stay here?" Jesse asked. "This place is reasonably safe and we could sure use you, especially when the kids come back. It would be nice to have a real doctor in the house, not to mention another adult."

"Well, you do work fast, don't you soldier boy," she teased, smiling brightly at him. "Known me all of two days and *already* asking me to move in. You do that to all the girls you meet?"

"Well, I ...er, that. . .no," Jesse managed to stammer an answer to her direct question.

"Take it easy," Kingston's laughter echoed in the room. "I'm just messing with you. Although, there are some good points to being in a place like this," she admitted. "But, I still have to make rounds, and help the sick and injured, at least as much as I can with what I have left to work with. Being here, so far out, might present a problem."

"With travel you mean?" Jesse asked, and she nodded.

"Nah, we can handle that," Jesse promised. "We should be able to set you up a route and provide an escort while you're making your rounds. Say once a week, barring an emergency?"

"That. . .that would work," it was Kingston's turn to look a little nonplussed. "Seriously, though, there's a lot of equipment and supplies I'd need to move, if I came out here. And where would I work, and live?" she asked.

"Well, here," Jesse waved his arms around. "There's plenty of room. If we keep growing we may have to double up some," he admitted. "But I'm sure Maria and Terri and Deena wouldn't mind sharing a room with you. All three of them seem to hit it off with you right away."

"And Angie would probably be overjoyed at having someone more qualified than her to handle the medical front. Plus, Miss Andrews looks like she's going to stay, and she's a nurse."

"A good one, too," Jennifer nodded her agreement. "Melissa works hard, and she's smart."

"As to your equipment and supplies, we can take a truck and go get everything you want to move. Set it up for you, here, to your specs. We've got power, and we'll try to get more UV stuff set up as well. The school's large enough, even with all the kids here, to probably let you have a small clinic room for patients. Maria would know that better than me, though," he admitted.

"Well, why don't I think about it while we run," Jennifer offered. Removing her lab coat, she revealed her own running clothes. Clothes that hugged her form very enticingly, and set Jesse's mouth to watering.

"Uh, yeah, that's sounds. . .I mean that's. . .sure, why not," Jesse finally managed.

"If you beat me, I'll move in with you, soldier boy," she batted her eyelashes at him. "Does that give you any incentive at all?"

"Lot of incentive," Jesse almost whispered.

"Then let's see this track of yours."

~*~

ROLAND

Roland was looking for the dog. He was tired of being treated like a simpleton. He knew there was a dog around here somewhere, and when he found it again he was going to make sure everyone saw her. Hence the rope he was carrying.

Roland had already scoured the building once, so he decided to go outside. He hadn't found any doggy waste anywhere in the building, so the dog had to have a way in and out of the building. If she wasn't inside, she had to be on the grounds.

Using the front door, Roland made a circuit of the school grounds. He passed the ball field, where he saw Jesse and the Doctor running on the track. Jesse seemed to be lagging behind the good doctor, who would occasionally turn to taunt the former soldier. From Jesse's reaction it was all in good fun, and Roland wondered if the two might have a thing for each other. Jesse was a good looking guy, and smart as a whip, while Kingston was about as shapely and attractive as any guy could ask for, *and* a Doctor.

He wished them both well. In this world, the way it was now, if two people could find happiness together, they needed to grab it with both hands and hang on.

Thinking that made him consider his relationship with Maria. He had mixed feelings still, expecting any moment for her to come to her senses and realize that he really wasn't much of a knight in shiny armor.

But, she should have already known that, really. He hadn't made any secret about that. And she had already seen him when he wasn't really trying to impress anyone. He thought back to when they had first met, and to their often contentious working relationship. It still surprised him that the two of them could even be friends, let alone that she could develop feelings for him.

And what about him? Roland considered that as he ambled along, no longer in any hurry. Did he return her feelings?

She was attractive, that was certain. A man could look far and wide and not find a more pretty woman. She was a hard worker, too, and had worked night and day to care for all the children. At times he had worried about her health as she seemed to always be awake and working.

She was also smart. Not just book smart, which she was to be sure. Maria had a head full of common sense, too. She seemed to be able to find a solution to any problem that cropped up, without resorting to some complicated, overly complex plan. She simply looked at the problem, and came up with a workable fix.

In these new times, that was worth a lot. He shook his head at that. Why was he trying to evaluate her? He wasn't hiring her for a job, for goodness sake. He was thinking about what his feelings for her might be.

Not so long ago, he hated her. Had actively hoped for the day when she would leave. He didn't want that *now*, of course. They had gotten along much better after settling into the school. And there was no point in denying that he was attracted to her. Maria was gorgeous. And she had a good heart. She had stayed to help with the children despite her inherent distrust and fear of Roland. That said a lot about her character, too.

Yes sir, a man could look a long time and not find a better woman than Maria. That being said then, why was he still thinking about it? Why not just go with it, and see what happened?

Yep, that's the thing to do, he decided. See where it goes, what happens. He started walking a bit faster at that, as if making that decision had made him pick up his pace.

He was just approaching Ralph's 'lab' when the teenager burst through the door, running as fast as his legs would carry him.

"Duck Mister Roland!"

~*~

"Ralph, what are you doing now?" Roland asked, as he and Ralph finally managed to get the fire out. It hadn't been too bad, to be honest. The explosion, though, that had been pretty spectacular. Fortunately, Ralph had used the same outbuilding where his bomb miscalculation had occurred, so the damage wasn't nearly as bad as it could have been.

"Well, I heard everybody talkin' 'bout how we ain't got much gas," Ralph replied, slapping a ragged towel at a last few embers. "And I got to thinkin' how maybe I could help with that, and I wondered if I had what I needed out here to make a still, and since we ain't gonna be drinkin' it, I didn't have to worry about usin' copper, or worryin' 'bout if there was impurities in it, and so I found an old water heater in the shed and decided that would work well enough to test things, and so..."

"Ralph!"

"Yes sir?"

"Short version!" Roland didn't quite snap.

"It blew up," Ralph said simply, shrugging. "Happens sometimes," he added philosophically.

"What happened to telling *...asking*, adults before you did any experimenting?"

"Uh, I thought that was just the bomb thing," Ralph answered. "And I wasn't so much experimentin', Mister Roland. I know how to make shine all right. Just. . .well, maybe that ole water heater wasn't the best alternative. But that's okay, 'cause I found..."

"No, no, no," Roland slapped his hands over his ears. "Don't tell me!"

"Uh, okay," Ralph replied. "Um, does that mean I can go ahead and..."

ROLAND

"I said don't tell me!" Roland repeated. "Please, *please* Ralph, don't.
. .blow yourself, or anyone else, up. Will you promise me that much?"

"Well, sure!" Ralph grinned. "No problem!"

"I'm going now," Roland said, shaking his head, walking back
toward the school building.

"Don't forget your rope, Mister Roland!"

~*~

"Well, I don't know where she is," James sighed. "Imagine
somewhere taking a nap."

"Well, you need to rest, too," Melissa scolded lightly. "It's time you
went to the radio room, wherever that is."

"This way," James motioned, and limped in that direction, Melissa at
his side.

"Say, Melissa," James said casually as they walked along.

"Yes?"

"I was wondering, and you don't have to answer if you don't want to,
but, well, I think you're awful pretty, and... well, there's no way around
here to have a real date, but, I was thinking we could do something
together, sometime."

"And just what did you have in mind?" she asked, eyebrows raised.
James looked at her, then slowly started to blush as her words sank in.

"I didn't mean it like that!" he objected. "I was just. . .well, I was
looking for a way to spend time with you, that's all," he shrugged. "Sorry.
I didn't mean to offend you like that."

"God, you're so easy," Melissa suddenly laughed. "And I'd love to
spend time with you, James. I'd like the opportunity to get to know you
better. Learn more about you."

"Really?" James looked surprised, but pleased.

"Really," Melissa nodded, and slipped her arm through his. "We can
start by you showing me this radio room, and explaining what goes on
there."

"I can do that."

~*~

"Maria's right," Roland said aloud as he walked through the back
door into the school. "I need a rest. I'm not getting enough sleep. That's
part of the problem. I need to just relax for a day or so, and then..." He
stopped.

Right there in front of him sat the dog. Looking at him steadily. Not
moving.

"Hello, girl," Roland said easily, and the dog wagged her tail.

"C'mere, girl," Roland said, holding his hand out. The dog got to her feet and walked over to him. He let her smell his hand, then slowly moved his hand up to scratch her head. She leaned into the contact, tail still wagging.

"Well, ain't you a friendly thing," Roland smiled. "Now, I'm gonna just loop this old rope around you so I can lead you into the-"

In the kitchen, only a short distance from where they stood, someone apparently dropped several pans, the clatter sounding almost as if the roof was falling in. Before Roland could react, the dog was gone.

"Wait!" he called, looking around. Nothing.

"Dammit," he muttered. "At least I know I'm not crazy." He walked along a little further, ignoring the spirited language coming from the kitchen. He decided he'd lie down a while. He'd feel better after a nice nap.

Yeah. That'd do it.

Just a nice little nap.

ROLAND

CHAPTER FORTY-FIVE

"Just so we're clear," Kingston said, "if you can't hold up your end of this bargain, tell me now. I can't just abandon everyone."

"We can, at least for now," Roland nodded. It was the next morning, and despite the fact that the pretty doctor had handily beat Jesse on the track, she had decided that the school was not only a safer place than town, but it would let her accomplish more than she could on her on.

Her requirements had been few, but non-negotiable. Once a week she would be taken into town to see the patients she had been caring for since the collapse. One room of the school would be set aside as a clinic 'ward' where patients could be housed that needed more acute care. No one would be refused medical aid if they came to the school seeking it.

Roland had balked at that one.

"We're not going to treat any of these scumbags that have been terrorizing the community," he told her flatly. "Anyone who is a known thief or predator will not be allowed on these grounds. Period. And that's final," he added, when Kingston started to reply.

"I was actually going to say I can live with that," Kingston shot back primly. "I'm a doctor, not a saint. I'm not going to waste precious medical supplies on vermin, Roland."

"Then we got a deal," Roland smiled. "I like your attitude, Jennifer. And I'm in your debt, anyway, after you patched up James."

"Nah," she grinned. "He's a good kid. I like him."

"He's a hell of a man," Roland nodded. "I wish we had ten more just like him."

"If wishes were nickels," she shrugged. "Oh, and I want Jesse to be the one who escorts me," she grinned.

"Oh?" Roland raised an eyebrow. "Anything I should know?"

"Not a thing," she laughed, heading out of the office. "I'll be ready in a few minutes." Roland chuckled, shaking his head as she left. Jesse was in for a time, if Roland was any judge. It seemed like the good doctor had set her cap for his friend and she didn't strike him as someone who did anything by halves.

"Jesse, come to the office," he called over the radio. "Vaughan, you too." Both replied affirmative, and two minutes later were standing in front of him.

"You're taking the doctor into town to get her gear," he informed them. "Round up two, maybe three guys to help you. You'll need one of the trucks I guess, and you may want to take the Hummer. I'll leave that up to you."

"Jesse, I want you to take Ralph with you," he continued. "He's a mechanical genius, but he needs stuff to work with. Let him see what's available, and we'll see what kind of a deal we can work out with whoever has it. He really needs some tools, though, for one thing."

"Got it," Jesse nodded. "You know, maybe you should talk to Tom. Mackey, I mean. He may know where there's a lot of stuff we can use just laying around. Either abandoned, or else the owners are passed on. No need to barter for what we can get for just labor."

"Good idea," Roland nodded. "Ask him to come in here on your way out. Leave Ralph here this trip, I guess. Just take a look around at what's available. And you guys be careful, all right?"

"You got it, boss." The two came to attention and saluted, resulting in Roland chasing them from the office, spitting a stream of expletives in their wake.

ROLAND

~*~

"So, I saw you and Roland at breakfast," Deena said slyly. She and Terri were side by side, as usual, and had 'cornered' Maria in the storeroom where she was doing an inventory.

"Yes, you did," Maria nodded, a faint blush coloring her cheeks.

"Well, give!" Terri demanded.

"Give what?" Maria asked.

"Oh, don't hand us that!" Deena chided. "You know what we mean!"

"Has he kissed you yet?" Terri asked, a goofy grin on her face.

"That is none of your business!" Maria replied, turning away to hide her blush.

"Then he hasn't," Deena giggled. "Why not?"

"You would have to ask him," Maria replied without thinking. Truthfully, she had been wondering the same thing.

"Well, that's out," Terri sighed. "I can see why you've got the hots for him. He is *totally* dreamy." The goofy look got worse, if that were possible.

"I do not have any hots..." Maria started to fire back, but Deena cut her off.

"Oh, bull-oney," the teen waved Maria's protest away. "You started looking at him funny at least three weeks ago. And that's just when I noticed. For all we know, you've been gaga over him from the start, girlfriend!"

Maria sighed, shaking her head.

"You know that isn't true," she said calmly, sitting down on a nearby box. "At first, I really thought I hated him. I may have, even."

"Really?" both girls spoke in unison as they joined her on boxes of their own.

"What changed?" Terri asked.

"I don't really know," Maria admitted. "And that's the truth," she added when Deena started to object. "I *don't* know. I. . .I think it was seeing him so tired and disheveled when he got back from. . .attacking those people. I think then I realized how worried I had been. . .no, that's not true. I was worried the entire time, for both he and James."

"But. . .for some reason, that worry hit home when I realized how truly dangerous those days had been. We. . .*I*, might have lost him. And that made me think about it, I suppose."

"Wow," both said softly. "That's sooo dreamy," Terri added.

"We have spoken of it," Maria admitted. "He knows how I feel, or at least how I think I feel," she qualified. "And he thinks I'm pretty," she said in a softer tone.

"Well, you are!" both replied together.

263

"Girl, with your figure, and that black hair framing your pretty face like that, you're a doll!" Deena giggled. "I'm surprised he hasn't already tried to sweep you off your feet!" Maria blushed furiously.

"I told you, it's somewhat complicated," she pointed out. "We spent the first several weeks literally hating one another. That's not easy to get over. I said some rather mean things to him, too."

"Really?" Again, in unison.

"Yes, really," Maria nodded. "I was. . .afraid of him," she admitted. She briefly explained what had happened to her family, and what had transpired when Roland had taken her home. Both girls were goggle eyed.

"He killed them because they threatened you?" Terri gasped. "My God that's so - "

"If you say dreamy one more time, I'm coating your next cupcake with Ex-Lax," Deena warned. Terri *hmphed*, but didn't add the word.

"I have to admit though," Deena went on, "that is pretty awesome. To think that he was thinking of you, and what those guys might do to you. What I wouldn't give to have a man that thought of me like that," she sighed.

"He protects you too," Maria objected.

"He protects us all," Terri nodded. "But. . .Maria, that's just. . .I mean, to have someone who is willing and able to do that when you're in danger. It makes my knees weak just thinking about it," the teenager admitted, longingly.

"It's like something out of a romance novel," Deena nodded her agreement. "And Roland is all man, girlfriend. I'm happy for you, sister!" she beamed, and before Maria realized what was happening, Deena had embraced her tightly. Terri joined in a second later. The two pulled back, tears glistening in both pairs of eyes.

"Why are you crying?" Maria asked, though her own eyes were damp.

"We're happy!" both replied at once. "Don't you see?" Deena added. "This. . .this is normal! Life should be like this, not what we've gone through lately! And, hey! If things are getting back to normal, then we might just find someone too!"

"Yeah," Terri nodded. "James is off the market of course, but - "

"What?" Maria asked, confused.

"Oh, honey, where have you. . .never mind," Deena said with an impish grin. "Forgot you've been busy. That Melissa? The nurse that came in with the freed prisoners the other day? She's got it *bad* for James. And if I'm any judge, he's the same way with her. I'm fairly certain that boy is hooked, and good."

ROLAND

For the next little while, the three sat talking about normal things. Normal teenage girl things.

And for that little while, life was good.

Normal, even.

~*~

"Well," Tom Mackey scratched his jaw, "I'm sure there's a right smart o' stuff just layin' around. I hate to think about what happened to some of the folks that used to own it."

"Does it bother you to think about us using it?" Roland asked.

"Nah, not especially," Tom shrugged a bit. "I mean, if we need it, and the folks that owned it ain't about to use it no more, makes sense to get some use of it, I'd think."

"Good," Roland sighed. "I wasn't sure how you'd feel, and I didn't want to ask you to do something you were uncomfortable with."

"After all you two have done for us, I can't honestly think of a thing I wouldn't help you do," Tom admitted. "Things have changed, and we gotta change with 'em."

"I can't help but wonder how they got you," Roland shook his head. "You're just too smart an old fox for that bunch." Mackey chuckled.

"Caught me unawares," he admitted. "I was workin' on something, and 'fore I knowed it, I was surrounded. Wasn't no point in fightin'. Always a chance so long as you're alive, so I went along and waited."

"Nice play," Roland admitted. "And that ain't the first time I've heard that," he observed.

"Probably won't be the last, either," Tom shrugged, ignoring Roland's almost question. Roland didn't press him.

"Well, what should we do first, Tom?" he asked instead.

"First thing, I guess," Mackey sighed, "is to take one o' these trucks and head over to my place."

~*~

Tom guided Roland, Ralph, James Edwards, Gavin Douglas, two of the young men who had stayed behind when so many others left, and Rich Williams, the older man who, along with his wife, had also refused to abandon the school, to his home place. Terri and Deena also came along, glad for the opportunity to be out of the school for a little while.

"Looks like that bunch would have taken anything usable when they got you, Tom," Roland said, as they drove into the yard. Mack and Angie had stayed behind to provide security for the school. Everyone on the trip was armed, including the teens.

"Would have if the dumb sons o' bitches had known where to look," the older man smirked. "Fortunately, they're pretty much a bunch of idiots."

"One or two of 'em seemed to have some sense," Roland remarked, thinking back to his pursuit.

"Oh, the leader, he's pretty smart," Tom warned. "And one of his chief lieutenants is almost as smart. But by and large the rest are cannon fodder. A few men looked like they knew what they were doing, but the rest are just common biker trash for the most part. Course, a bullet from their gun'l kill you just as dead as a professional soldier's will."

Roland nodded. He'd heard that expression before, too. There was a lot more to Tom Mackey than the older man was willing to reveal. He wondered how much Mack knew about his Uncle.

"Roll on up to the barn," Tom ordered. "They did ransack the house. I'll go in 'fore we leave and see what they left me, but what we really want is out here."

Roland did as ordered, and Harrison followed in the bus. Tom had wanted to have plenty of room, but that was all he would say. Roland backed the truck into the barn door and stopped. Everyone got out, looking around for any sign of trouble.

"C'mon," Tom motioned, going inside. They followed him inside where Ralph was immediately distracted by the selection of tools.

"Holy Moley!" he breathed. "You got ever'thing, Mister Tom!"

"Well, not everything," Tom chuckled, "but there is a right bit. We'll have you outfitted 'fore we leave," he promised. "Roland, a little help, if you will." He pointed to one of the barn stalls, and tossed Roland a pitchfork. "This hay has to go."

It was the work of only a couple minutes to clear the hay away, revealing a door in the floor of the barn.

"Huh," Roland grunted.

"Fallout shelter," Tom told him. "Hoped I'd never need it, but prepare for the worst, I always

say." He reached down, felt his way to a hidden lever, and pulled. The door hissed open smoothly on hydraulics, rising to stand at a ninety-degree angle.

"Neat!" Ralph exclaimed.

"Cool," Terri and Deena said in unison.

"That it is," Roland agreed. The others nodded their own agreements.

"Well, I figured I might need to get in here hurt or sick, so this was what I came up with," Tom replied. Another switch turned a light on, revealing stairs leading down.

ROLAND

"Well, let's see what we got here," Tom said, heading down the stairs. Roland followed, along with Ralph, the other two staying put to keep watch.

At the foot of the stairs, Tom hit a series of switches, and lights began coming on. Revealing shelves and shelves of. . .everything.

"Wow," was all Roland could think of to say.

"Took years of doing," Tom admitted. "Had a larger family, then," he added wistfully. "Wanted to be prepared, you know. Be able to care for 'em, no matter what happened."

"What did happen?" Roland asked softly.

"Car wreck," Tom said simply. "Wife, son, daughter, all gone in a blink. Truck driver high on speed or such like. Doubt they felt a thing."

"Tom, I'm so sorry," Roland said softly.

"Been a while back," Tom shrugged. "Ain't no help for it now, I reckon."

"Looks like you stocked for them pretty well," Roland told him. "Shows a lot of love." Tom looked at him gratefully.

"Thank you," he nodded. "Anyway," he sniffed, the moment gone, "ain't no sense in it just sittin' here, unused. I spent a lotta money on this stuff, proceeds o' more than one good harvest the Lord blessed me with. Reckon we can make good use of it now, though."

"Tom, why didn't. . .I mean, I'm grateful," Roland said, "but I can't understand why..."

"Why I didn't just come down here and sit things out?" Tom asked, smiling.

"Well, yeah," Roland nodded.

"For what?" Tom shrugged. "This ain't no way to live. And you're doin' a good thing, Roland Stang. A good thing. Reminds me. . .well, that's no never mind," he waved the comment away. "Thing is, you boys helped me. And I want to help you in return. And, truth be told, I think I can help you with more than just this stuff, but like I said. I spent a lotta time and money doing this. Might as well get some use out of it."

"Thank you, Tom," Roland said sincerely.

"Well, let's get to work," Tom declared. "Lots to get done, and we're wastin' daylight. Last thing we'll do is pull the gennie and the tanks that feed it."

"Propane?" Roland asked. Tom nodded.

"Yep. Ten thousand gallons or so, give or take."

"Good gravy," Roland shook his head.

"Let's get started," Tom repeated. "There's a lot to see."

~*~

There was indeed a lot to see. Tom had provisioned his shelter well. Roland couldn't help but be impressed by it.

Shelf after shelf of freeze dried foods, enough to feed his family and six more for five years. A dozen barrels each of rice, wheat, corn, and beans, grown on his own farm and stored against ruin in food grade barrels. Boxes of medical supplies, some of them far above mere first aid.

"Wife was a nurse," Tom shrugged when Roland asked about it.

Clothing, paper goods, feminine supplies, which made both teen girls squeal, radiation detectors, you name it, Tom had stocked it. Roland had never seen, nor heard, of a better set-up than Tom Mackey had built under his barn.

"Did it myself," Tom said during a break, when Roland asked him how he'd built the place. "Took a little bobcat and started digging. Widened it out, placed some supports, and then started pouring concrete. After that it was just finishing work. Getting the concrete in place overhead, and that door, was harder'n anything else. Well, aside from gettin' all that stuff down there in the first place," he chuckled.

Tom left some things behind, as a last resort kind of deal for whoever might need it. After everything else was loaded, Tom sent everyone out except Roland, who he led to a wall in back of the shelter.

"This here, this is. . .well, just have a look," he settled for saying. Pressing a lever that Roland couldn't see, a spot on the wall popped open, revealing a keypad. Tom punched in a series of numbers, and the wall slid open.

Revealing a small armory.

"There's a half dozen AK's in here," he told Roland. "They're full auto, too. Got 'bout ten thousand rounds for 'em, and plenty o' mags. Got a couple .308 rifles set up for long distance work, and a few Czech made hand guns. There's four 870's too, with about a thousand rounds o' slug and buckshot, and maybe three hundred game loads. Finally, there's three Ruger .22 rifles, one of 'em a bolt action, the other two autos, and a couple Browning Buckmark pistols. I don't even know how many rounds of .22 there are," he admitted. "There for a while, I bought a brick ever time I went to town."

"Figured I had all this, better have a way to defend it," he shrugged at the look on Roland's face.

"You want to take all this with us?" Roland asked.

"Figured to leave one AK, one pistol, and one shotgun, with ammo," Tom replied. "The rest, well, I figure we need it more at the school than sittin' here drawing dust." That had to be a figure of speech, Roland decided, since there wasn't a speck of dust anywhere.

ROLAND

"Let's slide what's goin' out, and then I'll close'er up," Tom ordered. "You and the rest of them strong young backs can load this while I see what's left in my house."

"Sounds like a plan," Roland agreed, and got to work.

~*~

By the time the last of Tom's 'armory' was loaded, he had finished looking through his home. He carried a duffle bag, along with a backpack and a suitcase. He placed the duffle and the suitcase into the shelter, and closed the door. He and Roland spent a few minutes hiding the shelter once more, and then he took one last look around.

"Reckon Ralph'll be some pleased," he said dryly, looking at his now empty tool area.

"That boy is a danger to public safety," Roland shook his head. "But I've yet to see anything he can't do. If we had another six like him I'd fear for the future, but I'd sure be glad to have them."

"He's a good kid," Tom agreed. "Seems smart as a whip, too, for his age."

"He had a very interesting grandfather, apparently," Roland said. "I'm not sure I really want to know what all he taught Ralph."

"Well, you're makin' good use of whatever he did teach him," Tom observed. "And that means the old man's work was worth it."

"Amen," Roland nodded.

"Well, seems we don't have anything left to load," Tom sighed. "Have to come back some time for the gennies, and the propane."

"Good place to leave them until we need them," Roland nodded. "Are you ready to go?"

"Yeah," Tom sighed again. "Ain't no reason to stay, and plenty to go. Let's head back."

Tom was fairly quiet on the ride back, and Roland didn't intrude on the silence. A large part of Tom's life was gone, and now he was using this last connection to those days to help others. Roland figured that was deserving of all the respect he could give the other man.

CHAPTER FORTY-SIX

Roland had called a meeting of everyone still at the school. Some of the people they had rescued had departed with family members who were notified through a complex system of radios, visits, and word of mouth. Thankfully, Shirley Pippins had been one of those, although Roland was sure he detected some reluctance on the part of her niece to accept the habitually complaining Pippins. He knew for a fact that no one at the school was sorry to see her go. Tom, Melissa, Susan, another woman from the group named Marie Hilliard, and the two girls, who turned out to be thirteen-year-old fraternal twins name Mindy and Mandy Barnes, had remained. Melissa stayed for reasons of her own, the others because they lacked anywhere else to go.

He looked the group over. Vaughan, Mack, and Angie were on guard, with Angie manning the radio room. Everyone else was here.

"You all know the score," he said simply. "We'll be attacked sooner or later. There's no real way around that. You new people are concerned about that, and you should be, but we are prepared for them."

"You've seen all the defensive positions, building reinforcements, and weapons here. There are five trained soldiers in this group and several others who are more than able to take a hand in defending this place."

"From now on, no one goes outside alone. I know that's going to cramp our style," Roland raised his hands defensively to mute the objections already forming, "but it's for our own safety. Starting today, we'll be running security around the clock. We've always had someone on watch, but now we'll start keeping a full watch on."

"What I need to know is, how many of you new folks have ever fired a weapon, and are willing to help defend this place?"

All three of the men from Nashville raised their hands, as did Fiona Richards, the older of the two women who had stayed. The Williams' both added theirs their hands as well. Melissa raised her hand, of course, but Roland shook his head.

"Sorry, Melissa," he said kindly. "You're the only nurse we have and that's where you'll have to serve. We'll have wounded to treat if it comes to a real battle." That sobered everyone, but no one changed their minds.

Susan Powers' hand was up, and Roland nodded to her. In the last two days the young woman had been working every waking moment to learn all she could about her new weaponry. She could field strip her AK and her pistol, and reassemble them in minutes. Not, perhaps, like a soldier could, but for someone who had shot for the first time just two days ago, it was nothing short of amazing.

"The rest of you need to learn to use at least a pistol for self-defense," he said. "Even you two," he told the twins, who nodded silently. "There's plenty of work for those who can't really aid in our defense. In a protracted battle, people will need ammo, food, and water brought to them. Wounded will need to be moved to the clinic area. Things like that. Everyone who can't fight can still help, so don't think you're useless or dead weight. Everyone counts here."

"Thanks to Tom, we've got some .22 rifles and pistols and plenty of ammo for training and practice. Trooper Vaughan will set up a training schedule later this morning and we'll work in two's and three's until everyone is up to speed as much as possible."

"We've made pretty much all the preparations we can, but I want everyone to be thinking as they walk through the school, what else can we do, okay? There's no bad idea. If you think of it, speak up. It might be something really important that we've overlooked. Even if we don't use the idea, don't stop giving them."

"Okay, I know everyone has work to do so go ahead. Remember that Vaughan will be assigning some of you to guard teams for the new watches. Don't forget about them, please."

People started filing out, until only Maria, James and Melissa remained.

"Roland, how bad will this be?" Maria asked.

"I expect it to be very bad," Roland didn't lie. "They'll have blood in their eye and hate in their hearts. We've killed a bunch of them already, and they won't forget that."

"I will go and look around the school," Maria nodded, and departed. James stood.

"Well, I can't stand the watch, but I can man the radio room. And I'll be good for the watch in a few days," he promised.

"When you can," was all Roland said. "One of the problems is we don't know when they'll hit. They could just wait and watch for a while, let us get tired of waiting, get careless, and then hit us when we think the problem's over."

"The one's I've. . .met," Melissa frowned, "aren't that patient."

"I've got a feeling their boss man is," Roland shook his head.

"And he's smart," James put in. "He'll come all right, and he'll think he's got an advantage of some kind when he does. He'll hit us when he thinks it's best for him."

"Right," Roland nodded firmly, pleased with James' insight. "Our job is to not let that happen."

"We'll do it," James nodded, determined. "Anyway, I need to go relieve Angie."

"I'll go with you," Melissa said, then blushed slightly. "He's teaching me to -"

"I'm sure he is," Roland remarked dryly. Melissa looked surprised for a moment, then laughed.

"Well, he is," she told him, still laughing. "I can help with that, if nothing else."

Roland couldn't help but smile as the pair, dare he say couple? walked out of the room. He followed seconds later. He too had things to do.

~*~

"Ralph, are you sure this is going to work?" Roland asked for at least the tenth time.

"Yes, sir!" Ralph beamed at him. "I *gur-uhn-tee it, or your money back!*"

"That is not comforting," Roland murmured. "How does this. . .thing, work again?"

Ralph had 'salvaged' the school's switchboard to use as a control panel to trigger his mines. As Roland looked at the Frankenstein board, with switches and relays, and who knew what else Ralph, wired into it. He tried, and failed, to suppress a shudder.

"Well, I thought 'bout how I was gonna be able to set 'em off one atta time, 'stead o' all at once," Ralph replied, still working. "See, they only need a teensy bit o' spark to fire the magnesium, which'll light up and set off the ANFO, and then go boom, and I figured a battery would gimme enough spark to do that, only we ain't got all that many batteries, and I don't want a bad battery to keep one from cookin' off, but then I remembered them ol' cars had batteries, and so I charged one o' them up with a water wheel and a alternator off one o' the cars. . .did you know there was a spring in that little lake outback? oh you did. Well, anyway..."

ROLAND

"Ralph," Roland sighed, rubbing his temples.

"Yes, sir?" the boy looked up.

"Short version," Roland ordered patiently.

"Battery powers the switch board, and the switchboard sparks the magnesium," Ralph replied.

"I assume you have a way to test this?" Roland asked, not quite fearfully.

"Yep!" Ralph nodded firmly. "Take a look outside."

"I don't want to," Roland tried not to whine. "What will I see?"

"Just lights," Ralph waved the question aside. "Ain't none o' the mines hooked up yet." Roland took faith in that, and looked out the window where he was horrified to see Terri, Deena, and the Barnes twins holding lamps at different places in the yard.

"Ralph, are you sure, I mean absolutely, one hundred percent, no possibility of a mistake *sure*, that none of those explosives are wired?" he asked.

"Yes, sir," Ralph nodded. "Nothing even wired inyet except the lamps. Promise. Cross my heart, even." He made the appropriate gesture.

"All right," Roland nodded, reluctantly. "Go ahead." Ralph hit a switch.

"That should be Deena," he said. Roland looked, and sure enough...

"My lamp's on Ralph!" Deena shouted. "You did it!"

"Terri," Ralph threw the other switches, "Mindy, and... Mandy," he finished. All the girls shouted in the proper order as Roland watched the bulbs light up.

"Okay girls, that's fine!" Roland called. They gathered up their lamps and went inside.

"I don't aim to wire up any o' the bombs unless we get attacked," Ralph told him. "Reckon that's okay?"

"Oh, I think that's a fine idea, Ralph. I *really* do."

~*~

"Roland?"

Roland looked up at the sound of Maria's voice. He was in his small room resting while he looked over a map.

"Can we talk for a minute?" she asked hesitantly.

"Sure," Roland agreed at once. "You want to come in, or go somewhere else?" he asked, putting the map aside.

"Here is fine," Maria nodded. Walking inside she sat down beside him.

"Are you. . .I mean, I need to know. . .what I'm trying to say is..." she trailed off, frustrated.

"Do I return your feelings?" Roland asked gently. Maria nodded, refusing to look at him.

"Well, that's a good question," Roland sighed. "The truth is I want to, but I'm a little afraid to." Maria's head shot up at that.

"Afraid to? Why?" she demanded.

"Well, that's a little complicated," he admitted. "See, I got some problems, Maria. I was getting help for 'em before all this happened, but now. . .well, there's no more help, and the medicine they were treating me with. . .it's pretty much gone, I imagine."

"Are you sick?" Maria asked worriedly. "If you are then perhaps Jennifer..."

"I'm not sick, exactly," Roland cut her off gently. "I'm just a little, well, different from most people."

"I do not need you to tell me that," Maria said softly, a ghost of a smile appearing on her face.

"Well, that's sweet, but not what I meant," Roland chuckled. "Maria, I have a… let's call it a chemical problem," he tried.

"You're an addict?" Maria looked shocked.

"No, I'm not an addict!" Roland snorted. This wasn't working out. Might as well out with it.

"Look, Maria, there are certain chemicals in the brain that, when they work correctly, they moderate behavior. Only my brain, the. . .the chemicals don't work right. They're outta whack, and that makes me a bit. . .well, unpredictable was the nicest way anyone ever put it," he finished lamely.

"So you're crazy," Maria said, her voice flat.

"No, I'm not!" Roland replied defensively. "I'm just. . .well, hell, you've seen me. I'm a very violent man, Maria. *Extremely* violent. You've seen it yourself, like I said. The meds helped me regulate that, and the shrink helped me deal with things better, but I don't have those anymore. And, so, I'm back to what I mostly was before," he admitted.

"And what was that?" Maria asked calmly.

"I'm a killer," he said flatly.

"I already knew that, as you said," Maria replied, her head high.

"And that don't. . .it don't make you stop to. . .that don't give you pause?"

"It does not," her answer was firm and final.

"Well, it should," Roland told her.

"Why? Because you might one day hurt me?"

"I'd never hurt you!" Roland was horrified at the thought of anyone, let alone himself, harming one lustrous hair on...

And that was when it hit him.

ROLAND

Yes, he really *did* return her feelings. Without thinking, he leaned into her and kissed her soundly on the mouth. Shocked, Maria struggled for an instant, then suddenly wrapped her arms around his neck and responded in kind. Eventually they were forced to come up for air.

"Jesse's Gran told me I'd meet you," Roland breathed. "Only. . .I already had, and didn't know it."

"You're a very good kisser," Maria smiled.

"You aren't so bad either," Roland smiled back.

"May I assume, now, that things are no longer. . .complicated?" Maria asked, looking into his eyes. Her own were deep pools of black; mesmerizing.

"Uh. . .no, I think we've uncomplicated things just, um, just fine," he managed to stammer, unable to tear his eyes away from her's.

"Excellent," she replied. "Then you may kiss me some more."

~*~

"Well?" BD asked, as Manny walked up.

"They're in place," Manny nodded. "Why don't we just hit them now, Boss? Why wait and watch like this? There aren't that many of..." He trailed off as BD raised his hand.

"I know that," he said evenly. "But they pulled a real number on us, Manny. Twenty-nine men dead, six more crippled, and eight still recovering. These aren't amateurs. Whoever this is, at least whoever is in charge, is a professional. That means he's waiting for us to just rush in wild."

"He used Claymore mines against us on our own road," BD continued. "They had to have watched us for days before they acted, and we still haven't found from where. They're that good."

"That means we have to be careful. We have to hit them hard, and final, but we have to do it *smart*. We can't afford to let someone stand up to us like this. Word will get around. People talk, and then the next thing you know, we go in somewhere for our fees and we're met with people with guns. That's not good for business."

"There's no one in any of our towns that can threaten us, Boss," Manny didn't quite scoff. "We can wipe 'em all out, we wanted to."

"And then who does the work?" BD asked calmly. "Who provides us with food, fuel, whatever else we want? Do you want to farm, Manny? Raise your own food?"

"No," Manny snorted. "No, Boss, I don't. Okay, I get it," he nodded. "I hadn't thought all that through. Sorry."

"No need," BD assured him. "I understand how this looks. That's why when we do this place, we do it right, and leave a smoking, smoldering ruin of it *and* the people inside." He stood suddenly.

"As an abject lesson to anyone else who thinks it's a good idea to stand up to our. . .business dealings. Understand, now?"

"Yes, Boss," Manny nodded. "I do."

"Good," BD nodded. "You're my right hand, Manny. I want, I *need*, for you to understand. I need to be able to count on you to make decisions in my absence. To do that, you have to know how I'm thinking."

"And I'm thinking about the long haul, Manny," BD smiled. "I'm thinking about what things will be like in a year. Five years. Twenty years."

"Most of the guys don't think past their next drink, or their next broad," Manny admitted. "I try to think ahead, but I admit I hadn't thought that far ahead."

"That's all right," BD assured him. "But now it's time you do. We're building a future for ourselves, Manny. One where we're kings." His look turned grim.

"And once in a while, the King has to remind the peasants of their place."

ROLAND

CHAPTER FORTY-SEVEN

Two days after Roland's talk with the assembled school occupants, they received visitors. Very unexpected visitors in the form of Derrick Turnbow, his wife Rose, and another couple.

They arrived in Turnbow's truck, pulling slowly into the front parking lot under the watchful eyes of James Golden. This was his first day back on his feet, so to speak, and he was standing the watch from a chair in the shade offered by the overhang at the school's front door. Not only did that keep the sun off him and out of his eyes, it also made it harder to spot him.

As the pickup pulled in, he radioed Roland and stood, leaning against the wall but still in the shadows. He watched as Turnbow cautiously stepped out of his truck and walked forward. Before he reached the door Roland was there.

"Mister Turnbow," he said evenly. "What brings you our way today?"

"Roland," Turnbow nodded. "Reckon I came to eat some crow, young man," the old preacher replied honestly. "I thought we could visit a while, talk, and try to mend our fences so to speak. If that's agreeable, of course."

Roland looked at the man for a moment. Jenkins had told him of Turnbow's apparent change of heart concerning Roland and his charges, but Roland was the kind of man who liked to make up his own mind about things. The fact that Turnbow had shown up offering to make peace said a lot. Maybe.

"Sounds good to me," he replied. "Ya'll come on inside," he waved. He nodded to James and opened the door, waiting for the group to enter. He followed, and led them to the office.

"Looks like you've made a lot o' changes," Turnbow offered, looking around.

"Trying to get more comfortable," Roland nodded, non-committal.

"Or get ready for an attack?" the other man asked from where he and his wife, Roland presumed, were following.

"If needed," Roland settled for saying.

"This is John Haggard and his wife Flora. And this is my wife, Rose," Turnbow offered introductions.

"Sir, Ladies," Roland nodded. He allowed them to precede him into the office. "Take a seat, and be comfortable," he offered. "Can I offer you some water?"

"No, no, we're fine, thanks," Turnbow shook his head. "Might as well get right to it, I suppose, and offer you an apology, Roland," Turnbow continued. "A sincere one I hope you can accept. I.. in my defense, I really did think you might be gypsies, or something similar. That doesn't make how I treated you right, but I hope it explains my actions."

"Wilson mentioned that to me," Roland nodded. "I didn't even know such things still existed, let alone here in America, but he set me straight about that, too. I can understand your concerns. And yes, your apology is accepted."

There was no reason not to accept it, and Wilson had told him more than once that while Turnbow was cantankerous, and often argumentative, he was, at the base of it, a good man and a good neighbor.

"I appreciate that," Turnbow nodded. "Tom told me that there's a group of ruffians about that plan on placing us under their heel at some point, and that you had already struck out at them."

"Yes, sir," Roland nodded. "I'm afraid that's all true. A rather large and well organized group, probably built around a motorcycle gang from before the collapse. They're pretty well armed, too, I hate to add."

"I assumed as much," Turnbow nodded heavily. "That Jenkins, he and his men spent most of a day helping us fix up some defenses of our own. We decided to fortify our church building as a fall back. There's a full basement there, completely protected, and we've stocked a good bit of food and water there, along with medicines, bedding and the like."

"Sounds like a good plan," Roland nodded. "I'm not familiar with your church building, but it sounds like the right place the way you describe it."

"We hope so," Turnbow nodded. "We've placed our faith in it, and each other, and made what preparations we know to make. That's about all we can do under the circumstances."

"We're trying to set up a radio as well," he went on. "We have a tower at the church, one we used to use to broadcast our Sunday sermons with, so we can get an antenna up a little ways. Could use some advice on what else to do, though," he added hopefully.

"What kind of advice?" Roland asked.

"Well, it would be. . .I mean if you can, of course, it would be a blessing if you, or someone you trust, could come and look our situation over. Tell us what you think. We've decided to use the church bell as a warning system, and we keep someone in the bell tower with binoculars all the time now on watch. Well, during the day anyway. There's not much point in it at night, although we do keep someone up and awake at the church to sound the alarm if they hear anything not normal."

"That sounds reasonable," Roland mused. "How well are you people armed?" he asked.

"Well, we've all got a deer rifle or a shotgun, pretty much, and there's several handguns. Thing is, most ever' body only has one, or maybe two boxes of shells for 'em. One fella has an old Garand he uses to deer hunt, but he's only got the one clip for it. It's a mixed bag, to be sure. Ever'one who has more than one firearm has placed at least one, along with its ammunition, at the church." He shrugged. "It's not much, but it's the best we can do with what we have."

"Well, it sounds like you're doing pretty good at that," Roland allowed. And they were, he figured. They just didn't have much.

"One boy has one of those little Ruger ranch rifles," Haggard put in. "He's got a couple of those big clips for it, but not enough shells to fill both of 'em."

"Good rifle," Roland nodded. "Feed just about any kind of ammo you can find for it, too."

"If we had a dozen, and the ammunition to go with them, I'd agree," Haggard replied. "Still, one is better than nothing I suppose," he added with a helpless shrug.

"Well, I don't have anything that will help you there," Roland shook his head. "We don't have any rifles like that, and I sure don't have any en bloc clips for a Garand. They're nice rifles, though, if a bit heavy." He leaned back for a moment, considering. He had a few rifles he could lend, and maybe a pistol or two, but would anyone there know how to use them?

"I tell you what," he said finally. "I'll take a run up there and see what you've got, and maybe I can scare up some stuff to help you with too, I don't know." He looked at his watch, seeing that it was just after ten.

"Why don't I try to get up there after lunchtime? Say about one, ish?"

"Today?" Turnbow asked, eyebrows raised.

"Sooner the better," Roland nodded. "We may have plenty of time, and they might hit us before the days out. Need to make hay while the sun's out."

"We'd really appreciate that, Roland," Turnbow said earnestly. "And it's more than we can rightfully ask after the way things got started between us."

"I won't worry about that if you don't," Roland told him. "I understand your concerns, at least *now* I do. And I don't blame you for worrying about your people. Both of us were suspicious of the other, and with good reason considering our situation. If you're willing to let by gones be, then so am I. We all need to be working together, and not just because of this threat."

"When that bunch is taken care of there'll be plenty of work to do. We can all help each other, one way or another. For instance, we don't have a single soul that I know of who knows how to preserve food."

"Why, we could help with that!" Rose Turnbow spoke for the first time, looking at Flora Haggard who nodded at once in agreement.

"See what I mean?" Roland smiled. "There's probably a lot more areas we can help each other out in, if we sit down and work on it. I'll get a couple of my people, you get a couple of yours, they can make notes, and then sit down to work on the details. But that's for after we deal with what's in front of us," he concluded, standing. "I don't want to get the cart 'fore the horse."

"Good idea," Haggard nodded. "I like it."

"Well, then how 'bout I see you after lunch, then?" Roland extended his hand.

"We'll be waiting for you," Turnbow promised, taking the hand.

~*~

"You're not really goin', are ya?" Jesse demanded. "After that bunch -"

"Water under the bridge, Jess," Roland cut him off. "We need friends. So do they. We need *their* help, too, you know. It's not a one-way street."

"Well," Jesse considered that. "Still, I don't want you going alone," he demanded.

"I won't be," Roland smiled. "I'm taking Maria, and I think I'll see if James and Melissa want to ride along. And maybe Susan Powers, too," he added.

"Why her?" Jesse asked.

"Well, a couple reasons," Roland replied. "One, she needs to get out of her comfort zone. Learning to shoot is helping her, but she's got to snap out of that shell she's in. This might help. Second, she's already learned enough to be helpful defending this place. I want that bunch up there to see that. That you don't have to be a soldier to be able to fight for your home, and your family."

"You know," Jesse nodded after a minute, "that makes good sense. I hadn't thought about it like that. It's pretty much the same thing we did."

ROLAND

"Right," Roland nodded his agreement. "I figure we can spare three rifles, with the mags and ammo. You agree?"

"Yeah," Jesse nodded. "I'd take a couple of those AK's too, if Tom's okay with it. They're pretty good rifles, and he's got plenty of ammo for'em. And they're simpler to use than an AR or M-4, too."

"Point," Roland agreed. "I'll talk to him."

"Talk to who?" Tom walked up just then. Roland briefly explained what he had in mind, and Tom nodded at once.

"Absolutely. I'll gather'em up a care package right now," he added, and headed off to do just that.

"I think I'll take Ralph, too," Roland decided. "Let him take a look at what they have to work with. He might be able to make a difference for them."

"All of you won't fit in that Hummer," Jesse told him.

"Well, we've got that truck," Roland considered. They had a pickup truck that had been left with the keys inside that had been put into use around the school. A four door Ford 150, it would hold at least five people.

"We'll take it and the Hummer," Roland decided. "And, I'll take. . .Gavin with me, too, since James is still limping." Gavin Douglas was the man who'd stood up in the first meeting, refusing to consider leaving when the threat of an attack had been exposed. He was a fair shot and had a cool head about him.

"You know, it might be a good idea to bring whoever's gonna get the rifles down here for a day or two for some training," Jesse pointed out. "Turning loose a buncha untrained folks with that kinda firepower might not be the best idea ever."

"You know, that's not a bad idea," Roland nodded thoughtfully. "Maybe we should do that, and then let them take the rifles back with them once we've shown them how to operate and care for them."

"I think that's the way to go," Jesse nodded.

"Well, that's settled, then," Roland sighed. "Time to get something to eat. Hey, have you seen a dog runnin' around here? I been meanin' to ask, but I've been busy..."

~*~

"I *told* you there was a dog!"

"You're going to be insufferable about this, aren't you?" Maria sighed theatrically.

"Well, no," Roland almost huffed. "Just. . .well, this proves I wasn't seeing things."

"True," she allowed, nodding. "So where is this phantom, chocolate dog?"

"No one knows, exactly," Jesse replied. "James found her. . .well, actually, she was one of the dogs tracking him in the woods the day he was wounded. She just. . .decided to change people, I guess. She made the trip back with us, but I lost track of her in all the commotion. Forgot about her, really," he shrugged. "James has looked for her last couple days, but so far, nothing."

"That's odd," Maria frowned. "She must need food, and water of course. Where is she getting it?"

"Well, there's a lake right out back," Jesse pointed out. "And she's a hunter. A hunting dog, I mean. She's probably eating squirrel, or rabbit, or anything else she can..."

"What?" Maria looked horrified.

"What?" Roland looked at her.

"How can you let her eat such things!" she demanded.

"Well, Maria, it's not like it's bad for her," Roland explained. "Dogs actually like wild game when..."

"I mean the *squirrels!*" Maria shot back. "We have to find her, and stop her from eating any more of them!"

"Why?" Roland and Jesse asked at the same time.

"It's. . .it's *horrible!*" Maria exclaimed. "Those poor squirrels! Being, being. . .eaten like that!"

"Uh, nothin' wrong with eatin' squirrels," Jesse said uncomfortably, and Roland looked away at something on the wall that suddenly fascinated him. Maria narrowed her eyes at that, then they widened as the import of the words hit her.

"You wouldn't!"

"Well, yeah, I...we, would," Jesse told her. "Squirrel is pretty good, especially when you're hungry. Roland, you remember that time at Fort..." he broke off, seeing Roland slashing a finger across his throat frantically, and shaking his head. He stopped suddenly when Maria looked his way, but she saw it.

"So, the two of you killed and ate cute little defenseless animals," she ground out. "Why does this not surprise me?" she huffed.

"Hey, now," Roland complained. "That's a little harsh, ain't it?"

"Ask the squirrels," Maria told him flatly.

"Now, Maria," Roland almost whined, "that ain't right. We were just raised different, that's all. Country boys kill and eat their own meat all the time. Deer, hog, squirrel, turkey, you name it. There's nothing wrong with that."

"How could look at such a cute, furry- did you say *deer?*" Maria cut herself off, eyes narrowing again.

ROLAND

Roland just groaned, dropping his head to the table. This was going to be a long day.

~*~

The two vehicle convoy left around twelve-thirty, Roland figuring that would give them plenty of travel time to arrive on schedule. He, Maria, James and Melissa rode in the Hummer, while Gavin drove the truck with Susan Powers and Ralph riding with him.

Susan had agreed at once to make the trip when Roland approached her about it, much to his surprise. He had expected her to resist the idea. Instead, she seemed to be looking forward to it. Maybe she was getting better.

Ralph of course was elated.

The community was called Greenwood. It wasn't a true town, per se, as it was unincorporated at the time of the financial collapse that had effectively ended the world as they knew it. It was a rather tight knit little community, however. The majority of folks in and around the area were either farmers or ranchers in some form, though many had held outside jobs as well before things had gone south.

There was a general store along the main road through town that had carried everything from feed to fertilizer, clothes, boots, dry goods, and had a small grocery section. Most of the stock was now gone, but the owner had kept the building open as a meeting place for the community, and a barter/trade operation had been set up there. The church, just across the street, and the store had become the nerve centers of the entire area.

The arrival of the two vehicles attracted more than just passing attention from those gathered about, and as Roland and the rest exited their vehicles, a stir ran through the crowd at the armament displayed so casually by so many.

"They do not seem overly friendly," Maria noted softly, standing by Roland, though clear of his rifle.

"Well, they're a bit on edge, I 'magine," was his drawled reply. James stayed toward the rear of the vehicle, Melissa to his side, between him and the Hummer. Gavin and Susan, Ralph between them, advanced slowly to stand on the other side of the vehicle. No one spoke, from either side, until Turnbow came bustling out of the church.

"Over here, Roland!" he called, smiling. "Good to see you. Well, ain't you ever seen visitors before?" he demanded of his own people. "Have some manners and start introducing yourselves! These folks are here to help us, if they can. Don't be rude."

Slowly the people who had been staring did just that, walking over to the group in twos and threes, offering their names, usually with a hand, to the others. Roland stood back, looking over the place.

"There's the church," Turnbow offered unnecessarily. "Come on and I'll give you the tour you want," he added.

"Maria, you want to come along?" he asked softly. She smiled and nodded, joining them.

"Ralph, take a look around, see what you think," Roland ordered. "James, keep an eye on him, if you will. You two stay here," he ordered Gavin and Susan. Both nodded.

"What's the boy looking for?" Turnbow asked.

"He's just taking a look at how the land lays," Roland replied. "Kid's a pure genius. If there's a way to make things stronger, or to make some kind of defensive effort that you've not got yet, he'll find it. You might want someone along with him, in case he's got any questions."

"Okay," Turnbow nodded. Turning, he called out to a young couple, telling them to do just that. Both nodded and hurried off in pursuit. The three of them entered the church together.

Roland had to admit they had done pretty well. At every window were boards, nails, and hammer, ready to close off the windows. The pews had been rearranged to add strength to the walls, and a pair of them sat near every entrance, apparently to be used as door stops.

"The stairs up to the bell tower are behind the pulpit," Turnbow informed him. "Really wasn't any honest need for havin' it, but it's come in handy these days," he admitted. "The stairs down to the basement are there, too." He led them to the stairs, and then down to the basement.

Boxes of canned and boxed food sat stacked around the walls, along with containers filled with water. Bedding, candles, flashlights, all neatly prepared, sat along the tables.

"We've got a well, little ways out back," Turnbow told them. "Since we use a solar pump we still have water, but we thought to store as much as we could in case something happened to the pump, or the solar panel."

"Good idea," Roland nodded. "Honestly, Mister Turnbow, this looks pretty good. I don't see any holes in your preparations that just jump out at me. Upstairs, you might want to consider going ahead and boarding the windows from the outside. Might save the window glass if it came to a fight."

"If we do that, this place becomes a furnace," Turnbow shook his head sadly. "We need to be able to open the windows, or we can't stand it in here. Down here, it's not so bad, since this is all below ground, but you can see for yourself it's still not ideal without the air conditioning."

ROLAND

"If you must stay down here for any length of time, you will need a fan," Maria chimed in. "Find a bicycle, remove its rear wheel, and attach the drive chain to a large fan. Someone can ride the bicycle and power the fan. It will at least give you some air circulation, and provide exercise for the people down... What?" she added, seeing how Roland was looking at her.

"That's a hell of an idea," he told her, smiling, then, "beg pardon, sir," to Turnbow.

"No harm," Turnbow smiled. "And it is a good suggestion. We'll see to that right away, too. I've been wondering how to cope with that problem, and that's an ideal answer, young lady."

"How many people will you have down here?" Roland asked.

"Depends on the situation," Turnbow replied. "Anyone able to fight will be upstairs, of course. Any wounded would likely be brought down here, though. And the total number depends on who all can get here before we have to seal the place up. Those who are very far out should just stay in place, or hide and wait to see what happens." Roland nodded again.

"About your armament," Roland told him. "We can spare five rifles, and three pistols, with plenty of ammunition for them. Also, that ammunition will fit at least one of your rifles, the Ruger. I'd suggest that you pick your best, most able and dependable people, and send them to the school tomorrow for some training. One of my men can put them through a course showing them how to operate the weapons and care for them."

"It's not ideal, but they should boost your firepower by quite a bit." Turnbow looked as if he could kiss him.

"I... that's mighty generous," he said gratefully. "And I'm truly grateful to you for helping my people like that, Roland."

"We all got to help each other, Mister Turnbow," Roland shook his head. "We're all each other's got, anymore. If we don't stand together, we'll fall into the dust. No one'll ever remember we were here."

"Now, let's go see what Ralph has come up with and take a look at the rest of your area. Might be we can make some suggestions for you."

CHAPTER FORTY-EIGHT

"They're doing okay," Vaughan informed Roland at lunch the next day. "I'd say he picked good people. And he was smart enough to send more people than there are rifles. According to them, they had a meeting last night and the rifles will be kept in the church instead of with the shooters. That way, no matter who makes it inside, the rifles will be there."

"That's a good idea," Roland nodded. "Anyone in the group you'd say no to?"

"No, not really," Vaughan shook his head. "It's a pretty solid group."

"Good deal, then," Roland replied. "Thanks."

"Hey, it's what I do," Vaughan grinned, departing.

The group had stayed until nearly dark the day before, leaving with just enough time to get home before dusk. The time had been well spent, as friendships had been made, and a good start toward a healthy relationship between the two groups had been achieved.

Ralph had stayed overnight, working on a plan to provide the little community with some extra security, including two cameras powered off solar batteries taken from road signs. He had also used some modeling clay and ball bearings to create a half dozen homemade Claymores that had been placed around the school as a last ditch defense.

It had been Ralph who had spotted the worst threat to the church, too.

"What you gonna do they set the place on fire?" he had asked, looking at the structure. Turnbow had, by that time, seen firsthand how sharp Ralph was.

"What would you do?" he asked.

"Need a water tank on that roof," Ralph pointed to the top of the church. "Take some PVC pipe and run it from the tank along the arch o' the roof, holes drilled through each side at say. . .six inches at most. Happen they got to throwing fireballs at ya, just turn that water on, and let gravity feed the water into the pipes, and down onto the roof. Plus, when it's hot it'll cool off the building some."

The men of the community had worked through the late evening erecting a small platform behind the church on which a two hundred gallon tank had been placed to do just that. Before Ralph had left with the shooters the next morning on his way home everything was in place and working.

While the construction was being done, Ralph had helped the store owner with setting up a set of PV panels. The man who owned the store had kept the panels in storage, having originally gotten them to resell. He didn't know how they worked, but Ralph did. Scavenging car and boat batteries that were no longer in use, Ralph had managed to set up a system that gave them some power, allowing them to charge batteries for hand tools, radios, and to have minimal light in the evening.

His reward for that had been a Leatherman brand 'Super Tool', the last one the owner had in stock. Ralph had been tempted to take it at once, but instead refused, saying it wasn't right. The store owner had insisted.

"You did the work, you deserve the pay," the man told him, handing it over. Ralph seemed more proud of the tool because he'd earned it himself.

"We got it all done," the teenager had announced upon his arrival at the school with the group selected for firearms training. "Reckon I'm goin' to bed," he added, yawning.

"You earned it, buddy," Roland nodded. "Thanks."

"Just doin' my job," Ralph had grinned, heading for his room.

~*~

"Any luck?" Roland asked Angie as he walked into the radio room. She had been trying to raise Jenkins, or anyone else at the Nashville Armory, to see how the kids were doing and just generally see what was what.

"Not so much," she sighed. "I've tried everything we have, but. . .honestly? We just don't really have enough power, I think. That's got to be it, Roland. The air waves are pretty clear, nowadays, so it's got to be the antennae and the wattage. If we had a tower, or a stronger radio, then I'm sure we could talk to them."

"Oh, well," Roland shrugged. "It was worth a try, right? Anyway, you hearing anything on that HAM?"

"Sporadic stuff, mostly," Angie replied, looking at a pad on the table. "Mostly it's crackpots talking about the wrath of someone or other, blaming all this on God, or else it's a 'hate the" and you fill in the blank. Every now and then you hear something interesting, though. There's one report from. . .yeah, Pennsylvania, reporting some kind of new flu virus. According to the woman I heard, it's a local epidemic already, and getting worse. Doesn't respond to usual antibiotics, high mortality rate, that kind of thing."

"Anything we need to worry about?" Roland wanted to know.

"There's always worry about something like this," the paramedic shrugged. "But this is the only report I've heard, and that's a long way off. It's definitely something to keep an eye on, and an ear to the ground over."

"Then we'll do it," Roland told. "Last thing we need is something like that running though here."

"Amen."

~*~

"What's the news?" BD asked as Manny walked up to him.

"There's about thirty people at the school," Manny told him, looking at his notes. "Twenty-one confirmed as individuals, and the additional as people moving inside or around the building, but too far away to ID as someone they'd already seen. I told them to be very careful not to under estimate the number," he added, looking up.

"Very good," BD nodded. "Anything else?"

"Met with people from Greenwood," Manny went on. "Some of them took a visit up there, apparently, no idea what for, of course. Other than that, their schedule hasn't changed in a week. They all seem to have chores to do each day, and do them. Our guys can see one man on guard at the front at all times, and another on the roof. There's enough of them that the guard isn't the same every day, too."

"Women?" BD asked.

"Several, and a bunch of'em are lookers," the biker grinned. "And our guys saw two of our former prisoners there, too. That hot little blonde nurse, and the girl that Teddy and Brick, um, entertained, the night before all this started, or thereabouts."

"Interesting," BD mused. "That confirms that we're in the right place. All right, then. It's time. Let's start getting set up. If we don't hear anything new, or see drastic changes in their operation before then, we'll hit them a week from today, early. Right after sun-up."

"Yes, Boss."

~*~

"We're bein' watched."

The words were soft, and Roland at first thought he'd imagined it. Tom Mackey was beside him as the two looked out the front doors.

"I know," Roland answered. "It's recent, I think. I made a turn all around here not long ago, and found nothing. But that just means they weren't there then. For all I know they could have set up watch starting that afternoon."

"Have you thought about what you'll do?" Tom asked.

"What *can* I do?" Roland shrugged. "If I go out there and eliminate them, then the others know we're on to them."

"Then use'em," Tom suggested softly. "Let'em see what you want'em to see. Use that to draw'em out."

"Invite an attack?" Roland asked.

"You know they're gonna hit you," Tom reasoned. "Try to influence when they do it. Set'em up."

Roland thought about that. In a true military situation, he'd have already done just that. But here, with so many civilians, he had hesitated to do that. Maybe that was a mistake.

Everyone here was a target, one way or another. That was just the way it was. There was no more risk in following Tom's advice that there was in just waiting on the enemy to strike. There might even be *less* risk, if things were done right.

The trick would be to convince the watchers they were weaker than they actually were, he decided. Nothing else would influence BD to hit them before he wanted to. But if he saw a perceived weakness, even for a day...

"I might have an idea," Roland spoke aloud. "I might just know how to do what you said, Tom. It's a risk, but..."

"All life is a risk, Roland," Tom said. "Who dares, wins." Roland shot Tom a look at that remark, but the older man was still looking out the window.

"Maybe it's time we dared a little."

~*~

"I want you to park the bus right here, where the door of the bus meets this side door," Roland explained to Rich. "I want you close enough that when you open the door it almost touches the wall."

"Why?" Rich asked, confused.

"There's probably people watching us," Roland told him. "I want them to get used to that bus sitting here."

"Okay," Rich shrugged. He was still confused, but he trusted Roland to know his business.

~*~

"Traffic on the road, military by the look of it."

"Understood," Roland replied at once. "Everyone in position." Hopefully this was Jenkins coming to call, and it probably was. Even so, it was a good training exercise, and with enough realism thrown in to make it more than just a drill.

It was day two into Roland's plan, and he had been about to put it into action, but that would have to wait, now. Hopefully Jenkins, if it was him, was bringing good news.

"Four vehicles, Roland," James called from the roof. *"Two trucks, MRAP, and Hummer. Hummer's pulling a trailer. . .no, the trucks are pulling. . .it looks like tanks. Water tanks, I mean,"* he added hastily.

"Water Buffaloes," Roland replied. "Used to haul drinking water to the front." He stepped out onto the front walk, waiting. Other than James, on his post on the roof, no one else was visible.

The vehicles pulled into the school, and Jenkins was the first one to dismount.

Lieutenant Jenkins.

"Well, well, well," Roland grinned. "And here I thought you was an honest workin' man."

"Up yours," Jenkins growled, but then grinned and fist bumped Roland. "How's it going?" he asked.

"We're probably under observation," Roland told him. He explained, briefly, what had happened since Jenkins' last visit.

ROLAND

"Sounds like you've got trouble ahead," Jenkins nodded. "I wish I could give you some men to help out, but we're wrung out right now chasing down bandits. I did bring you some stuff, though," he added, grinning.

"Yeah?" Roland asked.

"Trucks are food and other goodies," Jenkins nodded. "We've accessed some other armories around the state, and we've gotten some more men but they're being used hard right now. We do have extra supplies though, and we've been salvaging some stuff. I finally had enough men available at one time to make this trip down."

"How're my kids?" Roland asked.

"They're safe, and cared for," Jenkins promised. "And they all want to come 'home'," he added. Roland nodded.

"Maybe soon," he said. "I figure this will break, one way or another, in another week, tops. Which reminds me, we need a way to communicate -"

"Got it with me," Jenkins assured him.

"What's with the buffs?" Roland asked, nodding to the tanks.

"Think you can spare us some clean water?" Jenkins asked. "We keep getting new people, and we're not getting more water," he said. "And with the kids..."

"Sure," Roland nodded his understanding. "Least we can do, for all you've done for us. Probably take a while to fill three of'em, though, with -"

"Brought a generator and a pump," Jenkins assured him. "Both of which we're leaving. Getting water from you was one of the ways I talked the Captain into letting me make the trip. Things are really busy right now," he added. "The thugs are starting to get organized, and in a big way. We've about doubled our manpower, but our commitments have increased just as much. And now, with this flu thing..."

"I thought that was in Pennsylvania," Roland frowned. "At least, we heard one woman from there on a HAM receiver talking about it."

"It's not isolated," Jenkins shook his head. "It's spreading like wildfire up north. No cases reported here that we *know* of, but then, how *would* we know? With the comm situation like it is, there's just no effective way to keep on top of things."

"We've recruited some couriers who travel by motorcycle, and by horse, just to keep up with the outlying areas around Nashville."

"What about fuel?" Roland asked.

"Plenty for now," Jenkins shrugged. "After the die off, there's gas in almost every station, waiting to be salvaged. Some of it's already gone, of course, taken by the bandits, or by people who are trying to survive just like us. There's not much left in the way of authority or organization anymore. Lots of places much worse off than we are at the moment." Roland knew that was true just from the reports they'd heard over the HAM.

"Well," Jenkins sighed. "Let's get started unloading and I'll have my boys set up the pump. Okay for us to bivouac here tonight?"

"Course," Roland nodded at once. "Let's get going."

ROLAND

~*~

"Captain eventually wants to spread out some and put outposts around. Maybe one fire team and two civilian law officers. This place is high on that list, too, if that's okay?" he added.

"That'd be fine," Roland assured him. "I think we can spare the room. Even when the kids are back."

"Good to know," Jenkins nodded. "Anyway, he wants to eventually have a network of posts like that all around. As and when we can, we'll add to them. There's a limit as to how far we can go on our own, but we aren't the only people working. We've been in touch with outfits in Atlanta, Huntsville, Birmingham, and Knoxville, so far, who are all trying to do similar. We've been sharing Intel, and made a few equipment exchanges."

"But they're facing the same reality we are. The plain fact is, people have gone feral a lot faster than anyone would have guessed. Absent authority, folks with low morals are gaining ground in a hurry, and there's a lot more of them than there are of us."

"That's always the way of it," Roland nodded.

"We're still trying to get organized, while they're running circles around us," Jenkins sighed. "It's not that we're not trying, it's just. . .every time we think we're caught up, another fire breaks out somewhere. And every time, well, almost every time, we end up losing men and equipment before we get it put out."

"We've been lucky, here," Roland nodded. "But that won't last. Not if we're attacked in force, anyway."

"Well, like I said, we can't spare any manpower, much as I'd like to, but we did bring you some extra firepower. Two dozen M-4's, twenty thousand rounds, and two crates of mags. We also threw in some field gear, and another dozen M-9's. There's also some civilian rifles, shotguns, and handguns, and several thousand rounds of assorted ammo for them."

"We can use some of that to help Turnbow's people," Roland nodded.

"Work things out with him, did you?" Jenkins looked hopeful.

"I believe so," Roland replied. "He came here, asking for our help to look over his defenses. We helped him some, and gave them a few rifles we could spare. Trained his people to use them, too. They're going to help us with canning for the winter."

"How 'bout that," Jenkins smiled. "Man, that's great news. And just so happens, one of those trucks has a lot of canning supplies on it. Captain wants to help as many as he can make it through the winter. Also, come next year, we'll be lookin' to trade for some of that food."

"Don't know how much there'll be, with no fuel for equipment," Roland warned. "Maybe if we can get some horse drawn stuff, I guess."

293

"Captain thought of that," Jenkins looked smug. "Well, I did, and then he made a plan for it. There's several thousand gallons of diesel being held in Nashville specifically for planting and harvest. He hopes we can plant as much as we normally would but since there's a lot fewer mouths to feed that it'll go further."

"Hopefully by the time that runs out we'll be set up well enough that everyone is growing their own. Meanwhile, a few egg heads in Nashville are working to figure out how to power at least some equipment with resources we have here. Locally."

"Build a still," Roland snorted. At Jenkins look of confusion, he explained about Ralph's still idea.

"How old is this kid, again?" Jenkins asked.

"Fifteen, goin' on fifty," Roland chuckled. "I don't know what we'd do without him, to be honest."

"Sounds like a good kid to have around," the soldier grunted his agreement. "Well, anyway. You can see we're planning. Maybe at least some of it will bear fruit."

"I hope so," Roland replied. "I've been so busy just trying to keep things running here, and be ready for an attack I expect literally at any minute. I admit I haven't had time to think much about what's down the road. I need to start doing that."

"Well, now's a good time to start," Jenkins told him. "I brought you a whole bunch of books. Herbal medicine, medicinal plants, edible plants, homesteading, food preservation, blacksmithing, you name it, we probably got it. Also brought knives, axes, multi-tools, hats, boots, clothes and gloves. There's any and all sizes, mind you, and we didn't sort stuff. Just don't have the manpower. There's also several reams of paper and pencils, pens, notebooks, and folders, all kinds of clerical stuff you need to get and stay organized."

"Wow," Roland was stunned. "That'll be a big help."

"Learn to be self-sufficient, Roland," Jenkins advised. "Once the stuff in the stores and warehouses is gone, it's gone. Won't be back, most like." Just then Ralph walked in.

"I hear you got trouble cleanin' water?" he asked. "Sorry, did I butt in?" he added, realizing the two men were talking.

"No, Ralph, we were just talking about what needs to be done," Roland promised. "Come on in."

"We do have trouble cleaning water," Jenkins nodded. "Any suggestions?" He really didn't expect anything usable, but he figured he would test Roland's golden child.

"Tried using a sand and rock filter?" Ralph asked. Jenkins blinked.

"Ah, not that I know of," he shot a glance at Roland, who just smirked in reply.

"Well, I drew this for ya," Ralph handed over a sheet of paper taken from a child's notebook, probably found in the school somewhere. "Build ya one o' these and it'll clean the water for ya. If you can find some charcoal, add that in between, and it might be clean enough to drink right outta this. If not, it'll still make the job easier for that processin' plant you got." He stood up.

"Well, that's all I wanted," he said, taking his leave.

"Well I'll be damned."

"Could be," was all Roland said.

CHAPTER FORTY-NINE

Jenkins and his men were able to leave right after sun-up the next morning. Two of his men had set up the new radio and left the books and manuals for it, along with a code book to be used when times were perilous, but not for regular traffic.

Jennifer Kingston had been thrilled with the medical supplies they had brought, and wasn't shy in saying so. With the two crates Jenkins had unloaded she could take much better care of the people in the area. But she was especially glad to have another book of herbal remedies.

"I have two of my own," she admitted. "But not this one, and it's one of the best. Very hard to find. Pricey, too."

"Got it for free," Jenkins had smiled. "If you think of any other books you need, make a list and have it sent to me. I'll try and find them."

Roland had James and Gavin load up ten M-4's, sixty magazines, and five thousand rounds, and take to Greenwood. Looking over the cache of civilian weapon, he kept three bolt action Remington 700's in .308, four combat shotguns, and four revolvers, for anyone who couldn't master an auto-loader. He also kept a pair of small .380 autos and the ammo for them, intending to give those to the Barnes twins. Two .410 shotguns, both Mossbergs, were also set aside for the teens.

At the last minute he set aside two shotguns that were set up for bird hunting, some turkey and game loads, and two rifles chambered for .270 to hunt with. The rest he would send to Greenwood along with their own contribution.

In the end, Melissa and Susan had decided to go along as well, and the four piled into the pickup truck and departed.

Ralph spent the morning installing three of the four sets of PV panels delivered by the convoy, and tying their batteries into the limited power circuits used by the school. Their electric power was increased dramatically. The final set would be sent to Greenwood at some point in the near future when Ralph had time to go set it up.

Roland didn't want to make too many more trips to the small farming community until after the threat to them had been dealt with. But there was always the chance that the bikers would hit Greenwood first so helping them was important. The two groups needed each other to survive.

The load had also included a pair of chainsaws and the necessary spare parts to keep them running, as well as dozens of hand tools including rakes, shovels, axes, hammers, and two large boxes of various size files. Jenkins had really taken care in selecting what would be brought and then loaded the trucks to the gills.

Roland decided to see if he could find a way to heat at least part of the building with wood at some point, and on impulse, told Ralph.

"Outdoor furnace," Ralph nodded. "Good idea, Mister Roland. Heat the building, and can heat water, too, if you get the right one. We can tie it into the ventilation system and use it all winter."

"Dare I ask if you know how to do that?" Roland asked.

"Sure do," Ralph grinned.

"Ralph, I can't tell you how glad I am that you're here," Roland said earnestly, and the boy lit up like a Christmas tree.

"Thanks Mister Roland!"

Maria and the other women had been encouraged to find several large boxes of 'woman things', as Jenkins had put it, in the shipment. Roland hadn't asked any questions about that. And wouldn't.

Ever.

~*~

With Jenkins and his men gone, it was time Roland to put his deception plan into action.

~*~

"Everyone understand?" Roland asked the assembled group. Everyone nodded, somber.

"All right, then. Rich, let's get this rodeo going," he ordered. Twelve people loaded onto the bus through the doorway, the bus doors effectively blocking any chance of someone watching being able to see.

The bus then pulled away, everyone on the bus making themselves visible. Rich drove the bus ten miles away, and parked it for twenty minutes. With everyone hiding in the seats or floor, he then returned to the school, parking the bus in the same exact place. With the doors left open, everyone crawled off the bus back into the building.

"Why are we doing this again?" Maria asked, dusting herself off.

"Whoever is watching will see a pattern over the next three or four days," Roland explained. "Each day all of you will sink lower and lower into the bus, as if tired, or still sleeping. After a few days, maybe three, or four at most, we'll start just rigging makeshift dummies on the bus."

"And whoever is watching thinks we are still leaving every morning," Maria nodded her understanding. "That's very inventive, *mi amor*," she smiled brightly. "We must reward you somehow."

"Yeah?" Roland's eyebrows shot up. "How's that?"

"I'm sure I can think of something," she smiled over her shoulder, walking away. Roland watched her out of sight, smiling in spite of himself.

~*~

James and the others delivered the new weapons and supplies to a grateful Greenwood community. The crowd was glad to have the extra hardware, and James made sure they knew it was Jenkins who provided it.

"We sure appreciate it," Turnbow assured him.

"Have ya'll got a radio working?" James asked.

"Two of them," Turnbow nodded. "A HAM 2 meter, and a CB."

"We've got the same, and monitor these frequencies," James told him, handing the slip of paper that Angie had given him. "We can't promise anything, but if you get into a bind, try and contact us. We'll do what we can, if we can."

"We'll do the same," Turnbow promised. "I'm sorry I misjudged you folks, son," he added. James shrugged.

"Water down the river," he said in reply. "We're all just trying to get by, sir."

"I appreciate that, and everything else," the older man nodded. "You all hungry?"

"We can't stay, Mister Turnbow," Melissa replied. "We've got too much work to do to linger. Roland just wanted you to have all this as soon as possible."

"Well, we're grateful," the preacher assured her. "We might just make it, with your help."

"Good luck, sir," James said, shaking hands and then heading to the truck.

"He did say he was sorry," Melissa mentioned.

"So he did," James nodded.

"But you still hold a grudge," Melissa pressed.

"I don't hold grudges," James replied, looking at her. "But leopards don't change their spots, either. He's friendly now 'cause he needs us.

ROLAND

When I see how friendly he is when *we* need *him*, then I'll decide whether we can trust him or not."

"You still brought the guns," she shot back with an impish grin.

"I trust Roland," James said simply. "That buys Turnbow a lot with me that Roland said do it."

Melissa nodded her understanding, climbing in beside him in the truck as Susan and Gavin loaded into the back. James was a lot more mature than his age, she knew, and what he'd just said only added to that impression.

She was very pleased with her decision. James was the right choice for her.

Now she'd have to make sure he knew she was the right one for him.

~*~

For three days the group practiced their 'plan', the bus going out and coming back each day. On the fourth day Roland decided to try the homemade mannequins.

Old clothing stuffed with worn bedding, straw, empty box material, anything that added bulk, were made to look like workers off for another day of hard labor. Hats scavenged from any and every where possible were thrown on them, and pulled down tight. A pair of Styrofoam heads used to model wigs taken from a local beauty shop no longer in service, wigs and all, were used as well. Anything the group could think of to add any realism to the dummies.

Rich was about to get on the bus when Roland turned up, along with Gerry Fisk.

"Rich, I want to make sure you know how dangerous this is," Roland said softly. "If they decide to hit the bus, then they'll be expecting a dozen people."

"Yeah, I worked that out," the older man grimaced. "Still, this is a good idea. And," he added, "if I were them, I'd wait until the bus got back, empty, to attack. Make sure the workers weren't coming back unexpected like."

"Point," Roland mused. "Good one at that. Anyway, I want you to take Gerry with you. You guys know what to do, and how to get it done. Be. Careful. If you get the sense something's not right, abandon the plan and head straight back here."

"Will do," Rich nodded. He and Gerry stepped onto the bus, and were soon on their way. James was hidden on the roof, had been there since before dawn in an attempt to make the watchers think the school was getting sloppy.

But James was there, watching closely to make sure that no one was following the bus.

Roland stood outside and watched the bus depart, waving just as he always did. He was careful to keep to the same routine, every time.

He decided he'd have made a decent actor. Never a star, but a solid, dependable B-lister for sure.

Well, maybe C-lister.

ROLAND

~*~

"This is four days in a row, Boss," Manny reported to BD, referring to his notebook. "Dozen people from the school are on some kind of work detail, apparently. They're usually gone six to nine hours, depending on the weather. On really hot days, six is about normal. Cooler days, up to nine. Once."

"Four days isn't much of a pattern," BD mused, more to himself than anything else. "Still, it is a pattern. How many men are in the group?"

"Usually seven, from what our guys can see."

"Good," BD nodded. "All right, Manny, I think it's time we got ready to conclude our. . .business, in this area. Have everyone prepped and ready. If that bus goes out again tomorrow, then we'll hit the school the day after tomorrow as soon as the bus is gone for a half-hour. That way, even if they have communication, they can't make it back in time to help. Just to be defeated in detail."

"I'll see to it, Boss," Manny nodded, and set out to get it done. BD watched him go, then turned to look out again over the valley. The prisoners were working in the fields, all wearing chains now. There wouldn't be any more escapes. He needed that labor.

He needed all the labor and tribute he could get. The men who followed him did so for a number of reasons, chief among them that BD provided for them. Food, drink, women, whatever they wanted, he saw to it they got it. If he *couldn't* provide those things, his little army might just abandon him.

He'd worried he might lose some anyway after the casualties they had suffered, but after a few days of shaky ground the group had settled down and were now focused on getting revenge for their fallen comrades. BD had been circulating among them, slowly stoking that fire, commiserating with those who had lost friends or family in the attacks. Focusing their anger on their attackers, rather than on himself.

So far it had worked, as had the distractions of hard drink, food, and 'entertainment'. He had lost three women prisoners to abuse in the last week, but found it a small price to pay for the continued loyalty of his men.

He needed that loyalty. Already word of the losses had spread, and some of the outlying communities under his heel had started to resist seeing their food and supplies taken from them. He'd lost two more men killed, and three wounded in an ambush three days ago. He had yet to find the responsible party or parties, but once he'd dealt with the school, he'd root out the attackers and use them as an example, too.

He had too much riding on his operations to allow anyone to stand up to him.

Anyone.

~*~

"I got a bad feeling," Jesse said, as he and Roland sat out front the next evening, as they normally did. Tom Mackey had taken to joining them lately as well.

"Got one myself," the older man agreed. "Can't seem to shake it, neither."

"Might as well admit I do too, then," Roland sighed. "Reckon they'll hit us tomorrow."

"Think so," Jesse nodded. "I figure they got two choices. If they bought the bus action, then they'll hit after it leaves. Probably wait a little bit so they can't just turn around and come back to help out, but that's just what I would do, so I don't know."

"Otherwise, they hit us at sun-up, working their way into whatever positions they can before light. They might have night gear too."

"Thought about that," Roland replied, as calmly as if they were discussing how to change a tire. "Weather seems to be cooling tonight, too," he added. "Might be foggy in the morning."

"That works against us," Tom observed. "My old knees say it's gonna keep gettin' cooler though. And probably rain."

"Tomorrow, you think?" Roland asked.

"Nah, not till later on, anyway," Mackey shook his head. "Probably a cold front comin' through, though. Might be nice weather for a few days."

"I'm not opposed to that," said Jesse. "I'm too delicate for all this hot weather."

"Yeah, 'spect you are," Roland chuckled. "I'm honestly surprised you ain't on sick detail ever mornin' since Jennifer started staying here."

"I do feel a *cough* cold comin' *cough, cough* on, now that you *cough* mention it," Jesse replied, grinning.

"You ain't foolin' nobody," Mackey chuckled. "That woman's a looker, son, and smart as they get. She'll do right by you, you can catch her."

"That's what I thought, too," Jesse admitted, more seriously.

"Now that sounds like a man doing some serious contemplating," Tom laughed.

"Well, I guess," Jesse shrugged. "She's just. . .different, that's all. And I really like her, too."

"Well, I'd say it's mutual," Roland replied.

"Yeah?" Jesse gave his friend his undivided attention.

ROLAND

"Why you think you're always the one escortin' her around?" Roland asked.

"I just assumed you. . .wait, are you sayin' she *asked* you for that?" Jesse asked suddenly.

"Yep," Roland leaned back stretching. "Sure did."

"Why didn't you tell me!" Jesse demanded.

"I've had too much fun watching you try to get on her good side," Roland admitted. "You've done more work these last few days than I think I've ever seen. Good to get some *pro-duck-tivi-tay* outta you for once."

"That's. . .that's cold, Roland, even for you," Jesse said in a mock hurt tone.

"Nah, just funny," Roland snorted, then stood.

"Reckon we need to make sure everything's ready," he said, serious now. "This feeling ain't goin' away, so I'd say we're on the edge. Let's make sure that weapons and ammo are set to go, and we should chain the doors tonight, I expect."

"Jesse, make sure we don't have any empty water containers, too. And have James make sure the PV panels are covered. We really don't want them damaged if we can help it."

"Tom, you might just. . .make a round, you know?" Roland settled for saying. "Make sure everything looks right. I'm pretty sure this is the real deal, and we got little to no Intel on this bunch."

"All right," Tom rose, taking his chair inside as went.

"You think this is it, huh?" Jesse asked, folding his own chair.

"Yeah, I do," Roland nodded. "Feels like the night before we got-"

"Yeah," Jesse nodded. "Well, I got work to do," he said, taking his chair and going inside. Roland stayed behind another minute, looking out into the dark.

"I hope you bastards are getting a good look," he whispered. "And that you're as dumb as I think. Maybe tomorrow we'll have a surprise for you sure enough."

CHAPTER FIFTY

Everyone in the school was awake by three-thirty. Lighting was low, lanterns only, along with a handful of lights in the kitchen. Breakfast today was simple and hearty, oatmeal with apple slices. It was easy, quick, and would stick with them through the morning.

Roland shared his breakfast quietly with Maria. Neither spoke, simply enjoying the easy silence between them. Both knew that today could hold a great many losses before it ended.

Others did the same. There was low chatter here and there, last minute advice for those less experienced, encouragement for those who were scared. In truth everyone was scared or worried on one level or another, but some were better than others.

The soldiers among the group were in a heightened state of awareness, an alertness that others might mistake as nerves. They had all been here before.

Tom Mackey might as well have been preparing for another day's work. He had eaten early, then turned to his kit. His personal rifle was a Springfield M1A. He had the top level package, and his BDU held a dozen mags for it. There was also a 1911 pistol, and a wicked looking knife that caught Roland's eye.

"Tom, is that a Khukri?"

"Yep," the older man nodded. He hesitated for a moment, then drew the large knife and offered it, hilt first, for inspection. Roland took it carefully, examining the weapon.

It wasn't new, but it was in immaculate condition. The grips were an exotic wood of some kind that Roland had never seen. The blade wasn't shiny but a dull gray color, and Roland could tell without looking at it that the blade was strong. He looked closer at the hilt and could see very faint marks along the edges of the wood grips. *Many* faint marks. He looked at Tom.

"Yes," Tom said evenly. "That's what they are," he nodded, taking the blade back and securing it in its sheath. "I wasn't always a farmer, Roland. Surprised? Disappointed?"

"Neither," Roland almost smiled. "I'm just glad you're here." The old man smiled at that.

"I think I'll be on the roof," the farmer told him, standing. "I assume you want to let them announce themselves?"

"That's the plan."

"Very well, then. Call me if you need me."

"Thank you, Tom. For everything." Roland extended his hand.

"I wouldn't miss it for anything," the older man smiled wider, his hand shake firm. With that he moved off. Roland shook his head in wonder, and moved along to the next thing.

~*~

It was time for the bus to go. Roland was surprised when Glenda showed up with her husband Rich instead of Gerry Fisk.

"Thought we'd take a drive," Rich smiled. "Maybe have a picnic."

"Rich, I..."

"Roland, whatever happens, we'll be together," Glenda smiled, cradling the rifle she'd learned to use not long ago. "Now, you have plenty to do and Gerry's worth more here that I would be anyway. You go on dear, and leave us to this."

"Godspeed, you two," Roland smiled sadly.

"God be with you, son," Rich replied, shaking hands. With that the older couple boarded the bus, making sure the 'workers' were all seated, and then they were gone.

~*~

BD watched as the bus pulled away. It was too dark to see how many people were aboard, but he could see at least one person moving around, and the silhouettes of several others. He nodded to himself. They'd deal with the bus later.

He had fifty-three men in his group. He had planned to have more, but there were other problems in his 'kingdom' requiring attention, so these would have to do. He'd divided his force into five teams of ten, appointing his best men as team leaders.

"We'll stick to the plan," he ordered those five, gathered around him with Manny. "Team's one and five will hit from the front. Team three will hit the east side and four, the west. Team Two will be in reserve. You have fifteen minutes to get into position without being seen. Go."

All five moved away, gathering their men and heading for their positions. Manny watched them go, frowning.

"Something wrong, Manny?" BD asked.

"I… I'm just not sure we should be doin' this, Boss, that's all," Manny shrugged.

"And why is that?" BD's tone was calm, but Manny wasn't fooled. He didn't like being questioned.

"These people aren't going nowhere," Manny shrugged. "With the other problems we been having, just seems like we'd be better off takin' care of that, *then* hittin' this place. That's all." BD considered that for a moment, then nodded.

"I can see where you would think that, and it's not a bad plan. The thing is, this group," he pointed to the school, "is becoming a rallying point. As long as they're here, they're a point to rally around, to look to for inspiration if not outright assistance. They have to go before others start to rebel. That's why we're here this morning, instead of taking on the other problems."

"We'll see to them soon enough," he promised.

"Okay, Boss," Manny nodded. "Thanks for explaining. Helps me to understand how you think. How you want things done."

BD merely nodded, pleased with Manny. As his second, BD had told Manny that he would have to start thinking ahead. He was learning how.

"Five minutes, Boss," BD's radio man whispered.

"Good."

~*~

"They're moving into position," Vaughan whispered, watching the various enemy 'units' moving in the pre-dawn darkness through a night vision monocular.

"Roger that," Roland replied. "Let me know when they start to move forward."

"Roger," Vaughan acknowledged. *"Looks like twenty-five, maybe thirty out front, and at least ten moving to each flank. No sign of heavy weapons, either."*

"Best news so far," Roland sighed. "Keep us posted."

"You got it," Vaughan promised. Roland looked at the assembled people around him.

ROLAND

"Everyone to your posts," he ordered calmly. "They're coming. James, you and Susan cover the west, right?" The teen nodded, and he and Susan headed that way.

"Mack, take Gerry and Jim, cover the east." The trooper nodded, motioned for the men to follow, and left.

"Jesse, you and I will take the front. We've got the SAW, so take it. If nothing else, it'll give'em a good shock."

"All *righty* then!" Jesse grinned, rubbing his hands together.

"Try not to sound so happy," Roland sighed.

"Happy? I'm not happy," Jesse looked hurt. "I'm just. . .prepared. That's all."

"Great. Go and prepare."

With his friend moving to get the SAW, he turned to find Maria behind him.

"What do you want me to do?" she asked simply.

"Stay with the others," Roland told her. "I think the kitchen should be the safest place, but if you decide something else, I'll go with it. You and the girls are basically our reserve," he grimaced. "Take good positions with cover and don't leave them unless you have to. Remember your training."

"Please be careful," Maria said softly. Before he could answer she stood on tip toes and kissed him gently, then turned and hurried away before he could say anything.

Heading to the front, Roland felt anger at the entire, useless situation. So many already dead, so many more yet to perish in a world that had come apart at the seams, and here they were, about to be attacked by fifty or more perfectly healthy men who could have, *should have*, been helping to rebuild what had been lost.

How many of his own people would die today because of one man's insane need to garner personal power, no matter what it cost?

Try as he might, he couldn't force the anger aside. By the time he reached his post, he was almost overwhelmed with fury.

~*~

"Ralph, are you ready?" Roland asked softly over the radio.

"Sure am, Mister Roland," came the cheery reply.

"We've got enemy troops moving against our flanks, about where mines 11-15, and 1-5 are located."

"Ready to fire on your command, sir," Ralph tried to sound like a soldier.

"James will call for them on the right, Mack on the left, okay?"

"Roger," Ralph replied, and Roland could almost hear the teenager grin.

"Vaughan?"

"They're on their way, boss," Vaughan's whispered reply came back at once. *"The flankers are in position, looks like. The front. . .okay, they're moving again. It's showtime."*

"Everyone on your toes," Roland ordered. "It'll start anytime, now. Keep your cool, and we'll win."

The silence following Roland's last orders seemed to stretch on forever. All around the school, people who had never known the harsh realities of combat gripped weapons they had only recently learned to use, a gamut of emotion gripping them as tightly as they held to those same weapons.

Fear. Not only of what was to come, but of failure. Fear of death. Fear of captivity. Pain, suffering, despair. Some had already experienced the tender mercies of the men now creeping forward in the dark to do them harm, and were terrified of returning to it.

Strangely, the fear, the despair, the dread of such a thing happening again strengthened weakening hearts, stiffened spines, and allowed the school defenders to find their courage.

The soldiers among them also gave them courage. The cold eyed looks the veterans among them sported reminded the civilians that not all hard men, or women, were evil. No, indeed, some were good, were honorable, and would stand against the evil of the world, no matter the odds.

And so the defenders tightened their hold on their weapons, offered fervent prayers for strength, courage, and mercy, and waited.

~*~

James was the one to start things off.

"NOW RALPH!" he called, and Ralph instantly hit the switch for the western mines.

Five ANFO bombs, each weighing between three and five pounds and wrapped in steel shrapnel, exploded right in the faces of the western attackers. Three of the ten men on the west simply ceased to exist, caught full on by the homemade land mines. Two more were mortally wounded, and two others were injured less severely. Just like that, the western attackers had lost seventy percent of their strength.

"Fire frontals now, Ralph!" Vaughan called at once. With the element of surprise gone, it was use 'em or lose 'em. Ralph fumbled

slightly, but managed to get one of the two switches flicked before the front force could react.

In front, the assault force BD had sent against the school had pulled up short at the explosions on their flank, shocked at the bright flash and loud report. They couldn't hear the screams of their comrades over the ringing in their ears, but the smarter among them knew what had happened.

Ralph had placed ten mines in front of the building. Five of them detonated, shredding five men who were still standing exposed, gawking at the previous explosions. Five more were injured slightly, but not severely. The rest managed to find the presence of mind to hit the ground flat just as Ralph managed to detonate the other five. As a result, only two more were killed, and one injured.

"Ralph!" Mack called a second later, and Ralph hit his final switch. The eastern flanking force fared better, with warning time. One man lost and another injured left them strong enough to continue their mission.

Ralph had one more surprise, and Roland was quick to use it.

"Lights! NVG's *off!"*

The area around the school was suddenly bathed in harsh white light.

CHAPTER FIFTY-ONE

The lights came as a rude surprise to the attackers. They had counted on the cover of darkness to hide them until they were ready to attack. Bathed now in harsh, bright light they froze in place for just a vital second.

"Open fire!" Roland ordered.

Jesse immediately fired the SAW, rounds stitching over the yard, raking the prone figures without mercy. Some were almost certainly dead already from the blasts, but Jesse was a cautious man who believed in being sure of things when they were important.

People trying to kill him, or his friends, he judged important.

Others were also shooting, but other than the soldiers, and Tom Mackey, mostly they were just shooting wildly, their training largely forgotten in the ensuing panic. Aiming only in the general sense of the word, they simply shot at anything that moved. It wasn't the best way to repel an attack, but Roland had allowed for this, and was satisfied simply with the volume of fire. It was a waste of ammunition, true, but he counted on the heavy fire to have a disheartening effect on their attackers.

It did.

"We're being wiped out!" one of the squad leaders screamed into his radio.

ROLAND

~*~

BD sat perfectly still, stunned into stillness by the sudden turn of events. He had not seen this coming. In hindsight, his inner mind noted, he should have. This group was led by the same guys that had killed so many of his men, using Claymores, booby traps, and plain, old-fashioned aimed fire.

"Boss?!" Manny was shaking his arm, drawing him out of his shock.

"Move the reserve up front," BD ordered, "Tell him to send three men around to reinforce the west side, and take the rest toward the front."

The radio man nodded, and started giving the orders.

"Tell the East to keep up their attack, to try and take some pressure off the front," he added, thinking furiously. He had lost a lot of men, which meant a loss of face. He had to get that back, and fast, or someone would probably decide that a change of leadership was in order.

"Manny, get down there and take command of the frontal assault," he ordered his lieutenant, "Get them under some cover, and start laying suppression fire against the front. Never mind if they hit anything or not, just keep their attention, and their heads down. I'm going East and lead that team inside the school."

"Okay, Boss!" Manny nodded, and set off. BD headed in the other direction, motioning for his radio man to follow.

~*~

"They had a reserve squad, moving to the front now," Vaughan reported from his position. He had yet to fire, Roland having ordered him not to call attention to himself.

Tom Mackey had no such orders, and was keeping up a steady rate of fire from his position twenty feet away. Lying prone on the roof, a few feet from the edge, Mackey was a hard target to hit.

He changed positions after every third shot, too.

Below, Jesse continued to fire well-controlled bursts over the lit up front yard. His fire was pretty accurate, but it had been a long time since he'd used a SAW, and his aim wasn't all it could have been. Nevertheless, his fire was doing what it was supposed to do. The attackers along the front were pinned down.

On the western side of the school, James and Susan were in position, and trading shots with the remaining enemy on that side. James knew that he had taken two down hard right after the blast, but wasn't sure how many were left. He'd lost count in the smoke and confusion.

N.C. REED

He and Susan had discussed this, however, and held fast in their positions. Both had good cover and concealment, and their muzzle flashes weren't easy to spot with the lights blinding their opponents.

But the lights wouldn't last long. Ralph had done his best but so many lights would drain the battery reserve quickly.

Still, he would use the advantage while he had it. Despite how well things had gone so far, they were still in a bad situation. One that could go quickly from bad, to worse.

~*~

Tom Mackey was changing magazines when movement caught his eye. Behind the enemy to his front he could see two figures moving around the flank. He threw his rifle up and fired three quick shots before the two were concealed by shadows and brush.

Not knowing if he had managed to score a hit or not, he turned his attention back to the men in front of him. Whoever it was, he'd at least scared them, he decided.

~*~

BD heard the impact behind him, the sound of a large caliber bullet hitting meat and muscle. He dropped low, turning. His radio man, known only by the nickname Gadget, was down, a hole in the side of his chest BD could put his fist inside of. Cursing at the loss of his best technician, BD grabbed the radio Gadget had carried only to find a similar sized hole in it, the side covered with what could only be Gadget's blood. Tossing the radio aside in rage, BD continued to make his way toward his flanking team.

~*~

Maria, Terri, and Deena huddled in the kitchen behind the steel prep tables, peering beneath them, over the pots and pans stored on the shelves below. This was the best place to be, they decided, since it placed a lot of steel between them and the door.

"That's a lot of shooting," Deena said softly, eyes wide.

"Sure is," Terri nodded.

"Quiet," Maria shushed them.

~*~

ROLAND

Manny somehow managed to make his way down to the front without getting shot. He didn't know how, exactly, and didn't question it.

"Why are you just layin' here?!" he demanded, looking at the men around him. "Find some damn cover, and start shootin' back, morons! You just lay here, they gonna get you one by one!"

"They already got a bunch of us!" someone yelled out.

"More for the rest of us!" Manny encouraged. "You want the women, the food, the guns, you got to work for it! Now return fire!"

The little pep talk worked. Slowly but steadily, the remaining men of the frontal assault, bolstered by the reserve, began to fight back. Manny didn't know if it was doing damage, but they were making a lot of noise, like the boss had wanted.

~*~

"They're working to get around us," Mack said softly as he dropped the magazine from his M-4 and replaced it, "We can't let 'em flank us, or they'll get inside. Jim, get around the other side, and make sure we aren't flanked. Me and Gerry'll hold 'em here. Gets too hot, sing out. We may have to get some help." Edwards nodded, and slipped out of the room, moving low to his new position.

"Lot o' bad guys," Gerry commented.

"More targets," Mack corrected with a growl. "Let's get some."

~*~

James frowned. Something didn't add up.

"What is it?" Susan asked, noticing the look.

"There's too many," he said quietly.

"What? You mean we can't win?"

"No, not that," James shook his head, "I mean there's too many left here. Ralph's blast got at

least four, maybe five, down hard. Since then we've took four more between us. That should leave no more than two."

"And?" Susan asked, twisting around to get a new magazine from her web gear.

"There's at least five people shooting at us," he told her. "Five separate muzzle flashes. They've been reinforced."

"Maybe they had more men than we thought?" Susan offered, slamming the magazine home and hitting the bolt release.

"No, Vaughan was where he could see good. 'Ten men', he said. They've added at least three since the bomb blast. We gotta be careful," he looked concerned. "They're trying to shift more people toward you and me. Like they know where we're weak." He looked over at Susan.

"I don't have to tell you what happens, they get past us."

"No," Susan growled, shifting her gaze back outside, "You don't."

~*~

Roland was actually not doing much shooting himself, working as he was to keep up with what was happening on the outside. It was an unusual situation for him, one he'd never actually been in before.

He warred with the desire to be on the radio, demanding to know how everyone was doing. As an operator, he had hated that kind of elbow jogging. He had to trust the people he'd placed in defensive positions. If they needed his help, they would call.

But in the meantime he had to be patient. And patient wasn't something Roland did all that well.

~*~

BD made it to where his men on the east side of the school were returning fire with the defenders on that side of the building, almost being shot by one of his own men in the process.

"Sorry, Boss," the man apologized, "Didn't know you were coming."

"Radio got busted," BD shrugged. "What's the situation?" he asked the team leader, a short, thick man with a shaved head who went by the moniker, 'Cube'.

"We lost Chains, and Bobber is down, but we got his bleedin' stopped," Cube's answer was short, and just a little insolent. "Had no idea they had explosives." His voice held an accusatory tone.

"Told you they used mines on us," BD reminded him. "Warned you they could have more."

"This wasn't no Claymores," Cube shook his head. "Smells like an ANFO bomb. 'Bout wiped out the west side, I think."

"They're still shooting," BD commented. "Draws heat off of us. So are the front guys. We're goin' inside," he added, drawing his pistol.

"How we get inside?" Cube demanded to know.

"We're going right over the top of them," BD told him. "But not here." He quickly outlined his plan. Cube nodded.

"We can do that," he agreed. "Tee, Roy, you stay with me. Keep up a hot fire on 'em. Rest of you are with the Boss."

BD led the remaining five men around to the right.

ROLAND

~*~

Jim Edwards didn't like being alone in his new position, but it did seem that Mack had gotten it wrong. There was no one in his line of sight, at least not at the moment.

Edwards had never been shot at before, nor had he ever had to fight for his very survival. To say he was scared would be like saying the economic collapse had been a mild recession.

He tightened the grip on his rifle, then realized how sweaty his hands were. Not wanting to have the rifle slip from his hands, he laid the rifle on the floor in front of him, hastily wiping his hands on his shirt. Satisfied they were dry again, he found his rifle and looked back up, out the window in front of him.

~*~

BD shot the man through the window, right between the eyes. Even as the defender fell to the floor BD was scrambling through the window, followed by the five men from Cube's team.

"Time for some payback," he told them, and heard growls of agreement.

"Leave 'em," BD ordered as the men behind him started toward the other two defenders. "Cube's got them pinned down. If they try to follow, then he and the others'll take care of 'em. Let's go."

BD was grateful for the heavy hammering of fire from the defenders, since it masked any noise he and his men might have made. He needed to get inside, deep inside, the school. When he did, he and his men would simply start shooting. Together they could clean out this nest once and for all.

After that, it was just clean-up.

~*~

Jennifer Kingston was a doctor. She'd taken an oath.

She was also a woman with common sense and a strong survival instinct. Her oath, now, was to people she could care for. Like these people. People who had risked an attack just like this one to help others. Other people they had no obligation to, didn't even know.

She and Melissa were crouched in the infirmary, waiting out of the way until they were needed.

It was pointless to think they wouldn't be, she knew, but hoped for it just the same. It didn't cost her anything after all, and she had nothing else to do at the moment.

Outside the door she saw movement. She started to stand up and go to the door, but Melissa stopped her by taking her arm. Jennifer turned to look at her, about to demand to know what she thought she was doing, but Melissa shook her head frantically and made a shushing motion, then indicated they should stay hidden.

James' last minute instructions were to do just that. He had told her that if anyone needed the doctor and nurse team, they would call out.

No one had called out.

Suddenly the curtain over the doorway was shoved aside, and an all too familiar face looked inside. Melissa bit her lip to keep from crying out at the sudden appearance of BD, while keeping her grip on Kingston's arm. The young doctor was about to protest until she saw the absolute fear in Melissa's eyes.

Finally realizing what had happened, her own eyes widened, and she sank down, further out of sight. The two held their breath for what seemed like hours as the leader of their attackers scanned the room, then withdrew.

Both carefully took a breath, and Jennifer reached for her radio.

Melissa drew the small pistol James had given her and pointed it toward the door.

~*~

"Roland, they're inside!" Kingston's urgent call was heard all over the school. Maria quickly slapped her hand to the radio on her hip, muffling the sound. Roland turned to look down the hallway that led to the infirmary.

James almost left his position, but caught himself. Mack realized at once that Jim Edwards was probably dead. Susan Powers simply turned and ran inside the school. She knew that James could handle this.

~*~

Deena had stood up slightly in the kitchen, trying to see out the doorway.

"Deena, get down!" Maria hissed, "We must stay hidden. Wait for them to come to..." She never got the chance to finish.

"Look out!" Terri cried, running to push Deena down as a strange man looked inside the kitchen door and fired.

Maria raised up, braced her arms on the table, and shot the man through the chest with a three round burst from her rifle. She heard Deena grunt in pain as she hit the floor but resisted the urge to check on her, knowing that others might enter any second.

ROLAND

~*~

BD heard the shooting, and shook his head. So much for surprise. He had sent three men up the far hallway, taking the other two with him. In between the two hallways lay the cafeteria, though he wasn't aware of it. He directed the two men following him to keep watch and approached the doorway, intending to see what had happened.

~*~

Susan saw the three men as she entered the hallway from the gym lobby. Without pausing, she flicked the selector switch on her AK to 'auto', something Vaughan had stressed she should never do save in times of dire trouble.

To her, this was dire trouble.

The two men covering BD never knew what hit them, as a veritable storm of bullets filled the hallway. The hit ratio was low, two striking the front man, and three the follower, the rest blasting concrete and paint chips off the walls, ripping up floor tiles, and shredding ceiling tiles.

But the hallway was clear.

Almost.

BD peered out of the cafeteria door, and saw his two men down. He turned to look down the hallway, and saw...

"Well, looky what we got here," he sneered, "If it ain't out very own lit--"

He never finished the sentence. Susan was on him by then, empty rifle discarded. A tomahawk in one hand, combat knife in the other, she hit BD like a hurricane.

~*~

Maria heard the commotion outside the other doorway, but couldn't spare a glance that way. In front of her, she heard Deena grunting with effort.

"Terri, get off me!" she hissed, "We've got. . .Terri? Terri!"

No response.

"Terri!" Deena screeched, "Maria, we need the doctor! Terri's hurt! I think. . .oh my God, *she's been shot!"*

Maria didn't respond. Nor did she take her eyes off the doorway. She moved her hand to make an adjustment to her rifle and then simply waited. Her patience was rewarded three seconds later as two men ripped the double doors open and ran into the room.

Maria held the trigger down until the gun clicked empty. It took some time for her to realize the rifle was empty. It would take longer still for her to release the trigger.

~*~

Roland found her like that, following Deena's screams as she tried to wake her friend Terri.

Roland ordered Fiona Hughes to bring Jennifer and Melissa to the kitchen and called Angie as well.

Firing had slowed outside he noted, and he called Vaughan.

~*~

"We've hit them hard, sir," Vaughan informed him. *"I think they're pulling back. I... on second thought, there's not really any organization to it. I think we may have broken them."*

"Keep hitting them until they're out of sight," Roland ordered. "Ralph, can you hear me?"

"Yes, sir, Mister Roland!" the teen's voice answered at once.

"Call Turnbow's people, tell them what happened. This bunch may head their way as they leave out."

"On it!"

Roland released his radio, looking down at Maria. He carefully reached out and took her rifle in his hands.

The motion jarred her from her trance and she looked up at him, eyes almost wild.

"Ro... Roland I..."

"You did just fine," Roland soothed. He lay the empty rifle down on the table and helped Maria to her feet, then held her steady as she wobbled.

"I...it was so fast," she told him, her voice eerily calm. "There was no time to think! I just..."

"You did what had to be done," Roland told her, turning her face to where he could look into her eyes. "You did exactly what you had to do, Maria. I think it's all over now," he added.

And then Maria folded, the last of her calm gone. She simply folded into him, crying her eyes out.

Angie ran into the room, sliding down to her knees where Deena was still trying to get Terri to respond. Ignoring the screaming teen she assessed Terri quickly and efficiently, then sat back on her heels. Looking up, she saw Roland looking at her, and shook her head slowly.

Roland closed his eyes. He had lost another child.

ROLAND

CHAPTER FIFTY-TWO

The sun was well into the sky before the area was officially cleared. The surviving civilians simply sat still, shocked and exhausted by the events of the morning. None had ever been through anything quite like it. Their minds would be a long time processing what had happened here today.

The soldiers among them *had* been through it. They fell into an old, well-used routine. Gallows humor, cleaning and clearing equipment, returning to battery. Actions that could be done literally blindfolded. Familiar actions. Comforting actions.

Looking out over the body-strewn yard, Tom Mackey had walked outside to make sure that all the dead bodies were actually *dead* bodies. James exchanged a look with Susan, and they soon joined him.

James had gotten a look at what was left of BD before Susan had grabbed a tablecloth and covered him with it. She looked at him, eyes still a little wild, as if daring him to comment. James had simply nodded once, firmly. That seemed to reassure the woman and she relaxed after that.

James did make a note to speak to Roland about it. Susan had done a real number on BD. She might bear watching for a day or two. Or more.

Maria was too busy comforting Deena to assess her own feelings. It would come later, in Roland's arms, as she cried herself to sleep. She had killed three men, on top of everything else, today.

Deena was beside herself with grief, knowing that her friend, the girl she called 'soul sister', had died saving her. Saving her from a stupid act that Deena had known better than to do. As far as Deena was concerned, she might as well have shot Terri herself.

Roland watched the grim detail of Tom, James, and Susan going through the bodies. Anything of use was stripped from them, carried back to the school for later inventory.

ROLAND

Roland had done his own grisly inventory after the shooting ended. The bill had been high, this time. Very high.

Jim Edwards. Marie Hilliard. Cathy Larkin. All gone. Gone with Terri. Sweet, lovable, always Chipper, Terri. Nor had they heard from Rich and Glenda, yet.

Most of the survivors were injured to some degree, though thankfully, not badly. James had a bullet crease along his left arm. Mack had chips of concrete embedded along the right side of his face from a near miss. Jesse had a bruised shoulder from the SAW, and a nasty cut below his left eye from a ricochet. Susan Powers had several cuts, scrapes and bruises from her battle with BD. Fiona Richards had a flesh wound in her right leg. Vaughan a sprained ankle, gotten when he had moved across the graveled roof to assist James. Tom Mackey had a bruised and bleeding face from a shower of that same gravel thrown into his face by a close call shot from the attackers.

It seemed like a sick joke to say they were lucky, but Roland knew that they had been. If not for the presence of so many steady people and Ralph's handiwork, things could have gone much, much worse.

The building had taken a good bit of damage as well. Many windows were broken and the brick exterior would never look right again. What the attackers lacked in skill and brains they had tried very hard to make up for in sheer volume of fire. There would be a lot of work to do.

Roland sighed. So much loss, and so much still to do. It never ended. He wondered if it ever would.

~*~

"Well, soldier boy, I think you'll live," Jennifer Kingston tried to be upbeat, but it was hard. Her own brush with the invaders, topped with so many injured, to say nothing of those for whom she could do nothing, had left her mentally and emotionally exhausted.

"I've had worse," Jesse said simply. Adrenaline was still pumping through him, and he was careful to hold himself in check. He really liked the lady doctor.

"I'm sure you have," Jennifer nodded, her left hand absently tracing a scar down the left side of Jesse's abdomen.

"Ah, that was a long time ago," he said ruefully, "Misspent youth and all that."

"And the one on your leg?" she asked.

"Iraq," Jesse said simply, shrugging. "The one on my shoulder was Afghanistan," he added,

"Ambush."

"Such a rough life," she said softly, her hand caressing his shoulder.

"Ain't been that bad," Jesse shrugged, "Only one I had," He managed to grin.

"Well, I got work to do, and I guess you do too," Jennifer said, almost reluctant to take her hand back. She did finally, and Jesse shrugged back into his shirt.

"Yeah, no rest for the wicked."

"No wickedness here, soldier," she shook her head. "All of you, fighting to. . .no, no wickedness," she finished softly. "Come see me later?"

"It's a promise," Jesse nodded. On impulse he leaned down to kiss her cheek. He was surprised when his lips met hers, Jennifer having turned her head at the last second.

"Later," she said again, then turned to her work. Jesse left, shaking his head.

~*~

"Sir," Turnbow's runner was teary-eyed.

"Yeah?" Roland asked.

"Sir, we sent out a patrol after your message, to try and get a handle on the rest. We. . .well, sir, we found your bus. It…it was shot full o' holes, and been burned. There was. . .was two bodies inside," the young man's eyes were misty.

"I see," Roland felt a heavy hand settle on him.

"They fought, sir," the man went on, "We found five dead bikers around the bus, and another in

the door. They. . .they went hard."

"Thanks, son," Roland nodded. "Can you take us to it? We need to do right by 'em."

"Yes, sir. S'why the Reverend sent me. Allowed you'd want to do it y'all's selves."

"Give us a minute."

~*~

It was near sunset when the survivors gathered outside. Fresh graves had been dug near Cassandra's.

"Lord, we don't know why this happened," Jesse said softly, his voice carrying. "We don't know why our friends had to die like this, at the hands of criminals." Deena was sobbing, supported on one side by Maria, and the other by Melissa Andrews.

ROLAND

"We *do* know that these were good people, Lord," Jesse went on, "We know that because when things were hard, when things were dangerous, they didn't shirk their duty to their fellow men. They worked, they fought, and they died beside us, for the right."

"We ask, Oh Lord, that they inherit their place with You, where You'll keep them against that day when we can all see each other once more. We ask, too, Oh Lord, that You keep the rest of us in Your protected care, against that day. Forgive us, Oh Lord, when we sin, that we shall see that day.

Amen."

"Amen," the assembled group repeated. Slowly the bodies were lowered into the ground.

Several stepped forward to drop flowers or mementos into the graves. Deena softly dropped Terri's diary, along with her favorite hair ribbon into her friend's grave. Suddenly she turned and ran away, crying all the while. Maria looked at Roland for a second, then went after her, Melissa following.

The task done, James, ever present and loyal James, used the backhoe to finish the job. In twos and threes, the men and women of the school trooped back inside.

Roland walked around the school, silently looking for something he might have done different.

Something that might have made a difference in the body count.

Something that would justify the guilt he was feeling.

By dark, he still hadn't found it.

~*~

The night was still. No one had spoken much during the evening meal, whether from exhaustion, shock, or a combination of the two. There just didn't seem to be anything to say.

Every one of the old crew missed Terri terribly. Deena was the worst, of course, acting as if she had lost a part of herself. And, maybe she had.

Tom and James were on watch, and Melissa had fixed the two of them a tray, carrying their supper to them, then eating her own with James as he stood watch at the front. The young couple sat in silence. Even alone, no one had anything to say.

Roland assigned watches to the most dependable and able-bodied remaining people, two hour Shifts, max. Everyone needed rest. Needed time. He decided at the spur of the moment that the following day would be a down day. No work other than what was absolutely needed to keep things running, and minimum security. After weeks on edge, long days and nights of waiting for the attack, and then the brutality of the actual attack itself, everyone needed rest, and any relaxation they could get.

Including Roland himself.

~*~

The next morning dawned clear and a little cool, a gentle breeze blowing across the land.

Roland, as was his practice, was awake early. He very carefully extracted himself from Maria, rising from the bed the two had shared. She had always slept in her own bed, since the two of them had. . .well, since they'd admitted to liking each other. Couldn't really say they were dating, could he?

Last night she had come to his room, and was there waiting when he arrived from the shower.

They hadn't said much, beyond establishing that Deena was with Melissa Andrews and Jennifer Kingston, and she didn't want to be alone. Didn't think she *could be* alone.

Roland had nodded his understanding, taking her in his arms. Less than a minute later Maria had broken down completely. Roland patiently held her until at last she had cried herself to sleep.

It had taken him longer, but he'd finally drifted off.

Looking down now at her peacefully sleeping form, he smiled gently. She worked so hard, worried so much, and now it was starting to tell. She was exhausted.

He gathered his things quietly and left, closing the door behind him. He hoped she'd sleep for a while, knowing she needed it.

Dressed, he walked around the school in the approaching daylight. The bodies were gone but the damage was still there. He would ask Ralph to make an assessment of the building later, maybe tomorrow, and see what they had to do.

He wandered around front where Mack and Angela were standing, well, sitting, guard duty at the front door.

"Morning," he said gently. The two broke apart, startled.

"Morning, Roland," Mack smiled, realizing who it was.

"Hi," Angela smiled.

"You guys okay?" Roland asked. Both nodded.

"Ain't nothin' we ain't did before," Mack replied.

"Not anything we haven't done before," Angela corrected him, scowling.

"What I said," Mack nodded.

"How long you guys been out?" Roland asked, grinning.

"Just got here," Mack informed him. "Maybe twenty minutes. Relieved James, and Susan."

"Good deal," Roland nodded. "We're down, today. Nothing but absolutely essential work gets done today. I want everyone to have a good, long, easy day, hopefully free of. . .complications."

"That sounds like a gift from heaven," Angela smiled. "From your lips to God's ears."

"Doubt He'd listen to me," Roland said simply. "Certainly ain't no reason to."

"God loves soldiers, too, Roland," Angela said firmly.

"You guys take care," Roland said, and moved on.

~*~

He was sitting out front again, enjoying the sun, when Maria found him.

"Why did you leave me asleep?" she asked, sitting down beside him.

"You needed it," he said simply as she took his hand.

"You do, too," she said softly.

"I'm getting what I need," Roland told her. "I'm relaxing. Resting. Just like everyone else is.

Only the most necessary work is getting done today. We're all taking a much needed, much *deserved*, day off."

"I like this idea," Maria smiled. She lay down beside him on the blanket he'd spread across the grass.

Soon, both were dozing lightly.

~*~

The next morning Turnbow and a dozen townspeople showed up, arriving by eight.

Announcing that they were there to help, they went to work repairing as much of the damage to the building as they could. Broken windows were boarded, debris swept up and shoveled into buckets.

The work went quickly with so many willing hands. Roland tried to thank Turnbow, but the older man shook his head.

"If that bunch had hit us like they did you, we'd be done for," the preacher said. "As it is, I'm sorry you lost so many good people, son. I wish we'd been here to help you, even knowing some of us

would probably have met our maker in the doing."

"No way you could help us, sir," Roland shrugged. "They might just as easily have hit you.

We'll work together to form a defense of some kind later on though, if you'd like. In case something like this happens again."

"I would, and so would the others," Turnbow nodded firmly. "I admit, I really thought that things would right themselves. Been too long in the country I guess. I didn't realize until I talked to that young soldier just how bad things were."

"We can't thank you enough for helping out," Roland told him.

"We're just returning the favor," Turnbow told him, "And I'd like to think that maybe we've moved beyond trading favors, comes to that."

"I'd like that myself," Roland smiled for the first time in several days. "I really would."

"Well, we're needed at home," Turnbow sighed. "Ain't never enough light, these days."

"No sir, there ain't," Roland extended his hand, and Turnbow took it. "See you later."

~*~

Five days later, things back to normal as they would ever be, Roland and several others stood out front as a small convoy pulled into the front of the school. Two buses, three Army deuce-and-a-halfs, four box trucks, an ambulance, and four Hummers pulling trailers. There was also a semi pulling a mobile home, two RVs, and a fuel truck the size of those that made deliveries to small filling stations and farms. A pair of MRAPs guarded the convoy, fore and aft.

The children were on one of those buses and spilled out running to Maria, Deena, and Ralph as if they were starved to see them.

Jenkins approached Roland with a tired grin.

"Good to see you, Gerald," Roland returned the smile.

"Same to you, Roland. How are you?"

"We're. . .gettin' there," Roland settled for saying. "Lost a lot of good people."

"I know, and I'm sorry," Jenkins grimaced slightly. "It's that way everywhere right now. You aren't alone."

"Looks like you've brought more than just children this trip," Roland nodded to the convoy, wanting to change the subject.

"I have," the soldier nodded in return. "Let's go someplace quiet so we can talk."

~*~

ROLAND

"I'm sorry," Jenkins sighed as Roland came to the end of his after-action report. He had written a report for Captain Thomas, which he handed over to Jenkins.

"Nothing for it," Roland shrugged. "I think the gang is broken," he went on, "There's some of them still out there, but the leader is dead, along with a good many of his men. No idea who'll wind up in charge, but I think they'll stay clear of us, at least for a while."

"We'll try and get the word around to other places," Jenkins promised.

"So, what's with all the hardware?" Roland asked, sitting back in his chair.

"Well, we've had some changes," Jenkins leaned back in his own chair. "Thomas is now a light Colonel, in charge of the Middle Tennessee Military District."

"Interesting," Roland mused.

"Pentagon has made a move," Jenkins nodded. "There's no civilian leadership worthy of the name at the Federal level anymore. At least no one that anyone's willing to listen to."

"General Wheeler, the Chairman of the JCS, has issued orders to all military units to assist any local level leaders in their area."

"To what end?" Roland asked, leaning forward.

"Restoration of services as far as practicable, support for local law enforcement officials still on the job, securing infrastructure to ensure free flowing transportation and safe travel, and elimination of the 'undesirable element' now spreading terror and violence throughout the nation. End quote."

"Damn," Roland whistled lightly, "That's a tall marching order."

"Ain't it though," Jenkins sighed. "Good news is, a lot of guys are returning to the colors, bringing their families and any 'borrowed' equipment with them."

"No charges?" Roland asked, thinking of himself.

"Nope," Jenkins grinned, "Oh, and as of now, you've been honorably discharged from the Army, and are now a full-fledged member of the Tennessee National Guard," he announced, handing over an envelope with the Guard's letterhead on it.

Opening it, Roland read the short note from Captain, or rather Lieutenant Colonel, Thomas, ordering him to maintain his current post as OIC, and commander of the County Military Detachment A. Inside he found the yellow 'butter bar' of a 2nd Lieutenant.

"You're kidding," he looked as Jenkins, the bars in his hand.

"Nope," Jenkins grinned evilly.

"He couldn't have made me a First Sergeant?" Roland complained, "Someone with some real authority?"

"Hey!" Jenkins looked offended.

"Just sayin'," Roland muttered. "Thanks, though," he added, "It's a relief to know that I'm not -"

"You earned it, brother," Jenkins replied seriously. "The Colonel made that point rather strongly to your last CO."

"Please tell him thank you," Roland said sincerely, "For everything. And what's Detachment A?"

"Actually it's your only detachment," Jenkins shrugged. "This is a small county, so one's all you get. I told you we were going to place detachments in places like yours to help locals, right?" Roland nodded.

"Well, that was actually where Wheeler got the idea. Cap'n told him what we were doin', and he liked it so much he passed it on in his General Order Number One." You could hear the capital letters.

"You've got four men with an armored HUMVEE. Good sergeant leading the team. Their job will be to assist the local sheriff. Wilson still sheriff?" At Roland's nod, Jenkins nodded and continued, "Good. Sergeant Drake and his crew will assist him with patrol and back him up when needed.

He'll need to provide local sworn officers to accompany them, though. We're strictly here to assist.

Locals *have* to take the lead," he emphasized.

"Well, he'll be glad for that," Roland nodded, thinking what a difference these men might have made less than a week ago.

"Okay, now that that's taken care of, moving on," Jenkins went on, "There's another team along, two engineers and their escorts. Their job is to help get things like water services working again and to help set up some solar power systems. They're actually building some PV panels. No idea how it works, but it *does* work. They'll need manpower, which I will leave to you," he grinned, "as the local commander."

"Ass," Roland snorted.

"Ass, *sir*," Jenkins corrected straight-faced. He held the glare for all of five seconds before losing it in a struggle with a belly laugh.

"Anyway, take good care of them. You're getting them ahead of several larger places just because, well, you're you."

"What's that mean?" Roland asked.

"Hey, man, I don't think you realize how much you've helped us," Jenkins told him. "Some of your ideas are the reason we were able to start feeding and equipping people. Got the city cleaned out.

We owe you, and we pay our debts."

"You don't owe me," Roland shook his head.

"Anyway," Jenkins decided to end this before it started. "Give them whatever help they need.

ROLAND

What else?" he asked himself as he looked at his notebook.

"Supplies! Four box trucks full of canned and dry goods. Might be the last," he looked up, making sure Roland understood, "Use it well. One truck also has a lot of seeds for next year, and more canning equipment and supplies. Also might be the last," he warned, "Take care of them."

"Brought you some ammo, and replacement equipment as well. Have to let the Detachment draw supply from there, but there's a lot of it. There's several cases of MREs, but there won't be any more for a while. We're running low, and saving the rest for patrols. Supposed to be getting some more soon, and the General has already got resupply going out from dumps and plants all over the country. Supposedly the Air Force is even flying stuff home. We'll see." He checked his note book again.

"Medicines," he checked off another entry. "You've got a doctor now so we've sent everything she should need to set up a clinic. Have to share," he said pointedly. "She's not just for you guys, right?"

"No, we're taking her on her rounds each week."

"Great! One more thing already done," he made another check mark. "Let's see. . .fuel truck is staying, but the security guys will be using it too. There'll be another, larger truck coming soon, loaded with diesel for the harvest and hopefully enough for planting the next crop. You'll need to recruit a local leader for that," he added.

"There's a couple guys I know that might be able to handle that," Roland nodded, thinking of both Derrick Turnbow and Tom Mackey.

"Better and better," Jenkins nodded. "Some clothing on board, no idea what sizes, it's all just tossed in there, including skivvies," he added, "Some BDUs too, and some are camo, taken from warehouses. Civilian wear, but suitable for deployment. Web gear, a lot of civilian stuff but it looks pretty good."

"More hand tools, including some knives this time, and some machetes. Some multi-tools. I've got most of the better hardware separated so you can assign it to your operators if you want." He checked his notes. Looking up, he leaned back again.

"That kid's water filter works, by the way," he announced. "For the life of me, I can't figure out why none of us, *no one*, thought of it. I brought him a few goodies, too, to say thanks."

"Nothing that explodes or shoots, I hope," Roland snorted, only half joking.

"Hey, sounds to me like he's done right by you," Jenkins shrugged, "But, no. Some parts and supplies that he should be able to make use of. He was particularly interested in electrical wire, duct and electrical tape, wire connectors, and for some reason, copper tubing?"

"Oh, no," Roland felt a headache coming, "For his still."

"Seriously?"

"Oh, yes."

"Well, that explains the two-hundred-gallon water tank," Jenkins chuckled.

"How do you know he wanted all this?" Roland asked.

"He gave me a list, last time I was here," Jenkins replied. "Since the water filter worked, I decided to bring him everything I could find."

"Now he's building a network," Roland groaned.

"I've seen supply sergeants who couldn't do better," Jenkins agreed. "Keep a tight grip on that kid, Roland. He's worth his weight in gold these days."

"You can bet on it."

"Well, I guess we need to meet your troops," Jenkins stood.

"One more thing," Roland said, "I'd like for Jesse to be added to the rolls, as my Sergeant, and second-in-command. He'll need real authority with soldiers posted here now."

Jenkins reproduced his notebook, scribbled himself a note, and took Jesse's information.

"Go ahead and appoint him, on my authority," Jenkins ordered. "I'll clear it with the Colonel as soon as I get back."

"Thanks."

~*~

Tom Wilson arrived just as Roland and Jenkins were about to meet the men of the Detachment A.

"Tom," Roland nodded.

"Roland. Sorry I'm late."

"Right on time," Jenkins smiled. "Sheriff Wilson, may I present Sergeant Kenneth Drake. He will lead the team assigned to your office to help secure your area."

"Sergeant, it's a pleasure to meet you," Wilson said sincerely.

"We're here to help, sir," Drake promised. "We'll need a liaison for the team, who will be in charge. Our tasking is to provide support for your office."

"They've been given a crash course in Civil Affairs and Military Policing for Civilians," Jenkins added, "but they are *not* civilian peace officers. They are here to provide you with manpower, and, if needed, firepower."

"I can sure use the help," Wilson nodded. "Sergeant Drake, what say you and I, tomorrow, make the rounds. I can introduce you to the community leaders in the area, and my own people, and get you acquainted with the area."

"Sounds like a plan, sir," Drake nodded.

"Outstanding," Wilson agreed.

"Gentlemen, this is Lieutenant Roland Stang, late of the One-oh-One, and your new commanding officer," Jenkins introduced. "He and the people here just fought a major engagement five days or so ago against at least fifty attackers."

"Sir," Drake saluted. Roland returned it, feeling fraudulent.

"Sergeant," he nodded, shaking hand with each. "I'm sure the Sheriff is glad to have your help, and so am I. We took a lot of casualties in our fight. Had we had you and your men with us, I'm sure it would have gone better."

"Thank you, sir," Drake replied. "If there's a next time, we'll be here."

"Hopefully there won't be one as bad as that," Roland told him, "But I'm sure the Sheriff's office has its own troubles. You'll be a great service to him and the people here, I'm sure."

"Well, now that we've all met," Jenkins declared, "it's time to start getting some work done."

~*~

"Major Albert, and Captain Cristina Carpenter," Jenkins introduced, "this is Lieutenant Roland Stang, the Area Detachment Commander. Roland, the engineers I was telling you about."

"Pleasure to meet you folks," Roland shook hands. "We're glad to see you."

"Glad to be here," Albert smiled. "We'll see what we can do about getting you some systems restored, L-T."

"Just Roland, sir," Roland insisted, "I've been a Lieutenant for about," he checked his watch, "forty-five minutes," he grinned.

"Lot of that going around," Albert nodded. "My wife and I were out-date when the shit hit the fan."

"Now we're in again," the brunette Captain smiled, "But, hey, it's a job."

"It sure will be," Roland nodded. "I'm sure the Sheriff can get you in touch with the right people. This is Sheriff Tom Wilson."

"Pleased to meet you," Wilson agreed.

"We'd like to spend tomorrow here at the school, Sheriff, if that's acceptable," Albert said at once. "There's a good bit we can do here to make the clinic better, and make the children more comfortable."

"That's fine by me," Wilson nodded. "Tomorrow's full for me, anyhow. And I can use this afternoon to round up the people you'll need to see, too."

"Sounds good," Albert said. "In that case, we'll get to work."

"Seem like good folks," Wilson mused.

"They are," Jenkins assured him, "And smart, too. They'll get you back online, as far as practicable anyway. A few TVA folks are working on restoring at least some power, but it means reworking a lot of stuff. Still, maybe another month, we'll have some limited electricity."

"Oh, that would be wonderful!" Wilson smiled, "Anything'd be a help, right now."

"We're working on it."

ROLAND

CHAPTER FIFTY-THREE

The next week passed in a blur. The carpenters were everywhere at once it seemed. The school was now about three-quarters powered thanks to their homemade solar panels and an inverter built by Ralph out of. . .well, Roland didn't want to know what. It worked, so that was all that mattered. The Carpenters had brought a dozen massive forklift batteries with them, and six were put in use at the school since there was also a clinic there. The carpenters 'enlisted' Ralph to accompany them for the rest of their work throughout the county, so impressed they had been with his work. Roland immediately assigned one of the men from Sergeant Drake's command to escort Ralph, and Ralph only. The soldier was informed in no uncertain terms that Ralph was his *only* priority.

Wilson was thrilled to get one of the large batteries and the solar rig at his office, since it gave him at least some communications ability, and also meant that he could house prisoners in somewhat better conditions.

Reverend Turnbow's group also received one at the church, for which they were very grateful.

The others went to other communities throughout the small county.

Two days' worth of work at the water plant with a large generator saw water once more being cleaned and purified. A water buffalo was pressed into service to transport the now clean water to various points throughout the county, where grateful residents gathered to receive it. One of Drake's men accompanied a deputy to provide security and ensure that everyone got a share.

There was bickering of course, as people began to complain that they should have more than others, their need was greater, they had a 'right' to clean water, and so on. When would they get power like the people had in other places? Why couldn't they get water in their homes, like before? The litany of complaints went on and on.

Jesse continued to escort Jennifer on her 'rounds', visiting those who were shut in or too sick to make it to her clinic. This too caused grumbling. Where was the medicine for the colds, the aches and pains, the sinus troubles, the blah, blah, blah? Jennifer was patient at first, explaining that there was no way to provide the same level of antibiotics or pain medicine as before, offering home grown substitutes that people could grow or make themselves.

'Why should we have to make our own medicine?' was the inevitable reply. It was her responsibility to provide the medicine they needed and requested. Marijuana was being grown all over the county now with no interference, to use as an analgesic. Some refused to use the 'devil weed', demanding prescription drugs instead, and becoming irate when told they weren't available.

No amount of explanations would placate some, especially those who were legally 'hooked' on prescription pain meds before the collapse. The hell of it was, for her, she knew that many of them really needed the pain relief to have any kind of meaningful life. She could tell who was an addict and who was really in pain, but it made no real difference. She didn't have the drugs to give.

Those who listened soon realized that the home cures the young doctor gave them worked.

Perhaps not as well as their old medicines had, but close enough. Those who didn't evolved from complaints to demands, then from demands to threats. The threats continued to escalate until Jesse deemed it only a matter of time before someone tried to attack the medical mission. Thus yet another trooper was detached to accompany the 'medical detail' once a week on its rounds.

~*~

"I don't like the mood we're starting to see, Roland," Jesse said. They were seated around their version of a conference table, where key personnel met once a week to discuss planning. Tom Wilson sat in on those whenever he could, and was present at this one.

"It's the same all over," he sighed wearily. "Whatever we manage to do, they want more."

"There's no more to give," Roland shrugged helplessly. The carpenters had done all they could in the week they had been there, but the engineering couple were now five weeks gone from their area.

And they weren't coming back.

"We've done, or we're doing, all that we can," Roland continued, "And we're overextended doing that. Sergeant Drake and his men are doing all they can and we never have more than one person on duty here in the daytime. At least not anymore. We're spread thin."

"My men are tired, sir," Drake spoke up. "We've been working without a single day off since we arrived. And some of those days have had long hours. If they don't get at least a day of down time, and soon, they'll be on sick call."

"Is there anything planned for tomorrow that requires their presence?" Roland asked.

"No water deliveries, anyway," Wilson shook his head. "Plant's got to have maintenance done so they'll be offline until morning after. It'll help save fuel on the genny anyway," he added with a shrug.

"Ralph may have something to help with that," Roland noted. "We'll get to that. Meanwhile, I see no reason that the security detachment can't stand down tomorrow. Agreed?"

"No problems I know of," Wilson nodded.

"Thank you, sir," Drake looked relieved.

"What's next?"

"We need to start thinking about how many people we'll need to get our garden in," Maria pointed out, "And we need to talk to Turnbow's people about the help canning and preserving they promised as well," she added.

"Okay," Roland nodded, making a note. "I was thinking we can offer to let them use the kitchen

here to do their own canning, or at least some of it, while helping us do ours. Any objections?"

"We will need to plan that ahead so that we can have simpler meals that will not need the stove tops," was all Maria said.

"No problem, I take it?" he asked.

"No, but we will need a day, preferably two, to get things prepared."

"I'll make sure you get it," Roland promised, making another note. "Next?"

"We're starting to see a good bit of theft, and even some senseless vandalism," Wilson sighed.

"We going to need more patrols, and for that we need gas, which we don't have."

"Again, we'll talk about gas after the meeting," Roland noted. "What else might help?"

"Well," Wilson scratched his head, "we could station Sergeant Drake's men around the county, to help--"

"That's a no go," Roland shook his head before Drake could speak up. "They *have* to have a civilian police officer with them at all times when they're doing the patrols, or enforcing any laws.

That's from On High, and it's not amenable."

"Have you considered a posse, sir?" Drake asked, drawing a few chuckles.

"I'm serious," Drake informed them, his glare cutting across the laughs. "It's a legitimate law enforcement tool. Assigning volunteer or reserve deputy status to trusted members of the community to help in situations just like this one. You have the power and authority to do that, sir."

"Are you sure?" Wilson asked, skeptical.

"I am," Drake nodded firmly. "And with men spread throughout the county, you can reduce your patrols some as well. Equip the deputies with radios, and let them call you only when it's something they can't handle. All you have to do is write up their op orders for them to follow in the field."

"Wait. What?" Wilson was lost.

"Rules of Engagement," Jesse provided. "You need a list of things they can deal with, and another of things where they need to notify you at once. Some things can be dealt with using citations and maybe get a judge around once a month to deal with them. No one's got money to pay fines with, anyway, so most of its gonna be community service."

"And you can use that to get help to the elderly or shut-ins who can't help themselves," Jennifer piped up, seeing a way to help at least some of her patients.

"Hm," Wilson mused. "That ain't no bad idea at all," he decided. "I like it. I'll see what Judge McCoy says about it. I'm sure he'd like to get things back in some kind of order himself. We're only holding the worst offenders right now, anyway, since there's nowhere to send anyone, even if they had a felony conviction. We've got to get some semblance of a justice system started back, and soon."

"All well and good, but that's not really something we should be involved in," Roland moved to get the meeting back on track. "Anyone have anything else that concerns us, or our area?"

"One more thing, Sheriff," Drake spoke up, "You should appoint at least one person here as a reserve deputy. Then, we can roll out from here to answer calls with him if there's a real problem."

"Yeah," Wilson seemed intrigued, and glanced at Roland.

"Not a chance," Roland said at once. "Besides, since I'm technically Drake's commanding officer and in active service for the duration, I don't qualify. Neither does Jesse. Come to think of it, Vaughn, Mack, and Angie won't either," Roland frowned.

"Figures," Wilson sighed.

"What about Tom Mackey?" Jesse asked.

"He still stayin' here?" Wilson asked.

ROLAND

"Yes," Roland nodded.

"Well, he'd make a fine one for sure, if he'll do it," Wilson nodded. "Reckon I'll talk to him after this."

"Which brings me back to my original question, does anyone have anything else?" Roland looked around. "Then we're adjourned," he declared, when no one answered. "Tom, about the fuel? Ralph is cooking up some, uh, fuel additive, of sorts."

"Fuel additive, huh?" the sheriff grinned. "First time I've ever heard that turn of phrase used for shine. And I thought I'd heard them all," he laughed.

"Well, if there's others in the county that can, uh, cook, I guess, you should get them on it," Roland suggested. "Ralph says it'll work just fine for gas in engines that are properly maintained."

"Good idea," Wilson agreed. "Should have already done it, but. . .well, hell, it's kinda hard to remember that some things are okay, now, that weren't. Spent my whole career fighting drugs and illegal stills, and now there's pot growing everywhere, and I'm encouragin' it," he shook his head.

"Yeah," Roland was sympathetic. "Still, we've got to adapt. Only way we'll get back to some kind of normal. Someday."

"Normal," Wilson tried the word out. "Don't even remember what it was like, no more," he said wearily.

"Tom, you need to get some of the other people with this county involved in some of this,"

Roland suggested. "You can't do it all and still do your own job."

"I know, but. . .too many *won't* help, some *can't*, and the few that can want armed guards, cars, radios, protection for their homes, and a whole lot o' other stuff I can't give 'em," the sheriff sighed, "And, since they ain't gettin' paid no more, I guess they don't have any obligation to do their jobs," he shrugged. "That leaves me."

"They swore an oath," Roland pointed out. "One that's still in effect," he added.

"Try gettin' them to admit that," Wilson snorted. "Anyway," he stood up slowly. "I'll make another stab at it, I reckon. Can't hurt."

"You need to take a day off, too," Roland advised. "Maybe a weekend."

"There's always something needs doin'," the other man shook his head.

"You've got deputies, let them deal for two days. Anyone has a problem that someone else used to handle, send the problem to that person. Let them handle it."

"Wish it were that easy." A tired grin.

"It is that easy," Roland told him. "If they won't do it, remind 'em we're under martial law, and you're a lot nicer than I am." Wilson gave him a shocked look. That slowly gave way to a nasty grin.

"Now that's something I can use," he cackled, heading for the door with Roland. "I think I just might do that."

"You need support, you let me know." Outside the room, one of the passing children fell into a round of coughing. Roland patted him gently on the back.

"You okay, buddy?" he asked. The boy, all of five, looked up at him, and nodded.

"Yes, sir," he replied quietly.

"Okay, then. If that cough keeps up, you tell Miss Jennifer, okay?"

"Yes, sir." Another nod.

"Good deal." The boy went on his way, and Roland watched him, smiling.

"You're pretty good with them," Tom noted.

"Not like I should be," was Roland's only reply.

~*~

Roland ate supper with Maria, which had become their common practice. They couldn't always eat breakfast or lunch together, but baring emergency they made a commitment to always take their evening meals together.

"It would seem that as people grow less afraid, they grow bolder," Maria noted that evening.

"Don't they just?" Roland snorted. "It's not like we don't have a million problems. It's all 'me, me, me'. I...I can almost understand it, I guess. I mean, we've got it a lot better than some."

"And we've worked hard for it, too," Maria replied, a little defensive.

"Yes, we have, and made too many sacrifices," Roland agreed. "Thing is, since Thomas hung this county's military district on me, now I have to try and deal with a lot of those issues too. I guess," he leaned back, thinking, "I really need to get out more. See what's what, you know?"

"But what about here?" Maria asked. "You're needed here, Roland!"

"Not really," Roland shook his head. "I mean, this place runs itself, mostly. All of you know what to do without me telling you. Most of you do better without me telling you. There's no reason I need to be here day in and day out for the school to function. And, I really should be taking a more active role in helping make changes. I don't like it, but I can't really tell Thomas no, either. He helped me a whole bunch, and not just with supplies and equipment, either."

"I know," Maria nodded. "It just seems unfair," she added, sadly.

"Well, maybe," Roland shrugged. "But then, there's a whole bunch o' 'not fair' goin' around,

right now, too." He thought about it for a minute.

"I think tomorrow I'll borrow Tom Mackey and take a turn around. First stop'l be Turnbow's, I

think, to make sure we're on the same page about them helping with the canning."

"Thank you," Maria smiled, but it faded quickly.

"Hey, now, don't get all serious on me," Roland teased. "Makes you feel better, I'll take Mack and Angie, as well. Nice and safe. Drake and his men will be here all day tomorrow, so there's no safety problem. Plus, Vaughan, James, and Susan will still be here. So will Jesse, since there's no med run tomorrow."

"It'll be fine," he promised.

"If it will be fine, then there's no reason I can't go with you," Maria said evenly. Roland looked at her a minute, and then smiled.

"No reason at all," he replied. "We'll take Vaughan with us instead of Mack and Angie. How 'bout that?"

"I think that sounds like a wonderful day," Maria smiled.

Behind them, one of the children coughed.

CHAPTER FIFTY-FOUR

Tom Mackey had agreed to Wilson's offer, albeit reluctantly. So it was in his new official capacity that he went with Roland on his 'turn around town,' as Roland was calling it. Anticipating being away most of the day, a cooler was placed in the back of the Hummer with lunch and water.

"You're in charge," Roland took great pleasure in telling Jesse. "Don't do anything I wouldn't do," he added with a grin.

"What does that rule out?" Jesse asked. "We'll be fine. You deserve a day off, anyway."

"It's not a day off," Roland informed him. "With my ascension to the lofty heights of greatness, I need to start being seen a bit out in the county. There's a lot of stuff not gettin' done, and Wilson's got to have some help. These people are gonna have to get with the program or get out of it, know what I mean?"

"I get ya," Jesse nodded. "Anyway, we got this. Get on outta here. Officers give me allergies anyway. *Sir.*"

"You'll pay for that," Roland warned grimly, "When you least expect it."

"Go already!" Jesse laughed.

~*~

"Where to first, Tom?" Vaughn asked as driver. Roland had intended to drive, but Vaughan wouldn't hear of it.

"Officers don't drive with an enlisted man in the vehicle."

"Is that supposed to be funny?" Roland growled.

"Not a bit," Vaughan promised. "This'll make you look like the man, that's all. Impression is half the battle sometimes, Roland. Don't worry," he added, smiling, "I won't treat you any different. To me you're still just a crazy man."

"Well," Roland had been slightly mollified at that, "Okay."

"Let's head to Turnbow's first," Roland ordered before Tom could speak. "I need to speak to him, and make some arrangements, so let's get that done first. Tom, you can be thinking about a route for us until then, if you will. I'd like to cover as much as we can, and talk to as many community leaders as we can."

"Sounds like a plan," Tom nodded.

The trip was occupied with discussions about what was happening, and what still needed to happen. Roland paid careful attention to the people around him. They were all smart and experienced.

Not for the first time he thought about how very fortunate he had been to have so many good people around him. He didn't like to think about where he and the others would be, if not for them.

Turnbow was actually out in the small town when they arrived, and headed for the Hummer as soon as it pulled up, smiling.

"Morning, Roland!" he called, offering his hand. "How ya'll doing?"

"Doing well, sir," Roland smiled, "How are things?"

"Passin' fair, Praise the Lord," Turnbow replied. "We're in pretty good shape all around, seems like. Really appreciate the help from the engineering folk. And that boy o' yours. That's one smart young'un, son."

"That he is," Roland smiled. "Maria was wanting to speak to some of your ladies about preparing for canning season," he continued, "and, we're wondering if you folks would want to make use of the school kitchen during canning time this year."

"Why, I don't know," Turnbow mused. "Have to just ask. Young lady, my missus and several other ladies just happen to be discussing the same thing, over to the church building. You want to go and speak to them?"

"That would be good, yes," Maria smiled. "Thank you. I will be as quick as I can, Roland," she looked over at him.

"Take whatever time you need."

She rewarded him with a dazzling smile, and started toward the church. Roland looked at Vaughan and nodded in her direction. Vaughan nodded his understanding, and set out behind her.

"Fine young woman, Roland," Turnbow said.

"One of a kind," Roland assured him. "Meantime, let's you, me, and Tom find a shady spot, and palaver."

~*~

Roland spent an hour talking with Turnbow and then with a few others in Greenwood, answering questions, discussing complaints, and explaining the facts of life. Most left with a new understanding of their situation, agreeing that they were far more fortunate than they had realized.

Turnbow had provided a few names to Tom Mackey as well, people in other areas of the county that he knew personally that were doing much the same as he was, trying to hold things together around them.

"Things are tough, there's no question," Turnbow shrugged, "and there is a lot of anger out there, Roland," he warned. "Not here, not after all you've done for us," he was quick to add, "but among others, well. . .there's a tendency to blame anyone who's handy. Especially anyone with any level of government."

"People are going to have to realize that the ones of us still trying are doing all we can," Roland's voice was calm, but firm for all that. "We're stretched as thin as we can go and in some cases a little farther. No matter how well-meaning, there's a limit to our resources, and we're there. In fact, we're past there in some areas."

"I know, I know," Turnbow raised his hands in a placating gesture, "I'm just telling you the lay of the land, Roland. I recognize how hard everyone's working. Which reminds me. Have you seen Tom

Wilson lately?"

"Yesterday morning," Roland nodded.

"Did he look, well..." Turnbow trailed off.

"Rode hard and put up wet?" Roland offered.

"Well, yeah."

"He did, and I mentioned it to him," Roland said firmly. "He needs time off and I told him so. But, there's a problem. Too many of the county's elected officials aren't taking up their slack. Just sittin' by and lettin' others do for 'em."

"I knew that I hadn't seen many out. The courthouse is open most days, but there ain't many people there," Turnbow mused.

"I advised Tom to take a weekend and do nothing unless there was a bonafide emergency," Roland informed him, "and I might as well tell you now. Since we're under Martial Law until we can get some kind of decent organization back, at least at the state levels, technically I'm in charge."

"Now, I'm not too keen on being in charge," Roland continued, "but if things don't start to change, and soon, I'll be taking steps to get people on board. If those who took an oath to perform their duties don't start steppin' up, I will replace them. And then they can get out here and scratch for what they need just like the rest of us."

"That'll upset more'n one apple cart," Turnbow chuckled. "Be almost worth the trouble to see that."

ROLAND

"I don't want the trouble," Roland shook his head, "but it's time for folks to step up, or step out, one or the other. If the people that were elected won't do their jobs, then there's someone, somewhere out here, that can and will."

"Sounds like a winner to me," Turnbow nodded. "You can count on our support, whatever you have to do."

"I appreciate that," Roland nodded, rising. He could see Maria coming toward him, "and with that, we need to be on the road. Got a lotta ground to try and cover today, if we can."

"Be careful, fellas," Turnbow said.

~*~

Maria had worked out a schedule with the women of Greenwood that worked for both groups. The women were understandably excited with the prospect of using the school's large kitchen.

"We were going to have to use outdoor kitchens and wood stoves," Rose Turnbow told her. "It's worth bringing everything down there to keep from doing that."

"I am glad we can assist," Maria told her "especially considering we would not be able to preserve our own food without your knowledge."

"We're glad to do it," Rose told her honestly.

"It is time for me to go," Maria announced. "We have much to do today."

"That Roland is a handsome man, child," an older woman smiled gently. "Are you and him an item?"

"We are," Maria blushed prettily. "He is a very good man."

"But a hard man," Rose mused. Seeing Maria's reaction, she clarified.

"I mean that in a good way, hon," she promised. "Times like these, you need good men who can be hard men when the need arises. And I suspect there aren't many who would be willing to take on the responsibility of all those children." She gave Maria an appraising look.

"Nor women, either, especially one so young as you," she smiled gently. "You're both doing a good thing. God's work. May both of you be blessed for doing it, I pray." The woman's sincerity was so evident it was almost tangible. Maria blushed again, her head bowed.

"Thank you, *señora*," she murmured.

"Now you go on, he's waiting," Rose urged, "and you be careful being out."

"We will."

~*~

"We'll go to Big Springs, first," Tom decided, as the Hummer left Greenwood. "It's closest anyway, and we can make a round through there and head south."

"Suits me," Roland nodded, "you know the land and the people."

"Some of these folks are okay, and some not so much," Tom warned the younger man. "They're not really bad, per se, but. . .well, 'asshole' might not be too strong a word."

"Have to take the good with the bad, I guess," Roland shrugged. It didn't sound any different to any other place he'd ever been.

"A very few of 'em are a little. . .well, a lot, fairly anti-government, Roland," Tom continued. "They'll be unfriendly to us at best. Some may be downright hostile, too," he added.

"Should we wait and visit them in greater strength?" Roland asked, pointedly not looking at Maria at his side.

"Don't think so," Tom shook his head. "In fact, this here just might be the best way to go about it, I think. A show of force will just prove to them that they've been right all along."

"Well, I think we can agree that the 'government' wasn't much to be proud of," Roland snorted. "They were wasteful, arrogant, and controlling. In all honesty, maybe the best thing to come out of all this was the practical dissolution of the worst areas of government."

"You might throw that in, when you speak to 'em," Tom grinned. "Truth is, I'm known to be pretty vocal about such things myself."

"Not you, Tom!" Roland feigned shock, "I just don't believe it."

"I might surprise ya."

~*~

Big Springs was simply a collection of houses, centered on a small country store, at the intersection of two back country roads. When the Hummer pulled up to the store, there were several people gathered about, milling, really, discussing whatever came to mind. Such conversations trailed away as the foursome exited the vehicle.

"Howdy, Ben," Tom called, and one of the men seated on the store's porch looked at him closer.

"Well, Tom Mackey!" 'Ben' exclaimed. "Thought you was dead for sure, by now!"

"Likely would be if not for Roland, here," Tom agreed. "Ben Nevers, this is Roland Stang. He's a Lieutenant with the State Guard, though he don't like to be reminded of it. He's the county's military liaison."

ROLAND

"Sir," Roland nodded. Nevers stood, looking him over as he advanced. He was a large man, broad-shouldered, with a mop of fiery red hair.

"Pleased to meet you, Roland," the man/bear hybrid smiled, offering his hand. Roland took it, glad when the bigger man didn't try to crush his much smaller hand.

"Same here, sir."

"Just Ben," Nevers waved his hand carelessly. "C'mon up, and sit a spell. Ain't got no Coke or coffee, but reckon we can scare up some apple juice or water."

"Water for me," Tom said. Roland nodded his agreement. Vaughan was standing by the Hummer, Maria nearby.

"So what brings you our way, Tom?" Ben asked.

"Just givin' Roland the lay o' the land, and introducin' him to the movers and shakers."

"And you stopped here?" Nevers cackled.

"First stop of the day," Tom grinned. "Roland ain't been doing this job but a week or so, and he wanted to see what was happenin', and maybe get a feel for what's needful."

"Pretty much everything," Ben shrugged.

"I don't have everything," Roland sighed a little. "I don't have much of anything, to be completely honest. But what I can provide, I will."

"Son, I know you mean that, just by lookin' at you," Ben said kindly, "but it's a little late for most. Many of our old timers has done passed on 'thout the meds they couldn't get. We do have some young'uns that could use some formula and diapers, I reckon. And most of us'd kill for conditioned air, or even the power to run a fan, let alone a workin' refrigerator."

"I can't do any of the electrical," Roland shrugged, "but I might can get hands on some formula. Meanwhile, we've been making cloth diapers for the kids that are still in them."

"You got kids?" Ben asked.

"He's got a passel o' kids," Tom interjected. "Young'uns whose folks has passed on, or who just plain left 'em. Roland's takin' care of near thirty kids, all totaled."

"None of 'em your'n?" Ben asked, eyes slightly narrowing.

"No, sir," Roland shook his head, "and I haven't done it all alone, either. Maria has been the one to look after the children, along with a couple others. I help when I can, but. . .well, I've kinda had my hands full, last little bit."

"Him and his folk killed a bunch o' biker trash that had been terrorizing the area of late," Tom informed everyone within hearing distance. "Same ones that took me and a bunch of others prisoner to make us work for 'em. Well, the men, anyway," he added darkly. Muted scowls appeared on the faces around them. They understood *exactly* what Mackey meant.

"Sounds like a fine piece o' work," Ben nodded. "We've been lucky in that regard, I reckon. No body botherin' us. Not a bit o' trouble." The words were a little forced, Roland thought. Several of the people around him looked. . .uncomfortable.

Roland decided to take a chance.

"Folks, let me put your mind to ease," he said calmly. "If you've had trouble of the kind I just had, and you handled it, I got no problem with that. I mostly just dumped my. . .troubles in a hole and covered 'em over real good." Several muted chuckles answered that, and Ben Nevers, along with some others, nodded in approval.

"Might be we had a little trouble," Nevers admitted cautiously, "but nothin' like what you had, sounds like."

"Guess I better mention that I'm a reserve deputy now, too," Mackey grinned. "Sheriff pretty much agrees with Roland. Fact being, he's wantin' good men to deputize in all the communities to handle minor problems that don't really call for jailin' a man. Reckon you got anybody out this way that can do that?"

The rest of the conversation flowed smoothly after that. People began to loosen up. And speak up. Before long, Roland had pressed Maria into service writing down requests, information, and suggestions. As the talk wound down after an hour or so, Roland stood.

"Folks, I'm glad for the opportunity to meet with you. Mister Nevers, you've got the radio frequencies we use. If you get into a bind, call us. Meanwhile, I'll get my technician to start working on getting you a solar set-up to power your radio, and maybe let your folks charge a few batteries and what not."

"That'd be a good thing," Nevers grinned. "Folks get tired o' pumpin' that bike genny after a while," he laughed.

"I imagine they do."

~*~

"I saved the best for last," Tom said dryly, as Vaughan negotiated a rutted out, pothole strewn back road. "We're almost to Terry. This is the mostly anti-, well, pretty much everything, bunch." He turned in his seat.

"Rumors are that this bunch are inbred," he said, his tone indicated his opinion of that. "I've met a few of them, over the years, and they're very stand-offish. They can be violent, but I've never heard of one of them instigating anything. They're in town every so often, but stay to

themselves and usually don't bother anyone. They do, however have some.
. .peculiar, let's call it, ideas, about some things." He looked at Maria.

"Better you stay with the car, this time," he warned.

"If it's that big a problem, let's do this later," Roland said, his hand instinctively going to Maria's.

"I think it'll be okay," Tom shrugged, "and it's the last bunch, too. Your call," he finished.

Roland thought about it.

"How far out are we?" he asked.

"Another five minutes or so."

Roland sighed. They had come a long way. To go back now would just be a waste of gas. He looked down at Maria.

"You armed?"

"Of course," she said calmly, "I always am."

"Okay," he sighed again, looking at Tom, "let's go ahead and get it over with."

In what seemed like no time they were pulling up to a collection of ramshackle houses and rundown-looking mobile homes. One largetwo story house dominated the collection. Children were running around the nearly barren yard with a pack of dogs, screeching and laughing. All were dirty-faced and barefoot, but then, they *were* outside, and playing. All looked happy and healthy.

The dogs, too numerous and quick-moving to really count, turned at the sound of the vehicle and started barking, heading straight for the Hummer. Vaughan slowed so as not to hit any of them.

"Stay in the car until and unless someone calls 'em off," Tom warned. After a few minutes a tall, rangy man with a short beard stepped onto the porch of the main house. Dressed in overalls and a wife-beater tee, he looked at them for a while, arms hanging at his side.

Finally, he yelled, and the dog pack instantly left the Hummer, returning to the house where they encircled the group of children.

"You and me, Roland," Tom said, opening his door.

"That's far enough," the man shouted. "Who are ya, and what'd'ya want?"

"Abel, it's Tom Mackey!" Tom called. "We wanted a word, you got time!"

"Got nothin' but time," Abel called back. "What I ain't got is interest. What you want?"

"I'm Roland Stang, the military commander for the county," Roland called out. "I'm just trying to get the lay of the land, and meet as many people as I can."

"Got no interest in talkin' to you," Abel shook his head. "Gov'ment folk ain't really welcome anywhere on my land. Best y'all git."

"I'm not really a 'gov'ment' man," Roland called back. "Sorta drafted into this 'cause I was in the Army once upon a time. I mean you no ill will, or harm. I'm trying to see what needs there are, and what I can do to fill them."

"Reckon we take care of ourselves just fine, soldier," Abel shook his head. "Don't want, nor need, no one else buttin' into our business."

"Not here to butt in," Roland assured him. "Just to help, if I can."

"Don't need it," Abel called back, "and I'm tired o' talkin'. Turn that thing around and git gone. Don't come back."

"Best do as he says," Tom sighed. "Fair enough, Abel. Happens you need us; you can call..."

But Abel was already going back inside, closing the door behind him.

"Well, that went well."

"I told you," Tom shrugged. "Anyway, we tried. I'd say it's time we call it a day. I'm tired."

"Works for me," Roland nodded.

ROLAND

CHAPTER FIFTY-FIVE

"Anyway Mister Nevers, this here set-up'll do you fine. I just ain't got the makin's for a solar panel. But it's a good way to get exercise," Ralph grinned. He'd just finished attaching a car alternator to a bicycle. It ran to a bank of six car batteries linked together, and would provide a small but steady source of power.

"Don't know why I didn't think of that," Nevers was shaking his head. "Reckon 'cause I'd bought that old Hallicrafter set-up for emergencies, and was locked into it."

"Ain't nothin' wrong with it," Ralph assured him as he put his tools away. The Barnes girls were helping him, and started carrying the boxes to the truck Jesse had driven them out there in.

"But this here set-up should work better, and plus, you need or want to use the radio, there's power ready all the time. Won't need to crank to keep it runnin'."

"I appreciate it, son," Nevers smiled. "You're welcome to move out here with us, you want. I got a fine young granddaughter your age." The Barnes girls frowned at that.

"Uh, thank you, sir, but I reckon I better stay on with Roland," Ralph replied. He noted the twin's reaction. They'd been awful. . .*clingy*, lately. He'd tried to ignore it, but that was getting harder to do. He'd have to try and talk to them, and soon.

"Appreciate the formula, young fella," Nevers was talking to Jesse, now. "And you, miss, for givin' us all the once over," he turned to Jennifer.

"My pleasure," she smiled. "I gave your wife a list of the home remedies we're using right now, so she should be able to start treating some of the more common problems we're seeing. If you have an emergency, someone is always monitoring the radio at the school."

"We're beholden," Nevers nodded.

"Not in any way," Jennifer shook her head. "I'm glad I'm able to help."

"You folks travel safe," Ben smiled, as they reached the truck, "and keep a sharp eye on that lad," he nodded to Ralph. "He's worth his weight, no doubt."

"We will," the twins replied in unison. Ralph cringed at that, but remained silent.

"Take care, sir," Jesse shook hands, and started the truck. Soon they were back on the road. Two of Drake's men, along with Tom Mackey, followed them.

"Anywhere else?" Jesse asked.

"That was the last," Jennifer shook her head. "We can head for the barn."

"Barn, huh?" Jesse grinned.

"I'm trying to fit in," the doctor told him. "Learning to speak the language."

"Going native, are ya?" Jesse teased.

"Well, it does have its attractions," she gave as good as she got.

~*~

"You can't do this!"

"Oh, yes I can, and I am," Roland replied to the outburst. "You were elected to manage this county, and you ain't been doin' your job. Ain't seen you one time working on anything. If you aren't going to do your job, then you won't have one."

The county mayor, one William 'call me Bill!' Harrison, was red-faced with anger.

"What is it you expect me to have done?" he demanded.

"*Anything* would be better than what you have done, which is *nothing*," Roland spat back. "The Sheriff has been working for months, day in and out, trying to keep people fed, housed and protected, let alone doing his own work. Where were you during that time?"

Harrison stammered for an answer, but Roland provided it for him.

"Sitting here on your ass, that's where!" he snarled. "So you're out. We'll find someone else. Go get your crap outta what used to be your office. Got 'til closing." With that, Roland turned on his heel, headed to the Hummer, where Vaughan was waiting.

"This isn't the last of this!" Harrison all but screamed.

"Wanna bet?" Roland called over his shoulder. Without another word, he climbed into the Hummer, leaving a still-sputtering Harrison behind.

"Just makin' friends everywhere you go," Vaughan commented.

"He's a jackass," Roland snorted. "He's the main one that's been riding Tom about guards and cars and drivers. Like he's too damn good to drive himself around. Or protect himself. Anyway, we need someone else in there."

"Like who?" Vaughan asked.

"I got no idea."

~*~

"Not bad," James nodded as Susan's tomahawk *thunked* into the target. The two had been training together since the attack, and had become friends of a sort. Susan had turned her inner turmoil into a determination unlike anything she'd ever known, and was becoming a warrior.

"Thanks," she nodded.

"You're pretty intense, Susan," James noted. "Relax a little. This can be fun, if you let it." He threw a knife at the target, and hit just millimeters from the bulls-eye.

"I don't have time for fun," Susan said flatly.

"You have to make time," James stressed. "You can't just. . .be angry all the time."

"I'm not angry," Susan said at once, "just. . .determined. *Focused.*"

"What'd you do before the fall?" James asked suddenly. The question caught her by surprise, and Susan stopped and looked at him.

"What?"

"What did you do before things collapsed?" James repeated. "You know, for work?"

"I...I was a secretary at the Court House," Susan replied, "in the Trustee's Office."

"Cool," James nodded, "did you like it?"

"Yes," Susan admitted, "it was a good job, and paid fairly well for around here. I met a lot of people, and was. . .hey, that's not fair," she almost growled.

"What is?" James asked.

"Making me think about better times," she complained.

"I think about them," James shrugged. "Might be like that again, someday. Hope so, anyway," he added.

"It won't be like that for me again," she said sadly, suddenly deflating.

"Won't be the same," James nodded, "but no reason it can't be good."

"I'm. . .I won't ever be the same. No," Susan stated, "I'm damaged goods now, James. No one will want me around. Not anymore."

"Being a little hard on yourself, aren't you?" James asked.

"Just telling the truth as I know it," Susan shrugged helplessly. "I…they hurt me, James," Susan said softly, and he realized that she was crying. "Hurt me bad. Jennifer, she. . .I always wanted a family, but…" Finally, she broke down, and fell onto him. James held her as she cried, soothing her as best he could.

"I'm sorry," he said. "I'm sorry we weren't there to stop it."

"Me, too," she sobbed into this chest, "but you saved me, at least," she added. "Thank you for that."

Saved her? James wondered.

~*~

Roland was about to eat when Angie came to him.

"Roland, I need to talk to you."

"Have a seat," he pointed.

"No, in private." Roland sighed. He opened his mouth to ask if he could eat.

"Now," she stressed. Roland nodded, and followed her out. He was surprised when she led him to the radio room.

"What's going on?" he asked.

"Jenkins is on the radio for you," Angie said evenly. Roland frowned. Something was wrong.

"This is Stang," he said, having forgotten his code.

"Roland, this is Gerald Jenkins," he heard. Apparently Jenkins had forgotten his, too.

"Nashville is quarantined. The flu has hit here, and a lot of other places, in the last three days. It's not like the regular flu, Roland, which would be bad enough."

"This new flu, something maybe akin to the old avian flu virus, is deadly. Starts with a dry cough, moves into the flu, and then usually into pneumonia. It's got a seventy to eighty percent mortality rate, Roland."

"Anything we can do to help?" Roland asked.

"No!" Jenkins almost shouted into the radio. *"Don't come near us! We're already sick, there's nothing to be done. Any survivors might need help at some point, but under no circumstance are you to come here until it's clear. We have a few patrols out, so they may show up looking for a home. Do what you can for them."*

"You got it. Are you sure there's nothing we can do, Gerald?" Roland felt helpless.

"Roland, there's nothing to do. Just try and stay healthy. The word we're getting is that the flu is everywhere. People are dying by the

ROLAND

thousands, Roland. Maybe tens of thousands. There's no vaccine that works, and antibiotics are useless. There's. . .there's just nothing. " Roland heard Jenkins cough before the other man released the transmit button. His voice was that of a man who was defeated.

Beaten.

"Let us know if that changes," Roland said.

"Remember what I said. Isolation is the key. Don't come here, or send anyone else here, and be careful who you have contact with. Good. . .good luck, Roland," Jenkins finished. That sounded final, Roland noted sadly. Almost like Gerald had really meant to say 'good-bye'.

"Same to you, Gerald," Roland replied. Jenkins was gone. Roland put the mike down and looked at Angie.

"Well, we're in for it now."

"We better tell Jennifer," Angie temporized. Her face was a conflict of emotion. Jenkins and the others in Nashville were friends. They had been in combat together. Not helping was. . .*wrong.*

"I'll go get her," Roland sighed.

~*~

Kingston was eating with Jesse when Roland reappeared in the mess hall. He bent down and whispered in her ear. The young doctor's face froze in mid bite. Rising from the table she left the room immediately, following Roland out.

Maria saw that and frowned. Something was wrong. She walked over to where Jesse was still looking at the door.

"What's happening?" she asked.

"I don't know," Jesse said, looking up at her. "She didn't say a word to me, and neither did Ro'."

"Let's go, then," Maria ordered. Jesse didn't even consider not following her. The two made their way to the clinic by unspoken agreement.

". . .we're going to do?" they heard Roland speaking.

"What can we do?" Kingston replied, her voice frustrated. "If we tell them, and don't have an answer, then there's panic. And we don't have an answer."

"What is the question?" Maria asked, as she entered.

"What to do about the new flu," Roland sighed. "Jenkins just called us. They've got it in Nashville. It's pretty much nationwide, now. With a high mortality rate and no treatment available."

"Not available, or just not available to us?" Jesse asked.

"Not available *period*," Jennifer replied to that one. "There's no known remedy. A new strain, likely a branch of Avian origins, but that's

353

not confirmed, last I heard. I need to go to the radio room and see if we can contact CDC." This to Roland.

"Go ahead," he nodded. Kingston left, brushing Jesse's cheek with her lips as she went.

"We got problems," Roland told the two of them. "There's no treatment, there's no vaccine, there's not enough of anything to treat people with. The flu will get here, sooner or later, and when it does all we can do is pray."

"We need to start warning everyone, I guess," Jesse sighed. "Print out some protective measures, preventive measures I mean, and get it circulated."

"We should, but I'm worried that will cause a panic," Roland pointed out. "I'm open to ideas."

"Be truthful," Maria said. "Tell them there's no vaccine, no treatment. Remind them that the preventive measures are all we have. Stay home, avoid others, wait for the virus to run its course.

There's little else we can do."

"She's right," Jesse nodded, thinking about Jennifer. She'd be exposed to this virus treating the sick. He couldn't protect her from something he couldn't even see.

"Maria, will you get that going?" Roland asked. "I'll round up Drake, and he and his men can start distributing the fliers. Two men per Hummer. Jesse, see if you can round up some staple guns.

Notices can be tacked up everywhere with them."

"Yes, Roland," Maria nodded.

"Got it," Jesse replied, and the two left. Roland walked outside to the trailer that Drake and his men used as a barracks. Knocking, he walked inside.

"Evening, sir," Drake stood from the desk as Roland walked in.

"Sergeant," Roland nodded, "we have a problem. There's a flu bug in Nashville. Well, it's actually pretty much nationwide by now. There's no effective treatment or vaccine for it, either. I need you and your men for a public service mission. Take your Hummer and mine, two men to a vehicle, and start posting fliers that we're making up everywhere you can. Hand out extras when you meet someone. Ask them to pass it along. Leave bundles at every meeting place, store, community halls, and the like."

"Yes, sir," Drake nodded, sketching a salute. "We'll get on it."

"Thank you," Roland nodded, and left.

As he walked slowly around the building, a habit now, Roland allowed his mind to wander.

ROLAND

How many of them would catch this flu? And how many would die? How would a nationwide, maybe a worldwide virus of this magnitude affect things?

They were right in the middle of starting to get things going again. Now, not only would that likely stop, but maybe begin to undo itself. If seventy to eighty percent of the world's population died, those left would be in dire straits, in his opinion. Influenza was not selective in who it killed. True, many of the worst people might perish, but so might many of the good ones. People with knowledge they needed. How would that affect the rebuilding? Had they survived all this time, worked this hard, to see it all die out with this new super flu?

So wrapped up in these thoughts was he, Roland never thought about the coughing fit a young boy had had the day before. Or the coughing child in the cafeteria the night before.

It would bring him no comfort later when he realized that even if he had, it wouldn't have mattered.

N.C. REED

CHAPTER FIFTY-SIX

James finished hammering the last stake for the new sign into the ground, then leaned on the sign itself, wiping sweat from his brow.

Five days had passed since the warning from Jenkins, but for the school at least, it was too late.

The children, at least some of them, seemed to have brought the flu back with them. The signs James had just finished putting up had a simple message: FLU PRESENT, STAY BACK.

Over half the children were already sick. Worse, precautions had not been put in place until it was far too late to do any good. Vaughan, Maria, Fiona, and Mindy Barnes were also infected, as were two of Drake's troopers.

Deena and Melissa were coughing. James' heart tightened at the thought of Melissa. He had come to love the nurse a great deal. Had even allowed himself to think about some kind of future with her.

That was all in jeopardy now.

According to what Jennifer had learned from the CDC, not everyone who developed the cough actually caught the flu. There was still hope for the three of them, but it was a small percentage.

Roland was pretty much shot. Seeing Maria fall so fast into sickness had stunned the man everyone around depended on. James had quietly risen to the occasion, filling in for Roland everywhere he could. Drake and Jesse had assumed responsibility for the military aspect of Roland's job, but there wasn't much to do, anyway. Since they had all been exposed, they were quarantined here at the school barring the most strenuous of emergencies.

Jennifer chafed at not being able to go into the community to treat others, but she herself had to bend to the quarantine. She'd been exposed too, after all. The risk of carrying the infection into areas not already stricken was too great. As a result, she spent hours each day on the radio, acting through proxies to help as many as she could.

The stress level was the highest James had seen it, including the apprehension everyone had felt waiting for the attack by the gang. At least they could prepare for the attack, and then defend themselves.

There was no defense against this. They couldn't fight something they couldn't even see. There was no treatment for the flu. All Jennifer and the others could do was treat the symptoms, try to keep fevers down, and guard against pneumonia.

James wiped his brow again and started back for the school building. He and Ralph had been working to keep things running, but it was getting harder and harder. They needed ice to combat the fever, and the school's ice maker couldn't always keep up. Worse, it needed to work almost continuously. This caused more than one problem.

The power needed to run the ice machine had to come from the generator, which meant it had to run pretty much all the time, which burned fuel. The promised additional fuel couldn't be counted on, now, with Nashville under the same quarantine they were under at the school.

The solar rig and batteries could and did provide power to the equipment Jennifer had to use, but the batteries were usually near drained each morning. Soon, they would actually run out before sunrise. James wasn't sure the generator would pull everything at once.

And, sooner or later, they'd get a cloudy day, or even rain, and the batteries wouldn't get a full charge. When that happened...

Well, James didn't know. He hoped he wouldn't have to find out.

~*~

"Roland, how are you?" Maria asked weakly. "You look tired, *mi amor*. You should rest."

"Don't worry about me," Roland smiled weakly. "Just worry about getting better. That's all you need to think about."

"Roland, you know that I may not *get* better," Maria chided gently. "You must accept that, *mi gringo,*" she added with a weak smile.

"Don't even think like that," Roland said sternly. "People *do* recover, Maria, and you're going to be one of them."

"Perhaps I will be," Maria was too tired to argue, "but it will do me no good to recover if you allow your health to suffer in the meanwhile. You must take care of yourself, Roland. For me, and for the others." She coughed then, talking having exhausted her. Roland gently wiped her mouth with a clean cloth, then took a washrag from a basin and sponged her damp forehead.

"I'll be fine," he promised as he ministered to her. "Don't you worry. And once you're better, I'm not going to spend so much time taking care of everyone else. You and me, we're going to have more time to spend together, no matter what goes undone."

"I look forward to it," she smiled, albeit weakly. "I'm sorry, Roland, but I'm so tired. I...I need to rest."

"You do that," he nodded. "I'll be right here, if you need anything."

"No," she shook her head, "you rest while I do. That way you can be here when I am awake. Go, now, and sleep, *mi corazon*. Return to me only after you have slept, eaten, and bathed. Go, now," she shooed him one-handed. "I will not rest unless you do," she played her trump card when he looked reluctant. He sighed.

"Very well," he agreed, kissing her wet forehead, "but I do this under protest."

"Of course."

~*~

Angie pretty much collapsed next to Mack in the small bed they shared. He wrapped her in his arms, holding her.

"I'm so tired," she almost moaned. "There's always something to do. And nothing we do helps any." She was as down as Mack had ever seen her.

"You're doing all you can, love," he replied gently. "That's all anyone can do."

"I know," she sobbed slightly. Suddenly she buried her face into his chest, and cried softly.

"S...so many *niños*," she mumbled. "So very sick, and hurting so much."

"I know baby," Mack tried to console her. He stroked her hair gently, crooning to her softly. He didn't know what else to do.

She cried until exhaustion claimed her, and she fell into a deep, troubled sleep. Mack continued his gentle touching, hoping it would help.

While he did, he prayed.

~*~

"James, wake up," Ralph said softly. James was awake in an instant, pistol in hand and aimed before he had time to think.

"No, no," Ralph shook his empty hands in front of his friend. "It's not like that."

ROLAND

"What is it, man?" James asked, lowering his pistol, wiping his free hand down his face.

"The ice machine's broken down," Ralph told him softly.

~*~

"Can you fix it?" James asked, as Ralph showed him the problem.

"It's the compressor," Ralph shook his head sadly. "One of the few things on here I can't jury

rig, man. It might just be out of Freon, but I smelled burnin' wire when I opened it up, so. . .I don't think that's it."

"Well, that's just great," James said dejectedly. "What'da we do now?"

"There's only one thing we can do," Ralph shrugged helplessly. "We gotta go get another compressor, and maybe some Freon. I might be wrong, after all."

"Ralph, you're never wrong," James sighed.

"First time for everything," Ralph said, almost hopeful. Without the ice...

"Well, we got to have the ice," James put his younger friend's thought into words. "So what do we do? We're quarantined and all that."

"We'll just have to bend the rules a bit," Ralph shrugged. "Probably need some help, too."

~*~

"You what?" Jesse managed not to shout. He'd just been awakened from a sound sleep after eighteen hours of work.

"We gotta go scrounge up a compressor," Ralph repeated, "and maybe some Freon. Ain't got no other options, neither, 'fore you ask. This is it."

"We're under quarantine," Jesse reminded them.

"And it's one in the morning," James rebutted. "We need the ice. Period. There's a place in town that does refrigeration repair. Even if we have to use two compressors, we can at least get the ice maker

running again. If we can pick up the Freon, so much the better."

"So you just wanna go out into the night and steal what we need?" Jesse asked with a raised eyebrow.

"No, we're *going* to go out and steal what we need," James corrected. "We'd like your help, and your blessing, but we don't *have* to have it." The teen stood his ground as Jesse gave him the 'look'.

Finally, Jesse sighed.

"Fine, but Ralph stays here," he ordered.

"Can't," Ralph shook his head. "I got to see what's there. I can't tell you what'll work and what won't. I got to see it."

"All we need is a couple of guys to help with security," James told Jesse flatly. "You're welcome to be one of 'em if you want, but I figured you'd want to stay here," he nodded to Jesse's room, where Jennifer still slept, dead to the world with exhaustion.

"Well, maybe so," Jesse admitted. "I'll get Drake to carry you. Good enough?"

"Long as he don't get in our way," James warned.

"I'll be sure and tell him that."

~*~

"Where are you going?"

Ralph almost screeched as Mandy Barnes' voice came from behind him. Whirling he saw the teen standing behind him, arms crossed.

"Got somethin' I got to do, that's all," he temporized, angry that she had made him jump.

"Such as?" the girl demanded. "In case you forgot, we're under quarantine."

"Ain't forgot," Ralph told her, turning back to his small bag. He checked to make sure he had all the tools he might need and then shut the bag tight.

"Then where are you going?" she demanded again.

"Out!" Ralph bit back a snarl. "I ain't gotta answer to you."

"Tell me, or I'll start waking people up," Mandy simply replied.

"You wouldn't dare," Ralph scoffed. Mandy inhaled a deep breath as if about to yell. Ralph, in a panic, leapt forward and covered her mouth with his hand.

"All right, all right!" he growled. "Dammit, I gotta go and find a compressor for the ice maker.

It quit workin'." Mandy's eyes widened at that news.

"But we need the ice to..."

"Now you know why I gotta go outside," Ralph nodded. "Why do you care anyhow?"

"Because I don't want anything to happen to you, stupid," Mandy replied, as if it should be obvious.

"What?" Ralph frowned. "Ain't nothin' gonna happen to me."

"You don't know that," Mandy told him. "I've lost too much as it is, and now Mindy. . .Mindy might..." The girl trailed off, and suddenly started crying. She leaned into him, startling Ralph. He put his arms around her on instinct, and Mandy almost collapsed. Ralph managed to hold on to her and keep them both upright, but it was a chore.

"Mindy's gonna be fine," Ralph tried soothing her, patting her back, "but that's just another reason I got to go. We gotta have ice."

"I'll go with you," Mandy finally managed, pulling away from him and wiping her face.

"Oh, no you won't," Ralph shook his head. "You're stayin' right here, girl. Me and James and two o' them soldiers is goin', and that's all."

"If you try to leave me here, I'll wake up Roland and tell on you," the twin threatened.

"And then we don't go get the part, and there's no ice, and what happens to Mindy when her fever goes up again?" Ralph countered. He was learning.

Mandy frowned. She didn't like it when Ralph stood up to her.

"You need to go back to sleep," Ralph continued. "Pretend this ain't never happened. Got it?"

His voice was firm, something Mandy wasn't accustomed to. She wasn't sure she liked it.

"I ain't kiddin'," he added, seeing the indecision on her face. Realizing that for once she wasn't going to buffalo Ralph, Mandy nodded, looking down.

"Just. . .be careful, okay?" she asked.

"No problem."

~*~

"What took you so long?" James demanded when Ralph arrived at the Humvee.

"Aw, dang Mandy had her drawers in a knot, wantin' to come with me," Ralph exclaimed.

James looked at his younger friend for a moment straight-faced, then burst into laughter.

"I don't see how that's funny," Ralph said.

"Dude, you got two girls, sisters, *twins* even, fightin' over you!" James laughed.

"They ain't been in no...what'd you mean, 'over me'?" Ralph cut himself off as James' words sunk in.

"Are you blind?" James demanded, still laughing. "Those two have their cap set on you, man.

Wouldn't surprise me they don't decide to just share you between 'em."

"Share me how?" Ralph demanded, then, as James' suggestion settled on him, blushed from head to toe.

"That ain't no kinda funny, man," he growled. "They ain't nothin' but trouble."

"Dude, we should all have that kind of 'trouble'," James chuckled.

"Yeah, and if Melissa was a twin?" Ralph shot back. James got a 'far away' look for a moment, and Ralph punched him in the arm.

"Dude, I'm tellin'," he jibed. James laughed again.

"C'mon, man," he said finally. "We're wasting moonlight."

"You gentlemen ready?" Sergeant Drake appeared out of the night.

"We are," James nodded.

"My orders are to provide security, and assist you in any way possible," Drake said. He clearly wasn't completely happy with Jesse's orders. James motioned the sergeant aside as Ralph climbed into the truck.

"Your job, your primary and most important job, is to protect that kid," James nodded back to the Hummer. "This group absolutely cannot afford to lose him, no matter what. I want one of you with him at all times, I don't care if he's just taking a leak. He's not trained for something like this. He's too valuable to risk."

"Then he shouldn't be on this mission," Drake pointed out.

"No choice," James shook his head. "He's got to look for what he needs, and there's no way for him to tell us. He has to look at what's available, and choose from that. And we've got to have that ice machine working. Period."

"Very well, then," Drake nodded. "Let's saddle up."

~*~

The Hummer eased down the small side street, coasting to a stop in front of a small building.

The sign atop the store front read "Rick's Refrigeration". James slid out of the door before the Hummer had come to a complete stop, looking around carefully. The town was quiet, nothing moving anywhere he could see. Motioning for Ralph to follow, James walked to the door. He stopped short, seeing the door had already been jimmied.

"Wait here," he ordered, and Ralph nodded. James motioned to trooper Dominic, the driver, to follow him. Dominic looked to Drake, who nodded, taking a position near Ralph, and the trooper nodded back.

James opened the door just enough to get inside. He could tell even without a light that the store had been rummaged through pretty thoroughly already. He hoped that whoever had been here had left what they needed. Moving quickly through the building, he found it clear and whistled sharply. Ralph entered, Drake staying with the vehicle.

ROLAND

"All right, man," James whispered. "Place is a mess, but maybe whatever you need is here." James shrugged off the empty duffle he'd been carrying, and handed it to Ralph. "Time's a wastin'."

"Right," Ralph nodded. He immediately started scrounging through what remained of the shop's contents. James looked at Dominic, pointed to his eyes, then at Ralph. Dominic nodded, and moved to where he was only a few steps from the teen. James eased out the front, where Drake was standing in the shadows, watching the street and their surroundings.

"All okay?" he asked. James nodded.

"He's looking. Place is a mess, so it may take a few minutes."

"We're clear here," Drake said, eyes never leaving their surroundings.

"Thanks for helping," James offered. Drake grunted.

"Orders is orders," was his reply.

"Still appreciate it," James shrugged. "Without ice, we'll lose people for sure. Gotta have a way to fight the fever." Drake nodded. Two of his men were in the clinic, after all. He wanted them to make it, too.

"You cleared the building pretty good," Drake complimented. "Where'd you get your training?"

"From Roland," James told him evenly. Drake spared him a look.

"You're not service?"

"No."

"Trained you pretty good, then," Drake mused.

"Yeah, he did," James nodded, "and I'm grateful. And to you guys, too. All of you."

"Just followin' orders," Drake said again.

"And you could have stopped anytime," James pointed out. "I'm glad you didn't." Drake gave him a long, appraising look, then nodded.

"So am I."

~*~

Ralph almost shouted in relief when he found what he was looking for. Two beautiful, shiny, new compressors, just like he needed. Sighing gratefully, he placed the two components into his bag.

He picked up four 'jugs' of Freon he had come across, and two transfer kits. Stopping long enough to grab a handful of tools he could use, he and Dominic gathered the Freon and parts and headed for the door.

"James," Ralph hissed softly. Instantly James was there at the door.

"I'm good," the boy said softly. James nodded and motioned for Ralph to get to the Hummer.

In less than two minutes the four were loaded and moving.

Mission accomplished.

~*~

Ralph wearily reached up and hit the switch, activating the ice maker. He sat and waited as the machine worked. It would take a while. Leaning back against the machine itself, he never realized it when he closed his eyes and drifted off to sleep.

He was startled awake by the sound of ice falling into the box. Jumping up, he raised the door and was greeted with a cold rush of air. Ice was still settling atop what had been left in the box.

"Oh, thank you, God," he breathed. The machine was working. He gathered his stuff and walked into the hall, where James was sitting, waiting.

"It… it's fixed," Ralph almost sobbed in relief, but managed not to cry in front of James, whom he respected and looked up to so much. Relief was palpable on James' haggard face.

"That's great, buddy," James sighed. "Get some rest, Ralph. You need it, and you damn sure earned it." Ralph nodded dumbly, and staggered to his room. Setting his tools down, he kicked his shoes off and fell into his bed, not even bothering to remove his clothing.

He never knew when Mandy came in, covered him with a blanket, and lay down beside him.

ROLAND

CHAPTER FIFTY-SEVEN

Vaughan was the first to die. The hardy trooper simply went to sleep, and didn't wake. Jennifer tried everything she knew, and every bit of advice the CDC, or what was left of it, recommended.

Nothing worked. Vaughan basically drowned in his own fluids.

The entire group was stunned. If any of them had been expected to make it, it was Vaughan.

Always working out, always cautious about what he ate when he could be, tough, strong, he had always seemed. . .invulnerable.

Mack and Angelina were especially hard hit by the trooper's death. They had been friends for a long time, and through some rough times at that.

James, ever reliable, dug Vaughan's grave. There was a brief service as they laid the soldier to rest, but few were in attendance. Many were sick, and others were busy caring for them. It was one of the saddest things James had ever seen.

Jesse spoke over the grave, but his heart wasn't in it. He had liked Vaughan, a kindred spirit. He felt a heavy weight on him as he walked back inside.

The day hadn't ended before two of the children succumbed to the fever, rather than the pneumonia. Jennifer, Melissa, and Angelina were in tears as six-year-old Cody, and nine-year-old Kimberly breathed their last, both having slipped into a coma during the night. Jennifer knew both had almost certainly suffered brain damage from the fever despite the cold water baths and ice packs.

Angelina broke down as she washed the little bodies. Once she was finished, Jennifer ordered her to take the entire next day off. She refused, but Jennifer Kingston could be domineering in a way only a doctor could be, and Angelina finally relented, agreeing to return to work for the midnight shift the next evening. She took a shower, ate, and then cried herself to sleep once more in Mack's arms.

Jesse, Ralph and James took care of the burial.

~*~

The next day saw one of Drake's sick troopers, Corporal Lance Jamieson, die along with four-year- old, Brandy Nixon. At the same time, two more children and Deena were placed in the clinic, having moved from symptomatic to sick.

During all of this, everyone pitched in as best they could, and Roland let them. He spent every waking moment at Maria's side, whether she was awake or not. He was constantly sponging her with cold water, or helping her drink water, or one of any other dozens of things that needed doing. In a way it wasn't fair, since no one else had a constant attendant, but no one was willing to say anything to Roland. He had done more than anyone. He had earned a respite, even one as bitter as this.

The third day after Vaughan's death, Fiona Richards died along with Mindy Barnes, Trooper Darrell Morrison, and eleven-year-old Frankie Munz. Roland left his post beside Maria's bedside long enough to assist with the burial detail.

Mandy Barnes was beside herself with grief, and Roland couldn't imagine what the teen was going through. Bad enough, he figured, to lose a sibling, but a twin? Someone who essentially shared the same DNA? He did note that Mandy was clinging to Ralph as she bawled her eyes out, and that Ralph was doing all he knew to do to support her. Ralph looked at Roland and Roland nodded to the boy in respect for his actions. Ralph blushed a little, but stood just a bit straighter as well.

He was becoming a man, Roland decided. He had already been doing a man's work, but now his emotional maturity was catching up.

As the service ended, Roland gave Jesse's shoulder a squeeze, silently thanking him for always being the one to conduct the service. Jesse tried to grin, but all he could manage was a grimace.

Looking over at James, Roland was shocked by how haggard the teenager looked. Dark circles under his bloodshot eyes, the distance-eating look in those same eyes, and the slump of his shoulders told Roland that the younger man was near his limit.

"James, you need to take the rest of the day, and rest," Roland ordered.

"Can't," James shook his head, "got too much to do, Roland."

"It'll wait until tomorrow," Roland said firmly. "You have to rest. And see Jennifer about a good dose of vitamins. We all need you healthy,

ROLAND

James. We depend on you, and Ralph, too much. You're surely a blessing to us all."

James shrugged. He appreciated the praise, but was too tired to do anything else.

"Do as I say," Roland pressed the point home. "Whatever needs doing will need doing tomorrow."

"Okay," James gave in. He was honestly too tired to argue.

Roland took the time to walk through the school, and was struck by the dark mood pressing in on everyone. The sickness, the deaths, the isolation, all were contributing to the situation. It was as if a great, dark cloud was hanging over them. Pressing down on them.

Roland wanted to try and pick them up, but knew it was useless. He felt the same way and there was absolutely nothing that could be done about it. This was a game of roulette that Mother Nature was playing, and they had no control at all over how it played out. Some would die, some would live, and there was no way to know who was who until it happened.

He ate a small meal, took a shower and changed clothes, and headed back to the clinic. He was surprised to see Jennifer waiting for him.

"I want you to get at least eight hours sleep tonight," he ordered before she could speak. "You're killing yourself, and it has to stop."

"Roland, I…"

"No arguing," Roland cut her off. Jennifer shook her head.

"It's not that, Roland," she said hesitantly. "It's. . .Roland, Maria just went into a coma."

~*~

Roland sat in his chair and watched Maria struggle to breathe. It hurt him every time she did, as her breathing was labored and harsh sounding. Every breath was accompanied by a hissing rattle that shook him to the core.

Melissa came in, mask in place, and checked Maria's vitals, noting them on the makeshift chart.

Roland looked at her.

"Her blood pressure's falling," she told him, tears in her eyes. "Her pulse is a bit more thready, and her respiration has fallen one. I'm so sorry, Roland," she added before she thought. "I wish I could do more, or be more -"

"It's all right," he told her quietly. "Thank you, though," he added. Melissa nodded, and then resumed her rounds. Roland leaned back in his chair, settling in for the night. Maria would come around, he knew.

When she did, he'd be here.

He was asleep when, two hours later, Maria took a final labored breath, sighed, and then her struggle was over.

ROLAND

CHAPTER FIFTY-EIGHT

The flu passed, finally. The final death toll for the school was thirteen. Deena and two children who had been infected recovered. No one else.

Melissa hadn't gone into the flu, and apparently wasn't a carrier since no one else was sick.

James was so relieved that he cried, something he hadn't done since Cassandra had drowned. Melissa held him while he sobbed, crying with him. The two had been through a great deal, but they had survived.

They would keep doing so.

~*~

Roland threw himself into getting things fixed up around the school. Constantly working, he seldom stopped except to eat and sleep, and did both very rarely.

Two weeks after the last burial, James found Roland going through his trailer, now hooked behind the Hummer.

"What'cha doing?" James asked.

"Checking the load out," Roland replied. "How you doing, kiddo?"

"I'm tired," James admitted, "but other than the garden, we're all caught up."

"Good to hear," Roland nodded absently. "Everything running pretty well right now, looks like.

You agree?"

"Uh, yeah," James said hesitantly. "Why?"

"Good a time as any for me to go, then."

"Go?" James repeated, stunned. "What the hell you mean, 'go'?"

"I'm leaving, James," Roland told him. "Time for me to move on, see what's left of the world.

You, Jesse, and I guess Ralph now, you can handle things here. Drake and Dominic are going to stay on permanent, too, so you'll have their help. You don't need me anymore."

"That. . .that's *bullshit*!" James spluttered. "We can't do this without you!"

"Of course you can," Roland snorted. "You have been, haven't you? You and Ralph pretty much ran things while I was…while I sat with…her."

"That don't mean we want to keep having to!" James objected.

"Well, that's too bad," Roland replied, but grinned, taking the sting from his words. "We all have to do things we don't want to, James. And you've got your life ahead of you, you and Melissa.

This is a good place for the two of you. Jesse and Jennifer will be here to help you. And looks like Ralph and Mandy will be too."

"Once things have settled down, you'll have to see who's left, reestablish contact with who you can. Haven't heard from Sheriff Wilson, so I don't know if he made it or not. Same with Turnbow. Did hear from Nevers. They lost three people, but otherwise they're okay. Left a list of the others, and Tom Mackey, he knows them all. He'll help."

"Roland, I…no," he shook his head, "you can't make me do this."

"Got no intention of making you," Roland surprised him. "Up to you whether you do it or not.

This is where the rubber meets the road, kid."

"But. . .*why?*"

Roland sat down in the open trailer door, sighing.

"I've had it, James," he said tiredly. "I can't stay here. Not now. Not after…" he stopped. "Not now," he started again. "There's probably more to do, out there," he swept his arm around vaguely.

"I'm going to head out, do what I can, where I can, for as long as I can. Every now and then, I may send you some folks, if I think you can trust them. We'll work out a code so you'll know I sent them."

"Roland, I understand, but…"

"Do you?" Roland replied. Not unkindly, but rather firmly. "I don't see how you can, but you might. And while you might could deal, I can't. I *won't*," he added, more firmly.

"I…I guess I can see that," James said glumly, "but I don't know what we'll do without you."

"Same thing you've been doing," Roland's voice was sure. "You'll do fine."

~*~

"You're leaving."

ROLAND

Roland turned to see Susan Powers looking at him.

"Yep," he nodded, knowing what was coming. He'd expected it, once word got around.

"I want to come with you," she said bluntly.

"Why?" he asked.

"I want. . .I *need*," she stressed, "to try and make a difference. I need what happened to me to matter."

"It already matters," Roland told her. "You defended this school. Killed their leader yourself.

You did that."

"It's not enough," Susan shook her head. "I...if I can keep what happened to me from happening to someone else, even just one someone, then. . .then it mattered. What happened to me, what it made me become, it will matter."

"Will that make what you went through worth it?" Roland asked.

"No, but it'll make it *matter*," she replied, her voice strong.

"I won't carry you," Roland said simply. "I won't coddle you, either. We'll be uncomfortable most of the time. Short on water, no showers, baths, and probably not too much in the way of prepared meals, either. We'll make camp where we can, scrounge what we can, live off the land, and whatever's left." He eyed her closely.

"Think you can handle that?"

"If I can't, you can always leave me behind," Susan shrugged, surprising him.

"Not a bad answer," Roland admitted. "All right, it'll be like you say. Gather your things. You may want to think about getting an AR, though, to go with that AK. Might have to make do with whatever we can find ammo for, 'fore it's all said and done."

"I'll do that," Susan nodded.

"Well, partner, like I said. Gather your gear."

~*~

"This is stupid," Jesse said bluntly.

"Well, I've never been overly bright," Roland shrugged. "It's what I got to do, Jess. That's all."

"You sure you ought to be taking her with you?" Jesse nodded in Susan's general direction.

"Think so," Roland mused. "She's hard, now. Maybe too hard to be here, with the kids that are left. She needs somewhere she can be. . .wild. I think I can give her that. Might keep her sane."

"That's worried me, too," Jesse admitted.

"Well, that's one less worry already," Roland almost smiled. Jesse grunted in amusement.

"Ro', don't do this," he said quietly. "Stay here. Rest. You earned it, bro. Don't walk away, man."

"I'm driving, not walking," Roland pointed out, and Jesse snorted.

"Smart ass, you know what I mean."

"Jess, you got a good thing here. You and Jennifer, I'm really happy for you. She's a great lady, and you're one of the finest men I've ever known. I'm proud to call you brother. You've got James and Melissa, too. Deena will deal with the kids, mostly, along with Mandy. And Mandy will help keep Ralph out of trouble," he added, a genuine smile coming at the thought.

"I'd imagine," Jesse laughed out loud at that.

"I can't stay here, Jess," Roland said earnestly. "Can't do it. I got to go."

"I know," Jesse sighed. "I'll miss you, brother."

"Same here."

~*~

Tom Mackey and James were the only two awake when Roland and Susan climbed into the Hummer. Fuel tanks were strapped along the trailer's sides, and the rear of the Hummer. Water was stored in the trailer, along with most, but not all, of their gear.

"You two take care," Tom Mackey said, shaking hands with Roland.

"You too, Tom," Roland replied. "James, I'm proud of you," Roland said, and surprised them both by drawing the younger man into an embrace. "Take care of yourself. And watch after Ralph and Deena."

"I will," James nodded. "Promise."

The two of them watched the Hummer out of sight.

~*~

Roland and Susan would never return to the Bethesda school house. Occasionally people would arrive at the school, usually people with children, and whisper 'Maria'. That was the word Roland had settled on. Everyone would gather around these people, eager to hear news of Roland and Susan. Where they were, how they were and what they were doing.

The two were traveling, covering a lot of ground, always on the lookout for people in need of help. Always stepping in to lend a hand. Always, *always*, protecting those who weren't able to do it themselves.

ROLAND

Sometimes the newcomers would have heard of them before they even arrived. Word was spreading about a man and woman who fought for those who couldn't fight for themselves. A man and woman who went out of their way to hunt down trouble, and eliminate it.

It was during one of these times that Roland acquired a new name.

A family group had been set upon by thugs while camping. Held near the fire they had been cooking over, the group had been forced to sit and watch the thugs eat their hard earned meal, with children in the group going hungry.

As the food ran out, the thugs turned their attention to the women in the group. Before they could act out, however, rifle fire from the dark had cut them down. A man and woman, faces painted and wearing body armor, had materialized from the dark, ensuring the trash was well and truly taken out.

One of the rescued had asked for the man's name. It was the woman who answered.

"Paladin," she told them. "Call him Paladin."

THE END

A Note from the Author

First of all, I hope you enjoyed the story of Roland. When I first started this story, I had no idea where it would go. There are so many things that can happen to any group of people who are on the edge of survival. Sometimes it's difficult to remember that we're usually only a few days away from starvation, lack of medicines, or any one of the dozens of things that can happen should order collapse.

Next, some of you with experience will no doubt note that occasionally in my more modern stories, information on certain weapons systems, capabilities of vehicles, or improvised munitions, among others, is sometimes, well, not completely accurate. I know that, I assure you. However, one thing I promised myself when I started my first novel long ago was that I would not place such information in my books for just anyone to find. Yes, most of it is available on the net, or even in local libraries. That doesn't mean I want to give anyone something for free. Someone who wants to do harm to others will likely find the information he or she needs somewhere, but I determined long ago that they wouldn't get it from me.

Lastly, if you enjoyed this book, I hope you'll do me the favor of leaving me a review. Also, feel free to visit my blog over at Wordpress, and leave a comment there if you'd like. I'm also on Facebook and Twitter, and the links are on my blog at https://badkarma00.wordpress.com/. There are other stories there, and intros to others books. And, occasionally, a rant or two about something that has gotten under my craw. Feel free to ignore those if you want, it's usually just a place to vent.

N.C. Reed

THANK YOU FOR READING

"ROLAND"

ENJOY THIS BOOK?

CHECK OUT THESE OTHER GREAT TITLES

by

N.C. REED!

Parno's Company
Tammy and Ringo
Odd Billy Todd
The Monster of Creasy's Hollow
The Kid

ALSO VISIT OUR WEBSITE
At
www.creativetexts.com

THANK YOU!